£5
11/5/25

DECK BOY

To Vic

With all best wishes.
I hope you like the
story (and won't be
too critical)

Alan Temperley

Christmas 2013

Alan Temperley is a Geordie who left grammar school aged sixteen to join the Merchant Navy. As cadet and deck officer he has spent years aboard ships not unlike *Pacific Trader* in this story. At other times he has sailed as able seaman and trawlerman. Following studies at Manchester and Edinburgh Universities, he became a teacher of English, notably in the Scottish Highlands, and also an author. His novels appear in eighteen languages, have been successfully televised and won a number of awards. He has one son, a solicitor in Edinburgh, and two granddaughters. He lives in a schoolhouse in rural Galloway.

Also by Alan Temperley:

Tales of the North Coast
Tales of Galloway
Murdo's War
Harry and the Wrinklies
Ragboy, Rats and the Surging Sea
The Simple Giant
The Brave Whale
Huntress of the Sea
The Magician of Samarkand
Harry and the Treasure of Eddie Carver
Scar Hill

DECK BOY

ALAN TEMPERLEY

A. T. BOOKS

First published : September, 2013
© 2013 Alan Temperley

All rights reserved. No part of this book may be reproduced, stored in a retrieval system, or transmitted by any means without the prior permission of the publisher.

All the characters and events in this publication are fictitious and any resemblance to real persons or actual happenings is purely coincidental.

ISBN 978-0-9575006-0-0

Cover illustration : Alan McGowan
Cover design : James Hutcheson
Typeset by Hope Services (Abingdon) Ltd.
Printed and bound on FSC accredited paper
by T. J. International Ltd, Padstow, Cornwall

A. T. Books,
Old Schoolhouse,
Rhonehouse,
Castle Douglas,
DG7 1SA
01556 680 341
alan.temperley@metronet.co.uk

When Ben Thomson, nearly fifteen, plays truant from his expensive boarding school, he has no idea that he will never return. All he intends is to visit his old home in Westport, but a chance encounter in a steamy workmen's café on the Dock Road turns his life on its head. Before he knows it, Ben finds himself escaping through a window, assaulted in an illegal drinking den, threatened by a murderer, changing his name and his appearance, forging documents, getting tattooed, making a host of new friends – and enemies – and outward bound on a voyage to the far side of the world. Surrounded by a crew of loyal, eccentric, gay and violent shipmates, Ben needs all his courage and resourcefulness to keep one step ahead of the law and something infinitely more dangerous.

Deck Boy is a full-blooded and often comical adventure set in the 1970s, the last great days of the British merchant fleet, when the dock basins were crowded with ships, navigation was by the stars, and the thronging crews were very different from the crowd you met in the high street.

Some reviews for Alan Temperley

Harry and the Wrinklies
A gloriously outrageous adventure : *Jacqueline Wilson*
I wish I'd written Harry and the Wrinklies. It's such a happy book : *Anne Fine*
A glorious romp of a book ... fast and furious fun ... Temperley is a talent to watch : *The Independent*

Murdo's War
The narrative is so vigorous, the action so breathless, the atmosphere so powerful ... vivid authenticity of the background : *Geoffrey Trease, Times Educational Supplement*
Best novel I've read in weeks ... straightforward curl-up-in-front-of-the-fire thriller : *Sunday Post*

Huntress of the Sea
The sea has always been a metaphor for the erotic, but here the imagery is sustained and developed with unforgettable beauty and horror ... a powerful and original novel : *New Statesman*
A taut, beautifully-written story : *Mail on Sunday*

The Magician of Samarkand
A true page-turner ... packed with beautifully-narrated action ... Temperley is a wonderful story-teller : *Guardian*
I defy anyone ... not to be caught up in the magic of this robust, thrilling adventure : *Scotsman*

Scar Hill
But this is more than an adventure. More than anything it is a love story – the unconditional love that binds Peter to his dad, his dog, his sister's child and the magnificent landscape of the far north-west of Scotland : *Herald*
Temperley is a consummate storyteller ... real edge-of-the-seat stuff : *Daily Telegraph*

Ragboy
Rattles along with more thrills, spills and chases than an Indiana Jones adventure : *Daily Telegraph*

I wish to thank the following people for their friendship, kindness and help in so many ways during the writing of this book: David Banks, Gordon Armstrong, Andrew Constable, Iris Patrick, Iain Alexander, Deirdre Lothian and Jim Hutcheson. A special mention, with love, to Jean Slaven, my lifelong friend and companion, who has supported and encouraged me from the start. To all my warmest gratitude.

For my son
Andrew

CONTENTS

PART ONE   WESTPORT
1

PART TWO   PACIFIC TRADER
61

PART THREE   OUTWARD BOUND : THE ATLANTIC
117

PART FOUR   THE GREAT OCEAN
173

PART FIVE   NEW ZEALAND
257

PART SIX   HOMEWARD BOUND
329

Glossary of Nautical Terms
454

PART ONE

WESTPORT

Café on the Dock Road

I SHOULDN'T have been in Westport; I should have been at *Frankie's*, the expensive boarding school I attended, a hundred and fifty miles away.

I shouldn't have been shivering in the bitter wind that blew down the Dock Road; I should have been perched on a warm stool in double chemistry.

And I shouldn't have been inhaling a mouth-watering aroma of sausage and chips; I should have been gasping in the laboratory stinks of sulphuretted hydrogen and whatever else my classmates were brewing up in their bubbling retorts.

But at lunchtime that Friday in early November I *was* in Westport, every moment expecting a heavy hand on my shoulder and a voice demanding to know why I wasn't in school.

A lorry sped past, whirling litter past the dingy shops on my side of the road. An empty can rattled to my feet. I kicked it back and gazed at the funnels and rigging of the ocean-going ships that rose above the warehouses opposite. A gull slanted past, battling against the wind.

I turned back to the café beside me. The windows ran with condensation. Dead flies floated on the inside ledge. The room was busy. Men in working jerseys and donkey jackets sat at Formica tables. A babble of voices and laughter, mingled with the rich scents of tea, bodies, cigarette smoke and those sausages, blew from the rattling extractor fan. I looked up at the name, Betty's, then down at the curling menu. With eighty pounds in my wallet, my entire savings, I could afford anything I wanted. Fourteen years old and very self-conscious, I pushed open the door.

A loud bell jangled on its spring but no one took any notice. The warmth and smells and steam closed round me.

Two men stood at the counter. As they were served I looked from the deep-fat fryer to the hissing coffee machine and yellowed menu above racks of crockery.

The men moved away.

"And what can I get you, my love?" A busty blonde woman mopped the counter with a dripping cloth.

"Sausage and chips, please."

"That the lot?" Vigorously she stirred a paddle in the frothing fat and took a drag from her cigarette. "Cup o' tea? Fried slice? Couple of eggs?"

I couldn't help noticing that her blouse was rather tight, tugging at the buttons. At every movement it bounced splendidly. My ears burned. "Eggs, please. And a cup of coffee."

"That's right. Keep you warm on a cold morning." She cracked eggs into a big black pan and clattered cutlery onto a tray. "Growing boy like you, got to keep your strength up. Off one of the ships, are you?"

"No, I'm er – " I hunted for the lie. "I'm with my dad. He had to go into town."

"So you're having your lunch here. That's nice." She shovelled two sausages and a mound of chips on to a plate and scooped the eggs on top. "Salt and vinegar on the table." She added my coffee to the tray and rang up the cash on a battered till.

I handed her the money. Her fingers were yellowed with nicotine, her hair dark at the roots. But it was the blouse that fascinated me.

"'Ere, saucy!" She laughed and slapped me across the shoulder with her drying cloth. "Keep your eyes to yourself. Your dad know you look at girls like that? Here's your change." She dropped it into my palm. "There's a table over there."

I turned away blushing. As I squeezed between the workmen's shoulders, I was startled to hear my name called aloud.

"Hey! Ben!"

Charlie

I LOOKED all round. Until nine months ago I had lived all my life in Westport. Who was it among those chatting, laughing, smoking, munching workmen down there on the Dock Road who knew me?

It must be a different Ben, I decided. But it wasn't.

"Over here." An Asian boy aged about seventeen was waving. He had a thin moustache, a gold ring in one ear and he was grinning broadly.

I wondered who he was.

"Come on, Ben, mate. It's me, Charlie. Charlie Sunderland."

"Charlie?" Suddenly I recognised him. "Hey, Charlie!" Delighted to find a friend, I pushed through the elbows of the diners.

"Watch where you're going, son!" A man slopped tea on his jeans.

"Sorry!"

Charlie shifted some shopping bags and cleared a space at the table. "What you doing here?"

It was too complicated to explain. I unloaded the tray. "You cut your hair. You look different."

"Yeah." He smoothed the sleek moustache and ran a hand over his black hair, cropped at the sides and permed into curls on top. "Smart, eh? What you think?" He turned to give me the full effect.

"Great."

"Drives the girls mental." He introduced me to the two men who sat opposite. "This is a pal o' mine, Ben Thomson. His dad was mate on the old *Boston Princess*. Ben done a trip with him a year back. I was deck boy."

We shook hands, thick fingers with chipped nails, very different from the hands of teachers.

"Can't stop, Charlie." One ground out his cigarette and stacked their plates.

"See a man." His companion rose. "Leave you to talk to your mate."

"Catch you in the Eight Bells."

They nodded to me. "Nice to meet you."

"Yeah, see you." Charlie watched them go. "Couple of ABs from my last ship. Still got seventeen days' leave, lucky beggars."

I arranged my lunch and reached for the sauce bottle. "You off again then?"

"Sign on, Monday. Sail Wednesday."

"What's the ship?"

Pacific Trader."

"Where you going?"

He shrugged and took a chip. "Oz, I think. Or South America. Somewhere like that. Anyway," he brightened. "Like I said, what you doin' here? Not the school holidays, is it?"

I shook my head. "Half term two weeks back."

"What, playin' hookey?"

"Sort of. Well yeah, but not like you mean."

"Naughty boy!" Charlie laughed. "I didn't reckon you for that sort o' game. What about that smashin' gran o' yours? She'll give you hell if she finds out."

"Not going to." I felt a familiar lump in my chest. "She died last winter."

"Oh, mate, I'm sorry."

"No, it's OK."

"What happened?"

"Fell on the ice. Broke a hip." I took a shaky breath. "Turned to pneumonia."

Charlie made a face. "She was great."

I nodded.

"Where you livin' now, then?"

"Dad came home to sort things out. There wasn't anyone else, really, not that I could live with full time. So I'm at boarding school up the country. Stay with my Auntie Marjorie in the holidays. Dad's aunt, really, my great aunt."

"What about your mum, her family?"

I don't like to talk about it. When I was two, my mother ran off with one of dad's shipmates, leaving me with my gran. I never saw her again. Last I heard, she had moved to Germany. "Dunno," I said.

Charlie helped himself to more chips. "So what you doin' back here? Just come to visit the old place?"

"I s'pose. See the house; put some flowers on gran's grave."

I'd already been to the house. The new owners had built a porch and garage, laid a block-paving drive, painted the woodwork blue.

I picked up a sausage with my fingers and dabbled it in sauce.

"Just down for the day?"

"Booked into one of those B and Bs down near the beach. Told them at *Frankie's* my auntie wanted me to come down for the weekend. She doesn't live here, though, she lives in Oxford. I'll take the train back on Sunday."

"You mean you just said like: 'Hey, I'm going down my Auntie Marjorie's, see you on Sunday'?"

"Not exactly. I had to write a letter."

"Ah! Signed 'Auntie Marjorie'. But didn't they ring her up?"

"Yeah, but she's away this week."

"And they know what an honest lad you are. Crafty devil. When I forged a letter sayin' I couldn't do gym, they just laughed an' give me press-ups and cold showers."

"I got one of the sixth-formers to write it, cost me two quid. They'll kill me if they ever find out. So will dad."

"I bet." Charlie thought about it. "Still use the cane in a place like that?"

"Occasionally."

"What's it like?"

"Only been there one and a bit terms. Never had it. Not yet."

"I meant the school."

"Oh!" I pictured the long, wooden corridors of *Frankie's* – or to give it its Sunday name, *The Sir Francis Drake School for the Sons of Merchant Navy and Airline Officers*. The pictures of famous seafarers and aviators on the walls; the four-to-a-room dormitory I shared with my best friend Anson and two other boys; the early morning runs; the rows of washbasins and lavatories; big boys flipping you with their towels; the uniform jerseys with a ship's wheel badge;

the tears of some of the younger boys. It was costing dad a bomb and I hated it, resented it, even half blamed it for gran's death, which was ridiculous.

"It's OK," I said and popped the yolk of my second egg. "Anyway, what have you been doing?"

"Me? Well, Ordinary Seaman now, aren't I? Gone up in the world." And Charlie launched into an account of the two trips he had made since we last met. Life at sea attracts all sorts of weird characters and crazy behaviour. Soon I was laughing so much that, for the moment at least, *Frankie's* and my reason for being in Westport were driven from my mind.

"Hey, but listen," he said at length. "You don't want to stay in some boring old guest house. Come an' stay with us. Now our Bill's away in the army you can have his room."

"What about your mother? Won't she – ?"

"Nah. Mum'll be tickled pink. She'll spoil you rotten. Come on, let's get your things."

I drank off the last of my coffee.

"Bye, Betty," Charlie called cheerfully.

"Bye, my darlin'," came the equally cheerful response. "Don't do anything I wouldn't."

The Landlady

OCEAN VIEW, whose only glimpse of the sea was a tiny triangle of blue from the bathroom window, was a guest house set several streets back from the beach.

Charlie followed me into the brown, cabbage-smelling hall. An array of notices announced:

Smoking strictly prohibited.
Front door will be locked at 10.30pm.
Departing guests must quit their rooms by 10.00am.
Breakfast served between 8.00am and 9.00am only.
PRIVATE : for attention ring the bell.

A doorway beside the *Private* notice was covered by a clicking bead curtain. Seconds after we arrived it was swished back and the landlady emerged from her hidden quarters. Vera Stringbaum (Mrs), as she was named on various documents, was a suspicious-looking woman of middle age. The first thing I noticed about her was her hair which was dyed an unnatural shade sometimes called ox-blood. In tight curls, like dark red snails, it clung about her bony head. Everything about her was thin: her nose, her lips, her chest, her legs. She wore a limp black dress and carpet slippers.

"Oh, it's you." Mrs Stringbaum's voice was as sharp as the matching red pencil line of her eyebrows.

"I, er – "

"We don't encourage guests to come and go at all hours. Do we, Mr Stringbaum?" She called through the curtain but there was no reply. "This isn't a hotel. I did tell you."

"Well, I only – "

"If you want to be in and out all day, you should have put up at the Grand." She surveyed Charlie, from the ring in his brown ear to the chain round his throat, the rings on his fingers and his striped jeans. Her nostrils flared. "You didn't tell me you had friends in Westport." She pointed to yet another notice: *No Visitors*.

I didn't know what to say.

"Go on then, if you want to fetch something from your room. He can wait down here. But I hope you're not planning to make a habit of it." She turned back through the clicking beads. "Your meal will be on the table at five-thirty as arranged."

"What the hell are you staying here for?" Charlie said when the coast was clear.

"It looked all right from the outside."

"Miserable old bag."

"Sorry." I was embarrassed. "Will you wait while I – "

"Course, that's what we come for. Not going to see my old mate stuck in a dump like this." He grinned. "Reckon you're up to telling her you've changed your mind?"

I made a face. "Dunno."

"If I was in your place I'd do a runner."

"What?"

"Nick off without paying. Mean-minded old cow."

"I can't, I've got my rucksack upstairs. All my spare clothes an' that are in it."

"Well, fetch it down an' just walk out."

"She'd see me. There'd be a terrific row."

"So what, you're bigger than she is. Anyway, there's two of us."

"What about Mr Stringbean?"

"Probably give us a hand – if he exists. Imagine being married to her." Charlie thought for a moment. "Is your room at the front?"

"I think so." I tried to remember.

"Well, chuck your bag out the window," Charlie said. "I'll go outside an' catch it. Then you come downstairs with a scarf or somethin' an' we just walk away."

"She's got my name in that book." I pointed to the register on the hall table. "And my auntie's address. I had to fill it in when I arrived."

"No prob." Charlie examined the book, ripped out the top sheet and crumpled it into his pocket. "OK now?" He grinned. "Go on, I'll wait on the pavement."

I was appalled and stared at him, then ran upstairs and let myself into my room. My pyjamas lay on the bed, toothbrush by the washbasin. Hastily I stuffed everything into my rucksack and pushed open the window. A smallish front garden lay beneath: red gravel, flowerbeds and a green iron railing.

Charlie beckoned from the pavement. "Come on, mate. Bombs away!"

It was the moment of no return. I took a deep breath. Leaning far out, I tossed the rucksack towards him.

It was a bad throw. I couldn't get a swing and one of the straps caught my thumb. With a crash it landed in a shrub well short of the pavement. Branches broke off, berries scattered.

Charlie swung his leg over the railing and retrieved it from the flowerbed. But somewhere beneath me there was a shriek. Mrs Stringbaum had spotted him through the net curtain. A door banged and she came leaping down the front steps.

"Stop!" Her skinny knees pumped beneath the black dress. "Stop! Give that 'ere." She sprinted across the gravel.

A strap tangled in the twigs. Charlie tugged it free, but before he could escape Mrs Stringbaum seized the strap that trailed behind. Charlie and the furious woman faced each other across the damaged bush, the rucksack tight between them.

"Let go!" Mrs Stringbaum gave a heave.

Charlie heaved back, dragging the landlady clear off her feet into the leaves and berries.

"Let go!" she screamed again, refusing to loosen her claw-like grip. "Runnin' off without payin'! I'll 'ave the police on the pair of you."

With an almighty wrench, Charlie tugged the rucksack free and scrambled back over the fence.

"Help! Police!" Mrs Stringbaum regained her feet and pushed down the dress to cover her shredded tights. "Vandal! Thief!"

But by this time Charlie was racing away, my rucksack trailing from his hand. Two gardens along he stopped.

Realising she had lost him, Mrs Stringbaum turned and stared up at the window where I stood frozen with horror. "I've got one of you anyway!" she cried vindictively. "*You'll* not escape that easy." On goat-like legs she ran back to the house.

I'd left my escape too late, she would confront me in the hallway. And to make matters worse, a skinny old man in a vest and braces had emerged at the top of the steps. I guessed this was Mr Stringbaum.

"What's going on, Vera?"

She screeched a reply.

In a panic I ran to the bedroom door. Where was the key? I couldn't see it. Feet came racing up the stairs. I grabbed the bed and shoved it against the door.

Next moment the handle turned. Somebody pushed. The bed shifted.

"Let me in!" Mrs Stringbaum hammered on the panels. "This instant! Do you hear me!"

Nothing could have made me open that door. I pushed the bed up hard and ran back to the window. Beneath me was a drop of five metres. I could jump – but what if I twisted an ankle? Then just to one side I spotted a drainpipe.

There were voices on the landing. The bed scraped back. I pulled a chair to the window and next moment was out through the gap, standing on the sill.

The door opened wide enough for Mrs Stringbaum to squeeze through. Uttering a hawk-like cry, she ran across the carpet.

I reached for the bracket that fastened the drainpipe to the guttering and swung my weight across. To my relief the bracket held. Bracing my feet against the wall, I began to descend.

"Come 'ere!" Mrs Stringbaum leaned from the window and grabbed for my jacket. "Rotten teenagers!"

She couldn't hold me. I was halfway down and made a jump for the gravel.

Charlie had returned. "Come on, mate."

I looked up at the window. Mrs Stringbaum had gone and Mr Stringbaum stood in her place. He was clutching a plate from the chest of drawers. Baring his false teeth, he flung it after me. It shattered on one of the rocks that surrounded the flowerbeds. He threw a jug.

My head was in a whirl. I scrambled over the wrought-iron railing to join Charlie and we ran off down the pavement. After fifty yards we paused to look back.

Mr Stringbaum was shouting from the window.

Mrs Stringbaum emerged from the gate. In one hand she brandished a flapping umbrella. "Bloody kids! Don't think you're getting away with this. I've got your address in my visitor's book remember."

Charlie looked at me and grinned. "What an exciting life you lead."

"Me!"

"Come on, let's go and see mum."

I took my rucksack and we jogged on through the autumn leaves.

Black Sunrise

"Are you listening, our Charlie?"

"Yeah, yeah."

"Never mind yeah, yeah. I mean it. You're to be back in this house by eleven-thirty."

The Sunderlands lived in a council house, or rather two semi's knocked into one. The front door was freshly painted, the garden was tidy, a punctured football belonging to a playful Rottweiler lay on the lawn.

To my surprise I knew Mrs Sunderland, Charlie's mum. She had been one of the dinner ladies at *Westport High*, the school I attended before my gran died. She was popular, and now I saw her at home she was one of the nicest women I'd ever met – fat, funny, loving and sensible. Surprisingly, too, having Charlie for a son, she was white.

Seventeen years earlier, with four boys and a girl of their own, the Sunderlands had adopted Charlie when he was a baby in need of a home. After much thought they had christened him Charles Mohammed, so that if he wished to have an Asian name or become a Moslem when he grew up, there would be no need to change his birth certificate. But the easygoing Charlie, surrounded by his family, never gave it a thought and Charlie Sunderland he had remained.

Only his brother Frank remained at home, the rest had moved away: Bill a soldier in Yorkshire, Philip a journalist in London, Danny a student in Manchester, and Penny still in Westport, married to a painter and decorator with a little girl of two and another baby on the way. Mr Sunderland, newly retired from the railways, was a small man who spent most of his time in the back garden with his cages of free-flying budgies, parakeets and African parrots. They were a sprawling, happy family, very different from me in my famous school, with no brothers or sisters, my mum run off, gran dead, dad away at sea, and a single unmarried auntie in Oxford whose passion in life was bridge, but saw it as her duty to give me a home during the school holidays.

"You can stay out until all hours yourself, Charlie," his mother continued, "I don't mind that. Goodness knows what you get up to when you're away on those ships – I don't even want to think about it. But Ben here's only fourteen and I want you back by eleven-thirty, not a minute later."

"I hear you."

"Yes, but are you listening? And stay away from those bars, you're not even eighteen yourself yet. All right?"

"OK! OK!" Charlie rolled his eyes then turned to examine himself in the hall mirror.

"Off to the disco then?" Mrs Sunderland straightened my collar. "That Black Sunrise place? Can't say I like the look of it myself, all those pictures of skeletons and witches outside. Still, I'm not a teenager any more. You look very nice, love. Unlike some I could mention with their perms and earrings."

"Ah, you're just jealous you didn't meet me when you were seventeen."

"With hair like that! You fancy yourself, don't you?"

"Certainly do, Mum." Charlie kissed her on the cheek.

"Bye, love."

"Bye, Mrs Sunderland," I said. "Thanks for the tea and that."

She squeezed my arm. "You go off and enjoy yourself, love. Don't let that one lead you astray."

I crouched to pat Doctor Death, the huge soft Rottweiler, who licked my face with a sloppy tongue.

"Doc's taken to you," Mrs Sunderland said as I scrubbed my lips with a sleeve. "Haven't you, you big daft lump." She pulled the dog roughly by his collar and Doctor Death rolled on his back in ecstasy. She rubbed his chest. "And don't you forget, our Charlie. Half past eleven. I'll be waiting up. And I'll be cross if you're late."

I trotted down the front steps and Charlie pulled the door shut. Daylight was almost gone. As we walked through the orange-lit estate, I tugged up my collar. The wind was colder and a thin drizzle blew from the sea. By the time we reached the main road it had turned to rain. Cars swept past, spray whirling in their wakes.

I looked for a bus stop.

"Let's take a taxi." Charlie ran out into the road with his arm raised. Cars swerved round him. A taxi sped past. The second taxi pulled in to the kerb.

"St Steven's," Charlie said as we climbed in.

"Off Lady Road? That new disco place, Black Sabbat or something?"

"That's it." Charlie rubbed the raindrops from his face.

It was a black city taxi and smelled of cigarettes. "Do you often do this?" I asked.

"Take a taxi? Not in Westport, all the time at sea though."

"Yeah?"

"Well, you've maybe only got a couple of nights ashore, don't want to waste them finding your way around. 'Sides, it's safer. Some of these places you could end up in an alley with your wallet gone an' a knife in your back. Go with your shipmates. Share the cost, bit of company, have a laugh."

I looked out at the wet pavements.

"That reminds me." Charlie dug in his pocket. "Dad said to give you this."

It was a ten pound note.

"Ah, no." I tried not to take it. "Look, I've got – "

Charlie pushed the note into my hand. "Too late now. 'Sides, he'd be black affronted. Tell you what, you pay the taxi, I'll get the disco."

St Steven's Church, no longer a place of worship, stood in a sidestreet near the city centre. It was surrounded by a tremendous wrought-iron fence. Open gates led to a broad flight of steps that mounted to the heavy doors. Phosphorescent images of skulls, open coffins, witches and the undead shone in the light of street lamps. Twelve demons, cavorting in neon flames, spelled out the name 'Black Sunrise'.

It was the newest and most popular disco in the city. No alcohol was served which meant it attracted all those teenagers who could not pass for eighteen.

We joined the queue halfway up the steps. Girls held bags and coats above their heads to ward off the rain. It wasn't enough. By the time they reached the entrance their hair hung in rats' tails and mascara made tracks down their cheeks. With shrieks of merriment and dismay, they hurried to the toilets to repair the damage.

I shook my head and saw the water fly off. Raindrops sparkled in Charlie's curls as he paid the entrance money. Perched on the end of a table, a girl with black lipstick, black eye-shadow and bitten black nails stamped the back of our hands.

"I thought you only did that if we go out," Charlie said.

"Whatever," she said in a bored voice and rolled her gum.

I examined the smeary stamp, a devil's head and the date. "This says the sixth." I checked my watch. "It's the thirteenth."

The girl sighed and looked away.

We gave our jackets to a man in the cloakroom and wandered into the vast open space of the disco.

The worshippers at St Steven's, which had ceased to be a church only three years earlier, could never have imagined such a scene. Strobe lights, high on the ancient walls, flickered across the darkness. Coloured beams criss-crossed the vaulted roof. Spotlit in the old organ loft, the disc jockey looked down on the swaying mass of teenagers. The throb of drums and raging chants of *Take my Love*, the current Number Two hit, were so loud you'd think the stained-glass windows must explode into the street:

> *Take my love and leave me never,*
> *Hold me and you'll live forever,*
> *Aaaaaahhhhhh !*

Five hundred heads shook wildly, five hundred mouths opened wide, five hundred voices united in the final scream.

Charlie put his mouth to my ear: "Fancy a Coke?"

I nodded and we made our way towards the altar end of the church where there was a crush of small tables. The noise there was a bit less and we joined the queue by the vestry door.

"Hey! Charlie boy!"

I looked round. A gangly youth about the same age as Charlie, tanned and gap-toothed, waved a can to attract his attention.

"It's Joey Bennett," Charlie said. "Hey, Joey!"

He beckoned and Joey pushed through the crowd, a girl clinging to his arm.

Joey Bennett

He was tall and skinny with his head shaved at the sides and a fantastic Mohican. Bright blue and orange, it jutted from his forehead and ran to the back of his neck. With his prominent nose, rubbery lips and an Adam's apple the size of Ben Nevis, it gave him a pleasant, slightly comical appearance. His clothes were tight to accentuate his thinness: a painted-on tropical shirt and black jeans hung with silver chains. He looked a bit like a giraffe with a cockatoo on its head.

He had slopped his can when he waved and sucked the back of his hand.

"Hi there, Joey boy!" Charlie punched him lightly on the chest. "Love the hair. When'd you get home?"

Joey sniffed. He had a cold. "Signed off the old *China Rose* three weeks back." He drew the girl forward. "This is Fizz."

She was nice. Ginger hair cut in spikes and a cartload of make-up. Smashing little figure.

"This here's Charlie." Joey shouted above the music. "Old pal from sea school."

She held out a hand. "Pleased to meet you."

"My mate Ben." Charlie introduced me.

"I'll get y' a drink," Joey shouted. "See if you can grab a table."

I followed Charlie to the altar area, magnificent stonework from three metres up, thronging teenagers below. All the tables were taken. Then a group rose from one against the wall.

"Charlie, over here." I pushed forward and reached it seconds ahead of two other boys.

"That's ours." The boy in front grabbed my shirt.

I resisted. "First come, first – "

"You deaf?" He tried to push past. " I said we – "

"Tony, leave it." His companion, a fair-haired boy a year or so younger, tried to intervene. "He was here first."

"Ah, shut it, Phil!" said my attacker. "Don't be a wimp all your life." His face was inches from mine: dark curls and high colouring, red lips, a spoiled expression. Aged seventeen or eighteen. I'd met boys like him at *Frankie's*: rich parents, public school accents, bullies. "Got it, butt-face? This is our table."

"'Fraid not." Charlie yanked him off me and threw him aside. One foot caught the leg of a chair, he cannoned into a table and fell to the floor. Drinks scattered. The people at the table sprang back. "Hey! Watch out! Bloody oaf!" They were angry, mopping skirts and trousers.

"Sorry, mates," Charlie said. "I'll buy you another round. This guy's trying to throw his weight around."

The boy called Tony pulled himself to his feet. He was livid. A wet stain covered the front of his shirt. Coke dripped from his fingers. In sudden rage he lunged forward and swung a punch. Charlie took the blow on his shoulder and grabbed him, pinioning both arms to his sides. Tony struggled and kicked out.

"Quieten down," Charlie said. "I'll tell you what. Are you listening? Hit me again an' I'll flatten your nose right across your face. All right? Now on you go like a good boy and find another table. We were here first."

He let go.

I was impressed. Charlie had always been such a joker.

Publicly humiliated, his face flaming, Tony stared at Charlie and abruptly thrust a hand deep into his pocket. I drew back, thinking he was going to pull a knife, but whatever was in there, Tony thought better of it. "I'll get you!" he said viciously. One finger jabbed like a stiletto. "When you leave here tonight you'd better watch your back. I'll be waiting." He turned on me. "You too. I'll have your guts for garters."

Guts for garters? Come on! Even though I was shaking, I gave him a V-sign.

"Good on you, kid," someone said.

At that moment two bouncers arrived, real Neanderthals with shaved skulls and arms hanging out from their sides. "All right, all right. What's the trouble? What's going on?" They glared around.

"Nothing." Charlie straightened the table and picked up a couple of chairs. "Somebody tripped, that's all."

"That right?"

"Yeah, that's about it, isn't it, *mate*?" Charlie said.

Tony nodded. If looks could kill, Charlie and I were dead on the spot.

"If that's what you're saying." But the bouncers weren't happy. "You, on your way." They turned Tony by the shoulders and pushed him back towards the dancing. "Any more trouble you're out o' here, the lot of you."

They departed, hanging bellies, six foot four.

"Sorry." Tony's companion, Phil, shrugged apologetically and followed in their wake.

The excitement died down. We gave the group at the next table some money for drinks and a couple of minutes later Joey and Fizz came pushing through the crowd. Charlie waved. Fizz spotted us.

"I know her," I said. "She was ahead of me at school here."

"You must know Joey then," Charlie said. "He was in the same class. Everyone knew Joey. Star of the school team. Got a trial for – Leeds or somewhere."

"Joey Bennett?" The name hadn't registered. "Can't be. He was a titchy guy, hair down to his shoulders. Spots."

"Yeah, I'd forgotten. But little guys turn into big guys."

"He was a weed."

"He still is, look at him."

"Yeah, but white-faced, starved-looking. That guy's nearly as brown as you are."

"Well, he's at sea now, isn't he. You heard him, just back from the tropics somewhere."

They reached the table. Joey passed round the cans and Fizz threw down some nibbles.

We were a chair short. Charlie went to a nearby table. "OK if I take this?"

Two girls sat there. "Yeah," said the dark one.

"Help yourself," said her blonde friend. "To anything. Gorgeous."

Charlie grinned and pulled the chair across.

Joey crammed his mouth with crackers. "What you been doing then, Charlie?"

"Same as you, I s'pose. Japan, Singapore, the Gulf. Big container job." Charlie opened his can and caught the foam. "That's my leave over now."

"Where you going next then?"

"Not sure. *Pacific Trader*. Sign on, Monday."

Crumbs fell from Joey's lips. "Hey, me too."

"Yeah?" What you sailing as?"

"Deck boy again. You?"

"O.S. now, aren't I. Hey, it'll be good, you an' me. Have some laughs."

"I guess." Joey was less enthusiastic, He sucked the gap of a missing tooth.

"What's up?"

"Well, there's Fizz here, in't there? Her and me gets along pretty well. Go off again, there's goin' to be other kids tryin' to muscle in. Great girl like you – eh, Fizz?"

"You're my guy, Joey." She snuggled up and kissed him on the ear.

He pulled her close. "That's what you say now. An' there's not many like me, I know, got the body and looks I got. But when I'm away four-five months an' it gets a bit lonely on a Sat'day? Sexy Steve an' Ronnie Rich start ringin' up? Who's goin' to waste her life watchin' telly when she could be out havin' a good time?" Joey's eyes, very blue in his long brown face, were sad. "Four months on, three weeks off. Don't give a guy much of a chance." He pulled out a wet-looking handkerchief to scrub his nose. "Rotten cold."

"That's the way it is," Charlie said. "You knew that before you started."

"Course I did. But I hadn't met Fizz then, had I?"

"What a pair," Charlie said. "I don't know. You wantin' to leave the sea, Ben here runnin' away from boarding school."

"How d'you mean?" Joey sat forward. "Tchoo!"

"He was at the High, couple of years behind you an' Fizz," Charlie said.

"What, an' you're doggin' it?"

"Not exactly." I told them a bit about *Frankie's* and gran.

"I met him at Betty's this morning," Charlie said. "Done a runner from an old bag keeps a B and B down near the shore. Now he's stayin' with me. That right, Ben?"

I nodded.

"Never a dull moment." Joey laughed. "But I don't quite get it. This some kind of sea school you're at?"

"No. Well, yes in a way. It's just a school, like, but for the sons of sailors and airmen. People away from home a lot."

"Francis Drake, yeah? Place like that you prob'ly do some sea stuff, navigation an' seamanship an' that."

"Two periods a week. They've got a Sea Cadets though. Go sailing in the Lakes sometimes."

"Ben done a trip with his dad a year back," Charlie said. "That's how I met him. I was deck boy, my first trip. His dad was first mate. Put him under the bosun, made him work with me."

"So you've done chippin' an' holy-stonin' an' splicin' an' stuff?"

"A bit, yeah."

"Don't listen to him," Charlie said. "He had his cabin up top, but his dad made him do the same as me. Only thirteen but see him sometimes, all clarted up wi' grease and muck at the end of the day. Got stuck right in there. Dead popular with the crew."

"Wasn't hard," I said. "I liked it. I don't mind that sort of work."

"Don't mind it?" Joey said "Don't mind scrubbin' out the crew bogs? Where'd you say you met him?" he asked Charlie. "Down the funny farm?"

"It's true," I said. "Maybe not the bogs but the rest of it. Working there with the crew. I enjoyed it."

"Dear, oh dear!" he shook his head. "A sad case. An' you can't tell by looking at him, can you? Seems to me," he sneezed explosively, "it's you should be goin' down the Dock Office on Monday. Signin' on *Pacific Trader* 'stead of me."

"I wouldn't mind." I laughed. "Better than going back to boring old *Frankie's*."

It was just one of those things you say. I didn't mean it, didn't even think about it. At least not right then, because at that moment the two girls at the nearby table came over and asked if we wanted to dance.

A Few Beers

"She was disgusting!" Yet again I scrubbed my lips. "She tasted of cigarettes. And I didn't want to kiss her anyway."

"You can not be serious!" Joey rebuked me. "This is Jayne McVicar you're talking about. The sexpot of 4C."

"You don't have to remind me," I said. "Jayne the pain. She was horrible at school an' she's horrible now. What did she want to kiss *me* for anyway? The place was packed with older guys."

"It's obvious," Charlie said. "She's a baby-snatcher."

"Thanks very much."

"I can tell you why," Fizz said. "Ben's better looking, that's why."

"What! Him good-looking?"

"Of course. Not as good-looking as my Joey though."

I scarcely heard them. "She doesn't half fancy herself. I'd rather kiss Driller Killer."

"Who?"

"Charlie's dog. A big Rottweiler."

Charlie laughed. "Doctor Death."

"Yeah, well, Doctor Death. I'd rather kiss Doctor Death than Ciggy Jayne, any day."

We had left the howl of Black Sunrise for somewhere quieter. As we descended the church steps I spotted a movement in the shadows. It was Tony. When he saw there were four of us, he melted back into the disco.

"That's one gargoyle less," Charlie shouted at his back. "Gutless wonder!"

The rain had stopped. As we walked to the Railway Inn, down near the docks, the streets grew darker and narrower. The barman was a harder nut to crack than Jayne McVicar:

"Eighteen? Gimme a break. Coming up eleven more like. Go on, hoppit!"

The Anchor and The Dancing Monkey brought no better luck and St Mary's youth club was shut. In the end, carrying cans, pizzas and fish and chips, we took a taxi to Joey's, a council house at the far side of town. The house was empty, his mother out for the night with her engineer boyfriend. Charlie and I sprawled comfortably in armchairs, jackets on the floor. Joey and Fizz sat with arms round each other on the big settee. *Match of the Day*, sound switched off, flickered on a TV in the corner.

Joey coughed and spat into a kitchen towel. "What you were saying there in the taxi." He broke off a corner of pizza. "D'you you mean it? Would you really like to sign-on Monday? Go away 'stead o' me?"

I thought. "Yeah, why not?"

"Deck boy?"

"I've done it before." I spoke recklessly, a can of Merrydown at my lips.

"I'll tell you this." Joey washed down his pizza with a lager. "If you fancy it, I bet I fancy it a lot more."

"Yeah, but it's all talk, isn't it," I said. "I mean, I'm fourteen years old, you're what – sixteen, seventeen? I can't even leave school for a year and a bit. You've got papers an' that. I don't look anything like you."

Joey sighed deeply. "It would be good though, wouldn't it. You get to leave that school you don't like. I get to stay here wi' Fizz." He tugged her hair affectionately and she snuggled closer.

Charlie said, "Are you two serious or just talking daft?"

"Talking daft," I said.

"More's the pity."

"'Cause if you did really mean it, I'm not sure we couldn't work it out. That's if Ben's up for a bit of adventure."

"Get on!" Joey sneezed. "How?"

"Where's your Discharge Book an' Union Card, all that stuff?"

"Upstairs. Why?"

"Fetch it down."

Joey hesitated.

"Don't worry, she'll be here when you come back."

Joey unwound himself, Mohican erect, and left the room. A minute later he returned, a tatty envelope in one hand.

"Right." He settled himself and tipped out the contents. "Discharge Book, Identity Card, Vaccination Certificate ..." One by one he passed them across.

"What a terrible photo, Joey," Fizz cried. "Look at your hair. It's nothing like you."

Charlie sucked his fingers and took the cards from him. "Same as mine." He turned the pages. "Identical, 'cept your vaccination's a different colour. But look," he laid them open on the coffee table. "They could almost be anybody's. Registration Card – nothing but your name and signature. Union Card – signature. Vaccination – signature. It's only these two," he glanced at the covers, "Discharge Book and Identity Card. They're the only ones have any description."

"But look at his photo," I said. "I don't look anything like him."

"Hang on, don't get your knickers in a twist." Charlie read from the bright red Seaman's Identity Card: "*Height : five foot ten.* Taller than that aren't you, Joey?"

"Six-one now. I had a spurt my first trip."

"Doesn't say that here. What about you, Ben?"

"Five-eight, five-nine," I said.

"And growing all the time. Who's going to notice two inches if you stand up straight? Now, *Colour of eyes : blue.* You've got blue eyes, haven't you?"

"Yes, but not like his."

"It doesn't say like anything, just blue, an' your eyes are blue." A thought struck him. "Hey, your eyesight's OK? I mean, you're not short-sighted or colour blind or anything?"

"No."

"Right." Charlie read on: "*Distinguishing marks : tattoo left shoulder, anchor.* Let's see, Joey."

Joey unbuttoned his shirt. Right on the muscle was a blue and red anchor with a leaping dolphin. Across the middle, in a decorative scroll, stood the single word *Mum*.

"Hey, neat," Charlie said.

"Goin' to get one the other side for Fizz."

She hugged him tight.

Charlie turned to me. "You wouldn't mind a tattoo like that, would you?"

"Not *Mum*."

"It doesn't say that here." He checked. "Just an anchor. You could have *Dracula* in it if you wanted."

"*Jayne McVicar*." Fizz giggled.

Charlie cast his eye down the page: "*Date of birth ... Place of birth ...* an' that's the lot." He set the Identity Card aside and picked up Joey's blue Discharge Book. Carefully he studied the first few pages. "Nothing new, just the ships you've been on and the same details as before: *height ... colour of eyes ...*"

"And a photo," I said.

"I suppose that's a bit of a problem but it seems to me like it's the only one. "You can easy learn to copy Joey's signature; your eyes are the right colour; no one's going to notice the height; an' you can get a tattoo tomorrow. The only thing left's the photograph."

"It's got an embossed stamp." I pointed. "Half on the photo and half on the page." I turned it over. "Right through."

"I can see that."

"An' it's strong glue." I picked at a corner. "You can't just peel it off or stick another one on top."

"Give us time, give us time," Charlie said. "We've not even thought about it yet."

"I know somebody might do it," Joey said. "That's if he's home right now. Guy I sailed with last trip. Smoky Crisp, one of the ABs. Fantastic artist."

"Do you know where he lives?"

"Easy find out."

"Anyway," Charlie took a cold chip, looked at it and put it back. "No point even thinking about it till there's an answer to the big question – the only question left really. Are the two of you serious about all this?"

And all at once we weren't just talking, it wasn't a 'what-if' game. I was scared and took another pull of Merrydown. My head gave a lurch.

"You're wrong, it's not the only question," I said. "What about my dad – and Auntie Marjorie? They'd be worried sick. What if there's somebody on the *Pacific Trader* sailed with Joey last trip? What if something went wrong? It was OK on the *Boston Princess* 'cause dad was there. This time I'd be on my own."

"Hey! Hey! Nobody's trying to *make* you do it," Charlie said. "It was your own idea. But if you do decide, you could prob'ly share a cabin with me. Deck boys and ordinary seamen double up all the time. It would be good, I'd tell 'em we're best mates."

"And if somebody knows Joey?"

"Who's going to see your papers? None of the crew anyroad. Call yourself something different. Got a middle name, Joey?"

"Yeah, Alvin."

"Alvin!" I said.

"They called me Jabbo at school," Joey said. "My initials like."

"I remember that," Charlie said. "When you played for the team. All the kids shouting, 'Ja-bbo! Ja-bbo'!"

The memory made Joey sad.

Fizz twined her fingers in his. "You boys are so thick," she said. "Joey's name's Bennett, right? And you're called Ben. Think about it. You do this crazy thing, you don't need to change your name at all, just use the one you've got – Ben."

"Of course, Ben for Bennett." Charlie sat up. "You're right, people use their second names all the time."

"Like who?" I said.

"Smithy, Mac, Chalky White – half the people I know. Hey, I'm getting a feeling about this."

"Ben Bennett," I said. "And what happens if I get found out - at least, *when* I get found out?"

"Well, they can't flog you or hang you, can they? It's not like you murdered anybody. Just give you a slap on the wrist an' send you back to school. You can live with that."

Charlie drained his beer and reached for another. At the same moment a clock on the mantelpiece began a long series of chimes. He glanced across.

"Midnight! That can't be right." He checked his watch. "Oh, help! Mum'll be on the warpath." He grabbed his jacket. "C'me on, Ben. It's all your fault!" Snatching a handful of crisps, he crammed them into his mouth and headed for the door.

"See you tomorrow," Joey shouted.

"If mum lets me live that long. Listen, 521387 – write it down – 521387. Give me a ring. If I don't hear we'll see you down at Betty's half ten. Come *on*, Ben."

Jackets flapping, we tumbled from the door and ran down the abandoned garden. The fresh air hit me. I felt a bit peculiar.

"Half-ten, Betty's. *Be* there!"

We emerged from the lopsided gate. Joey and Fizz were lost behind hedges.

"Don't forget to bring your papers!" Charlie's shouts rang along the deserted street. "Be good!"

A bedroom light came on. Somewhere in the night a dog began to bark.

We ran on.

"Taxi! Taxi!"

The New Image

"Same again?" The barber, a wizened gnome of seventy, tucked the sheet round my neck. "Just tidy it up a bit?"

"No, er," I cleared my throat. "I'd like it different this time."

He viewed my reflection. "Suits you like that."

My eyes, smudged with too little sleep and a mild hangover, gazed back from the mirror. My hair had always been the same: fair, springy, parted on the left. I gripped my fingers. "I'd just like a change."

The barber sighed. "Ah, well, you're the customer. How d'you want it then?"

I knew exactly. I'd always fancied a Steve McQueen. I'd been thinking about it since the night before when Charlie and I – Charlie in his pyjamas on the edge of my bed – had sat talking into the early hours. Tattoos, shipwork, my gran, forging Joey's signature, foreign ports, Mrs Stringbaum, my age, how to avoid a hangover, *Frankie's*, the trouble at the disco, a haircut to make me look older, Joey and Fizz – we talked about many things. And would have talked longer had not Mrs Sunderland, finally losing patience, called along the landing: "Are you never going to bed, our Charlie? It's past two. There's people here have to get up in the morning."

I met the barber's currant eyes. "No parting, please, an' quite short – not too short." I hesitated. "You know what Steve McQueen looks like?"

He snorted: "It'll be a few years before you look like Steve McQueen, son. Still, if that's what you want."

He gripped my head with fingers like steel, snapped his scissors a millimetre from my ear and got to work. The hair tumbled down my chest and fell to the floor. As he worked, the little man muttered beneath his breath, pushing my head roughly to right and left. But he was a good barber and in ten minutes the job was finished. He sprayed my hair with water and attacked it with a stiff brush.

"It'll take a few washes to get rid of the parting. Had it all your life?"

I nodded.

"Well, see what your mum thinks. Suits you better than I expected."

I turned my head this way and that, startled at the change in my appearance. He held up a mirror. A short scar, the result of a bike accident years before, showed up as a white line at the back of my head.

"Hey, fantastic!" Charlie joined me as I paid at the desk. "I love it. You look like a deck boy already."

I wriggled my shoulders. Half the hair had found its way down my T-shirt.

"Thanks." I took the change. As we left the shop I examined my reflection in the window and ran a hand over the top of my head. Ben Thomson? I looked like some other person, a young soldier maybe, and felt everyone was looking at me.

It wasn't far to the ship's chandler's, an old building on Nelson Street with chipped black paintwork and mesh across the windows. It sold anything and everything to do with ships: rope, soap, blocks, binoculars, holystones, buckets, blankets, chains, canvas, knives, chipping hammers, red lead, prisms, grease, lifeboat supplies – and seamen's clothes.

"What about these?" I stood before a rack of jeans, not sand-washed for comfort but hard blue denim.

"How much are they?"

"Half the price of the others – less."

"They'll do fine. A couple of washes'll knock the stiffness out of them."

I pulled two pairs off the rail and took them to a booth to try on.

"New deck boy," Charlie said to the middle-aged assistant, a man with an eye-patch and brown dust coat, who hovered to see we didn't pocket any knives or hand compasses. "He'll be wanting some other stuff."

Charlie followed me into the booth. I shook the hair from my T-shirt and pulled on the jeans. They were horrible, chafing and ice-cold against my legs, but at least they fitted at the waist. With a rattle of curtain rings we emerged and I laid them on the counter.

During the next half hour other garments were heaped on top, the cheapest we could find: two denim jackets with brass buttons, two thick jerseys, work shirts, rubber boots, cotton shorts, yellow PVC oilskins, a sou'wester, a knitted navy-blue hat, underpants, socks and heavy work shoes.

The assistant rang them up on his ancient till. The total came to almost a hundred pounds, more than my entire savings. Notes and coins spread on the counter, I looked round helplessly.

"No worry, mate." Charlie felt in his back pocket. As if it were nothing, he dropped an extra twenty to pay for my purchases and handed two tens to me. "Here, pay me back when you're rolling in it. Deck boys get paid, you know."

I knew his shore money was getting low. "Are you sure you can – ?"

"Yeah! Rockefeller, that's me. No prob."

To my surprise the assistant was sympathetic. "Ten percent off for cash, son. That fair enough?"

The till shot open. He gave me change and folded the clothes into poly bags.

"Good luck." He smiled. "What ship you joining?"

"*Pacific Trader*." I glanced at Charlie. "Both of us."

"That right? We had two others in a couple of days back. Panama – New Zealand. Lucky beggars, you'll miss the winter."

We pulled the bags from the counter. "Thanks."

"A word in your lugs though." He followed us to the entrance. "Just in the way of an old shipmate like. I hear you've got a new bosun this trip, name of Ryland. You want to watch your backs wi' that one."

We turned.

"I sailed with him when he was AB. Nasty piece of work."

"How?" Charlie said. "What's up with him?"

"Always hatching some scam. Violent temper. Knock your block off first, ask questions later."

"That's nice," Charlie said. "Ben's first trip, my third. Really encouraging that."

The man pulled up a sleeve revealing a thick blue scar above his wrist. "It was him done this to me. Said it was an accident but he meant it all right."

We stared.

"More recent, a steward drowned a year back. Calcutta. Nothing proved mind. But the word goes round."

"What happened?"

"Bit of a mystery. Nice young fella, they say. Not much older than you two. Bad blood between them. Steward threatened to put the finger on him. Bit of a fight. Next morning they're pullin' him out the River Hooghly. Not much left after a night with the crocs – biggest in the world over there."

It wasn't something I wanted to think about.

"An' now this guy's bosun," Charlie said. "What's his name again?"

"John Ryland – better known as Jumbo. Easy recognised, birth mark over one eye, can't miss it."

Charlie gazed down Nelson Street, past the cranes and warehouses and funnels of the big ships, to the thin brown line of the estuary. "Aye, well. He lays a finger on me, the old man'll hear about it 'fore you can say Jack Tar."

"Just thought I'd warn you, a word never goes amiss." The man squeezed my arm. "You'll be all right, your mate looks as if he knows his way around. Off you go an' make the most of it. It's a great life." He turned back into the gloom of the shop. "All that sunshine; blue seas and foreign ports. I wish it was me sixteen again, I'll tell you that."

We went to Boots for the photos.

I examined myself in the mirror outside the booth. "What do you think?"

Charlie considered. "Put on one of them working jerseys and a denim jacket."

I dug in the bags and changed quickly.

"That's more like it." He pushed my hair about. "Try to scowl a bit. Think about someone you'd like to give a good thumping."

I turned back to the mirror. Even to my own eyes I could pass for a young – very young – deckhand. I smiled at my reflection, frowned, wrinkled my forehead, gawped like an idiot.

"Are you going in?" A well-dressed man stood waiting.

"Er, yes." I blushed scarlet.

"Get a move on." Charlie laughed. "We're going to be late."

I ducked through the curtain and spun the seat. My ghostly reflection appeared in the glass panel. Carefully I read the instructions, pushed coins into the slot and sat back. A red light came on. I stared into the panel and waited. And waited. My face muscles felt stiff. I blinked – *flash!* I was dazzled. Blast! One wasted. I licked my lips and waited for the red warning light to – *flash!* … *Flash!* Only one to go. I stared hard into the – *flash!*

Cross that I had got it wrong, I emerged into the busy shop. At once the man took my place. Shielded by Charlie, I changed back into my regular clothes.

The photos dropped down. I was appalled. Blinking, startled, scowling, a rough-headed working boy gazed back at me. Was this the polite Ben Thomson my gran had loved for fourteen years? I passed them to Charlie.

"Hey, do I know this boy?" He pointed to one. "Jack the Ripper – I wouldn't like to meet *him* on a dark night. And Loopy Leonard!" He looked more closely. "But the other two are great. Perfect."

"Look sixteen?"

"Yeah, I reckon. Fifteen – sixteen. Some kids of sixteen look about twelve." He passed them back and glanced at his watch.

"Come on, Joey's waiting. Got to get down to Betty's."

Smoky at Home

FORTIFIED BY coffee and hot buttered toast with fried eggs – not to mention Betty's spectacular boobs and back-chat – we boarded a bus which took us past shabby and boarded-up shops to the far side of town. This was the rough end of Westport, the part the police knew best. We jumped off and turned down a side-street. Broken glass lay in the gutters, litter flourished in abandoned gardens. A group of teenagers fell silent as we approached.

"Azalea Terrace somewhere round here?" Joey said.

One pointed with his cigarette: "First right, first left."

"Thanks."

We walked on, listening for footsteps at our backs.

Azalea Terrace, despite its name, was as neglected as the streets around, and 15a was no different from its neighbours. Net curtains, lopsided and torn, covered the windows. The door stood open. Two children stood in the entrance. The older, a girl of about four with tear-filled eyes and a food-stained dress, chewed a finger of cold pizza. The other, a boy with a runny nose, sucked a lollipop. A third child, younger still, slept in a pushchair in the hallway. Angry shouts, a woman's voice, issued from some inner room.

I looked at Joey. "You sure about this?"

He shrugged. "It's the address they give me. If it is Smoky lives here, he did those pictures I told you about on the old *China Rose*."

A woman appeared, fat and pregnant in a purple dress, her hair hanging in rats' tails. "I'm just fed up, Barry. Not even the price of a packet o' fags. All gone at the boozer, you an' them mates o' yours. An' I'm stuck here in the house wi' the telly an' the rotten kids. It's not fair! You're just a lousy …" She spotted the three of us standing in the path. "What d'you lot want? You 'is pals, are you? Down there spendin' the last of 'is wages, chuckin' it down your mis'rable throats?"

"No, er – " Joey took a step back. "Can you tell me, does Smoky Crisp live here?"

"Smoky? Aye, smoky all right. Gone up in smoke! Might as well've burned it, all the good it's done me an' the kids."

We were silent.

"What you lookin' at me like that for? Bloody cheek! Aye, he lives here, Barry rotten Crisp. Whenever he thinks to come 'ome, that is. When he's not away on them ships, or drinkin' hissel' mindless down the Eight Bells. I've 'ad enough, I'll tell you that." She shouted up the hallway: "D'you 'ear that, *Smoky*, darling? There's three mates 'ere to see you. I'm off. I'm out of 'ere. See you tonight, if you're lucky." She started down the path, tripping over a broken tricycle. "Louise an' Gerry want their dinner, all right? An' Tom needs changin'!"

She was gone, dress straining. "Rotten men!" Her voice reached us as she crossed the road and let herself into the house of a friend who lived opposite.

Charlie blew out his cheeks.

Joey knocked on the door. "Hello? Smoky? Are you there? It's Joey, Joey Bennett off the old *China Rose*. Got a couple o' pals with me. OK if we come in?"

There was a rattling smoker's cough and a man appeared at the end of the passage. He was about forty, hollow-chested and thin, with bags beneath his eyes and several days' growth of stubble. He wore unwashed jeans, bunched at the waist and a paint-streaked shirt.

"Hey there, Joey." He removed a hand-rolled fag and gave a brown, broken-toothed smile. "How's it going?"

Joey introduced us. We shook hands.

"Come away in." He nudged the children aside with a bare foot. "Out the way, you two. You'll get your dinner in a while."

The house smelled of stale milk, nappies and cigarettes. We followed Smoky into the living-room. Clothes and toys, magazines, cans and unwashed dishes lay on every surface. He cleared some spaces and we sat down.

"Sorry about the welcome." He coughed deeply. "She's in a bit of a mood today. Now, how about a lager? There's some in the shed she doesn't know about."

"Not for me," I said, nursing the remains of my hangover.

"No? What else – rum? Vodka? Er – "

"Have you got a Coke?"

"Coke? I've no idea. The kids might have some. Hey, Louise! We got any Coke?"

"Fanta." Four years old and a voice like a fishwife.

"Where?"

"In the fridge."

"Well fetch us one."

"I can't reach."

"Course you can. Stand on a chair or somethin'. I've got to go out the garden a minute."

Louise appeared in the doorway, hands and face smeared red with pizza. "Mum knows about the lager. I told 'er. She's took them out the shed an' hid them somewhere else."

"Rotten little snoop. Where?"

"Cost yer." She swung on the edge of the door.

"What you want?"

"One o' them mint bars on the high shelf."

"All right, I'll give you a mint bar. Now where's she put the lager?"

"Bar first."

Smoky heaved himself to his feet. "You'll grow up to be a criminal, you know that? A blackmailer."

He fetched the green-wrapped chocolate bar. At once the little girl pulled off the paper and pushed the bar into her mouth.

"Right, where's the lager?" said her father.

"In the shed!" She shrieked and fled back along the corridor.

"You said your mother – "

"I never!" Louise's triumphant cry reached us as she ran from the front door.

"Little liar!" Smoky shouted after her then shrugged and grinned. "Kids, eh?"

We saw him through the window as he crossed the back garden and disappeared into a shed. While he was gone I looked around the room. Despite the mess I hated it: the cheap furniture, multi-coloured carpet, chrome spotlights. The walls, in contrast, were hung with beautiful sea paintings: a sunrise with icebergs, warships amid the smoke of battle, the *Cutty Sark* in a typhoon.

"Good, eh?" Joey nodded towards a picture of a rocky coast with seabirds circling. "Did that one last trip."

I was very impressed. Whatever else might be said about him, Smoky was a wonderful artist.

You Can Change a Nappy

"Let's see if I got this right." Smoky nipped off the end of his skinny cigarette. "You're fourteen years old. You want out o' school. You done a trip wi' your dad an' know a bit about deck work. You want to swap with Joey so he can stay ashore with his bit o' skirt. An' you're asking me to forge the photos on his papers."

"I'll be fifteen next month," I said.

"Fifteen, no less." He lit up and was clouded in smoke.

"What do you think?" Joey said.

"What do I think? As a respectable British seaman that's not been in jail above four times in his life?" He gave a crooked, brown-toothed grin. "I love it."

I caught Charlie's eye. He gave me a wink.

"Let's have another dekko." Smoky stretched out a thin brown hand.

Joey passed him his documents.

"Where's my reading glasses?" Cigarette wedged in a corner of his mouth, Smoky searched the coffee table, sideboard, window sill and unearthed a pair of dirty spectacles with a cracked lens and one arm repaired with tape. Holding the photos near the window, he examined the stamps. "Shouldn't be no problem. I'll need a magnifying glass – got one somewhere around. An' a couple o' scalpels. Have to take a bit o' care." He looked up. "Got the new pictures?"

I pointed to the two he should use.

Smoky compared the size. "Good, manage a little bit of overlap. I'll rest 'em on a sheet of blotting paper, find something to do the embossing." He ground the stub of his cigarette into a brimming ashtray. "Yeah, do that for you. When d'you want it? 'Fore Monday, obviously. How 'bout tomorrow afternoon, round teatime?"

"Great!" Charlie said. "We'll pick 'em up then."

"Cost you, mind."

"How much?"

"Well, I got to buy some stuff. Can't make no mistakes. Thirty quid?"

"Yeah, fine," Charlie said at once. "No problem."

I thought of the money I owed already.

"Don't you go sayin' nothin' to the missus, mind." Smoky tossed off the last of his lager. "Right, if you want it tomorrow I got to go into town 'fore the shops shut." He felt in his pockets and seemed surprised. "Dead skint. Need an advance."

Charlie glanced at Joey. "We'll get 'em tomorrow, definite?" he said. "Can't be no messing about."

"Said so, didn't I?"

"How much d'you want?"

"Fifteen. No, say twenty, jus' to be on the safe side."

Charlie hesitated. "Yeah, OK." He nodded to me and I handed over the two tens he had lent me.

"Thanks." Smoky stuffed them into a back pocket. "Won't be long. See you when I get back." He pulled his jacket from the debris. "You'll stay here, right? Keep an eye on the kids."

"Can't." Charlie stood up. "Got to get Ben to the tattoo parlour 'fore it closes for the weekend."

"Which one you going to?"

"*Skin Deep*," Joey said. "Down Rum Lane."

"Sam Pearson?" Smoky said. "Oh, he'll open up for you anytime. Likes to catch 'em fresh off the ships or comin' out the pub. Prob'ly won't shut till six anyway. Tell him I sent you."

"You know him?" I said.

"You could say." He tugged up the back of his shirt. A single tattoo, a fantasy of leaves, flowers, macaws and other jungle creatures coiled up his spine and spilled across his bony shoulders.

"Hey, fantastic!" Charlie examined it.

Smoky showed us his chest. "Legs too. I design 'em, Sam draws 'em. Him an' me's old mates. He'll see you're OK." He straightened his clothes. "Right for a couple of hours then? Tea an' biscuits in the kitchen. TV control somewhere about." He headed for the door. "See you."

Joey ran after him. "What about the kids? Your wife said – "

"Oh, they'll not bother you. Give 'em a bite o' lunch, yeah? Stuff in the fridge. Stick a few chips an' fish fingers in the oven. They'll eat them till they're sick. Prob'ly want the lav sometime. Oh, an' Tom needs his nappy changing. He's the one in the pushchair. You'll find some stuff in the bathroom – or the kitchen, I don't know."

"Change his nappy!"

"Yeah, you were a kid once, weren't you? Nothin' to it. Jus' stick him on a towel on the floor, wash his bum an' put on a clean one. Any problem, the wife's across the road – Dolores. Better not bother her if you can help it though. Big woman. Gets a bit violent sometimes."

We stared at him.

"That's all, I think." Smoky patted his shirt pocket to make sure he had his tobacco tin. "I'm off, then. Ta-ta."

The Green-Eyed Tattooist

WE DIDN'T have to wait for Smoky's return which was just as well because he was gone twelve hours, and when a taxi driver tipped him out on the pavement at two the next morning, he was so drunk he could hardly stand. Nor did we have to cook lunch or, worst of all, change Tom's ominously heavy-looking nappy. For Smoky's wife saw him heading jauntily up the street and erupted from her friend's door with a scream of rage. At which Smoky, knowing better than to hang around, took off with a burst of speed that would not have disgraced an Olympic sprinter.

"That's right, y' idle, good-for-nothing! Off you go to your boozy mates. See if I care. An' don't bother comin' back neither. If you do, by heaven, I'll give you what-for! You drunken sot!" She shook a fist like a stevedore. "D'you 'ear!"

But Smoky, for the moment, was beyond her reach. Halting at an alley between broken fences, he looked back and blew an elaborate kiss. His wife's fury reached new heights. With a carefree shrug, Smoky hitched his jacket and vanished among the houses.

"Rotten no-good! All you sailors are alike. Swan off an' leave us women to do all the work, bring up your kids." Muttering, she turned to where Louise, fingers in her mouth, stood watching from the gate. "Come on, pet. Never mind him. Into the house and we'll see about some dinner. What d'you fancy, fish fingers and chips?"

Louise played for sympathy. She pushed up against her mother's fat legs and raised her arms to be lifted. Her mouth trembled, her eyes swam with tears.

"That's right, you come to mum. An' you too, my pet lamb," she added as Gerry, awash with snot, came running for a cuddle and whatever else was going. With powerful arms she swept one to her shoulder, took the other by the hand and waddled up the path.

Charlie, Joey and I stood apprehensively at the foot of the stairs.

"Left you to look after 'em, I s'pose." Her aggression returned as quickly as it had departed. "Well you can save yourselves the bother. This is my 'ouse an' I want you out of 'ere. Go on! 'Oppit!"

"We're only here 'cause Smoky – "

"Are you deaf? Out!" She set Louise on the carpet, looked round for a weapon, saw none and advanced with clenched fists.

Hastily we squeezed past her down the hallway. Last in line, I stumbled against the pushchair. Tom was jolted from his sleep. Startled and finding himself horribly uncomfortable, he commenced a loud howling.

"Now see what you've done!" Seizing his sticky rattle, his mother flung it after us. It struck Charlie on the ear and dropped to the path. Following close behind, I felt it crunch under my foot. I sprang aside and fell full length across the broken tricycle. My shin was bruised, my hand scraped, my ear full of muddy grass. Painfully I limped after the others.

"An' don't come back!" The terrifying Dolores stood in the doorway, arms akimbo. Louise and Gerry clung to their mother's dress.

The Skin Deep Tattoo and Body-Piercing Studio was situated in Rum Lane, a cobbled street that ran up from the docks. The door was shut although these were opening hours. I peered through the window and saw a row of chairs, a table piled with magazines and walls covered with designs: dragons, snakes, eagles, Nazi insignia, girls in (and out of) bikinis, football crests, flags, anchors, everything imaginable from whole-body tattooing to a tiny bee. One section advertised the body piercing: ears, noses, lips, navels and other parts that made me wince.

An electric bell invited customers to ring.

"What do you think?" I was scared.

"Yeah, why not?" Joey rubbed his shoulder. "Tattoo looks good."

"Up to you," Charlie said. "If you get it, that's the full house. Without it – well, who's going to notice? You take a chance."

I took a shaky breath and pressed the bell.

A teenage boy appeared beyond the glass. He wore jogger bottoms and a Newcastle FC jersey. I recognised him from my years at the Comp – Danny Pearson. We were part of the same crowd that kicked a football about every lunchtime. A bell jangled as the door swung open.

"Hey there, Ben boy."

"Hello, Danny."

"Long time no see. What can we do you for then?"

"Come for a tattoo," Charlie said.

"Yeah? Come on in." He let us past and swung the door shut. "Hey, Dad! Customers! See you, Ben."

Leaving us standing, he returned to the family room. Briefly I glimpsed a rugby match on the television, then Danny was gone and his father took his place.

I stared, we all did, for Sam Pearson, a tall, athletic-looking man with designer stubble, wore a long blue dress and silver slingbacks. His hair was thick and short. Pendant earrings and a matching necklace of peacock blue hung against his neck. A scatter of bracelets was around one muscular wrist and a man's platinum watch around the other. His make-up, jade-green eye shadow and dark ruby lipstick, was immaculate.

"Hi there, lads." He had a comfortable Geordie accent. "Lookin' for a tattoo then?"

Still we stared.

"Oh, me get-up like. Sometimes I dress like this at the weekend, helps us relax. Doesn't trouble ye, does it?"

Charlie was the first to find his voice. "No, not at all." A slow grin lit his face. "Bit surprising."

"Aye, I know that. Most folk feel the same way. Don't see why I should change me clothes just to suit them though. They soon get used to it. Don't mean nothin', I'm not gay like." He laughed. "Hardly, five bairns an' a bonny wife right through there. One of you knows our Danny, right?"

"Yes." I cleared my throat. "Me."

Sam rubbed an eye with his knuckle then abruptly examined it. His eyebrows were thick and his lashes so dark they had no need of mascara. He wiped off a green smear and looked at Charlie and Joey. "Which one of you is it wants the tattoo then?"

"Me," I said again.

"You! How old are you, son – fifteen?"

"Sixteen." I drew out Joey's Union Card.

"Not old enough, sorry. Got to be eighteen."

"I'm not eighteen," Joey said. "Nobody asked how old I was."

"Where was that then?"

Joey thought. "Lagos."

"Ah, well, that's different." Sam smiled. "Go down the waterfront Lagos, Calcutta, places like that, they'll tattoo you for your christening. Here in Britain you got to be eighteen. Sorry." He went to let us out.

It was disappointing.

Joey checked his watch and told me, "There's a place down the sea front does tattoos. Don't know what it's like but we could go and see."

"Moxie Clark?" Sam caught his words and turned back. "You can *not* go to Moxie Clark. He's not clean for a start." Despite the blue dress, there was nothing feminine about Sam Pearson. "Go there, God knows what disease you'll come out with. He can't even draw."

"Well, have you got any suggestions?" Charlie said. "Ben – I mean Joey here – he's got his heart set on a tattoo."

"Aye, I've got a suggestion. Wait till you're eighteen, son."

"That's years!" I said.

"That's the law," he said.

"You don't really have to hang on till you're eighteen," Joey told me. "Do like I did, wait till the ship hits Panama or wherever. Loads o' tattooists places like that."

It was Sam's turn to stare. "Are you deaf or daft? D'you *want* your pal to get sick?"

"Didn't affect me."

"Mebbe you're lucky."

I remembered something. "D'you know Smoky Crisp?"

"Barry? Aye, I know him. What's he got to do with it?"

"He told us to come here."

"Barry did?"

"We were in his house an hour back," I said. "I sailed with him last trip. He told me: *You want a tattoo, go to Skin Deep. Sam Pearson's a mate o' mine. He'll see you right.* That's why we're here, not some other place."

"Sixteen years old? Barry knows the law."

"You could ring him up," Charlie said. "'Cept his wife got a bit ratty an' he took off."

Sam laughed. "Aye, that sounds like Barry."

"He knows how keen Joey is." Charlie put a hand on my shoulder. "Prob'ly thought you'd do it, save him the risk of infection."

"Places like Calcutta an' that," I said.

"Only sixteen, a shipmate an' all." Joey fingered his crest.

"An' you did some great work on him" Charlie said. "He showed us."

"Not his bum, I hope."

"Eh?"

"All right, all right." Sam gave in. "If Barry sent you, I'll do it. But you got to keep your traps shut, right? People find out, I could lose my licence."

"OK," I nodded.

Charlie grinned.

"I mean it, mind." Sam tugged the shoulder of his dress and became businesslike. "One small tattoo, no charge. Keep it off the books."

"And an earring," I said.

Names, Needles and Ink

"Let's see you then." Sam gripped my shoulders and turned me to catch the light. "Fair skin, it'll take well, good strong colour. You sure you're sixteen?"

"I showed you my Union Card. Why?"

"You look on the young side. Nowt but a bit o' fluff on your top lip. Our Danny's got more than that and he's only fourteen." To my relief he didn't pursue it. "Anyroad, what sort of thing have you got in mind?"

"Something with an anchor – and a name inside."

He took a book from a shelf. "Like this?"

We gathered round. I caught a whiff of cologne.

"Or this?" He flipped over the pages. "This?"

"Hang on. Yes, I like that."

"No hurry, take your time." He surrendered the book. "A tattoo's for life. I'll leave you to think about it. A few more you might like round there. I'll come back in ten minutes."

High-shouldered, earrings dancing, he returned to the rugby.

Joey watched him go. "How about that?"

"He's OK, good guy. Don't bother me how he dresses." Charlie pulled out another book and turned the pages. "Hey! Wow! Look at these lizards. Fantastic! How about one of them up the side of my neck?"

I couldn't share his enthusiasm. The longer I looked at the bewildering displays, the more I liked my shoulders the way they were. Then I thought of becoming Joey. Working in the tropics with my shirt off. Getting into trouble in some foreign country and having my identity checked. Maybe it wouldn't be so bad.

Finally I settled on a simple anchor design with a short length of chain and a scroll through the middle.

Sam approved. "One of me favourites. A little classic. An' what name d'you want on the scroll?"

"My gran," I said.

"Gran – that's nice. Now," he turned his green gaze on Charlie and Joey. "Why don't you boys take yourselves off for half an hour. Good pub just up the lane, the Mermaid. This lad an' me'll go into the studio. What's your name again, son?"

"Joey Bennett," I said and felt myself blush.

"I've heard that name before somewhere." Sam tried to remember. "No, it's gone."

Charlie and Joey went off and I followed the tall tattooist into an adjoining room. It was small, white and simply furnished: upright chairs, pictures on the wall (I recognised one of Smoky's), a little cabinet like a dentist's, a stainless steel autoclave and two tables, one set with pens and paper, the other with a surgically clean tray of apparatus.

I eyed the complicated tattoo machine and didn't like it at all.

"It'll not hurt, I promise." Sam smiled with ruby lips. "Come an' sit over here."

Apprehensively I joined him at the drawing table.

"Now, where do you want it?"

I touched the top of my left arm.

"Perfect spot. Just on the outside there, on the muscle. Not too big – about this?" He held his forefinger and thumb about five centimetres apart.

I nodded.

"Right." He took a pen and a small square of tracing paper, slipped a carbon beneath, inkside up, and pushed back the sleeves of his dress. "Most people use transfers, I like to draw it by hand. Every one an original." With confident lines, never needing to correct, he drew an immaculate anchor, chain and diagonal scroll.

I was impressed.

"What do you think?"

"Looks good."

Very lightly, with coloured pens, he blocked in the spaces and pushed the drawing across. "Something like that?"

"Yeah."

"I think so." He made a minor adjustment. "Let's see how it looks on your shoulder. Slip off your T-shirt and sit down over there."

The room was warm but I hugged my chest as I took my place at the tattooing table.

"Just give your shoulder a shave. Take off any tiny hairs."

With a can of foam and a disposable razor it was soon done. Sam mixed some Dettol in a basin of steaming water and wiped me clean.

"Now." Carefully he positioned the tracing paper and pressed it against my shoulder with a damp pad. As he peeled the paper away, a perfect outline was left on my skin.

I turned my head to see. After fourteen years of skin-coloured shoulder the black design was startling. On the other hand it was simple and looked good.

"Aye, I like it." Sam considered. "An' you're sure you want it? Not just to impress your pals? You're a young lad for sixteen and now's the time to say. I don't mind."

I looked up into his eyes, almost as green as the eye-shadow, then back again at the tattoo. "Yes," I said.

"OK, then let's do it." He tore open a pack of surgical gloves and set out his equipment.

He had said it wouldn't hurt but I didn't believe him. I hated injections. How could stabbing my skin a million times fail to hurt? The sight of those rubber gloves made me think of dentists and surgeons. When he fitted the needle into his machine and sat beside me, the room began to spin. I gripped my fingers tight.

"Relax, son, relax. There's nowt to be scared of."

And Sam was right. After a momentary burn as he started the outline, it faded to a stinging sensation that didn't trouble me in the least.

It was all so interesting: the different needles in their cellophane packs, the little pots of ink, the buzzing machine, the developing picture and Sam's sure hand as he guided the needles across my skin. Black outline, then blocks of green and red, and GRAN in letters of glowing blue within the scroll. Carefully he wiped off the excess ink and blood with an antiseptic wad.

All too soon it was finished and he passed me a hand mirror like a barber's. My shoulder was pink and swollen. The new tattoo, like a multicoloured wound, stood out starkly against my skin.

"It'll quieten down in a day or two." He covered it with lint and sticking plaster. "Leave it on for a few hours. The scabs'll drop off in a couple of weeks. An' *don't pick*, you'll ruin the tattoo."

The bell rang as Charlie and Joey came back into the shop.

"Still want your ear pierced?"

"Please."

He took a box from a drawer. Within lay a gun and a score of titanium sleepers – each, like the needles, in a sterile pack. He loaded one into the gun and cleaned the lobe of my ear thoroughly. Carefully he made a tiny dot to mark the spot of the puncture and positioned the gun so that my earlobe fitted into a slot at the end.

It didn't really hurt but I gasped as Sam pulled the trigger, the bolt shot forward with a thud and the sleeper pierced my ear .

"There, nothin' to it." He fitted a clip at the back and rubbed my ear again with antiseptic. "Feel that button at the front?"

I put up a hand.

"Give that a bit turn a couple o' times a day. Just so's your ear doesn't heal against it. Leave it in six weeks or so then get yoursel' along to a jeweller an' choose a ring." He set the gun beside the tattoo equipment. "You can pay for that, no laws about piercing. Four quid."

I paid him and we returned to the waiting room. Charlie and Joey, smelling of beer, gathered round.

"All OK?"

"Yeah." I showed them the dressing and grinned, suddenly feeling I had come through an ordeal and was now one of the lads. In two days I would be signing on as deck boy aboard the *Pacific Trader*.

"Can I ask you something?" Joey turned to Sam Pearson. "Charlie an' me were just talking about it. When I was at the Comp your Danny came into the first year. I remember 'cause everyone said his dad used to be a professional footballer, played for Newcastle or Sunderland, somewhere up that way. Is that right?"

"Aye, I played up there – an' Manchester. Years ago now. Picked for England in me prime - eight caps. Int'rested in football then, are you?"

"Yeah, I used to play for the school team. An' Westport Juniors."

"You without the hair an' me without the dress, eh?" A sudden memory lit Sam's face. "That's it, I knew I'd seen you before. It's the hair put me off. You're that little skinny lad used to be striker. Everyone said you'd go places. What you doing now?"

"I'm at sea."

"But you got a trial for Leeds, wasn't it? What happened there?"

"Oh, I got the flu, then I hurt my knee. I don't know, somehow it never happened."

"It's a wicked waste that. I came to watch you a couple o' times, you were good. Doesn't grow on trees you know, talent like that."

Joey shrugged.

"What's your name again?"

"Joey Bennett."

"Aye, that's it. I knew it was familiar." Suddenly it struck him. "Joey Bennett?" He turned to me. "You said *your* name's Joey Bennett. Showed us your union card. Hey, what's goin' on here?"

We backed towards the door.

"Hang on a minute. If he's Joey Bennett, who're you?"

Charlie made a dash from the shop. Joey and I followed.

I called from the pavement. "Didn't mean any harm. The tattoo's great. Thanks."

Sam hitched up his dress and rushed at me but he was hampered by the slingbacks.

We ran off down the cobbled lane.

"You little toerags! Come back 'ere!"

I stopped at the bottom and looked back. Sam stood by his window. We turned the corner and jogged on into Nelson Street.

Joey, a smoker and wheezing, slowed to a walk. His long face was racked with disappointment. "Hey, man, I feel rotten. He was nice, remembering my football an' all. Coming to see us."

"What are you talking about?" Charlie was upbeat as ever. "You want to stay wi' Fizz, don't you? Didn't mind playin' a trick when you didn't know who he was. Anyway, Ben got his tattoo, that's the main thing."

He was right, but I felt bad too.

"Mebbe I'll go back sometime," Charlie said. "Make up with him an' get one of them lizards on my neck. Fantastic!" He gave a little skip. "Hey, I'm starving! Anyone fancy a curry?"

I'm Dying Here

CHARLIE AND I went to see Smoky on Sunday afternoon. The papers were not ready as he had promised. I wasn't surprised. Haggard with a hangover and sporting a black eye – the result, he told us later, of a magnificent left hook from his wife – he greeted us on the step.

"Sorry, lads." He spoke in a croaky whisper and puffed on his crumpled cigarette. "Best not invite you in. She's come round a bit but it's not safe yet."

A tuneless fragment of *Puppet on a String* issued from within the house.

"Don't let that fool you." He glanced over his shoulder. "She went for me like a mad rhino. Best be on your way, yeah?"

The rhino and the wino, it occurred to me.

"But Ben's *got* to have them," Charlie said. "He give you twenty quid. He's signing on tomorrow."

"Aye, well, like I said, sorry." Smoky retreated into the house and began to shut the door.

"I'll give you sorry!" Charlie went after him and grabbed him by the collar. "You took the money an' you promised."

"Don't hit me!" Smoky covered his head. "Not you as well."

"Scared of your wife? What are you, a man or a cockroach?"

He thought about it. "Cockroach, I reckon."

"No you're not, you painted that." Charlie pointed to a picture in the hall: children splashed on a beach, the water sparkled. "We're counting on you. Ben's got to have them papers, else he can't go away."

"Who's that, Barry?" His wife's voice rang down the stairs, accompanied by the scents of bath oil and shampoo.

"No one, Dolores, darling. Just a woman collecting for the Lifeboat." He put a finger to his lips.

"Well don't give her nothing. Collectors never off the bloody doorstep. Seem to think we're made of money."

Charlie had an idea. "Listen," he whispered. "You spent that dosh we give you, yeah?"

Smoky put a hand to his throbbing head.

"Skint?"

He nodded faintly.

"Hair o' the dog?"

He hung out his tongue like a desert explorer.

"Well, you go get Joey's books an' whatever else you need, an' we'll take you down the Eight Bells. You can do the job there."

Smoky's eyes filled with hope. "I got the scalpel an' stuff like I said I would. 'Fore I went to the pub."

"Good. Well you fetch it an' we'll wait for you out in the road."

Leaving Smoky to creep like a fugitive through his own house, we retreated down the garden and hid behind a hedge. A minute later he joined us on the pavement, ghastly pale, shoelaces untied, jacket in one hand and crumpled poly bag in the other.

"Got everything?"

"Yeah."

"Sure?"

Smoky checked. "I forgot the books!"

"Well go back and get them."

"Oh, God! A simple funeral. Here, hang on to these." He handed over what he was carrying and crept back up the path.

It was Louise who gave the game away. A sticky figure with half an orange, she spotted us from an upstairs window. "Mum! Them lads are 'ere again. The ones that come yesterday."

"What's that, love?"

"Them lads. The ones that give dad money."

"What!" There was an explosion of wrath. "Barry!"

As if her voice were gunpowder, Smoky shot out the front door. Joey's books and a brown manila envelope flailed from one hand. Halfway down the path a shoe flew off. For a moment he was tempted to leave it then ran back and snatched it from the lawn.

Behind him, swathed in towels and a stupendous bra, his wife appeared in the doorway. "Barry!"

He regained the pavement and sped past us. "Run for it!"

For a third time, Charlie and I fled from trouble. I wondered if his life was always like this.

A minute took us through the alley and round some corners to safety. Smoky halted, his chest heaving and hands on his knees.

"Ohh! Ohh! I think I'm going to be sick!" But he wasn't and soon, having got his breath back, he began to perk up. "Thanks, lads. Cor, I thought I'd 'ad me chips that time." He pulled on his shoe and fastened the laces.

We laughed and walked on.

"What'll happen when you go back?" Charlie asked. "Got the kitchen knives locked up?"

"Who said anythin' about going back?" Smoky halted a moment. "Oh, my 'ead!" He waved the tattered envelope. "Fetched my own Discharge Book an' all. Mebbe sign on wi' you two tomorrow morning. Prob'ly somebody not turn up. Get a sub, stay out on the town till she sails. What ship is it again?"

"*Pacific Trader*," I said.

"That's it, just the job. Bit o' the old bronzie." A hint of swagger appeared in his step.

It didn't last long. After quarter of a mile he slowed to a halt and slumped against an advertisement hoarding. "Come on, boys, gimme a break. I can't walk all the way down the docks. I'm dying here. Not got the money for a taxi?"

I looked at my watch. "Won't be open for two hours yet."

He gave a hacking cough and groped for his tobacco tin. "Depends who you know."

"They'll not let me in anyway."

"Why not?"

"I'm not old enough."

"Leave it to your Uncle Barry." He looked up. "You got your ear pierced."

"I got a tattoo an' all."

"While you were drinking yourself witless," Charlie said.

"Don't you start."

We found a taxi and a few minutes later it dropped us on the pavement outside the Eight Bells. A tug yelped in the river. The masts and superstructure of a cargo ship, big as a block of flats, slid past the warehouses.

Charlie paid the driver and we turned to the pub. It appeared deserted. The black door, chipped where it had been kicked by a thousand boots, was locked. The hanging sign squeaked in the breeze.

I Make an Enemy

"This way, lads." Smoky led us round the side and pushed open a gate that led to the inn yard. Empty crates and casks stood on every side. Abandoned furniture – cookers and tables and broken chairs – rotted in the corners. I shut the gate behind us while Smoky crossed the yard and knocked four times on the back door. There was silence, then a bolt slid back and the door opened. The barman, a big man with rolled-up sleeves, was smoking a stubby cigar.

"Cheers, Rolly." Smoky greeted him. "Brought a couple o' young pals along."

The man stood aside and we passed him into a gloomy, beer-smelling corridor. He bolted the door and led the way to the big public bar.

To my surprise, on that Sunday afternoon, the room was two-thirds full, the atmosphere boozy and easy-going. The curtains were drawn, cigarette smoke floated beneath the lights. The bar glowed with bottles and brasswork. By the entrance to the *Gents* a flashing slot machine promised fortunes. At old mahogany tables the customers, all men, sat with glasses, talking, laughing, silent, watching the football on a TV screen high in a corner.

"Shouldn't it be shut?" I whispered.

"It is shut," Charlie said. "These are just Rolly's friends, like you and me, invited in for a quiet drink."

"But I've never met him."

"Don't be stupid. That's the story if the cops come round: bar's shut, we're all his guests, no money involved. Costs a bomb, mind, if you want a pint."

I thought about it.

"Hi, there, Smoky." Heads turned. "You had a skinful last night. One of the walking wounded, yeah? What a shiner!" Someone pulled out a chair. "Come on, sit down before you fall down."

"Sorry, mate." With a firm hand Charlie led Smoky away. "Got to do a little job for us first. See you in a while, OK?"

I looked around me, knowing I should not be there. Three men sat at a nearby table. One, heavily built, was clearly the dominant figure of the trio. The second man, a bit older and once red-headed, was raw-boned and scruffily dressed. Their young companion, not much older than Charlie, was a body-builder with bright blond hair, a tight black T-shirt and black leather jeans.

The red-headed man sprawled in his seat, legs thrust out between the tables. As I passed, my eyes not yet fully adjusted, I caught his ankle with the toe of my trainer. Then three things happened very quickly: I stumbled against the man's chair; his arm jerked and beer spilled down his jersey; he sprang to his feet with an oath, brushed off the worst and struck me a tremendous clout across the head.

"Clumsy fool! Look at me!"

I clung to one of the bar-room pillars. Dizzily I was aware of him bearing down upon me.

But other men were on their feet.

"Less o' that!" The barman came to my aid. With powerful hands, cigar parked in the corner of his mouth, he grasped the man by wrist and collar and propelled him backwards into his chair. "It's not the lad's fault. What d'you expect if you stick your scabby legs out halfway across the docks?"

"Take your soddin' hands off of me!" The man struggled. "I'm tellin' you, if – "

"No, I'm telling you. Hitting young lads – we don't want your sort here. So just shut up, finish your drink an' get out."

The thick-set man rose, radiating violence. He had, I saw now, a port-wine birthmark on his face which twisted his right eye to a glitter. "Puttin' us out an' all?"

"That's up to you."

"If he goes, we go." He rested a thick hand with two gold rings upon the back of a chair. "An' if we go, there's likely to be a bit o' damage."

"That a threat?"

"Call it a fact. Added to which," he looked all round, "you'll have the fuzz batterin' on the door afore you finish that cigar."

Rollo examined his wet stub. "All right, he stays." He addressed the red-headed man. "But no more trouble. These boys," he indicated the drinkers who had gathered round, "have got ways of dealing with scum like you."

The man sneered and took another mouthful of beer. He turned malevolent eyes upon me.

Charlie stood at my shoulder. "What're you staring at?" he said aggressively and took my arm. "Come on, mate, take no notice. Miserable old git!" He led the way across the room. "There's a table over here."

Smoky and I followed meekly. While Charlie went to the bar, we pushed the table into a pool of light. Soon he was back, carrying two beers, a shandy, and three packets of crisps in his teeth. Carefully he set down the drinks and wiped the table with a bar towel.

"This pint an' one more," he said to Smoky. "That's all you're getting till the job's finished. After that we'll pay you the rest of what we owe."

Smoky stretched out a hand.

Charlie kept the beer from him. "Ben an' me, we really *need* this. We're counting on you."

"I said all right, didn't I?" Smoky tipped the contents of his poly bag on the table. "Strewth, you're worse than the old woman! Just give us the glass an' shove off."

We sat at an adjoining table. I looked across the bar-room. The two who had caused the trouble had their heads together. Their blond companion looked towards me, then the thug with the birthmark. His hot eyes held mine. I looked away. This *had* to be the new bosun, the man we'd been warned about, the man suspected of murder. What was his name?

"Jumbo Ryland," Charlie said. "Great start, eh?"

My ear still burned. I cracked my jaw and the sound came back.

The shandy was excellent, ice-cold and running with condensation. I tore open my crisps.

Smoky's head was bowed with concentration. His fag ash dropped on Joey's Discharge Book. His glass stood empty.

PART TWO

PACIFIC TRADER

Monday Morning

THEN IT was Monday and I had to lie to Charlie's mum. I felt really bad about it because she'd been great and thought I was an honest boy.

"Yeah, really, Mrs Sunderland. I rang the headmaster last night. I'll get gated and loads of extra homework an' that, but it'll be OK." I slung my schoolbag over my shoulder, underpants and dirty socks crushed into the bottom.

"Well, I don't like it," she said. "I can understand you being unhappy there and playing truant, telling those fibs about your auntie and coming back here to see your old home and your granny's grave. I'm not even going to *ask* what you and our Charlie have been up to this weekend. But now going back a day late. And with a stud in your ear! They'll make you take that out for a start, a school like what-you-call-it."

"*Frankie's*," I said and lied again. "No, quite a lot of the boys have got them – earrings I mean."

"Really? Well, I must say I'm very surprised." She looked at me with eyes that went right through you. "Mm … Anyway, it's been lovely having you here. And when you get back I hope you'll feel a lot happier. You must have friends, a nice lad like you." She gave me a squashy hug. "And be sure you come back and see us next time Charlie's home. Maybe it'll be your school holidays and you can stay a bit longer."

"Thanks, Mrs Sunderland. And for all the meals and that."

"You're more than welcome, love. It's a treat to have young folk about the house again. Me and the old man rattle around here like two peas in a tin kettle." She opened the door. "And you've got your sandwiches and everything for the journey?"

I patted my rucksack. "Yes, thanks."

Doctor Death trotted in from the garden. He saw I was leaving and jumped up, paws the size of plates on my chest. I staggered back against the banisters and put my face to his, smelling his sweet breath and *Doggy Brek*. With a sloshy tongue he licked me wherever he could reach.

"What a good boy!" I said and hugged him round the neck.

"Come on, you daft thing." Mrs Sunderland pulled him off me. "You'll see Ben when he comes back. Now into the kitchen with you."

I brushed the mud from my jacket and followed Charlie down the steps.

"What time did you say you're signing on, Charlie?" his mother called.

"Eleven, down the Dock Office. I'll see Ben off at the station an' go straight there."

"Back for lunch?"

"Depends how long they take. Likely meet a pal."

"I think dad's going out but I can leave something ready." She glanced at her watch. "Got to dash or I'll be late for work."

"Forget it," Charlie said. "I'll get something in town."

"Well, if you do come back there's the rest of that pie. Pop it in the microwave and do yourself some veg." She turned to me. "Bye, love. Good luck, hope it all works out. Drop us a card sometime, I'll be thinking of you."

"Thanks. Bye."

I hitched my rucksack and started down the path at Charlie's back. The door shut behind us.

I'd left my seagoing clothes in a locker at the station. A taxi took us to the *Mission to Seamen* down at the docks, an organisation known worldwide as *The Flying Angel*. The door was locked. I rang and the warden, a middle-aged man in navy-blue battledress, let us in. We followed him across a vinyl-floored vestibule to his office.

"Signing on today," Charlie said. "My pal needs a berth for a couple of nights."

The warden indicated some grey-metal chairs and we sat down. "What ship's that?"

"*Pacific Trader*. Both of us."

"Sailing Wednesday, right?"

"I think so."

An array of fifty or more curling postcards were pinned to the wall. Sydney, Abu Dhabi, Yokohama – lonely sailors writing to the Mission that had given them a home for a few days.

"So that's what?" the warden said. "Just him for two nights?"

"Yeah."

"What about you?"

"I live in town," Charlie said.

The man eyed him suspiciously. "Not planning to sleep on the floor are you? Save the price of a room?"

"No, I am not," Charlie said very definitely.

"All right, just asking. You'd be surprised what people get up to. Couple of months back I found seven kipping in one room."

"Not me. Got no gear anyway, have I?"

The warden opened his register. "Need some identification. Got your Discharge Book?"

I passed it over and glanced at Charlie. Despite his hangover, Smoky had done a great job. Time and again I had held the page to the light, picked at the photo and examined it from every angle. To my eyes, at least, it was impossible to tell it had been tampered with, that the embossed stamp was a forgery and the boy in the photograph was an imposter. All the same, I couldn't believe we'd get away with it and waited for the accusing stare, the harsh words, the hand on the telephone. They never came. With no more than a glance the warden entered the Discharge Book number in his register and flipped it open to my photo and Joey's address.

"I thought you lived out of town," he said. "Got a Westport address here."

We had discussed this. "I never said that." I talked a bit rough and tried not to blush. "Had a bust-up wi' my dad an' he put me out."

The warden surveyed me disapprovingly over the top of his glasses but made no comment.

"Right." He swung the register towards me and pointed to a line. "Sign there."

I took his pen and forged the signature I had practised a hundred times: *Joseph A. Bennett* and a flourish beneath.

"Thank you." He checked it against the Discharge Book and returned it to me. "Want to pay now or get a sub when you sign on?"

"I need a sub."

"All right, but I'd like you to pay when you come back tonight. You look an honest lad but I've had a few slip away. Lock up at eleven. TV and that in the common room. We've got coffee and biscuits; if you want a hot meal there's plenty of places up in town." He scanned a board and unhooked a key. "Room five. Through the fire doors there and up the stairs."

There were voices and a couple of Asian seamen passed us on their way out.

I picked up my rucksack and bags of working gear, suddenly all I possessed in the world. Charlie took the last one and we went up to my room. It was bare but clean: a bed, a locker, a washbasin, an upright chair, a window that looked down on dustbins in the yard.

"It'll do," Charlie said. "You only have to sleep here."

"I s'pose." Feeling empty, lonely, more than a little scared, I dropped the bags in a corner.

"A pity you couldn't have stayed on with us." Charlie turned a tap and the pipes gurgled. "But there was no way, mum would have sussed it out in a minute."

I tested the bed. The springs squeaked and sagged but the covers were fresh. I wondered who had slept there last. "It's fine." I took a deep breath and collected the rest of Joey's papers. "What's the time?"

"Coming up to ten."

"Time to go?" I twiddled the sleeper in my ear. It made me wince.

"Let's have a coffee first," Charlie said. "Betty'll be open. Better than the stuff you'll get here. Come on, my treat."

Leaving everything as it lay, I locked the door behind me, ran down the steps and emerged into the momentous morning.

The dock gates were thrown wide. We walked through. No one questioned us as we crossed the acres of cobbles and rail tracks that lay between the busy road and the quays. Transporter lorries growled beneath heavy loads. A stiff wind swirled dust around pallets and the corners of warehouses. The hulls of the ships were hidden, but the funnels and spider rigging of their masts rose above the warehouse roofs. Beyond them the sky was blue and white.

Betty's doughnuts made me belch.

A short distance ahead of us, two figures made their way in the same direction. One was squat and bow-legged. The other, slim and much younger, glanced round and spotted us. They waited for us to catch up.

"Excuse me," the younger man said in a light voice. "You're not signing on by any chance, are you?" He was about twenty, blond and vivid.

"*Pacific Trader*?"

He examined a piece of paper. "That's it."

"Yeah. Dock Office, eleven o'clock."

"You and your friend?"

Charlie grinned. "Both of us."

"Oh, that's good. Us too. I mean, you never know *who* you'll be sailing with, do you? Some of the crews …! Well, you wouldn't share your *flat* with just anyone, would you?"

We walked on together.

"Honestly," he chatted on, "I've been feeling depressed about it for days. And when I woke up this morning and realised this was *it*, this was *the day*, I could have screamed. Well, I did, didn't I?" He appealed to his companion. "I just felt like drinking a bottle of gin in a hot bath and opening my wrists. I did really. Ending it all! It only seems like yesterday I signed off the last one." He sighed, then abruptly, as if someone had pressed a switch, he brightened up and gave a skip. "But things are looking better already. What are you sailing as?" he asked Charlie.

"Junior ordinary seaman."

"Not pantry boy, what a pity." He gave a musical laugh and looked at me. "What about you? Don't tell me. Umm …" He rolled his eyes, bright blue. "Deck boy?"

"How'd you know?"

"Well, you're not exactly old enough to be the old man, dear. And your friend's a J.O.S. Out on deck with all those horrible hairy

ABs. Still ..." I caught a whiff of aftershave or body rub. "What's your name?"

"Ben."

"Ben. Ben the deck boy. And look, he's blushing! Oh, isn't he lovely!" He clung to his companion's arm.

———•———

Lively Friends

I HAD never met anyone like our new-found friend, and nobody had ever talked to me like that, but I liked him. He was funny and nice.

"And I'm called Charlie," Charlie said. "What about yourself?"

"Me?" He set fingertips against his chest. "Well, I'm Michael. Michael Goldie." He held out a pale hand, a hand with two monogrammed rings and a wrist festooned with friendship bracelets. I thought his hand would be soft and his handshake limp, but it was strong and muscular. He turned to his companion. "And this is Barbara."

I was startled. Anyone less like Barbara it was hard to imagine, a thickset figure of forty, not much higher than my shoulder, with shapeless trousers and the broken nose of a boxer.

"My pleasure." Barbara – Bob to his parents, I learned later – smiled shyly and extended a hand like a bear's paw.

"What are you sailing as?" Charlie said.

"Well, I'm officers' steward." Michael flapped his hand. "At least that's what they told me. And she's going as a greaser."

"Change for me," said Barbara, his voice soft and broad Norfolk.

"She used to be engineers' steward," Michael explained. "But after what happened, it was greaser or out."

"Yeah?" Charlie pricked up his ears. "What was that then?"

"You won't believe it." He skipped backwards.

"Come on, Michael," Barbara said, "that's not fair. We've not even signed on yet."

"She's right, stories later, when we're out on the briny with a bottle of gin." He fell into step, or not quite, for Michael's was a brighter, shorter step than Charlie's and mine. "Have you met any of the crew?"

"Not so far," Charlie said.

"Someone told us the bosun's a bit of a killer," I reminded him.

"Bosun!" Michael shrugged carelessly. "Bosuns don't bother us, do they, Barbara? It's the chief steward I want to know about."

"And the engineers," Barbara said. "And Ossie B."

"A pal," Michael explained. "Been ill. We heard he might be coming back as messman."

"Very ill," Barbara said. "Thought he might have to give up the sea."

"What, an accident?" Charlie asked.

"No, dear." Barbara tapped his bullet head. "Up here."

"Well, we'll know in a few minutes," Michael said. "By the way," he caught Charlie's sleeve, "I've got to tell you. I just love your haircut – that curly bit on top. And that earring with your dark skin. And those stripy jeans. Fabulous!"

"Thanks very much," Charlie said. "Ben just got a new haircut too."

"Oh, I noticed. Very butch, don't you think, Barbara?"

"Yes, very nice," said the chunky Barbara. He halted, looking right and left. "Which way now? Can you remember?"

We had been walking without paying attention. Directly ahead, moored stem to stern and two abreast, the magnificent ocean-going ships lay at the quayside. On that Monday morning all was bustle and activity: dockers called loudly, pallets of cargo swung from ship to shore and shore to ship, forklifts moved in and out of warehouses, barges drifted in the dock basin, a score of flags streamed stiffly in the wind.

"Not down there anyway," Michael said.

"Any idea which one's *Pacific Trader*?" I said.

Barbara studied the long, bristling lines of vessels and shook his head. "Can't be sure, not from here." He pointed. "That might be her, right down the far end. See, with the orange funnel. Wouldn't count on it, she might be in one of the other docks. Beautiful ship though. Moored right next to her one time in Hawaii. Crowd of us went aboard for a bit of a party. Very lively."

We circled the harbour buildings and after a few minutes came to a bruised wooden door with dirty panes of glass. Above it a peeling sign, once black and gold, proclaimed *Westport Dock*

Authority. A brass plate in need of polishing stated *Dock Office*. A long-dead seagull had been kicked to one side.

"Here we are," Charlie said cheerfully.

"Look at the state of it." Michael made a face. "What do they think we are, some down and outs? You'd think they could afford a lick of paint."

"Stop it, Michael," Barbara said, "it's just a door. You're such a drama queen."

He pushed through and we followed him into a shabby but clean-swept lobby. A painted finger directed seamen up a flight of stone steps, worn like the steps in a cathedral.

A notice, with the name of the ship chalked in, issued more precise instructions: *Crew signing aboard PACIFIC TRADER report to Room 2C.*

"Oh, very droll!" Michael commented. "2C! Give the man a banana. And so friendly – note the *please*. Still, never mind. This way for the *Skylark*."

He led the way to the stairs.

Ossie B

THE STAIRCASE led to a landing with posters on the wall. We went through a fire door. There was no need to search for 2C. A hubbub of voices issued from a crowded room.

It was spacious, strip lighting, a few plastic chairs and a line of desks near the back wall. Behind the desks a scatter of officials, some in uniform, were checking documents, getting the crew to sign ship's articles for the coming voyage. Twenty or more men, some little older than Charlie, others old enough to be grandfathers, waited to be called forward. The windows were shut, as if to keep at bay the wind that blew from the sea on that fine autumn morning. Cigarette smoke drifted in the air. It caught my throat and made me cough.

I did not belong. I felt like a very visible intruder. Back at *Frankie's* – I checked the time – my class would be in history with Mr Conway, working on a project about the Russian Revolution. After school there was a hockey match. I put it from my mind and studied my shipmates. Most looked pleasant enough but it was like entering another world. I spotted the baggy-eyed figure of Smoky Crisp, a scrap of toilet paper stuck to his chin where he had cut himself shaving. Our eyes met. He gave me a wink and perky thumbs-up then put a finger to his lips for secrecy.

A name was called. A balding man in a bright Mobil anorak made his way to one of the desks.

Michael was looking across the room. He touched Barbara's arm. "There's Ossie."

Barbara craned his neck. "I see him." He stood on tiptoe. "Looks a lot better."

"Calmer."

"More like his old self."

"I hope so."

Charlie said, "Who are you talking about?"

"That big chap over there."

"The black guy?"

"Behind him."

I could only see his head, a big pumpkin head and a pinky-white face. It was a face you'd remember, a bit like a baby's face with blond baby hair. His cheeks were soft, as if they never needed a razor. His eyes, hardly set back at all, were large and milky-blue; his lips so pink you might think he used lipstick.

"Odd-looking chap," Charlie said.

"Odd fish all round," Michael said.

Barbara said, "That's unkind, Michael. He wasn't well."

"Fair enough," Michael said. "But he's not normal like the rest of us, is he? All that gear he brought with him for a start, he had it before he joined the ship."

"Michael and me sailed with him two trips back," Barbara explained. "He went really crazy, you know. I mean half the people that go to sea are a bit doolally anyway, you know that for yourselves, but Ossie was scary. Into tarot and the occult. Took to dressing up as a priest. Ended up having a breakdown. When we got to – where was it, Michael?"

Michael didn't need to think. "Calcutta."

"Of course. Sorry, Michael." Barbara gave him a quick hug. "When we got to Calcutta they come for him with an ambulance. Had to be sedated. Took three men to hold him down. Took him away."

"I didn't catch his name," I said.

"Ossie. Ossie B."

"Ossie Bee? Like a wasp? That's a queer sort of name."

"No, the letter B. He doesn't use his surname – except times like this when he can't avoid it."

"Why not?" Charlie said. "Is he in trouble?"

"Not like you mean," Barbara said. "Not with the police. It's just – well, caused problems."

"How?"

"His name's Bagot," Michael said plainly.

"What's wrong with that?"

"It rhymes with maggot," Michael said. "People call him Maggot and he can't stand it."

"That's not so bad," Charlie said. "I get called stuff sometimes: Nora Pakora, Paki, you know, racist stuff. I can live with it."

"I think it's awful," Michael said. "But you look good. You're OK in the head. Ossie isn't, and he does look a bit, well – "

I could see what he meant: the pale skin, the fat. It was cruel.

"He lived with his mum," Barbara said. "She looked after him when he got out of hospital. Looked after him all his life really, never anyone else. He just worshipped her. Then a few months back she suddenly went and died. After all he'd been through. Right out the blue. Nearly killed him, I think."

At that moment the big man looked round the room and caught us gazing at him. His pumpkin face broke into a grin, gappy teeth like tombstones.

Michael waved him over.

He pushed through the crowd, jostling shoulders, standing on toes.

Voices were raised. "Hey, watch who you're pushing! Bloody oaf!"

"Sorry. Sorry." He reached us. "Hello, Michael. Barbara, my friend!" He hugged them like a bear, Barbara not up to his shoulder, and hugged them again. "Oh, I'm so glad you're here. I was frightened you might change your minds. I need a friendly face today."

I was startled, I'd never met a man with a voice like Ossie B. It was high-pitched, high as a boy whose voice has not yet broken, almost the voice of a girl.

"We weren't sure *you* were going to make it," Barbara said in his broad, friendly Norfolk. "What do the doctors say?"

"The one I like best reckons I'll be OK. I've got over what happened to mum. If I'm ever going back to sea, he says, now's the time. I've been ashore for eight months, can't put it off for ever. Just keep taking the pills and try not to get upset."

"That's wonderful, Ossie," Barbara said. "We're always thinking about you, you know, wondering how you're doing. And here you are, large as life. Don't worry, you'll be all right with Michael and me to keep an eye on you."

"You're my friends." Ossie smiled with pleasure.

Michael introduced us. "This is Ossie, an old shipmate – whoops, the 'o' word, sorry, Ossie." He laughed. "Sailed together on the *Star of Bengal*. And this here's Charlie, signing on as J.O.S. And Ben the deck boy. Isn't he gorgeous, just like the brother I never had. I'm going to be his big brother all trip and make sure he comes to no harm." He took my arm. "Aren't I, Ben?"

It was news to me.

We shook hands with Ossie.

"What are you sailing as?" Charlie asked.

"Messman, this'll be my tenth trip," Ossie replied. "Started out pantry boy. I liked it in the galley so – "

"Oswald Bagot?" An official voice reached us above the hubbub.

"Oh, help!" His eyes filled with alarm. "Barbara, will you – ?"

"No, you've got to do it yourself. On you go, Ossie boy. You'll be all right."

"I hope so." He gritted his teeth. "Meet you here after?"

"Of course."

"Wish me luck." He worked his way through the crowd and sat at the appointed desk.

"Will he be OK?" I said.

"Let's hope so." Barbara looked anxious. "He had a bad time on the *Star*. We all did."

I looked to Michael for details. But gay, merry Michael wasn't listening. He was staring across the room and the blood had drained from his face.

Curly

"What is it?" Barbara said.

Michael seemed not to hear.

"Michael!"

"Rat'bone," he said.

"What! Where?"

He nodded.

At first I saw only the crew. Then my stomach clenched as I recognised the man who had smacked me across the head in the Eight Bells. He was sitting at one of the desks.

"Charlie," I said.

"I see him."

"Is he signing on?"

"Looks like it." He touched Michael's arm. "He the one you mean, that scrawny guy in the denim jacket? Hair hanging over his collar."

"That's him, nasty, vicious … I hate him!"

"Ben and me know him."

"You *know* him?"

"Well, not exactly know him. He give Ben a thump."

"That sounds about right," Barbara said.

"I tripped over his foot," I said. "Slopped his beer."

"Lucky a thump's all he give you."

"What did you say his name was?"

"Lenny Rathbone," Michael said. "Known to those who love him as Rat'bone."

"What'll he be sailing as?"

"AB, I expect. Unless he's been made up to bosun. Not likely, no one would have him."

"I'll find out." Barbara pulled a French fisherman's cap from his pocket. Tugging the peak low, he crossed the room.

He was soon back. "AB," he said shortly.

"I can't stand him!" Michael said. "I never even wanted to hear his *name* again, never mind sail with him. He's evil. Oh, Barbara!" He turned to his friend. "What do you think?"

"I don't know." Barbara was perplexed. "I'll leave it to you, love. If you want to do a runner that's all right with me."

"Do you think we should?"

"Nothing to stop us, I suppose. Mind, that nice woman at the Pool said it's the only ship on the books with a berth for the two of us. And we have let the flat." He looked around the room. "No sign of Cyclops anyway. And we're here now. Can't let scum like Rat'bone rule our lives."

"You're right, of course. And there's poor Ossie signing on this minute. Look at him." Michael's eyes brimmed with tears. "We can't just abandon him."

Why was he so upset? Surely not, I thought, just because this Rat'bone was signing on as AB.

"Maybe if we make it plain from the start," Barbara said. "Get a few people behind us. Tell him we're not going to be pushed around."

"It's not going to be like the *Star*," Michael said.

"No way, or we'll go straight to the old man."

Michael looked at Charlie and me. "Here's these two lads for a start. You'll be on our side, won't you?"

"I thought you were going to be my big brother," I said.

"Oh, I will." He rubbed his eyes. "We'll look after each other, eh?"

"If it's against that horrible Rat'bone," I said.

Charlie said, "There's something going on here we don't know about. What happened that trip? On the *Star of Bengal*."

"Trouble," Barbara said briefly. "Big trouble. Ended with somebody dying. A friend."

"Not somebody, Barbara!" Michael's eyes spilled over. "Not *somebody*, it was Curly! Not *somebody*, it was *Curly*!"

"I'm sorry." Barbara took his hand. "Of course it was Curly. I was trying not to upset you."

Men were watching.

"Seen enough, have you?" Barbara said aggressively. "Happy now?"

They looked away.

"Curly was Michael's best friend," he explained in a softer voice. "Went to the same school. Sailed together for two years. Peas in a pod, lovely chap. Always laughing, head full of curls. Then that trip we all got caught up in some scam Rat'bone an' his mate were pulling."

"The guy you called Cyclops?" Charlie said.

"That's him. He was at the heart of it. Worse than Rat'bone even."

"Much worse," Michael said.

"Why Cyclops?"

"Why d'you think? Ugly great brute, one eye."

"One eye?"

"Well not in the middle of his forehead. He's got two eyes, need two eyes to be on deck. But one's all twisted, covered by a birthmark."

My heart gave a jump.

"What happened?" Charlie said. "To Curly, I mean."

"No one knows really. At least everyone knows but nobody saw anything, no one could prove anything." He glanced at Michael. "Things on board had been getting worse and worse. Cyclops was at the heart of it but there were others as well. I was threatened with a knife. Michael here got knocked down and given a kicking. Curly told them if anything else happened he was going to shop them, they'd end up in an Indian jail. Never had the chance. That night we were having a bit of a party, anchored off Calcutta. Hot as hell. He went along to the galley for some grub and – well, he never came back. Just disappeared."

"Over the side?" I said.

"Into the Hooghly?" Charlie added.

Michael sniffed back his tears. "How do you know that?"

"Something a guy told us when Ben was buying some gear. He said the – "

But Michael wasn't listening. "You don't think they could – "

"What?" Barbara said.

"Still be together."

"Cyclops and Rat'bone? How would I know? Surprising they're not both in jail, if you ask me." He stood on tiptoe to scan the crowd. "No sign of him."

"I couldn't bear it. I just couldn't bear it if they were both joining."

I remembered the three in the Eight Bells: Cyclops, as Michael called him, Rat'bone and the young bodybuilder. I remembered what we'd been told about the bosun's violent temper, and the 'nice young fella' torn apart by crocodiles.

At the far side of the room Rat'bone gathered his papers together and rose. Blinking in his own cigarette smoke, he elbowed a way through the crowd.

"Hey, you have no manners?" The voice was deep. "Watch who you're pushing." A middle-aged black man protested. He was the biggest man in the room, even bigger than Ossie, a dignified figure, his hair touched with grey. One tooth, I saw, had been capped with gold. He wore a suit for signing on, much worn but neatly pressed.

Rat'bone glanced at him contemptuously and ignored him. From the hostile looks he received, it was apparent that Rat'bone was known to some of the others. With a surly nod he acknowledged a couple on his way to the door. If he recognised Michael and Barbara, he gave no indication of it. But he saw me.

"Oh, my word." He removed the cigarette. "Small world. Not signing on the *Trader* are you? Not deck boy?" His eyes slipped to Charlie. "You too? Well, that's brightened a dull morning." He smiled nastily, revealing a set of over-large false teeth. "I'll see you later." A rank smell hung in the air as he headed from the room.

"Oh, Ben!" Michael was shaken. "What a beast! Do you think you'll be all right? I've got such bad vibes about this trip."

The Fight on the Landing

THE CROWD cleared slowly. As men signed on and departed, others arrived.

"Looks like we're going to be here for some time." Michael blew his nose on a crumpled tissue. "Got any plans for lunch?"

"We thought we'd go back to Betty's," Charlie said.

"Sweaty Betty!" Michael exclaimed. "She of the bouncing boobs. All those dockers stuffing themselves with pie and peas? You don't want to go there. Come on up town with us. We'll go to *Chez Marilyn*. They do these Italian dishes. Fabulous!"

Charlie looked at me. "Sounds a bit pricy," he said. "We'll think about it."

"And talking about fabulous Italian dishes," Michael was looking across the room. "What about him over there, Barbara?"

A young sailor with olive skin and dark eyes was combing his hair. Seeing us watching, he gave a shy smile.

"Isn't he gorgeous!" Michael said.

I was embarrassed. A hundred times I had heard boys say, *Cor, look at her, I wouldn't mind* … But I'd never heard a boy say, *Cor, look at him!*"

Charlie grinned.

Barbara said, "Michael, behave yourself."

There was time to hear no more because right then my name was called: "Joseph Bennett?"

A bald official in spectacles looked up from one of the tables. I took a deep breath and went forward.

"Sit down." The man held out his hand. "Got your Discharge Book?"

I passed it across.

He entered the number. Carefully he turned one page, then another and studied the entries. "Second trip?"

"Yes."

"Looking forward to it?" He stamped the ship's details in the first column.

I read it upside down. "Very much."

"Quite right too." He stamped the second column. I read that too: *Westport* and the date. "Fine life for a young lad like yourself." He wrote the words *Deck Boy* and set the Discharge Book aside. "I wish it was me going away again at your age. Vaccination Certificate?"

I handed it to him. We had been given jabs at school though I wasn't sure what for. And I'd been given loads when I went away with dad. Hopefully they were still working.

"That's fine." The man passed it back. "No problems where you're going."

"Where is that?"

"Didn't they tell you at the Pool?" He was surprised. "Out through Panama, call in at Fiji, discharge New Zealand. Miss the winter." He mused a moment. "Right, Union Card?"

The formalities were quickly concluded. A long and official-looking document lay at his side. He swung it towards me and pointed to the bottom line. "Sign there." The words *Deck Boy* had been typed in readiness. Trying to steady my hand, I signed *Joseph A Bennett* with Joey's flourish, and added the date.

"Good." The man glanced at it briefly, checked the signature against my Discharge Book and dropped the Discharge Book into a wire tray at his side. "That's it then. Report on board eleven a.m. Wednesday. Any questions?"

Charlie had told me what to say. "Can I have a sub?"

"Not my department." He pointed with the biro. "Desk over there."

"Thank you very much."

The man seemed surprised. "You're welcome. Have a good trip."

There was a queue by the sub desk and by the time I was finished – another signature, sixty pounds in my pocket – only a scatter of men remained. The officials stood drinking coffee, waiting for stragglers. Charlie and Michael, who had signed on more quickly, were standing by the door. Barbara joined us a moment later.

"It's all decided," Michael greeted me. "We're grabbing a quick sin and frolic at the Eight Bells then going up town to *Chez Marilyn* for lunch. You'll love it."

"Sin and frolic?"

"Gin and tonic," Barbara translated. "Nothing to be alarmed about, she always calls it that."

"Ossie and Luigi are meeting us there."

"Who's Luigi?"

"That young Italian." Michael rolled his eyes. "Talk about drop-dead gorgeous! Met him on his way out."

"Oh," I said.

"Ossie's got to pick up a few things at the chemist," Barbara said. "Says he'll not be long."

We drifted down the corridor.

Charlie held me back for a moment. "All OK?"

"Like clockwork." I couldn't believe it. "Deck boy."

"Yeah!" He punched the air. "Fantastic!"

"What's fantastic?" Michael turned.

"Nothing," I said.

"Oh, secrets." He tossed his head. "Well, I'm sure Barbara and I don't want to know anyway."

The fire doors had been wedged open to clear the air. Voices drifted up the well of the stairs. They were quite narrow and we waited on the landing. I was at the back but Michael gave a cry as the late arrivals turned a corner and started up the final flight. There were two: the bosun with a twisted eye – Jumbo Ryland, or 'Cyclops', as Michael called him – and his companion, the young bodybuilder.

"Well, well." Ryland smiled as he reached the top. "A welcoming party. Isn't that nice, Steve?"

"Yeah." Steve's hair seemed blonder than ever. Wearing another tight black T-shirt, jacket over his arm, he took in Charlie and me. "We seen these two yes'day, down the Eight Bells. Who's the others?"

"Oh, I know them. Both on the – what ship was it? India, anyway. This one's called Barbara. Get that, Barbara! Look at the state of him. An' the other one – can't remember his name, steward of some kind. One of the poofs. Mate of that guy I told you about, Curly something."

"The one was going to put the finger?"

"That's the one." Ryland's eye glittered. "These others aren't stewards though. Haven't got the look. Must be on deck."

I smelled whisky or beer.

He gripped me by the jaw. "What are you? Deck boy?"

I tried to pull free but he was strong and pushed me against the wall.

"Deck boy, yeah? Can't be much more, your age."

"Leave him alone!" Michael began shouting. "Take your hands off him, you ugly great – " He tugged at the bosun's sleeve.

"Oops!" Ryland laughed and let me go. With a thick arm he pushed Michael aside. "Going to hit me with your handbag, dearie?"

Michael gave a cry and flung himself at the powerful bosun, punching and scratching. I was astonished. So was Ryland. It was a gazelle attacking a lion – or a rhinoceros. But although Michael was slim and not much taller than myself, he was sinewy and several of his blows got through.

"Oh! Ow! Get off, you little – ! Are you mad!" Ryland grabbed an arm but Michael wrenched it free and struck him again. A long scratch appeared down the bosun's cheek

Steve tried to pull Michael off. Barbara stepped forward and gave him a savage kick on the back of his leg. With a cry of anguish, the bodybuilder fell to the floor. Clutching his thigh, he rolled to and fro. "You stay there," Barbara said.

Despite Michael's reckless courage, the fight could not last long. Ryland grasped him by the neck and shoulder and flung him aside. He put a hand to his face and saw the blood.

"You're a bloody maniac! You should be put away!" He started forward, murder in his eyes, but Barbara stepped between them and at the same moment two officials, alerted by the shouting, emerged from the office.

One was a uniformed officer with gold braid on his sleeve. The other was the bald, bespectacled man who had signed me on.

"What in God's name's going on?" the officer demanded.

"Fighting!" said his companion. "We'll have none of that here."

Michael picked himself from the floor. Steve, his leg locked and leather jeans split, dragged himself to one knee.

"We'll finish this on Wednesday." Ryland dabbed his cheek with a handkerchief.

Michael was shaking. "Cyclops!" he hissed and thrust his head forward. "Patch!"

"What!" Ryland started towards him. Chunky Barbara pushed him back.

"Stop it, you hear!" The officer placed himself between them. "That's enough. You'll finish nothing on Wednesday. I'm reporting this to Captain Bell. Any sign of trouble, he'll have you on a charge and off that ship before you can blink." He turned to the rest of us. "Now, you four. Finished signing on, yes?"

We nodded.

"Right then, on your bikes."

But the bald official was enjoying the situation. "Ryland, isn't it? You've been in trouble before. And," he tried to remember the name of his friend, "don't tell me – Petersen. *Mr Westport* back in the summer weren't you, Petersen? Flashing your muscles around the swimming pool, natty pair of trunks? Saw your picture in the *Argus*." His eyes twinkled. "The editor's a friend of mine, maybe I should give him a ring, always on the lookout for a story." He sketched a headline in the air: *"Brawling bosun and local beefcake duffed up by gay stewards."* Laughing, he returned to the office. "Come in when you've recovered and we'll see about getting you signed on. That's if Captain Bell doesn't mind having a couple of marshmallows like you on board."

Glad of his support but scared what it might mean for the future, I headed downstairs with the others. At the first landing we jostled to a halt for Michael had gone limp and seemed hardly able to stand. Helpless with tears, he clung to Charlie for support.

"Don't worry," Barbara reassured me. "She'll be all right. It's just the shock."

I also was shaken. I had never been threatened in my life, certainly not by a grown-up who gripped me by the face and shoved me against a wall.

Michael showed no sign of letting go. Charlie began to work himself free.

What sort of people were these, I wondered as we set off a minute later. What on earth was I doing there? What had I got myself into?

Letters from the *Flying Angel*

I COULD see that our new-found friends might like *Chez Marilyn* but it wasn't the sort of place dad used to take me at all: big swags on the curtains, waiters in black trousers and coloured shirts, and right in the middle a life-size statue of Marilyn Monroe with a fountain playing in front of her. The food was tasty enough but only tiny helpings on big plates with a slice of lime on one side, a strand of watercress on the other, and a scribble of brown sauce to fill the gaps. When I told Michael it cost a pound a bite he told me not to be so *bourgeois* and anyway he and Barbara were paying so just *enjoy*!

Ossie and Luigi had joined us so we were a group of six. Ossie was there when we arrived, standing outside on the pavement. He was so excited, his big moon face so happy to be with friends, that no one had the heart to tell him about Rat'bone and Ryland.

Luigi arrived late and caused a flutter among the waiters. I think he'd been unsure about coming because he knew nobody and his English was poor. From what I could make out he came from the foot of Italy and this was his first voyage on a British ship. He was a quiet, likable man. With his mouth closed, Luigi might have been one of the Hollywood stars whose photographs adorned the walls of *Chez Marilyn*. His teeth let him down, they were so strong and crooked that every time he smiled he turned into a werewolf.

But this was Michael and Barbara's occasion. They were in their element, telling stories, swapping backchat with the waiters and keeping us laughing all the way through. It was a happy and memorable lunch although, to be honest, my stomach kept clamouring for Betty's sausage, egg and chips, or pie and peas with the dockers.

*

Afterwards we split up. For the first time since I had run into Charlie – only three days ago though it seemed half a lifetime – I found myself alone. I wasn't sorry because I needed time to sort things out in my mind and I had some shopping to do.

An hour later, poly bag in one hand and a bunch of red and yellow chrysanthemums in the other, I took a bus to the edge of town and walked to my gran's grave. This, as much as anything, was my reason for coming to Westport. She had been cremated but dad and I had scattered her ashes on the family plot where my grandpa and dad's baby sister were buried. Since I left the city, gran's inscription had been added to the gravestone:

Also Edith Mary,
beloved wife, mother and grandmother,
R.I.P.

There were some glass containers by a tap at the graveyard wall. I rinsed one, arranged the flowers and set them in front of the cross. Then I just crouched on my hunkers and remembered her, at home but mostly in the hospital before she died, and thought about my own strength and how I had wished I could give some of it to her. With my eyes shut I said a prayer then found my thoughts wandering.

What would she have made of my present escapade? There wasn't any doubt: thoughtless, hurtful, headstrong and foolish. "Tell your friend you're sorry and get yourself back to school this minute, Ben," she would have said, fixing me with those blue eyes. She was absolutely right. Yet somewhere in my belly I felt a stubborn resistance. I hadn't come this far to go back now. "Sorry, Gran," I said guiltily. "I'll be all right, really I will. Don't worry."

For five minutes I lingered but she was slipping away. Sadly I ran my fingers over the sharp new inscription and realised it was time to leave. After twenty paces her grave was merging with the others. After another twenty it was gone. Then I spotted the brave chrysanthemums and knew that whatever I did gran would never have stopped loving me.

*

By the time I returned to the *Flying Angel* it was five o'clock. It didn't take long to arrange the things in my room and take a hot shower, hoping no one would come into the bathroom while I was there. Afterwards, wearing a clean T-shirt, my hair gelled and set in the new style, I wandered down to the common room.

Although I was on my own there was no danger of being lonely for other seamen, singly and in groups, drifted into the Mission after their evening meal. Spotting the deck boy sitting by himself, they invited me to games of table tennis, darts and crib for matchsticks.

As the waterfront bars began to liven up, the common room emptied. A crowd invited me to join them and could not have been kinder, but I didn't want to go. Besides, I had letters to write and fetched a pen and notepaper from my room.

I knew what I wanted to say but it was hard to find the right words, much worse than writing essays for old Spitty Barker who took us for English. Each one took several attempts, sitting alone in that sailors' common room with half-filled ashtrays and posters on the walls. Screwed-up balls of paper littered the table. In the end this is what I wrote, the first to the headmaster of *Frankie's*:

> Dear Captain Winchester,
>
> When I left school on Friday I expected to be back by 1600 or 1700 hours on Sunday, in time for tea. But because of unexpected events this weekend I won't be returning at all. Please will you phone my Auntie Dorothy Thomson at Oxford 680291, or my dad at the Hong Kong Shipping Company, who's number is London 736 4141. He is mate on the London Pride.
>
> Will you send all my belongings to my Auntie.
>
> Please don't worry about me or search. I am well and have got a job in Yorkshire. Everybody at school has been very kind and I do not want to cause any trouble but I did not feel right there.
>
> Yours faithfully,
> Benjamin Thomson

> Dear Auntie Dorothy,
>
> I have to make a confession to you. I told them at school I was staying the weekend with you in Oxford. Really I came to

Yorkshire where I have got a pen pal. I had to show them a letter from you and got somebody to write it for me.

Don't be angry please. I have got a job and am not going back to Frankie's. I don't like it there very much as you know. I think you will be annoyed I am causing you trouble and I am very sorry. But it is a good job and I will write every month so you will know I am alright.

Tell Dad not to worry. I am not a baby any more, I am nearly fifteen and know what I am doing.

Love and thanks,

Ben

Dear Dad,

By the time you get this letter I think you will have heard from Auntie Dorothy and Captain Winchester. It was hard for you after Gran died and I know you are doing your very best. Frankie's is a great school and some of the boys like it very much. It is not your fault that I was not happy there. I know you will be worried but please don't !!! I have got this job in Yorkshire with nice people. They think I am sixteen which I will be in a bit over a year. I have given them a different name so they don't know I am Ben Thomson.

It is great here and I am well. I will write to Auntie Barbara every month because you might be at sea but you can phone her to know that I am alright. I will write to you as well, of course.

I miss you.

Lots of love,

Ben

It was nearly eleven o'clock by the time I had finished and written the envelopes. The warden was locking up for the night. A few seamen had come back to the Mission, a couple the worse for drink. The rest, I suppose, returned to their ships. Anyway, I stamped the letters and put all three into a bigger envelope addressed to Charlie's brother Bill, who was a soldier up at Catterick camp in Yorkshire. Charlie had told him what we were doing and sworn him to secrecy. Bill thought it was great and had agreed to post any letters I sent him, now and during the trip, from the nearby town of Richmond. I wanted to get the bundle away so I would not lie awake half the night worrying about it. Just before the warden locked the door I ran down the road and dropped the envelope into a postbox at the corner.

It was done. My last task.

Nothing remained but to report aboard the *Pacific Trader* in two days' time.

Pizza and Kisses

THAT WAS Monday.

On Tuesday Charlie couldn't meet me because the Sunderlands were having a family day, a big get-together before he went back to sea.

I spent the morning in the city library and a coffee shop, studying Charlie's book of seamanship. In the afternoon I went to the pictures with Joey and Fizz. When we came out it was teatime, the light was fading, so we went to Alfredo's for a pizza.

I told them all that had happened and described my new shipmates: Michael and Barbara, Ossie and Luigi, Ryland, Rat'bone and Steve.

"Blimey!" Joey said. "All them names. Sounds like you're halfway across the Atlantic already. Don't waste no time, do you?"

"I didn't go looking," I said and speared a mouthful topped with olives and chorizo. "Just the way it turned out."

"Well I don't like the sound of it," Fizz said. "It sounds dangerous. I wouldn't want a fourteen-year-old brother of mine going away with people like that." She had taken off her dazzling PVC jacket and wore a sexy top with a halter neck. "All those men fighting. Two of them actually hitting you. And this Cyclops person probably *killed* someone. You're not even on board yet. What's it going to be like when you get to sea?"

I shrugged.

"Sounds great to me," Joey said. "Hey, gimme back my Discharge Book, I've changed my mind."

"Joey Bennett!" Fizz slapped his arm. "Don't you dare!"

But Joey was kidding. In the two days since I'd seen him he had changed. He was talking about giving up smoking and getting fit again. The startling Mohican was gone, his hair trimmed to a soft brown stubble. With his big nose and rubbery lips, his little head perched on that long neck, he looked like a kindly vulture.

"I went back to see Sam yes'day." His voice was eager. "You know, Sam Pearson at the tattoo parlour. Not in a dress no more, just jeans an' a sweatshirt now. Told him we was sorry about the tattoo but I was thinking about giving up the sea an' taking up football again. He says once I've got the fags and booze out my system, he'll take me along to the Rovers' training sessions. See how I get on."

Fizz smiled, nice eyes and pretty white teeth.

But Joey's mind was on the football. "Great, eh?"

"Yeah, big chance." I was pleased for him but thinking more about joining the ship next morning.

Fizz read my mind. "You will be OK?" She was anxious. "It's not too late, you know. You don't *have* to go. Just don't turn up. Go back to that school an' no one'll ever know. All they've got's your picture, no name nor nothing. Joey's the one could get into trouble, but he can easy say he lost his papers, or somebody nicked 'em. They're not going to lock him up."

"Not go?" I managed a carefree smile. "What are you talking about? It's going to be brilliant."

"D'you mean it, mate?" Joey said. "I've been feelin' a bit like – guilty, you know. Me stayin' ashore wi' Fizz, you getting out o' that school – it were just an idea. Then Charlie takes over an' suddenly here's you on the briny an' me tryin' to get back into football."

"Course I mean it," I said. "Panama, Fiji, New Zealand – and getting paid for it. Who'd turn down a chance like that?"

Fizz put down her knife and fork. Unexpectedly she leaned across and kissed me full on the lips. It was like being KO'd by a velvet hammer.

"You – are – terrific." She cupped the back of my neck. "Good looking. Style. I've been wanting to do that for a long time. If it wasn't for Joey, I'd run off with you myself."

Michael used the word 'gorgeous' a lot. He didn't know what he was talking about. *This* was gorgeous. My face burned.

"Here, take your hands off him. That's my mate." Joey pulled the back of her jeans. "But listen, sailing tomorrow, yeah? We were planning on coming to see you off but I reckon we'd better not, OK? I might know some o' the crew. No point runnin' risks."

His voice was clear enough but I never heard a word because right then Fizz began kissing me again.

I Join *Pacific Trader*

At half past ten, his gear in two holdalls, Charlie picked me up in a taxi. Minutes later it dropped us by the gangway.

Pacific Trader lay starboard side to the quay. She was a beautiful ship, a hundred and sixty metres long, thirteen thousand tons, elegant black hull, white superstructure, tan and black funnel. I had walked the length of her the previous day and loved her at first sight. It was hard to believe that in a few hours' time this would be my home, and I would be crossing the Atlantic, steaming through Panama and heading west into the vast Pacific as one of the crew. But now here I was, lugging my bags beneath the towering legs of the cranes.

The gangway was almost horizontal, the treads stood upright. Trying to quell the grumble in my guts and look as if joining a ship was no big deal, I followed Charlie on board.

Figures hurried to and fro with paint rollers, clipboards, pots of grease and small pieces of machinery. Pallets of cargo disappeared into the holds. Pallets of supplies stood on deck. Lifeboat covers were thrown back. Oil pipes and water pipes snaked aboard from the quay. Wreaths of smoke from the funnel were torn sideways by the wind. Up on the foremast, the fluttering Blue Peter announced that the ship would be sailing that very day.

The day watchman nodded as we came aboard. Two figures stood by the gangway. I recognised both and was filled with alarm. One was Jumbo Ryland, the bosun, thick arms folded across his chest. The second was a cadet, little older than Charlie, in officer's uniform with a gold flash on his lapel. He was the boy with whom we had quarrelled at the disco, a fleshy, handsome youth with high colouring and dark glossy curls. He murmured something to the bosun and they laughed.

Ryland's twisted eye flashed towards us. He jerked his head. "Come here, the pair o' you."

We crossed the deck, bags bumping our legs.

"You've met Mr Fanshott-Williams." He cocked a thumb. "Senior cadet on this ship. You'll treat him with respect, right? You've met me, an' all. I don't like you an' I don't like the company you keep, poofs and troublemakers. So I know *what* you are, a couple of toerags, but not *who* you are." He consulted a grubby list.

"Sunderland," Charlie said.

"Bennett."

Laboriously he crossed off our names with a stub of pencil. "J.O.S. an' Deck Boy. Right," he looked up. "My name's Ryland. I'm the bosun on this ship an' don't you forget it. Give me any hassle, any grief, any jokes about this," he touched his face, "an' I'll squash you like a couple o' bilge rats. Understood?"

Not two minutes on board. I was transfixed by his malevolence.

"I said do you understand?"

"Yes, Bosun," Charlie muttered.

"You?"

I nodded.

"You tryin' me on with dumb insolence?"

"No."

"No, *Bosun*."

"No, Bosun," I said.

"Better not, neither." He hitched his thick belt. "Right then, leave your gear in the crew mess and report to the mate."

"Where is he?" Charlie said.

"Find him, Cocoa, find him."

Charlie stared at him. "You call me that again, Bosun, ever, I'll report you."

"Ooooo!" Ryland laughed dismissively. "On your way."

The cadet laughed with him: red lips, dark eyes, arrogant.

Side by side they watched us go.

We found the mate in the officers' saloon. He was younger than my dad, slim, neat, dark hair brushed across, three rings on an immaculate sleeve. Company reps lolled nearby. The table was strewn with papers: bills of lading, schedules, cargo plans. Cigarette smoke and whisky fumes, acrid after the breeze on deck, made my eyes prick.

The mate finished a story before he paid us any attention. "And you are?"

"Sunderland, J.O.S."

"Bennett, sir. Deck Boy."

He glanced at his watch, a gold Oyster, and annotated the list at his side. "Right." He half rose and held out a hand. "My name's Rose, Mr Rose. Good to have you aboard."

After the rough welcome by the bosun I was relieved.

He subsided and drew on a cigarette, squinting through the smoke. He had those eyebrows that almost meet in the middle. "Hard work and a happy ship, that's the name of the game. Think you can manage that?"

"I think so, sir," Charlie said.

"You *think* so?"

"Well, *we* can."

The mate's gaze sharpened. "And somebody else can't?"

Charlie shrugged.

The mate didn't like it. "You keep your noses clean, that's good enough for me. Any problems, report them to the bosun."

My eyes met Charlie's. He raised his brows. "Very good," he said. "Sir."

The mate looked at me. "You don't say much."

"No, sir."

"First trip?"

"Second, sir."

"You look very young."

I didn't reply.

"Everything all right?"

"Yes, thank you."

He looked at me narrowly. "You speak very well for a deck boy."

My cheeks burned. "Thank you, sir."

"Nothing I should know is there," he consulted the list, "Bennett?"

"I don't think so, sir."

He sat back. "All right, find your cabins and settle in. Lunch at twelve. Turn-to after. Any questions?"

"One, if you don't mind, sir," Charlie said. "Can you tell us how many deck boys there's going to be?"

The mate consulted his list. "Meant to be two but Sanderson's in hospital. Motorbike smash apparently. So just the one this trip, Bennett here."

"Well, could Ben and me share the deck boys' cabin, me being ordinary seaman now? We're pals see."

The mate considered. "Don't see why not. You'll probably have to muck in as peggy anyway. Can't see the other J.O.S. objecting."

"Thanks very much."

"Thank you, sir," I said.

Again the mate turned curious eyes upon me. He flipped through a jumble of Discharge Books in a wire tray and pulled one out. As he glanced through the details I saw my photograph. I held my breath but all seemed to be in order.

"Right, on you go." Still holding the cigarette, he reached for his whisky glass. A signet ring on his little finger winked in the light.

Charlie and I went back on deck and cleared our lungs in the wind that blew from the river.

"Great!" he said. "At least the mate's OK. A good guy."

"What's he mean, peggy?" I said. "Who's Peggy?"

"Well," Charlie was serious. "It's like when you have to wear a frilly apron and – "

"What!"

He burst out laughing. "No, peggy's when you have to work below decks – washrooms, alleyways, cleaning and that. All deck boys have to do it. Word from the old days, centuries back."

"Phew!" I said. "That's a relief."

Familiar Faces – and Aaron

AFTER FIVE weeks' coasting with dock workers wandering through to the toilets, shore crews dossing down and no cleaners of any sort, the accommodation was filthy. I guessed whose job it would be to clean it up. We lugged our gear down the long starboard alleyway. With a heavy heart I surveyed the greasy smears on the paintwork, the dirt and diesel trodden into the deck. Within the cabins, bunks were littered with cans and newspapers, washbasins left half full of scummy water. Doors hung open, others were shut, radiators on full blast.

The cabin at the after end, opposite the washroom and just for'ard of the storm door leading out onto the crew deck, was for deck boys. The one before it was labelled *Junior Ordinary Seamen*. A boy was in there, Charlie's age, bending over an open suitcase.

"Hello." Charlie stood in the doorway.

He turned. "Oh, hi. Didn't hear you." He was average height and strongly built: fresh open face, blue eyes, springy blond hair.

"J.O.S.?"

"Yeah." He rubbed sweat from his forehead.

"Me too. Charlie." Charlie held out his hand. "This is Ben. Deck boy."

"Aaron. Hello." Clothes everywhere. Photos of girls on the locker. He pushed his suitcase to one side. "Want in now?"

"Not really. Look, Ben and me are pals an' he's the only deck boy this trip. I thought we'd shack up together – if that's OK with you?"

"Cabin to myself?" Aaron looked round. "Yeah, great. Be like the Ritz. Fix it up with the bosun?"

"Mate give us permission. Who's the redhead?"

Aaron looked down. "Abbie – no, Rita."

Charlie grinned. "Girl in every port?"

"One's no good, what if she's not home?"

"You can have the other one, Rita'll do me fine." Charlie stepped back. "See you later, yeah?"

The deck boys' cabin was a mirror image of the one next door. Like the rest, it was a tip: stale blankets, sticky deck, pizza remnants in the washbasin. A big ginger tom cat lay on the bottom bunk. It yawned, showing needle teeth, and stretched out to be patted. I rubbed its marmalade belly. When I stopped it jumped down and wandered out.

"I'm not bringing my gear into this dump," Charlie said. "Let's clean it up a bit."

With wet cloths, disinfectant and bags for the rubbish it didn't take long. I hooked open the porthole.

"Top bunk or bottom?"

I considered. "Don't mind."

"Good, I like top." Charlie swung up and tested the mattress. "Great!" He bounced a few times and traced a rusty stain overhead with his finger. "Soon get used to this."

When I sailed with dad I'd been given a cabin in the officers' quarters, high up on the airy deck. Living below decks, amid the radiator heat, smell of diesel and throb of the engines, was going to be very different. Washroom opposite, Aaron next door, Charlie sleeping above me. I loved it already.

There were six drawers, two narrow lockers, two hooks on the bulkhead. We divided them evenly, stowed our belongings and changed into working gear. Aaron joined us and we took our empty bags to the storage locker. The second steward gave us clean blankets, mattress covers and so on and we made up the bunks, hung towels by the washbasin.

There were twenty minutes to kill before lunch so we explored the ship. Charlie and Aaron, seventeen years old and on their third trip, seemed quite at home. I envied them their ease, regular merchant seamen who had every right to be there, whilst I was an imposter, a fourteen-year-old schoolboy with forged documents. Without warning, as if I had developed a sudden fever, I began to shiver with nerves. I had experienced several small panic attacks over the past few days but nothing like this. My chest felt tight, my vision blurred, my guts turned to water. As we clambered over gear on the foredeck, looked down from the fo'csle head and climbed ladders to see the lifeboats, I trailed behind. Whichever way I turned, men seemed to be watching me. Clumsily I caught my toe on a deck bracket and fell. As I stood up, rubbing my elbow, I felt dizzy. And when I saw Rat'bone come aboard, savage-faced and lugging a heavy holdall, I could have been sick.

"You all right, Ben, mate?" Charlie was concerned. "You're white as a sheet."

"Fine." I drew a shaky breath. "Just caught my funny bone."

He knew I was lying. "Be OK when you've had some dinner, yeah?"

"I guess."

"You're sweating," Aaron said.

I wiped my brow. "Maybe something I ate. Got to go to the bog. See you back in the cabin." I hurried away.

The feeling passed but it left me shaken.

Lunch was tasty, not as good as Betty's but filling: stew and potatoes, apricot sponge and custard. The three of us sat together. While I ate I examined the faces surrounding me. These were the men I would be sailing with. A few I recognised already: the big black man who had protested to Rat'bone in the dock office; Steve Petersen, yellow hair to his shoulders, muscles bulging in another tight T-shirt; Barbara looking deeply depressed; Smoky nursing a massive hangover.

A hand fell on my shoulder. A refreshing scent of eau-de-Cologne mingled with the smells of diesel and food:

"Charlie! Ben! Such a *relief* to find a friendly face. Isn't it all just ghastly! Nightmare!"

The atmosphere brightened. I grinned and looked up. Michael wore black trousers, a white shirt with the sleeves rolled halfway to his elbows, and a red silk handkerchief around his throat. "When we had that *fracas* with Cyclops the other day I felt like throwing the whole thing up, really I did. But after that lovely lunch at *Chez Marilyn* – wasn't it gorgeous! – and the thought of sailing with you two boys, I said to myself, well why not? I'm not going to let any ugly old bosun spoil my life. So here I am!" He threw his arms in the air. "And it's not two of you now, I see, it's three."

Aaron was startled. I introduced them. "Pleased to meet you," Aaron said uncertainly.

"Oh, what a lovely dry handshake," Michael said. "I can tell we're going to be great friends. But look, I can't stay. Barbara's really down in the dumps. She went to see the engine room, you know, down all those oily ladders, and she just *hates* it. Well, who can blame her? I'd drink poison here and now if it was me." He lowered his voice conspiratorially. "Except she's got Luigi with her down there, you remember? I mean, how unfair is that? I could scratch her eyes out."

He was gone, a swirl of perfume, dodging between the tables. We resumed our dinners.

"How d'you know *him*?" Aaron said.

Charlie told the story, pointed out Rat'bone, squat Barbara.

"You should have seen the way he went for Cyclops," I said.

"Who's Cyclops?"

"The bosun. That's what Michael calls him – ugly one-eyed monster."

"And Barbara flattened his mate," Charlie said. "Him over there, the body-builder."

"Steve Petersen," I said. "Would you like to look like that? I bet he takes steroids. Steroid Steve!"

Charlie laughed. "Pete the Meat."

I pushed back my plate and started pudding.

"Right, you lot." The bosun stood scowling, sleeves pushed up his massive forearms. He spoke to Aaron. "Finish that then go and find Chippy. Three and four holds have finished loading. Give him a hand to batten down."

He turned to Charlie and me. "You two go peggy the next couple o' days. Place is like a pigsty. You, Abdul or whatever your name is, finish your chapati and get along to my cabin. I want it scrubbed out, top to bottom. Make up the bunk – best blankets mind. I want that place like a new pin. An' you, Babyface, give the messman a hand in here then get yourself along to the crew washroom. It's like the black hole of Calcutta. Make a start on that – showers, bulkheads, bogs, the lot."

Charlie was seething. I nodded dumbly.

"Cat got your tongue?"

"No, Bosun."

"Well answer when you're spoken to. Bloody deck boys! Be trusted with that can you, cleaning out the bogs?"

"Yes."

"Yes, *Bosun*."

"Yes, Bosun."

Hostility crackled from every hair. He seemed about to say something else then realised half the mess was listening. "Right, get a move on. An' there'd better be no slacking. I've got my eye on you two."

A clear, courageous voice piped up in the silence. It was Michael. "Which eye would that be – Bosun?"

The Messman's Cabin

I HELPED Ossie to clear up and scrub out the messroom. He was frightened. Unlike the happy man I had met signing on and who had lunched with us in town, his pumpkin face seemed on the point of collapse. His lips trembled, his pale eyes swam with tears.

"Oh, Ben! Both of them!" That high-pitched voice. "Not just Ryland, Rat'bone as well!"

He had not served lunch but that would be his job in future. As messman he wore white: a freshly-laundered jacket, apron and trousers. "Aaah!" He cried aloud as a gravy-covered plate slipped from his fingers and smashed on the deck.

"Ben, be a pal." He leaned on the serving counter and took several deep breaths. "Fetch my pills from the cabin." He fumbled for a key. "Top drawer on the right. Long yellow ones – a bottle."

"Of course. Which cabin is it?"

"Number seven – Messman." He subsided onto a chair.

I hurried through the alleyways. His room was fresh and tidy. The ginger cat, whose name was Attila, lay on the bunk and watched me with sleepy eyes. The locker door had swung open. Among Ossie's neatly-hung jackets and trousers, I spotted a flowing black garment, not unlike the cassock of a priest. I couldn't resist a quick look. As far as I could tell it was precisely that. What did he want a cassock for? In the bottom of the locker, behind his enormous shoes and flip-flops, was a container shaped like an urn, made of bronze-coloured plastic. Next to it stood a beautiful old Ouija board with the letters of the alphabet painted ornately in a double arc and the numbers one to zero in a line underneath. I recognised it because one of the boys had taken a Ouija board to *Frankie's* and we'd had fun with it at night, swigging from a cheap bottle of sherry and the dorm lit by candles – until

Captain Winchester, the headmaster, found out and there was a sensational row. Perhaps we would be playing with it at sea; I hoped so.

But I should not have been prying into Ossie's locker. Quickly I tidied the jackets and turned to the pill drawer. I had imagined a couple of bottles and maybe a packet or two, but this was a chemist's shop: antiseptic, plasters, cold cures, homeopathic remedies, foot spray, hand cream, eye wash, mouth wash, a blood pressure machine, tubes of ointment – and stacked neatly at one side, two dozen or more packets of pills, powders and capsules. The drawer was two-thirds full. A clean, astringent smell wafted out at me. There was no doubt which were the yellow pills Ossie needed. I tucked the bottle into my pocket, locked the door and hurried back to the messroom.

A glass of water stood ready. Shakily Ossie tipped a tablet, then a second one, into his palm and gulped them down. His face was greasy, hectic spots of red burned in his cheeks. "Sorry, Ben. I'll be all right in a minute." He took another sip and spilled the water down his chest.

"Are you really OK?" I sat beside him. "Do you want me to get Barbara – or the chief steward?"

"No, no." He waved his hands. "Don't tell anyone. Keep this between the two of us – do you mind?"

"Of course not, if that's what you want."

"Thank you, Ben. Such a friend." He took my hand. "It was seeing the two of them together. After the *Star* and everything that happened there. One would be bad enough, but both – !" His breath came quickly. "I've not been well. Did Barbara tell you?"

"Michael said something about it."

"I'll be all right as long as I don't get upset."

I eased my fingers from his big soft grasp. "Look, you stay there and I'll make a start."

He rested the hand on his chest. "I'll be all right in a few minutes."

I stacked the chairs on tables, the way we did at school, and fetched a broom from the cleaning locker. Ossie calmed down as the pills kicked in and for an hour we worked together. Dead chips and cigarette butts were swept from the deck. Crusty spills were scraped and washed away. After weeks of neglect the stainless steel and Formica began to shine.

The messroom clock showed two-fifteen. "You'd better go," Ossie said. "Make a start on the washroom or the bosun'll be after your blood."

"Cyclops, that's what Michael calls him." I tried to make a joke of it.

"Cyclops, Heinz, Quasimodo, I've heard them all. Don't play games with that one, Ben." Ossie was earnest. "He's not funny, he's dangerous."

"He's certainly been pretty nasty to me."

"I didn't say nasty, I said dangerous. Of course he's nasty." He hesitated, seemed uncertain whether to say more. "Jumbo Ryland's a *wicked* man. Wicked like it says in the Bible. Evil."

I stared at him.

"Keep out of his way as much as possible."

"I'll do my best."

"A young boy like you, I don't want you to get hurt."

Get hurt? What did he mean? Was he comparing me with Curly? I'd done nothing. Of all my recent experiences there was none stranger than this, standing in that half-cleaned messroom, a bucket of dirty water in my hand, listening to a lumbering man dressed all in white, who warned me about evil and danger. It was too much to take in. I needed to talk to Charlie about it.

"Thanks, Ossie. I'll not forget." I tipped my bucket down the sluice in the galley and wrung out the cloth. "Sure you're OK now?"

"I'll be fine," he said and certainly seemed better than when I arrived.

"I'm off then. See you at smoko."

"Bye, Ben."

I hurried away.

Incident in the Washroom

THE LAMPTRIMMER, or Lampie as he was known, was a tiny bandy-legged man with a wrinkled face. His name was Jockey White. It was his job to look after the deck stores and dole them out from his locker in the fo'csle. Paint, deck scrubbers, ropes, chains, holystones, tar, grease, wires, shackles, everything that might be needed on deck to keep a ship in good repair was in his charge.

With a gummy scowl – for when he wasn't eating, Lampie kept his teeth in the top pocket of his overalls – he handed me a cloth, a lopsided bucket and several scoops of suji, a powerful cleaning powder, in an old can. I was on my own. Feeling years older than the schoolboy I had been at *Frankie's*, I carried it to the crew washroom.

Like everywhere else, the washroom was a mess: basins scummy, smears and hand marks all over the bulkheads, the white tile deck trodden black. I looked in the showers and lavatories. Most, to my relief, weren't too bad. With a sigh, I mixed the suji with hot water and made a start.

It was a job I did not enjoy. The suji inflamed my fingers, a small cut on the back of my hand stung like fire, but it cut through the dirt like a TV advert. As I worked my way along the row of washbasins, the porcelain gleamed white in my wake, the taps shone silver. Now and again one of the crew came in to use the toilets. Aaron looked in to see how I was getting on.

"Looks good," he said, then saw the creamy-grey slosh of suji in the bottom of my bucket. "Hey, man, how much did you put in?"

I told him.

"Quarter of that's plenty," he said. "Strip your skin off if you use it that strong. See if Lampie'll give you rubber gloves."

I rinsed my hands beneath a cold tap to ease the sting.

"Bosun's fairly got it in for you and Charlie, hasn't he? You should have heard the way he tore a strip off him when he stepped out on deck for a minute. He was raging. What's all that about?"

I told him about Rat'bone at the Eight Bells, how he had hit me and the barman had threatened to throw them out. "Then when we were signing on, the bosun picked a fight with Michael, you know, the gay steward, and – "

"An' what?" The huge figure of Ryland stood in the doorway. "An' what, eh?" He came across the oily tiles. "Smarmy little git! You start tellin' them lies round this ship, you'll not last long." He turned on Aaron. "What the 'ell you doin' 'ere? I left you workin' wi' Chippy, chocking up number five. Hop it! If I catch you hangin' round 'ere again, you'll feel the weight o' my fist. Understand?"

"Yes, right." Aaron backed away.

"An' shut that door when you go."

"Shut the door?"

"You 'eard me."

"What for?"

"'Cause I said so."

"But – " Aaron's eyes flicked to me.

"Give me strength! Are you deaf?"

The washroom door was hooked wide. Washroom doors are permanently open, like cabin doors at sea, with a curtain pulled across. Reluctantly Aaron shut it behind him.

"Right," the bosun turned. "You an' me's goin' to have a little talk. First," he glanced at the bright washbasins, "who taught you this way to clean a place out? Jus' do the easy bits? That might be the way you did it your last ship, it's not the way you'll do it 'ere. P'raps you wasn't listenin': deckhead, bulkheads, showers, bogs, the lot. Start at the top an' work your way down. Get some steps. Get yoursel' wet."

He advanced upon me. "Now, that other, what you saw Monday. That screamin' queen tryin' to scratch my eyes out. I wasn't jokin' what I said a minute back. I learn you been spreadin' that around, one night you'll find yoursel' with a two thousand mile swim. It's happened afore, it'll happen again. You ask your queer pals, ask 'em about that Curly."

He caught the front of my T-shirt with a big fist and pushed me against the washbasins. "Let me tell you somethin'. I'm bosun here, an' I hate deck boys! Lowest form of sea-life that ever crawled, an' you'd better remember that. Only thing I hate more than deck boys is deck boys wi' la-di-dah accents as thinks they're better than the rest of us; deck boys as knocks about wi' poofs; deck boys as looks about ten; deck boys as should still 'ave a dummy tit in their chops." His grip tightened, his fist came up under my chin. "Innocent deck boys!"

I felt myself choking and struggled. Almost lifting me from the deck, he battered me against the mirrors above the basins.

What would have happened next I don't know for the door suddenly crashed open and a group of seamen burst into the washroom. Aaron was in the lead, close behind him the black AB – whose name I discovered was Samuel – then Smoky and two others.

"What going on here?" Samuel's voice was deep. He pushed past Aaron. "Leave the boy alone. Let go of him." He tugged the bosun's hands away.

I slid down from the washbasins.

With stern eyes Samuel regarded my tormentor. "Never you lay hand on another man. Never! You know that."

"You keep your nose out o' this." The bosun reacted quickly. "Bloody ship's full o' nig-nogs and queers. Get your 'ands off of me!" He pulled away. "Give me cheek, the little toerag. Deck boy, still wet be'ind the ears, tells me to f— off."

I stared at him.

"Next time I'll take you up to the mate," he warned me. "See what he has to say. Dock you a week's pay. Black mark in your Discharge Book." He straightened his jersey, twisted the thick ring on his thick finger. "So watch your dirty lip. You 'ear?"

"We all hear," Samuel said. "And you lie. He never swear at you. Why you tell this other boy shut the door?" He was a giant man, calm and self-assured. "Now I tell you. Never you lay finger on him again. Or his friend you got cleaning your cabin. Or any of us. You do, you the one taken to the mate. No, to the captain. And you have *me* to deal with. You remember that."

The rest gathered round him. Five to one.

There was silence. Then the bosun said, "Oh, to hell!" and barged through them to the door. "Get back to work, the lot o' you."

He was gone.

My neck hurt. I tugged my T-shirt straight.

"Back to work? What time is it?" Samuel pulled a battered watch from his pocket and flipped up the cover. "Two minutes to three. Smoko. Come on, young – what's your name?"

"Ben," I said.

"Benjamin – the youngest."

"Yes, I know."

"Ben what?"

"Ben – " I caught myself just in time. "That's only what people call me. It's Joey, really, Joey Bennett." My cheeks burned. "Ben from Bennett. It started at school, there was another boy called Joey in the same class." The lies sprang from my lips.

He eyed me keenly and looked around. "All these good names from the Bible: Benjamin, Joseph, Aaron, Samuel. You think this means we are going to be friends? I hope so." He held out a big hand, dirty with rust and grease.

I shook it.

"Come on, Benjamin the youngest. Everything stop for smoko. See if the baker sober enough to make any tabnabs yet. I am partial to a currant bun." As we left the washroom he rested his hand on my shoulder. "Don't you worry about this bosun. He not touch you again, he not dare. If he do, we take him to the bridge. He lose his job, end up in court. Never bosun again."

He did his best to reassure me but I wasn't too worried about a punch in the stomach or a smack on the ear. I was imagining that swim in the cold black waves, two thousand miles from land.

Word had reached Charlie and he came running down the alleyway. "You OK, mate?"

"Course." I drew a shaky breath. "Don't know what all the fuss is about. It's only ol' Cyclops."

His eyes held mine. Slowly he broke into his big white grin.

I did my best to smile back..

Charlie turned to my rescuer. "Did you say something about tea and tabnabs, Sammy? Sounds good to me."

He hung an arm round my shoulders as we started up the alleyway.

"Not Sammy, please." A deep voice came from behind. "My name is Samuel, Samuel Isaiah Jones."

The Curry Ladle

On ships all over the world, the morning and afternoon breaks to which hardworking sailors look forward so much are called smokoes. There is fresh tea in the pot and snacks that are known as tabnabs.

On board *Pacific Trader*, the tabnabs were a lottery. Sometimes when we turned up dirty from work there were plates of pastries that would have graced the Ritz. Other times we were presented with teacakes burned to charcoal and doughnuts so undercooked that the middles were yellow liquid. The reason was simple: Kenny the baker was an alcoholic. Occasionally this led to a fight which poor skinny Kenny, his hair thinning and a can in his hand, always lost – except on one famous occasion when he laid his attacker cold with a baking tray. This first afternoon was a good day with fresh cream éclairs and coloured cupcakes with icing-sugar writing on the top. Mine said *Bon Voyage* and *Good Luck.* It cheered everyone up and we returned to work with a lighter heart.

Lampie gave me clumsy rubber gloves and a set of steps with a little platform on top. I carried them to the washroom and mixed fresh suji. Then, bucket in one hand, cloth in the other, I began to wash the painted ceiling – or deckhead.

If it had been one of the labours of Hercules I could not have hated it more. The caustic suji dripped in my hair and stung my eyes, ran up my arms and spilled down my T-shirt, turning icy-cold and making it stick. My jeans got wet and twisted round my legs. It was a horrible job.

As I worked I wondered why the bosun hated me so much. Was it personal, because of the way I talked, because I'd been brought up to be polite? Was it because of Michael, so camp and gay, a friend of the dead Curly? Or the trouble at the Eight Bells? Or the fight on the landing where I had seen him humiliated? Or did he genuinely hate all ships' boys, as he had said, simply because we were young and happy?

At last it was knocking-off time. Sailors tramped into the washroom, dirty from their work on deck.

"Come on, mate, down tools. On overtime are you? ... What's your name? Ben? You're doing a good job, Ben. ... Here, give us your bucket."

The last of the suji vanished down a toilet. Steps and bucket were dumped in the alleyway.

Greatly relieved, I retreated to the cabin and stripped off my clothes. Dye from the cheap jeans had turned my legs blue. Towel round my waist, I returned to the washroom and took a shower. Despite a determined soaping, my legs retained their denim hue. Dripping, I collected both pairs of jeans from the cabin, dumped them in the shower and trampled them underfoot. Blue as ink, the dye flowed away down the plughole. Still in my towel, I carried them to the drying-room and draped them over a wooden spar. It was like walking into an oven. My shoulders scorched.

I dressed and wandered out on deck. Loading was complete. While I laboured in the washroom most of the hatches had been closed, all but a few of the derricks lowered, debris taken ashore, pallets of stores carried below deck. The ship had a keener, cleaner look, as if eager to cast off her moorings and head for the open sea.

At the head of the gangway a cadet in uniform, younger than Tony Fanshott-Williams, was lashing the sailing board to a rail. Details had been chalked in. I read past his shoulders:

This vessel will depart for
FIJI AND NEW ZEALAND
via
PANAMA
at 2230 *hours*

He straightened, slightly-built and fair-haired. I recognised him as the boy who had been with Tony at the disco.

I nodded at the board. "Thought we were sailing in the morning."

"Nope. Finished ahead of time. Catch the night tide." He wiped off a smudge and hurried away.

The detestable Rat'bone was on gangway duty. "Heard you got wrong side o' the bosun this afternoon."

"Not on purpose." I wandered off and leaned on the rail.

"Hoity-toity! Not on purpose!" His voice pursued me. "You look very tidy. Finished for the day?"

"Have to turn-to after dinner I expect." I gazed across the wharf.

"Aye, I expect you're right. Just as well we've got you on board, eh? Show the rest of us what to do."

I didn't reply.

"Any idea what we're getting?"

"For dinner?" I shook my head. "Smells good though." I tested my eyesight – right eye, left eye – on the advertisement hoardings, far off on Dock Road.

"Smells like dead dogs to me."

He was disgusting and I wished he'd leave me alone. After the events of the afternoon I didn't want to talk to anyone, certainly not Rat'bone or one of his pals. I walked round to the far side of the ship. The last of the setting sun shone through a gap in the clouds. Smoke from our funnel blew across the brown water. Diesel fumes caught my throat. I moved to a better spot.

My knuckles were inflamed with the caustic. Idly I gazed from the vessels opposite to the lock gates and factory chimneys beyond the river. What was I *doing* here?

Fifteen minutes passed. A distant bell announced that dinner was ready. I glanced at my watch and went below.

A savoury smell of chops and curry issued from the galley. My mouth watered. Voices were raised in the messroom. As I approached, I recognised the high distressed tones of Ossie B. The other was Lenny Rat'bone. He had been relieved on the gangway and now vented his nasty humour on the hapless Ossie.

"What you call this?" He thrust out a plate on which curry had spilled to the rim and covered his thumb. "Are we goin' to have this kind of slop all trip?"

"I'm sorry, Lenny." Ossie was placating. "I just tried to give you a good helping."

"Did I ask for a big helping? Look, it's gone all underneath." He clattered the plate on the counter. "Give us another one." He snatched a tea-towel from Ossie's shoulder and scrubbed his fingers clean. As he threw it back, the cloth landed half in the tray of curry.

"Sorry, Lenny," Ossie said again. Hastily he cleared up the mess.

"Take more care feeding the dog than they do in this place," Rat'bone said.

"Come on! Get a move on!" A dozen men stood waiting.

"I sailed with this bag o' lard before." Rat'bone turned to face them and showed his long teeth. "'Ere, d'you know what we called him? Maggot! Get it – Maggot. 'Cause that's his name, see – Bagot. Ossie Bagot." He laughed. "Come on, Maggot. You heard 'em. Get a move on. There's men waitin' here."

"Leave him be," came a voice. "What d'you want to upset him like that for?"

"What for? 'Cause he's a nut case, look at 'im."

Even before we set sail, Ossie's worst fears had come to pass. He slumped against a tray-rack at his back. The curry ladle dripped on the deck.

"Come on, Ossie, mate." Charlie pushed round the end of the counter. "I'll take over here. You go off to your cabin."

Limply Ossie surrendered the ladle. "Thanks, Charlie." Then he pushed himself upright. "No, it's my job. But could you lend a hand?"

"Sure, if that's what you want." Charlie took stock. "I'll serve the first course, how about that? You look after the puddings."

Ossie nodded. He groped in his pocket and I saw the yellow pills.

"Right," Charlie was brisk. "What can I get you?"

"I told him," Rat'bone said.

"All right, so now you tell me."

"Don't half fancy yourself. Bloody J.O.S."

"Listen, Lenny, I'm being polite. There's a crowd of sailors here. They're tired, they're impatient, they want their dinners. Now what do you *want*?"

"Curry, on a clean plate. Reckon you can manage that?" He looked round for approval. "Your sort of nosh, yeah? Paki git!"

Before he could move, Charlie whacked him across the side of the head with the curry ladle. Rat'bone staggered back. Charlie leaned across the counter. "I was being polite. I've said to the bosun and now I'll tell you." He pointed a threatening finger. "One more crack, just one, I'll be on that bridge shoutin' so loud the lawyers'll hear me from here to Karachi. Got it?"

"Good on you, son," came a scatter of voices. "Ignorant scruff."

"Thanks." Charlie was blazing. "What can I get you?" he said to the next man.

"Chop an' peas."

The queue shuffled forward. Ossie prepared to dispense apple tart and fresh fruit salad.

Several places back, Rat'bone mopped curry from his ear and regarded Charlie with venomous eyes.

———•———

PART THREE

OUTWARD BOUND: THE ATLANTIC

Stations Aft

Straight after dinner Charlie went off to work on deck. I had been given no instructions, so I gave Ossie a hand to clear up in the messroom then went out to join him.

From stem to stern the ship was floodlit and an anthill of activity. Hatch boards were being dropped into place, the last derricks lowered into their cradles, cargo lights unplugged and stored away in deck lockers, shore pipes uncoupled, lifeboats made secure, navigation lights tested, windlass checked, the pilot ladder carried out on deck and lashed to the rails.

"Here, Benjamin the youngest." Samuel called me to number two hatch. "If you're doing nothing else, give Chippy and me a hand to batten down."

So I helped them to spread the three layers of heavy canvas – oldest on the bottom, newest on top – across the hatch boards and secure them with iron battens and wooden chocks. We moved aft to hatches five and six.

By the time we were finished most of the crew had gone below decks to shower and tidy their cabins for families to come aboard for an hour. Children sat with their dads, unmarried sailors hugged their girlfriends, tearful mums sipped gin and gazed about them. Samuel introduced me to his wife and two lovely children. A whole crowd, clutching bottles and shrieking at the strangeness of everything, arrived to give Michael and Barbara a cheerful send-off.

Charlie had warned me to be on the lookout for his parents but I didn't expect them to turn up on the boat deck. Luckily I spotted them before they saw me. I pulled the woollen hat low over my eyes and fled to the stern.

For a while I sat on a coil of rope and watched the lights on the water.

Smoky joined me. "No one to see you off?" He pulled out his tobacco tin.

"Hardly."

"How do you mean?"

"Well you should know."

"Oh, aye." He gave his gap-toothed grin. "Suppose they couldn't."

"What about you?"

"Never mentioned the bloody ship but the wife sniffed it out somehow. Nose like a blood'ound." He nodded towards his cabin. "She's in there with the kids."

"Aren't you going to – ?"

"An' get my block knocked off? Not on your life." He struck a light. "Keep out the road, that's my motto. No point lookin' for trouble. They'll kick her off in a bit."

We fell silent. Clouds covered the stars and after a while it came on to rain. Smoky moved to shelter. I crept back to the washroom and locked myself in a cubicle with an abandoned magazine.

I was there for over an hour. Even at *Frankie's* I had never felt so lonely.

By ten o'clock all visitors were ashore. A deck officer with the two cadets searched the ship for stowaways. The gangway was raised. A few minutes later we were summoned to stations.

I changed into working gear. My jeans had dried in the baking heat. I pulled a pair on, hard as crumpled packing cases.

Charlie was sent for'ard with Jumbo Ryland and some others to work under the mate. Aaron and I went aft with Lampie and the second mate's gang. He was the friendliest of the deck officers, a short, cheerful young man with red hair, prematurely balding, though for the moment this was hidden by his officer's white cap. His name was Tim Nettles.

The rain had stopped. A scatter of relatives stood on the puddled quay, lit by the orange dock lights. Aaron leaned over the rail and talked to his girlfriend, a tearful, pretty girl with short fair hair. Samuel's children stood at their mother's side. Charlie's mum and dad had gone home.

"Hey, Ben!"

Where had the shout come from?

"Over here." A couple stood waving by a pile of crates, one tall as a lamp-post, the other barely up to his shoulder. Their faces were hidden by party masks: Frankenstein's monster and a kiss-me-quick blonde with rosy cheeks and yellow curls.

"Everything OK, mate?" Joey's bellow was like a foghorn.

"Yeah, great!" I gave a thumbs-up.

"Watch out for the girls," Fizz called. "I've heard what all you sailors get up to."

I grinned, happy to have friends to see me off. All at once the months ahead seemed brighter.

"Good luck with the – "

"Ahhh!" A shriek pierced the night. "I see you there, Barry Crisp!"

Smoky, who was sitting on his heels behind a coil of rope, ducked lower.

"I'm not blind, you know – though God knows I must have been to marry a useless article like you."

Realising he was out of reach, Smoky decided to brave it out. "Is that you, Dolores, darling?" Puffing jauntily on his cigarette, he crossed to the rail. "I didn't know you were coming down. You should have told me. You haven't been on board?"

"Been on board? What do you think? Of course we've been on board."

"Why didn't you come to the cabin?" He held up a thin, nicotine-stained hand. "As Davy Jones is my witness, I had no idea."

"No idea! Oh, you liar! You're rotten, Barry, just rotten. My, if I got my hands on you this minute you'd know about it." She looked around. A broken shackle, a lump of iron big as two fists, lay by her feet. Dolores was a strong woman; she snatched it up and flung it at her husband's head. Had it struck, it would have dashed his brains out. But her aim was poor. Missing Smoky by several feet, the heavy shackle rebounded off a piece of machinery and hit the second mate on the leg.

"Ah! Ah!" Clutching his shin, he hopped around the deck and pulled up his trouser leg to examine the damage.

"Sorry, Second," Smoky said. "You OK? She gets a bit carried away sometimes." He looked back at the quay. "That wasn't very nice, love. What's the second done to you?"

"Aye, you're the funny one, our Barry." She yanked the squabbling children to her side and rocked the pushchair violently. "I'm going down the dock office first thing tomorrow morning. You'll be laughing the other side of your face by the time I've finished with you."

By this time the entire gang, with the exception of the second mate who was tying a handkerchief round his bleeding shin, had gathered along the rail.

"Aye, aye. Just as you say, love." Smoky nodded agreeably. "Bye, Louise. Bye, our Gerry. Be good children now. Look after your baby brother. Daddy'll be back soon."

At this they let out a loud wail and clung to their mother's coat.

I had almost forgotten about Joey and Fizz. Emboldened by their masks, they advanced to the ship's side.

"Just as well the gangway's up, Smoky," Joey said.

Dolores shot him a black look.

"Beautiful ship, Ben," Fizz called. "Nice cabin?"

"Yeah, I'm sharing with Charlie. He's up for'ard with the mate."

"What about the bosun?"

I made a face.

"But you're going to be all right? I mean – "

I lost the rest of it because at that moment the second mate's walkie-talkie crackled into life. He listened briefly, trouser-leg rolled to his knee, and passed on the message from the bridge.

"Here we go, Lampie. Take the tug rope. Port quarter."

A Close Shave

A POWERFUL tug, the *Maid of Westport*, had drifted alongside. The bow-legged little lamptrimmer summoned Smoky, another seaman and me and we crossed to the port quarter. Smoky threw a heaving-line to the tug crew who attached it to the heavy tow-rope. Hand over hand we hauled it across and dropped the eye over a pair of bitts. The tug took up the slack. We returned to the starboard side.

Joey and Fizz were still on the quay. "You'll write to us," Fizz shouted, "let us know how you get on."

"You too," I shouted back. "The football an' that."

Joey stuck up a thumb.

The walkie-talkie buzzed and crackled. A parrot voice issued from the bridge.

"Single-up, Lampie." The second mate passed on the order. "Down to the wire."

"Right you are, Second." Lampie called the crew from the rail. "Come on, let's be having you. We'll take that one first. Ease her off, Brian."

There were four mooring lines at the stern; three ropes leading aft and a wire called a backspring leading for'ard.

Brian, a middle-aged AB I hadn't met yet, threw the massive coils of rope off a pair of bitts. Soon only a single figure-of-eight remained and the mooring line, dragged down by its own weight, slumped into the water. Workers on the dockside threw the eye off a bollard. With a splash it slid into the dock. Then Brian and Aaron heaved the rope to a winch drum and wrapped it round twice. Samuel took the controls, the drum revolved and the dripping rope snaked aboard.

"All right, young what's-your-name," Lampie said. "Ben is it? Coil it down on the rest. That's your job."

Glad to be given a proper task, I sprang to it. The plaited mooring line was heavy as a dead anaconda, especially the twenty metres that had been in the water. It took all my strength to heave it across the deck and arrange the coils. By the time I had finished another rope was waiting, and then a third. Aaron and Samuel gave me a hand and soon the job was complete. The moorings at the stern were reduced to the single wire.

"Good work, Lampie." The second mate pressed a button on his walkie-talkie. "Singled up aft."

The radio crackled again. "Thanks, Two-oh. Going out bow-first. Leave it there a minute."

"Aye-aye."

The masts and rigging of *Pacific Trader* swung slowly across the sky. I leaned over the starboard rail. Black water, glinting in the lights, was opening between the bow and the quay. I wanted to see everything and crossed to the port quarter. The *Maid of Westport* pressed her buffered nose against our stern, holding it alongside. At the bow a second tug, the *Lancelot*, was heaving us out towards the middle of the dock, clear of the vessels double-moored ahead of us. The towrope was bar-tight. Smoke poured from the *Lancelot's* funnel. Dirty white water boiled at her stern. I returned to the others.

Soon we were at an angle of thirty or forty degrees to the quay. With a loud *crack* the backspring, the single line holding us to shore, jumped on the bitts. As *Pacific Trader* swung out, it was taking a lot of strain.

"Stand back, everybody. Ease her off a bit, Lampie."

"Aye-aye, Second."

Two men jumped forward to throw off a coil or two and let the wire slip. But someone had thrown a half-hitch over one of the bitts. The heavy wire had jammed.

"Come on, son. Feed it through, feed it through."

"Can't, Lampie." It was Aaron. "She's jammed solid."

"Here, out the way." Wearing gloves to protect his hands, the little lamptrimmer struggled with the wire. "Can't budge her, Second. Tell them to stop heaving or she'll go."

As if in response, the wire gave an ominous crack and jumped again.

"Stern to bridge. Stop heaving! Wire's jammed. Think she's going."

"Aye-aye, Two-oh."

The ship's whistle tooted a signal to the tug. But it was too late. *Pacific Trader*, twenty thousand tons fully loaded, continued swinging. The wire was thrumming, visibly vibrating. A cloud of ginger dust stood round it on all sides.

"Watch yourselves!"

With cries the seamen scattered. They were not a moment too soon. With a vicious *BANG*, loud as a pistol shot, the wire broke. The ragged end whipped back, too fast to see, so fierce it chopped straight through two iron rails and sent an oil drum flying. For seconds, like a beheaded snake, it thrashed about the deck.

I had been the last to dive for safety. The end of wire flashed past me.

"Anyone hurt?"

By good fortune nobody was. We gathered by the buckled and gaping rails. It was scary.

Smoky had a hand over his mouth. Abruptly he was sick over the side.

"You OK?" Samuel was concerned.

"Yeah." Smoky wiped his lips. "Happened before. On the old *Gypsy Queen*."

Samuel nodded. "Someone get hurt?"

"Pal o' mine, standing right beside me. Wire broke on the fo'csle. Took his leg off – good as, anyway." He rinsed his mouth with whisky and spat into the scupper.

"I heard of that sort of thing."

Smoky took another mouthful, swallowed this time and returned the half-bottle to his pocket. "Died inside five minutes. Couldn't stop the bleeding."

I stood listening.

Aaron said, "What happened to your jacket?"

I looked down and saw a long rip across the chest. The denim flapped. I had felt nothing. I pulled it off. My jersey too was torn. In a panic I hitched it up. Then my T-shirt. My skin was unmarked.

The crew gathered round. "By God, Deck Boy." Lampie sucked his gums. "You'll never have a closer shave than that."

The second mate double-checked that no one was hurt and

reported to the bridge. "Wire's gone, you probably heard it. Chopped up the rails a bit."

The radio crackled back.

"No, all OK, thank heaven. Deck boy had a near miss." He smiled at me to ease the tension. "Needs a new jacket. This one's cut to ribbons."

The parrot voice came again from the bridge.

"Will do," the second mate said. "No, he's fine. Thanks." He switched off. "Old man says get a working jacket from slops and buy yourself a new one when we get to New Zealand. Never mind the cost, company'll pay for it."

Very shaken, I smiled back. "Thanks."

"Sure you're all right?"

"Yes, I'm fine." I took a deep breath and glanced at the sky. "I guess somebody up there likes me."

It was a phrase of my gran's but his gaze sharpened, clear eyes fixed on my own. The way I spoke was betraying me again.

He let it pass. "Right, Lampie. Let's clear up then stand by"

Anxious voices came from the shore.

The second mate called back: "No, nobody hurt."

I waved to Joey and Fizz.

They capered like clowns. Fizz blew a kiss.

Toooot! Toot-toot! At a signal from the ship's whistle, the *Maid of Westport* backed off and began to heave. The gap between ship and quay widened.

Last shouts rang across the water.

"Good luck!" I recognised Joey's booming voice.

Soon we were mid-dock and turning. Samuel wiped tears from his cheek. Smoky sat shakily on one of the bitts. Brian rigged a rope across the broken rails.

Deep swirls broke the surface as the propellers nudged us forward. It was dark out there. A thousand confusing lights shone across the water. Occasional seamen on other vessels gave us a wave. After a while the lock appeared before us. The massive gates swung wide. Slowly we slipped through and were brought to a halt. The lock gates closed. A single mooring line at bow and stern held us alongside.

It was a moment I was to dream about, my last chance of escape.

I looked down at the wet cobbles. In seconds I could have swung my legs over the rail, jumped ashore and vanished into the shadows. I was a good runner, no one would have caught me. Only Charlie knew my real name – and Smoky. It would have been so easy.

But I didn't. Instead I watched as the deep currents bloomed around us and *Pacific Trader* rose up the oozing walls of the lock. Then the gates ahead of us opened and we slid out into the broad, black, glinting river.

The tugs were let go and steamed off into the darkness. The second mate relayed a message from the bridge: "Finished stations, Lampie."

The crew returned to their cabins but I stayed out on deck.

I shall never forget that night, leaning on the rail as we travelled downstream. The lights of Westport glittered from either bank. Flashing navigation lights, white, red and green, marked the channel. Dad had taught me what they meant and I tried to remember. The night wind blew my hair. Black water tugged at the ship's side beneath me. Infinitely slowly, or so it seemed, the lights of the city fell astern. The river broadened and became the dark estuary. A launch came alongside and took off the pilot. The engine note picked up. The wake widened as we gathered speed. I looked up at the steaming light on the mainmast. The filmy moon appeared through a gap in the clouds. Somewhere ahead, beyond the dimly-lit funnel and superstructure, lay the Atlantic.

As I turned to go indoors, two figures appeared on the boat deck above me. I recognised them immediately for they were the only women on board. One was the captain's wife, a happy and thick-waisted German lady called Heidi. The other was the mate's wife, younger than her husband with blonde curls and the figure of a film star. "There'll be trouble with that one before the trip's out," Lampie had predicted. Her name was Trish and it was said they were newly married. Her laugh reached me across the afterdeck. They passed from sight.

Charlie met me in the alleyway, mahogany brown with a towel round his waist. I followed him into the cabin. "Always like a shower when we sail. Wash off the dust of the streets." He had heard about the broken wire. "Yeah, Aaron told me."

I showed him my jacket.

"Boy, were you dead lucky." He clambered up to his bunk and slid beneath the blankets. "Great! Pass us that magazine, there's a pal." He switched on the reading light behind his head.

Ten minutes later, wearing clean boxers, I climbed into the bunk beneath. It was warm and comfortable. The soft roar of the engines vibrated through the ship's plates. The door curtain swung rhythmically as we met the first swell from the open sea.

Before I knew it I was asleep. Charlie told me later that he spoke to me, and spoke again quite loudly, and hung over his bunk to look down. I was dead to the world.

Thief

I soon settled into the routine of a deck boy's life. At seven o'clock each morning – six-thirty as we headed south and the days grew longer – Charlie and I rigged a hose and scrubbed down the decks from stem to stern. After breakfast we became peggies again, sujiing and scrubbing our way into every last corner of the crew and petty-officers' accommodation. It took three days. Once everything was spick and span, Charlie went off to work on deck and I was left to maintain it by myself. After lunch, when my peggy tasks were finished, I joined the rest of the crew, painting, chipping, holystoning, learning to splice, maintain equipment and all the other duties of a seaman.

There was a lot to do, but little by little, as I scoured and mopped and polished below decks, the accommodation began to shine. Brass portholes gleamed in the sun. Sailors who had been careless with their cigarette ends, stubbed them in ashtrays to keep the place clean. When they finished work, they scrubbed their shoes on mats I placed inside the doors.

"You're doing a great job!" A dozen times I was clapped on the shoulder. "Good to have a deck boy that's not afraid of a bit of honest sweat. Makes the place a bit more like home. Dirty little tykes, some of 'em, spend all day in their pits given half a chance."

But when I got things wrong, Ryland and his cronies were there to give me a hard time: "Stupid little toerag! Leaving a bucket there for anyone to trip over!" An ill-tempered kick sent the suji flooding across the deck. If no one was present, a fist struck at my head. "Get it cleaned up. Useless bloody deck boys." And at other times: "You an idiot or something? Did you learn *nothing* on your last ship?" Or "Hey, babyface, I left my fags up on number three. Fetch 'em down an' quick about it."

As the grey Atlantic slipped beneath our keel I learned what to do and what not to do, where to be and where not to be if I wanted to avoid trouble. My friendship with Charlie and Aaron grew stronger. As the sun climbed higher we played deck tennis and deck golf in the evenings. We wore shorts. My back turned dusky red and began to go brown.

A hundred times I thought about my dad and gran and Auntie Barbara. But as *Pacific Trader* took over my life and Westport retreated one thousand, two thousand miles astern, my feelings of guilt grew weaker. *Frankie's* was another existence. By the time we were approaching the Windward Isles, that necklace of islands that forms the eastern rim of the Caribbean, I had settled comfortably into my new life.

Or so it seemed to me.

How wrong I was. For unknown to everyone on board, a bigger drama than my own, a drama that was to affect many lives, had already commenced and was about to gather pace.

My own part in it began one night when we were a day's run short of the islands.

Normally I slept well. The moment my head hit the pillow I crashed out until a hand shook me awake at six-fifteen next morning.

That particular night, however, I woke some time after midnight with a feeling of unease. Had there been a flash of light? A noise? Was it the heat? The moon shining through a chink in the curtains? The shandy and toasted sardines I had eaten for supper? Whatever had disturbed me, I lay listening, my eyes wide in the semi-darkness. The feeling persisted. After a few minutes I swung my feet to the deck and pulled on shorts, T-shirt and trainers.

The cabin I shared with Charlie, as I have said, was at the after end of the crew alleyway. The washroom and drying room were situated more or less opposite. Astern stood a watertight metal door that led out on deck. In stormy weather this was kept shut and secured by clamps that operated from inside and out. In warm weather, such as we had at the moment, it was permanently hooked wide for ventilation. From the alleyway we looked directly out onto the crew deck with the sea and sky all around. The door had been open when I went to bed but now, to my surprise, it was shut, a single clamp pulled across. Perhaps it was the clang of the door that had wakened me. For some reason it made me uneasy. There was nothing sinister about a shut door – but why was it shut? Who had shut it? I pushed back the clamp and eased the door open.

The night was calm, the moon covered by patchy cloud. Before me lay the wooden crew deck – at least a section of it, bordered by the coaming and canvas of number four hatch to port and the ship's rail to starboard. Astern and below lay the iron afterdeck.

Why was I so on edge? Just because of the storm door? Surely my imagination was working overtime.

Then a short distance away, down on the afterdeck, I heard a thud and muffled oath. It could have been one of the watch, and yet ... I stepped over the sill, carefully shut the door at my back and pulled the clamp across. For a full minute I stood watching and listening. Nothing moved but the waves, a hanging rope, and the mainmast cutting arcs against the sky. The only sounds were the muted roar of the engines and creak of the ship.

No one accosted me, all remained peaceful. Softly I walked to the rail above the afterdeck. The position was exposed and I moved into the shadow created by a winch and samson post.

The afterdeck appeared deserted. After a while, clutching the handrail, I descended the steep metal steps.

Before me stood the winches and powerful cargo equipment of the afterdeck. Again I waited then walked on, my trainers silent as I passed number five hatch, the white mainmast housing, number six hatch and the poop. No one was there. Alone I stood at the stern rail. Had my imagination been playing tricks – the closed door, the bump, the muffled voice? I didn't think so. My heart hammered as I looked down at the white boil of the propellers and the restless Atlantic on every side.

The three-quarter moon emerged then vanished and appeared again as the clouds reformed. My white T-shirt shone like a beacon. I tugged it off, rolled it up small and tucked it into the waistband of my shorts. The soft wind tickled my skin as I returned along the deck.

Abruptly, almost at my side, the noise came again. A scrape, a soft grunt, a thump. I froze and looked about me. There was no one there. It came from a spot between number five hatch and the mainmast housing. Despite a confusion of shadows, I could see well enough. Nothing occupied the space but a rectangular booby hatch, a sort of raised manhole, eighty centimetres high, that gave access to the hold. In port the heavy lid was hooked up, for this was the entrance used by dockers. Every night it was lowered and locked to prevent pilfering. At sea it was locked permanently

Now, though the lid was shut, the padlock hung open from the hasp. Someone, or several people, were down among the cargo where they had no right to be. Was there an accomplice on deck, someone to keep lookout? I stared all round. Keeping well back, I circled the mainmast and scanned the upper decks. Nothing moved. No unaccounted shape deepened the shadows. I was alone, I was sure of it.

Softly I approached the booby hatch and listened. No voices, no sounds at all. I put my ear to the cold lid. Silence. Then after a while a mutter, a shuffle, a soft clink. Silence again, then a scrape of feet mounting the fixed metal ladder inside. A glimmer of light appeared round the lid.

I flitted the length of the hatch and disappeared into a hiding place I had selected, a corner behind a winch and under the steps by which I had descended from the crew deck.

It was not a second too soon. The lid of the booby hatch was raised. A cautious head appeared. I could not see who it was for he had switched off his torch and the lid cast shadow. The pale blotch of face turned left and right. All seemed safe. He hooked the iron lid open and descended again. A flicker of torchlight shone at the opening.

When he appeared again he was carrying something, or several things. Leaning over the trunk of the booby hatch, he set them on the deck. I heard a soft slap, the chink of glass. He swung his legs out and lowered the lid. There was a tiny clang and the rattle of keys. He straightened. At that instant I recognised him: Tony Fanshott-Williams, the senior cadet. As if to confirm it, the moon emerged from a wispy edge of cloud and bathed the afterdeck in light.

He wore black – at least it looked black in the moonlight – black jeans, black sweater, his head of curls dark too, good camouflage for the night but very visible against the white masthouse. Bending quickly, he collected whatever he had taken from the hold and ran towards me along the deck. I shrank back into my hiding place.

There was a glint of white teeth, Tony was smiling. Hooking a finger round the rail, for both hands were full, he started up the flight of steps. Had he looked down he might well have seen me, my shoulders paler than the shadow. But he didn't look down. Midway he paused, raising his head to scan the crew deck above. I was so close I could have reached out and touched his foot. The moonlight revealed what he was carrying: over one arm a snorkel, a face mask and a set of flippers, in his hands two bottles of whisky. I guessed it was whisky because we had loaded several hundred cases the day we sailed.

The deck was clear. He continued to the top of the steps. I heard a swift patter of feet. The sound faded For a minute I waited, terrified to be seen, then followed. I was alone. Tony had gone. The storm door, which had been shut, stood open.

I was shocked. The senior cadet, so confident and sneering, sneaking the hatch keys and robbing the cargo. A common thief.

It was a relief to reach my cabin. At the curtain I paused and looked back at the moonlit decks. Beyond the doorway all lay spread before me. Anyone doing the same – one of the watch, a sailor visiting the washroom – might easily have spotted Tony and wondered what he was up to. Shutting the door was an obvious precaution.

I was shivering, my head damp with perspiration. I scrubbed myself with a towel, tugged off my shorts and pulled on the crumpled T-shirt. My bunk was warm and comfortable. Charlie did not stir. I reached up and touched the base of his bunk with my fingertips, then turned on my side and pulled the bedclothes about my neck.

The Fight on Deck

"No," Charlie said. "I've told you what I think."

"But he's an officer – a junior officer anyway."

It was smoko the next morning and we were sailing through the Guadeloupe Passage into the Caribbean. Lush volcanic islands rose to port and starboard, our first sight of land in over a week. Charlie and I leaned on a rail and watched the smoking peak of Soufrière.

"So you keep saying," he said. "And a thief and a total pig, I agree. There's nothing I'd like better than to see him dragged off screaming. But think about it. If you hadn't woken up who'd be any the wiser? Do you want people to start taking an interest in you? Do you want to forge Joey's signature on a statement? Do you think the mate's going to thank you for stirring up trouble?" He took a mouthful of tea. "Let it go. He's not the first and he'll not be the last."

"I just hate it."

"Me too, but we're not talking about what's right, we're talking about the best thing to do."

I sighed and threw the remains of my burned tabnab into the waves.

Aaron arrived. "Hey, come an' look at this."

"What?"

"Never mind. Come on."

He led us up to the funnel deck. We hurried between the lifeboats and engine room ventilators.

"Sshhh!" Aaron put a finger to his lips then fell to his belly and wriggled forward. Two sailors, also lying on their bellies, glanced up as we arrived.

Below us lay number three hatch, just astern of the bridge and deck officers' accommodation. A beach towel was spread on the canvas. The mate's wife, known throughout the ship as Trish the

Dish, lay sunbathing. She wore the tiniest of bikinis and had loosened her straps for an even tan.

"Could I do with a basinful o' that?" murmured one of the ABs.

"Aye, wouldn't kick her out the bed," agreed his pal

She looked terrific. "Aren't you scared she'll see you?" I said.

"Already has, I reckon. Likes to know there's somebody watching."

"Got somethin' to show an' all."

Trish sat up, carefully holding her top in place, and adjusted a large pair of sunglasses. A tube of sunscreen and a long fruit drink lay at her side. She took a sip and lay down again, on her back this time, arm behind her head.

"What a brama!" Aaron said.

He was right but I didn't like being a peeping Tom, especially if Trish knew we were there.

"I'm going down."

"Me too," Charlie started backwards.

But before we would get away there was a shout from an open window and the mate came bursting from the officers' entrance.

"You men! What the hell do you think you're playing at? Get away aft." He shaded his eyes. "I see who you are. Even the deck boy – mucky little tyke. Get out of it, the lot of you. Catch you hanging round here again, I'll have you on a charge. Understand?"

We understood all right and scrambled away down the funnel deck. I was shocked but the others seemed not to mind.

"What a cracker!" Aaron said again.

"Got his hands full with that one," said one of the ABs.

"Wouldn't mind havin' my hands full neither," said the other. "Any time."

Behind us the mate's voice was raised in anger: "What d'you expect on a ship full of sailors? Have you got no sense? Didn't you see them all up there slavering down at you?"

I didn't catch her reply.

"Get away indoors," he said, "off the deck. Your shoulders are burning anyway. If you want to sunbathe go up on the monkey island. They'll have to climb the foremast to see you there – mind I wouldn't put it past them."

"Aye, but that's not her game, is it?" One of the ABs stood beside me. "She likes men looking at her. Mate should have more sense than marryin' a bit o' jail-bait like that, bringin' her on board with him."

That afternoon, Charlie and I were sent to holystone the boat deck. This involved spraying the planks with seawater, scattering them with sand, and scouring them with a heavy sandstone block on a long handle. A section had just been completed and I was rinsing the sand into the scuppers while Charlie went to fetch a broom from Lampie. The sun was hot. The water sparkled. Little drifts of sand tumbled away in the jet of my hose.

I was happy in my work and thinking about nothing in particular when Tony Fanshott-Williams appeared round the corner. The senior cadet was carrying some papers. He wore his officer's whites: blancoed shoes, socks to his knees, crisp white shorts and a short-sleeved shirt with epaulettes. His head was bare, dark curls gleaming. Expensive sunglasses.

What happened was an accident. The jet from the hose was quite powerful for I had opened the stopcock wide. As Tony walked past it hit a bracket on the deck and splashed his legs, not much but enough to make him jump back.

"Sorry!" Instantly I swung the jet away.

But the damage was done. Tony looked down at his knees and shorts. "Clumsy – ! Look at me! Clean on." He was hot-tempered, as I remembered from the night at Black Sunrise. "You did that on purpose!"

"I didn't even see you. It hit that – "

"Stupid bloody deck boy."

"I said sorry. What more d'you want me to – ?"

"Think you're funny, don't you."

"No."

"I've got a good mind to – "

"It was an accident!"

"Some accident!" And before I could resist, he snatched the hose out of my hands and turned it full force onto my belly and legs.

It didn't matter because I was only wearing a T-shirt, black cotton shorts and trainers. I was wet already and on that hot afternoon the cold seawater, though a bit of a shock, was refreshing. If Charlie had done it I would have laughed. But Tony wasn't laughing.

"There! See how *you* like it."

My own temper flared up. "What did you do that for?" Without thinking I rushed at him, battered by the water, and wrestled the hose from his grasp. Bright jets flew in every direction, sparkling in the sunshine. If he had been dressed as I was, I mightn't have succeeded but Tony wanted to keep his whites clean. So far only his legs were splashed. Not for long. Before he could dodge aside, I swung the nozzle and sprayed him head to foot. The jet smacked him full in the face and sent his sunglasses flying.

In the heat of the moment, neither of us spotted Smoky at the end of the deck. Fag in his mouth, pot of paint in his hand, he stood watching.

"There, how do *you* like it?" I swung the hose away. "That's quits."

Tony's hair hung over his face. His shirt clung to his chest. His underpants showed black through his shorts. Mouth open, he stood gaping. He could not believe what I had done. Then rage and pure poison came into his eyes and he flung himself at me.

It could have been funny, two boys fighting over a threshing hose, but this was in deadly earnest. Though I struggled and punched I had little chance for he was a good three years older, heavier and stronger. Also he fought dirty, kneeing and head-butting. Inside a minute I was flat on my back with Tony sitting astride my chest. He drew back a fist.

"Hit me an' I'll tell!" I cried.

"Tell what?"

"Thief!"

The blow never landed. "What do you mean?"

I bucked beneath him.

"What?" He slapped me across the head. "Eh?"

I spat in his face.

"Dirty little – !" He scrubbed his cheek and slapped me again, harder this time. "Tell me!"

"I saw you."

"Saw? Saw what? You saw nothing."

Footsteps came running. "What the hell's going on?" Charlie had returned. "Get off him." He grabbed Tony by the hair and yanked him aside. "You OK?" He crouched beside me.

"Yeah, I guess." I dabbed my mouth with the back of a hand. My lip was split. My left eye was closing.

Tony was unmarked though his uniform was filthy. Buttons had been torn from his shirt, an epaulette hung flapping.

Charlie was appalled. "What started all this?"

Before I could open my mouth, Tony jabbed a finger in my face. "You'll be on a charge!" He turned to Charlie. "Coming round the corner. Young toerag sees me and sprays my feet. I jump back, tell him to watch it. Before you can say squit he lets me have it right in the chest. Then when I go to take it off him he flies at me like a wildcat."

"That's not true!" I said.

"Aye, well. Let's take it to the mate, shall we? See who he believes."

"Can I come an' all?" For the first time I saw Smoky. "I seen the whole thing. It's you went for him, you lyin' git! Ben done nothin'. That first splash, it were an accident."

"You'd take his side anyway, wouldn't you? One of the crew, stands to reason."

"What about me?" A young engineer looked from his porthole. His hair was wet, drips fell from his chin. "I've been watching too – and listening. Good fight. But the young lad didn't start it, you did, an' you're lying in your teeth. If I were you I'd say sorry an' push off smartish, keep my trap shut. Cause if *he* wants to take it further, cadet picking a quarrel with a rating, you're in deep doo-doo."

Tony's face was dark. He pushed the curls from his eyes. "Ah, to hell with the lot of you." He picked up his soggy papers and turned away up the deck.

"Now will one of you turn off that damned hose," the engineer said. "Came right in through the porthole."

"Sorry," I said.

"No harm done. Mop it up with a towel." He vanished inside.

Charlie hosed me down to wash off the sand then turned the red wheel on the stopcock. The jet subsided to a trickle.

Smoky clapped my shoulder. "You're some fighter, boy."

"It's the last thing I wanted," I said.

"Anyway," Charlie looked round. "Let's keep it between the three of us."

I shivered and looked out at the sea.

Chocolates, Sausages and Ash

THAT SAME evening, shortly after seven, I went round to see Michael. His cabin, as usual, was crowded. Ossie sat on Michael's bunk with Attila, the big marmalade tom cat, purring at his side like an engine. Barbara, resplendent in a straw hat, Tahiti shirt and wrap-around, his legs as hairy as a gorilla, occupied the chair. Michael and Luigi sat on the day bed. A half-empty bottle of gin with ice, lemon and tonic stood on the table.

"Oh, Ben! Come in, we've just been talking about you." Michael gave a scream. "Darling, your face! They didn't say. Is it sore?"

I touched my lip and the bruise on my cheek. "No, I'm fine."

"Oh, that brute! Come and sit down." He shifted along the day bed and patted the seat. "Here, beside me. Now, we want to hear *all* about it."

"You mean this afternoon?"

"What else?"

"How did you know?"

"How did I know? Oh, isn't he lovely! The whole ship's abuzz, nobody's talking about anything else. How that horrible, stuck-up Miss Fanshott-Williams picked on you and you took her down a peg or two. Let her have it with the hose, right in the tropics."

"Quite right too." Barbara, who detested working in the engine room and wore six clean shirts a day, was cleaning his nails with a cocktail stick. "Swanning round the ship like God's gift."

"Well, I was just holystoning with Charlie …" I outlined what had happened.

"Brilliant!" Michael said. "I love it! Here," he reached for the gin bottle.

"Not for me."

"Just one. Come on, to celebrate."

I shook my head. "No, really."

"Michael, don't force him."

"I don't think I've got anything non-alcoholic." He rummaged in a locker. "Fanta, Coke – ugh! Got some chocolates." He produced the box we'd all been given first day at sea, a good-will gift from the captain. Mine was long finished. "All for you, Ben." He tore off the cellophane. "Stick in till ye stick oot, as my granny used to say. Just so long as you don't ruin that schoolgirl complexion."

I listened as they swapped stories. Luigi told us about his boyhood in Naples.

After a while Ossie tossed back the last of his gin and floundered from the bunk. "I've g-got to go."

His high-pitched voice still caught me unawares.

"You're coming back?" Michael said.

"If that's O-OK."

"Any time, Ossie. You know that."

"Thanks, M-Michael." He hovered beside me. "Can I have one of your ch-chocolates, B-Ben?"

"They're not mine, they're Michael's." I held the box out.

"Thanks." Carefully he selected one. "Strawberry c-creme. M-mum's favourite."

The curtain closed behind him.

"Poor old Ossie," Michael said.

It was cramped on the day bed. I took Ossie's place on the bunk. "What's happened to his voice? He didn't use to stutter."

"He did on the *Star*," Barbara said.

"Lost it by the time he signed-on here," Michael said. "All that hospital treatment, I suppose."

"Living on pills again," Barbara said. "Not surprised, picking on him the way they do."

It was true. Rat'bone mocked Ossie at every opportunity. Steve joined in. It was their cruel game, hunt the messman. Every day, as he served breakfast, lunch and dinner, he was the victim of their jibes:

"Ugh! I'm not eating that muck, there's a big white maggot been crawling all over it … Look, it's the blob … Tater-head! Oyster-eyes! Barmy Baggot! … Hey, handsome, Hollywood been on the phone yet?"

Ossie was helpless. His eyes filled, his hands shook. Several of us spoke up for him. Barbara said: "You don't have to put up with it, Ossie, love. Complain to the chief steward. You're a big man, fight back." But Ossie was one of life's victims. He just couldn't.

Until two days earlier when they'd pushed him too far.

"We missed it," Michael said regretfully. "Were you there?" He topped up his gin.

"There's all sorts of stories flying around," Barbara said. "Ossie won't talk about it."

Yes, I had been there, standing in the queue.

The meal was sausages or fish pie, with chips, potatoes and vegetables. As usual, Lenny Rat'bone and his sidekick, Steroid Steve Petersen, stood together.

"Look, it's the Mad Messman."

Steve laughed.

"Give it a break, Lenny," Aaron said. "Play some other record."

"That's right," Samuel agreed in his deep voice. "We sick of it."

"Dear, oh dear! Some people got no sense of humour." Rat'bone remembered something. "Here, Fatso, someone jus' told us your mum died. That right?"

Ossie kept his eyes lowered. Carefully he dished out a portion of pie.

"What she make of you then? Havin' a big fat maggot for a son?"

Ossie froze.

"That is enough." Samuel gripped Rat'bone's arm.

"Get off of me." He pulled away.

"Hey, if he's a maggot," Steve said, "does that make her a bluebottle?"

"That's right." Rat'bone bared his teeth. "A big, nasty bluebottle."

"Someone squash her, did they?"

Rat'bone slapped the counter. "Splat!"

Ossie cried aloud. "No! No! You'll not say that about my mum." In blind retaliation he flung the metal slice he was using at Rat'bone's chest. Snatching up the tray of hot sausages, he heaved it into his face and rushed round the counter. Seamen scattered. Rat'bone was not fast enough and Ossie, who towered over the little man, caught him by the shirt. Crying, "Ah! Ah!" he beat him with the empty tray. Rat'bone's false teeth fell to the deck. An ear was torn. Blood ran down his face. If they had been alone, Ossie might have killed him. It took several men to pull him off. Samuel held him tightly to stop the shaking.

The chief steward was summoned. There was an enquiry. Ossie was confined to his cabin for a day while Charlie took over as messman. Rat'bone and Steve were ordered to leave Ossie alone or they would find themselves on a charge.

"More or less what we'd heard," Barbara said.

"That about his mother," Michael dropped in the ice and lemon. "He'll brood about that for weeks."

"Were they close?"

"Close? He worshipped her. Passed away four months ago."

I thought about my gran. "Was it a long illness?"

"No, dead sudden."

"I hope that's not a joke, Michael," Barbara said.

"What?" Michael gave a shriek of laughter. "Dead sudden! No, they were sitting by the fire watching telly. One night, about nine I think, she didn't feel too grand so Ossie went through to the kitchen to make her a cup of tea. Came back, put it down on the table. Said did she want a tablet? No reply – there she was."

"Dead?"

"I hope so. They cremated her three days later." He shrieked again. "But he stayed with her all that night and all the next day. Curtains drawn, just the two of them. Didn't tell the doctor or anybody."

I didn't like to think about it.

"You know what he's doing now don't you?" Michael said.

"I thought he'd gone to the toilet."

"All this time?"

I looked from one to the other. "What is he doing then?"

"His mother's ashes," Barbara said. "He's brought them with him."

"Her ashes?"

"Got them in his cabin," Michael said. "In a casket. Horrible bronze plastic thing."

I remembered the container I'd seen in his locker. "What for?"

"It's weird."

"Everything about him's weird," I said. "Half the things on this ship are weird. I've never – "

"He didn't want to leave her behind," Barbara said. "She always wanted to travel, so he's brought her with him."

"That's not weird, it's creepy."

"Very creepy." Luigi pulled his shirt to the throat.

I thought about it. "Any idea what she was like?"

"I met her once," Barbara said. "Horrible old thing, big as Ossie with ropes of grey hair and a shawl. Sat in a wooden chair by one of them kitchen fires with bars across – you know, from the old days. Glass of Guinness. Stank like a stoat."

I pictured them hunched over the gloomy hearth. Ossie telling her about his voyages. Ornaments from Sydney and Rio.

"What's he doing now then?" I hardly liked to ask. "Talking to her? Showing her the sunset?"

"Sort of," Barbara said. "She wanted to travel, yeah? So every night he carries her ashes to the stern and scatters a bit over the side."

"With a coffee scoop!" Michael clapped a hand over his mouth. "It's the truth – a red plastic scoop. I never go to his cabin for a cup of coffee, I can tell you. Never know what you're going to get."

"Michael, stop it!" Barbara turned back to me. "He's made a little ceremony of it. He says the Lord's Prayer, then a prayer for his mother, and throws her ashes into the sea."

"Except they never reach the water," Michael cried. "They all blow back and get into his eyes. It's like a dust storm in the Sahara. When he gets back to the cabin he has to brush her out of his hair."

"That's not fair."

"He breathes her in and can't stop coughing! Spits her over the side half the time."

I joined in the laughter. "And is that what he's doing right now?"

"I think so."

"Is it OK if I go and watch?" I jumped down from the bunk.

"Provided you don't start asking a lot of questions. Ossie likes you."

I ran down to the afterdeck. In the last of the daylight it appeared deserted. Then I saw Ossie, right at the stern. He stood by the rail, a shapeless figure in crumpled white trousers and a cotton jacket. His head was lowered as if in church. I went forward then stopped because I didn't like to intrude. After a while he crouched to something at his feet. I guessed it was the urn. He straightened, looking from the horizon to something in his outstretched hand. He tossed it forward. A little cloud blossomed in the wind – and was gone.

I didn't feel in the least like laughing.

Swimming in the Green Caribbean

THE NEXT day we arrived in Curaçao, one of three small islands to the north of Venezuela. We were there to fill up with fuel from the nearby oilfields in the Gulf of Maracaibo.

The company agent brought mail. Seamen retired to their cabins to read letters from friends and the people they loved. I had hoped there might be a letter from Joey and Fizz but there was not.

Since it was a Saturday, Charlie and I had the afternoon free.

"Fancy a walk into town?" he said. "Bring your swimming gear, there's a pool in the rocks just over the headland."

"A pool in the rocks? You mean swimming in the sea?"

"Yeah, sandy beach and everything. It's great."

"Are you off your head? There's sharks! It's one of the worst places in the world."

"Nah, it's all fenced off. I was here last trip. Come on, you'll love it."

After the rolling decks of the ship, the dusty road seemed to move beneath my feet. It was a walk of two miles. On one side lay a deep sea inlet, on the other the hillsides were covered with refineries. A smell of oil hung over the island. Concrete and tarmac shimmered in the heat.

Willemstad, the capital, was a cheerful town, clean-swept and bright as a paintbox. Although it was Dutch, most people spoke English. We bought a few things and wandered the squares lined with palm trees and hung with bougainvillea. In a cool café open to the street we ordered malted milkshakes with double ice-cream, served in the dewed metal containers.

One of the crew was there before us. Philip, the junior cadet, sat with a big glass of orange. He led a lonely life on board, or so it seemed to me: not quite an officer, not allowed to make friends with the crew, bullied by the arrogant Tony. I had spoken to him several times on the way out and I liked him: lightly-built, shy, clever, hard-working. We joined him at the table.

"Philip, isn't it?" Charlie introduced us: "Charlie and Ben."

"Yes, I know. Hi."

He wore lime-green shorts, running shoes and a vest.

"Been jogging?"

"Running."

"In this heat?"

"I did cross-country at school." He carried a bottle of water. "Wet my hair and vest, keeps me cool."

"Better you than me."

It was a tourist café. A snooty waiter eyed us with disfavour. He wanted wealthy Americans, not hard-up young sailors. Charlie stared him out.

"We're going swimming." He blew bubbles into his milkshake. "Fancy coming along?"

Philip looked down. "Not got my trunks."

"What's wrong with your shorts? No one around, you can go skinny dipping."

He brightened. "Yeah, OK. Thanks."

Half an hour later we were climbing a stony track over the headland. Beneath us *Pacific Trader* lay at her mooring, yellow oil pipes snaking aboard. She looked terrific.

The heat was intense; puffs of dust rose at every step. The refineries with their massive oil tanks were left behind, crickets trilled, lizards whiplashed away into the baking scrub at our approach. We reached the crest. Before us the hillside dropped away to bays and the jewelled, blue-green Caribbean.

"Fantastic!" Charlie balanced his camera on a rock and took a photo of the three of us. Then we started downhill towards the beckoning water.

A lopsided horseshoe of posts and shark net indicated the safe area for swimming. The beach was a dazzling strip of sand broken by rocks.

Three figures stood above the water. They were facing us but at that distance I couldn't tell if they came from the *Trader*. One raised his hands and I caught the flash of binoculars. They were lowered and after a while the figures drifted to the head of the beach.

I thought no more about it and as we descended, a spur of the hillside hid the shore from view. A sea eagle launched into the air. We watched it circling until turning a bend we came face to face with the figures we had seen on the shore, labouring up the track towards us.

There were few people I wished to meet less: Jumbo Ryland, Steve Petersen and Tony Fanshott-Williams. All wore shorts and carried rolled towels. Ryland had binoculars round his neck. Never, I thought, had I seen anyone more like an ape with his thick bow legs and bulging stomach, all shaggy with dark hair. Tony was carrying the flippers, mask and snorkel he had stolen from the cargo. I saw they were blue. Steve carried an identical set, his were green.

I prepared myself for a confrontation. It never came. Tony and Ryland were laughing at some joke while Steve, untypically, seemed ill at ease.

"Afternoon," said the bosun.

I was startled. "Afternoon."

"Going for a swim?" Tony said.

Charlie said, "Yeah."

"Water's perfect."

"Yeah," Charlie said. "Looks great."

"See you back on board then." The bosun nodded. I had never seen him so friendly.

"Right."

"Have fun," Tony said.

"Thanks."

We passed on. After ten metres I looked back. They were laughing again. Tony caught my eye. I guessed they were making jokes at our expense.

But the beach was coming close, the sun was hot, the water too inviting to let people like that spoil the afternoon.

It took only seconds to kick off my clothes and pull on swimming shorts, in my case the paint-stained football shorts I wore for work. I ran down the beach past skeins of seaweed and flung myself into the water. It was brilliant.

The shark net extended about fifty metres from shore. A wooden platform, a bit over a metre wide and ten metres long, ran along the central section. I swam halfway out and duck-dived. Abruptly, at about two metres, the temperature changed. What had been warm was suddenly chill. Patches of weed on the sandy seabed looked menacing. I was glad to return to the surface and swam on out to the platform.

For a while we played, diving, wrestling on the hot sand, kicking spray into each other's faces.

Leaving Charlie spread out on shore like a starfish, Philip and I swam back to the platform. He looked down from the edge. "How deep d'you think it is?"

I shrugged. "Five metres?"

"Reckon you can touch the bottom?" His dive was immaculate. As the surface stilled I saw him beneath me, a pale figure swimming down and down. His hand touched, he turned, kicked off and arrowed back to the surface.

"More than five metres anyway." In a gush of water he sprang to the boards beside me. "More like eight. It's cold down there." He shivered. "You going to try?"

I looked past my feet. Eight metres! That dark weed! "Well, I could if I wanted," I said. "Easy-peasy, but it's hardly worth the bother. If it was twenty I might give it a go."

He laughed and jerked a thumb. "Twenty out there."

I looked seawards. The limpid green water of the shore darkened to the ultramarine of the horizon. Deep water, scary deep. Sharks, stingrays, jellyfish, drowning. "Some other time." I stretched out in the sun, arm behind my head.

Philip trailed his ankles in the water and for a while we chatted. It was, he told me, his second trip. He loved being at sea, found his studies easy, liked Tim Nettles, the second mate, didn't like the mate and loathed the senior cadet. He was religious, a committed Christian, his father a vicar. And he had also, though I had to drag it out of him, been county schoolboy champion in both cross-country and freestyle swimming. I was impressed. But more important than these things, from my point of view, I realised that Philip had become my friend.

"I'm going back." He rose. "Coming?"

I stretched luxuriously on the hot boards. "In a minute."

With scarcely a splash he was gone. Rolling on my side, I watched his easy arm movements, the turn of his head for air.

I spotted something else too.

Inside the net, thirty metres away and cutting through the water even more efficiently than Philip, was a large triangular fin.

Tiger Shark

"Philip!" I jumped my feet. "Philip! Shark!"

Charlie had seen it too and rushed down the beach, shouting and pointing.

Philip saw him and turned his head. The shark was closing. How he kept his cool I have no idea. Momentarily he stopped swimming. The shark cruised alongside, checking him out, and passed ahead. Had it wished, a slight angle of the tail, a lazy snap of the jaws and Philip would have been gone.

He swam on, twenty metres from shore. The shark circled and made a second pass, so close it must have brushed his side. Again, somehow, Philip hung motionless in the water.

Then he was in the shallows, racing frantically to the beach. The shark pursued him until the water could only have been thirty centimetres deep. Philip ran up onto the sand. The shark lay watching him, half out of the water. Deprived of its prey it turned away, thrashing the sea with its tail. Seconds later it sank from sight. Philip hung an arm round Charlie's neck, then his knees gave way and he slithered to the ground.

He was safe but what about me? Fifty metres out and a shark in the pool. It was like a film where the victim has locked all the doors and finds the murderer in the house with him. I couldn't swim back, that was certain. Outside the mesh a blue bladder, a Portuguese man o' war, drifted past with trailing stings. Deep down an eel, over a metre long, crossed a patch of sand. The only way to get ashore, as far as I could see, was to clamber round the outside of the net.

Half a metre, or maybe a little more, rose above the surface. I grasped the top, lowered a foot down the seaward side and hooked my toes in the steel mesh.

Charlie shouted, "Ben! Stay there. I'll get a boat."

"It's all right, I'll climb round."

It was awkward, either I had to lower my legs into the water or hang far out with my shorts touching. It wasn't hard otherwise, no worse than gym exercises at *Frankie's*, and work on the ship had made me strong.

At one point there was a jagged wire and it cut my foot. A tiny bloom of blood hung in the water. It stung like fire but my fear of the shark was so great that I scarcely noticed.

Every few metres the net was bolted to a concrete post sunk into the sea bed. Except for the top these were green, covered with shells and clinging weed. I passed two and clung to the third. Briefly, to ease the strain on my arms, I straightened.

The shark knew I was there. No fin broke the surface but as I looked down I saw it glide past. I was appalled. It was enormous, two to three times as long as myself with cold black eyes and a tapering tail. The faded stripes down its back made me think this was a tiger shark

It vanished beneath the surface dazzle. I started towards post number four.

There was no warning: no sound, no slicing fin, no disturbance of the water. Suddenly, with what seemed the speed and power of an express train, the shark smashed headfirst into the mesh where I was hanging. The net leaped, buckled, ballooned and I was flung backwards into the open sea. I was winded, dazed, bruised. Gasping for breath, I struggled back to the fence.

The shark had gone but the net was damaged. The mesh gaped, wires were broken. I scrambled away, half swimming, half dragging myself with my arms.

I was midway to the shore. The sea was shallower now, four or five metres. Less weed and rock, more sand.

The shark would attack again, I was sure of it. But if a creature so terrifying swam in the pool, what swam behind me in the open sea? I reached another post and pulled myself from the water to look around.

At that very moment, as my eyes were turned from the pool, the shark slammed into the wire right alongside the post. The post buckled, the concrete fractured. Bolts sprang out. The net burst free. I clung tight, my hand torn. Looking down, I saw the shark not a metre away. Its snout was bleeding. Its mouth gaped wide, showing serrated teeth that could have sliced off a limb with a single bite. Its alien eye regarded me with no feeling at all.

The shark circled away but before I could continue it lunged again. The weakened post threw me back into the sea. The gap was almost wide enough for the shark to squeeze through. I looked into its face with no mesh between us. The massive body, thick as two men, struggled to reach me.

In a panic I swam to the next post and pulled myself from the water. I was just in time for at my back the shark had reached the open sea. It was injured. Cuts and scratches bled into the water. Apparently feeling no pain, it turned towards me and in an instant could have snatched me by a leg. I flung myself back over the net into the pool and started swimming in a clumsy frenzy towards the shore. For several metres the shark kept pace alongside, batting the mesh with its terrible head, watching me with those dead eyes.

Then the fence came to an end. An outcrop of rocks protected the pool from the open sea. The shark glided to a halt. I stood up, the water to my shorts, and began wading. Charlie and Philip splashed to meet me.

"Are you hurt?" Charlie's arm went round my waist.

"Why should I be hurt?" I tried to smile. "It was just an old ... Happens all the ..."

I began shaking. From head to foot, though I stood in the blazing sun, it was as if my bones had turned to ice.

Beyond the fence, the shark turned as if it had all the time in the world and swam off into deep water.

"I feel so c-c-cold!" I hugged arms about my chest and sat on a rock a few metres up the beach. It was so hot it almost seared my skin but the heat was comforting and after a while my shivering died down.

"Striped," Charlie said. "That's a tiger shark. They're dangerous!"

"No, really?"

"Yeah, they – Oh!" He grinned.

"I thought you said you weren't hurt," Philip said. "What's that?"

I looked down. There was red on the rock. The sand on my left foot was caked with blood.

"Oh, yes." Now I saw it I felt the pain. I pulled my foot up. A ragged scratch, quite deep, ran across the sole. "I cut it on the wire."

"That's why it attacked you and not me," Philip said. "They can smell blood through the water. Switches on their feeding mechanism or something. They go into attack mode."

"Like Ben with sausages," Charlie said. "Will you be OK for walking back?"

Limping on my heel, I returned to the shallows and rinsed out the sand. The water stung and it started to bleed again. Charlie gave me a piggyback to the rocks to keep it clean. My hand was cut too, a gash across the fingers. While I waited for the bleeding to stop, the others explored the shore.

How, I wondered, had the shark got into the pool in the first place?

Charlie provided the answer. "Hey, look at this."

Philip was examining a desiccated seabird. He dropped it and went to see.

Charlie had found a large white board and was picking off strands of seaweed. He showed it to Philip.

"What is it?" I called.

He brought it across, a notice board with a warning painted red and black in four languages: Dutch, German, Spanish and English.

DANGER
SHARKS
DO NOT SWIM IN PROTECTED AREA.
VISITORS ARE ADVISED THAT THE NET IS
HOLED BENEATH THE SURFACE. THERE IS A
HIGH INCIDENCE OF SHARKS IN THIS AREA.

"I didn't see that," I said.

"Well you wouldn't, would you."

"Blown down?"

"No, it was hidden."

"Hidden?"

"You know what hidden means. Pulled off the post and covered by some weed an' dead branches an' stuff."

I stared at him.

"Look." He showed me the freshly-broken wood. "I saw a corner sticking out."

"You mean somebody – ?" I looked back at the spot where he had found the notice. There stood the white post. Jagged splinters projected from the top.

A similar post stood further away. Philip ran to look. An identical board lay near it. Fresh sand had been kicked over the top. He held it up for us to see.

"Well," Charlie said ironically. "Both of them, there's a coincidence. I wonder how that happened?"

An Ear at the Curtain

For a day we were famous. Everybody wanted to hear the story of the boys who were attacked by a tiger shark. It was even, we were told, reported in the Caribbean newspapers and back in the UK, although by that time we were far out in the Pacific Ocean.

Captain Bell interviewed us in his cabin. He was a kindly man close to retirement who wanted to enjoy his last year or two at sea. Running the ship was left in the hands of Mr Rose, the first officer.

"By God, boys, that was a close shave. And there were no warning signs or anything, you're sure about that?"

"Yes, sir," Philip said. "We looked before we came away. Two posts but no notices."

We'd agreed to keep quiet about it. If Ryland, Tony and Steve knew we'd found the boards torn down with splinters of fresh wood, they were bound to realise we'd be suspicious. We had no proof they'd done it, and there was no point making a bad situation worse. Perhaps they'd realise we'd had a fright and would leave us alone for a while.

"Well it won't do, won't do at all. Can't have half my crew vanishing down the throat of some bloody great shark." He took a turn around the cabin. "Who's going to run the ship apart from anything else?"

I laughed.

"And who's going to tell your mothers about it? Harbour master had better pull his bloody socks up. I'm going to give him a rocket up his backside, I can tell you." He remembered something. "You're the laddie got his coat cut by that broken wire aren't you?"

"Yes, sir."

"Got a black eye too."

"Yes, sir."

"Want to tell me about it?"

"I'd rather not."

"Mm. Thrive on danger do you?"

"Not really. I just want to get on and do my job, enjoy the trip."

He eyed me keenly. "You express yourself very well for a deck boy."

I'd done it again. "Thank you, sir."

He thought about it. "Well said, anyway. That's the attitude we want. I can see your hand's scabbing over. How's the foot?"

"A bit sore. It'll be all right."

"Good, good. I like a chap who doesn't make a fuss. Gives you something to write home about anyway."

It occurred to me that Philip and I were lucky to have hands to write home with.

"Carry on then."

"Thank you, sir."

As we filed from the cabin Mrs Bell, who had been sitting all this while with a piece of embroidery, offered us a chocolate.

We left Curaçao on Sunday, the bitts hot enough to fry eggs. Our next port of call was Colón, seven hundred miles away at the Caribbean end of the Panama Canal. We were scheduled to arrive late afternoon on Tuesday, allowing plenty of time to take on fresh water and give the crew a night ashore before making the nine-hour passage through the canal the following day.

Our route lay round the north coast of Colombia. The sea was calm, the sky was clear. That Sunday evening I leaned on the rail watching a school of twenty or more dolphins leaping in the bow wave and diving beneath the ship as the sun, a molten orb, slipped into the sea. Darkness came quickly. Fat stars appeared in the tropical sky. Around midnight, while I slept, we rounded Punta Gallinas and turned south-west on the long run down to Panama.

When I went on deck next morning, the snow-covered peaks of the Sierra Nevada, fifty or a hundred miles away on the port beam, floated like a mirage above the horizon.

In the mid afternoon Philip, who had been sent to the crow's nest to keep a lookout, shouted down to the bridge. A short distance ahead, sharp-cut as a brushful of paint, the sparkling sea turned brown. The great Rio Magdalena, running north between two arms of the Andes, reaches the sea at Barranquilla and keeps on flowing. Forty miles out we sailed into fresh water. At once Charlie, Aaron and I, who had rigged a deck hose and shut the portholes in readiness, were sent to spray the ship from top to bottom to wash away the salt. We had to work quickly and were just finished, happily wet from head to toe, when the sea turned crystal blue again.

That evening, after dinner, I played deck golf with three others. A course had been painted on the crew deck. It is a game a bit like croquet with wooden mallets, hardwood pucks and numbered circles. Halfway through, Aaron's puck cannoned into a ringbolt and flipped over the side. Since we had no spare, the game had to stop. The rest went to their cabins or the bar but I wandered up to the boat deck and leaned on a rail again to watch the sunset.

As the light faded I heard footsteps and saw Tony Fanshott-Williams disappear through a door and start down a stairway that led to the petty officers' accommodation. He was carrying a bottle. It was, I guessed, whisky he had stolen from the hold, either when I saw him or when he returned later, as he must have done, to get the snorkelling gear for Steve. I wondered if he was visiting the bosun. Curious, I went below decks and approached the bosun's cabin from the opposite direction.

Ryland's and the other petty officers' cabins stood apart from the crew accommodation. I knew them well for it was my job, as peggy, to keep them clean. I looked round a corner. The door curtains swung gently in and out but no one was to be seen. Faint voices reached me, a chink of glass, a sudden guffaw. They came, I was sure, from the bosun's cabin. Who was in there? What were they talking about? I longed to know. It would be so easy to tiptoe to the entrance and listen. But what if I were caught? A ready-made answer sprang to mind: I could say I was looking for Lampie to get a new puck. Softly I crept along the passage.

The curtain almost touched my knee. There were three in the cabin, at least it sounded like three: the bosun, Rat'bone and Tony. Their voices were muffled by the throb of the engines, but I could make out enough to follow the conversation.

"'Ow much?" This was Rat'bone.

"Twenty pallets," Tony said. "That's … cargo plan."
"Lovely stuff an' all, slips down a treat. Here …"
Another clink of glass.
"… get the key?"
"Any time, just … chartroom."
"… kids in a sweet shop."
"… bottles you want?"
"Not … bottles. Cases, son."
"Cases!"
"What you reckon, Lenny – thirty?"
"Whatever you … Jumbo."
"Who dares wins, eh?"
"… store them?"
"Loads of places. Just for a few … guy I know in Fiji."
"Pretty risky …"
"Nah … mid Pacific, everyone in their pits … dopy Steve to keep a lookout."
"… reckon you'll get – a case like?"
"Stuff like this, single malt? Fifty anyway. Maybe …"
"… dollars?"
"Quid I should hope. What's that add up …?"

Something brushed my ankle. I bit back a yell of fright. It was Attila, prowling the alleyway.

"Sshh!" I stroked his ginger head. He gave a little front-paw jump to greet me, and stalked through the curtain into the bosun's cabin.

I froze.

"Allo, a visitor."
"Puss-puss."
"… that mad messman."
"Come on then." Someone made a kissing sound. "Let's be 'aving you. Cor, he's a heavy brute."
"No wonder, the Maggot prob'ly gives 'im … an' we get the stringy bits."
"… sling him out the porthole."
"… kind o' person are you? That's cruel."
"'Ere, cats like whisky?"
"… be a prat, course they don't."

"... a try. Come on, Moggie, what's this? Now, now!"

Attila gave a dangerous growl.

"... bloody thing tried to scratch me."

"I told you, they don't ..."

"Come on, Jumbo ... for a laugh. You 'old 'is 'ead an' I'll ..."

A chair scraped.

"Should be rum, o' course ... ship's cat."

"... like this?"

"Cor, look at the teeth on 'im."

"Hurry up."

"'Old 'im steady now. Come on, puss, open wide. You try a drop o' – "

There was a wild squall and a commotion. Glass smashed, something fell. A babble of voices: "Bloody arm! My face! Aah!" Another screech from Attila as somebody kicked him. "Go on, you brute!" The curtain convulsed. Attila, not hurt too badly, shot from the cabin, skittered past my feet and vanished round the corner.

I fled after him.

Halfway down the alleyway, Philip stood outside Samuel's cabin. The mate had given permission for these two committed Christians to read the Bible together. "Hi!" He raised his hand as I came close, then Samuel appeared through the curtain and welcomed him inside. A choir was singing 'Jesus Loves Me' on the tape player: I knew most of the hymns through going to church with gran all my life. I hesitated then continued to my own cabin at the end.

Aaron and Michael were paying us a visit, Aaron fresh from the shower with a towel round his waist and Michael with a gin and lemon. He was talking about Ossie: "And now he's messing about with the occult – tarot cards and that ouija board. It's the *Star of Bengal* all over again. I'm frightened to think how it's all going to end."

They looked up as I came in.

"Ben, darling!" Michael changed mood like a chameleon. "Where have you been? We've missed you." His eyes widened. "Something's happened, I can tell. Are you all right? Come on, sit down here beside Aaron and tell us about it."

Night in Colón

At half past three on Tuesday afternoon we sailed between the tremendous breakwaters at the north-west end of the Panama Canal and entered Limon Bay. By five we were moored alongside in Colón, ready for an early start the next morning.

Strong scents blew from the land: steamy vegetation, spice, hot streets, fruit stalls, bars, drains, tropical flowers, fish. It was a heady, alluring mix that made everyone eager to go ashore.

The washroom was crowded: sailors shaving, showering, scrubbing paint from their hands, scrutinising themselves in mirrors, getting ready for a night out. To and fro they trotted along the alleyways, some half naked and still dripping, others in fresh shirts with rings on their fingers and money in their back pockets. The scents of the isthmus were obliterated by aftershave, hair gel and anti-perspirant. From a dozen cabins came the fumes of beer and whisky to set the nerves a-tingle and get the night started.

Not everyone waited for dinner. Eating wasted time, and food at that moment was not a priority. Beyond Panama lay the whole Pacific, a fortnight with not a glimpse of land. They planned to make the most of the hours ashore.

I was a sailor who did want his dinner. After a hard day's work I was starving. Also I was on my own. Charlie, in a flame-red shirt and his striped jeans, was planning to visit a barber and get his hairstyle sharpened up, then join a crowd in the waterfront bars. The last thing I wanted was to go drinking with men old enough to be my father, though we did make a sort of arrangement to meet at a place called Matteo's if I changed my mind. Aaron, who spent many hours writing to pretty pen pals in ports he was likely to be visiting, was off to meet Sophia, a dark-haired beauty of sixteen. Samuel was going to a church meeting. Philip was on duty. Michael had to serve dinner to the officers. Afterwards he, Barbara and

Luigi were heading for a club called Tamara's, several miles out of town.

He had described it to me: "It's fabulous! Right out in the jungle. Madame Tamara walking round with this leopard on a leash. Actually," he confided, "she used to be a stoker in the Royal Navy but you'd never know."

I met them on deck, a colourful trio in a haze of lotions. "Wish us luck," Michael called gaily. "If we don't come back you'll know the little brown men got us."

"What little brown men?"

"You know, poisoned darts and pointed teeth." He was high on excitement.

"Or the mosquitoes, or the rabid monkeys," Barbara said gloomily. "Or the snakes, or the piranhas, or the vampire bats, or the – "

"Oh, shut up!" said Michael. "You're such a drama queen! I've told you, you'll love it."

"Or'a the jungle juice," said Luigi who rarely spoke. He gave his fruit-bat smile.

"Or the taxi driver." Barbara was looking down.

A dilapidated vehicle with a wing hanging loose and what looked like bullet holes in the windscreen stood by the gangway. The driver, a murderous-looking man with dreadlocks, leaned on the bonnet.

"Oh, my God!" Michael said. "Still, come on, my jolly sailor lads. We can only die once." He ushered Barbara ahead of him.

Luigi, to my astonishment, gave me a big Italian hug. "Good'a bye, Ben. I love you like'a my brother. You enjoy'a yourself."

I watched them descend the gangway. The taxi, with a bang and enveloping cloud of smoke, shuddered into life. I heard Michael's scream of laughter. Pale hands fluttered from the window as it drew away.

I returned to my cabin. The alleyway was deserted. I had changed into my only decent shirt – my blue school shirt – and clean jeans. Now I pushed a few notes into my pocket, ran a wet comb through my hair and left the ship.

The city of Panama lies at the southern, Pacific end of the canal.

The docks at the Caribbean end adjoin the twin towns of Colón and Cristóbal. Daylight was fading as I limped along the quays, for my foot was not completely healed yet, and down the dusty road that led to town. Squashed fruit and withered palm fronds lay in the gutters. With the onset of dusk, cockroaches and crabs had emerged from the drains. On every side cicadas were chirruping. Tree frogs bubbled and croaked in the undergrowth. A big rat scuttled in front of me and vanished through a wall.

Soon I found myself on the edge of town – at least the part that seamen know. There were few streetlights. People sat on verandas, watching as I passed. As I reached the squares, light spilled from wooden buildings and concrete doorways. Above my head the ever-stirring palms were silhouetted against a sky of deep, intense blue.

Most of the shops were shut. A man who spoke little English, his teeth brown and last strands of hair greased back, sold me a strange-flavoured ice cream. I handed him a five-pound note and got a fistful of crumpled notes and coins in return. After a few licks I dropped the ice cream down a drain and wandered on.

Three local youths gathered in a doorway, watching as I drew close. One picked his teeth. Another, barefoot, sat on the step. My heart quickened, I got ready to run. But none moved or commented as I passed by and soon they were left behind.

The bars were livening up. A crowd of foreign seamen, chattering loudly and larking about, approached me down the pavement. With good-humour they parted to let me through.

A girl in a tight skirt stepped into the glow of a streetlight and gave me a smile. It was my biggest fright yet. I hurried across the road.

The walls of the bars were crudely painted to attract customers: big-busted señoritas with flowers in their hair, happy drunks, south-sea islands, blossoming trees, sailors in bell-bottoms, girls winking, couples dancing. *Meet your friends in here* read a sign beneath a bar-room scene of leering seamen with foaming pints and girls on their knees.

For half an hour I wandered the town. Bats flitted above a fountain. I bought a baseball cap with *Panama* printed across the front. One by one the last shops were closing. There wasn't much for me, I thought, in Colón and Cristóbal at this time of night, and turned back towards the docks.

A church doorway stood open and I went in. The holy statues and smell of incense were unfamiliar to me but I liked it, liked the peace, and sat for a few minutes. There in the gloom were the Virgin Mary, Christ on the Cross, the figures of saints I did not recognise. I found them comforting. A hunched old lady, the only other person in the church, sat saying her rosary. A cluster of candles flickered in the draught. On my way out I hesitated by a small stone font on the wall, uncertain whether a boy brought up in the Church of England was permitted, then dipped my fingers in the holy water and crossed myself. As I reached the pavement it was nice to feel a cold drop trickling between my eyebrows.

Charlie had told me where to find Matteo's but I had no idea where I was and had given it up, so it was a surprise to see the name flashing above a decoration of green neon palm trees, red neon stars and a blue neon lagoon not fifty metres away. I'd had enough of the town by that time and wasn't in the mood, but I thought at least I could look in. Tucking my money to the bottom of my pocket and drawing a very apprehensive breath, I ventured through the entrance.

At the age of fourteen I had never entered any bar by myself, let alone a tropical waterfront dive like Matteo's. At once the heat and noise enveloped me: loud music, sailors shouting, women screaming orders. The room was bursting at the seams and so, from what I could make out, was a darker room beyond. Every table was full. Waitresses in sexy clothes and money belts squeezed past with bottles and trays. Sailors grabbed their bottoms and caught their waists with hairy arms.

I circled the room looking for Charlie, Smoky or any of the *Trader* crowd. Accidentally I trod on the toes of one of the waitresses. She turned on me with flashing eyes and a torrent of furious Spanish. I backed away, apologising profusely, my cheeks on fire.

The people I knew were not there. I thought I would wait ten minutes and fought my way to the bar. The barman, fat and sweating, shouted at me angrily and pointed to a table. I didn't understand what he meant. He shouted again.

A woman stood at my shoulder. "You are Eenglish?"

"Yes," I said.

"He tell you it is table service only." She was thin as a stick and as old or older than the mothers of my friends, but with her hair dyed a matt black and a feathery green dress cut short, she didn't look like any of them. "You are lonely boy, yes?" She took my hand. "Come, I find you a place to sit. You buy me a drink." Her eyes scanned the room.

"No!" I pulled my hand away. "Thank you. I was just looking for a friend. I've got to go."

Careless how many waitresses I trampled, how many drinks I spilled, I hurried from the room and took to my heels across the square. Behind me the hubbub I had caused faded into the night.

Steve Twists his Ankle

"You're back early."

Philip was relieving the AB on gangway duty.

"Didn't fancy it much." I told him about my time ashore. "What's doing on board?"

"Quiet as the grave."

We were taking on fresh water. Two hoses from the quay pulsed rhythmically. An engineer checked one of the couplings.

"Not be so quiet when they start coming back."

"Off duty by then." He nodded. "Messman didn't go ashore."

A hunched figure sat on the fo'csle head. His crumpled white jacket and trousers glowed in the moonlight.

"Poor Ossie. Is he OK?"

"Seems happy enough. Just wants to be alone for a bit."

But I knew more than Philip. "I'll go up and have a chat. See you later."

Limon Bay was bathed in moonlight. The majestic ships lay at their moorings.

I crossed the foredeck and climbed to the fo'csle head. Ossie half-sat on the windlass, his pumpkin face uplifted to the moon. It was full and fat, riding high. Small clouds shone white against the night sky.

"Hello, Ben. Been ashore?"

"Mm. For an hour or so."

"Lovely night. So peaceful." After the bars and drunks and women of Colón, Ossie's voice was strangely pure. "I'm g-glad you've come. You or Barbara or one of the others."

"Hardly anyone left on board."

"Yes, I know." He hesitated. "B-Ben, can I ask you to give me a little hand with something?"

"Course. What is it?"

"I'll show you." He pushed himself to his feet. "But you've got to promise not to tell anyone."

"Depends what it is."

"Nothing bad. You d-don't even have to do anything, just keep a l-lookout for a couple of minutes."

"I don't want to get involved in any more trouble. Things are bad enough already."

"No one will even know." He turned and bumped into me. "Please, Ben! While everyone's ashore. It the only ch-chance I've got."

We made our way to his cabin. The door was locked. "And you won't tell anyone?"

"It's nothing bad?"

The baby-blue eyes slid away. "No."

"All right then, Ossie."

"Say it again. Say I p-promise not to tell."

"Oh, come on!" I said. "Get on with it."

As the door swung open a smell of joss-sticks and fish hit me in the face. I prepared myself for something strange.

He switched on the light.

At first glance, Ossie's cabin was much as I remembered it. Then I saw the casket containing his mother's ashes. It had been taken from his locker and now stood in pride of place on the chest of drawers with a squat candle at each corner. At that moment they were unlit.

He shut the door behind us. As I looked around I spotted other objects. Playing cards were spread on the coffee table. Several were named: The Magician, The High Priestess, The Hanged Man, The Fool. A well-thumbed book lay beside them: *The Tarot – Practice and Interpretation*.

His Ouija board was propped in a gap beside the day bed.

No wonder Michael was worried.

Attila lay on the bunk. A dish of water and another containing a fish head stood beneath the washbasin.

"Would you like me to r-read your fortune?" Ossie gathered up the cards.

"Not right now."

"No, but sometime. It's accurate, you know. You'll be surprised."

Attila stretched and yawned. He jumped down, brushing Ossie's ankles.

"All right, all right." Affectionately he rubbed the cat's ears. "You've had all you're g-getting. Off you go and find some mice." He opened the door and Attila slipped into the alleyway.

It was hot in the cabin. I loosened my shirt. "What do you want me to do?"

Ossie crouched to a drawer beneath his bunk. I saw work trousers, socks, underwear and what looked like a folded crimson cloth. With care he lifted out three objects wrapped in crumpled brown paper and set them on the coffee table.

They were dolls, puppets, crudely shaped out of wax. Unravelled string had been moulded into their heads for hair: one natural, one red as ink, the third coloured black. Staring dolls' eyes, blue, green and brown, had been pinned into their faces. It wasn't difficult to guess who they represented. The nearest, thick-set with the wax round an eye roughened, was plainly Jumbo Ryland. The second, with bulging arms and shoulders, was Steve Petersen. The third, and most carefully shaped, was Lenny Rathbone with his hollow chest and mean lines around his mouth.

A darning needle had been thrust through each.

"They wouldn't leave me alone so I m-made these."

Voodoo dolls. I didn't want to touch them.

"Can you tell who they are?"

"Yes." I cleared my throat. "Yes."

"You don't mind?"

"It depends what you're planning to do."

"They're not f-finished yet," he said.

"I can see that."

"No, I mean they've got to have something personal in them."

"What do you mean?"

"Belonging to whoever it is they r-represent."

"Like what?"

"Hair, rings, nail clippings, buttons, that sort of thing."

I thought about it. "And this is your chance to get it, while everyone's ashore?"

"Yes, but I need a lookout. Will you keep watch while I go into their c-cabins and see what I can find?"

"Then what, needles through the heart?"

"I don't know. I've not stabbed these through the heart, have I?"

I looked down at the table. Steve's doll was pierced through the foot, Lenny's through its mouth, the bosun's through an arm. Why those parts, I wondered, then guessed it was because of Steve's swaggering fitness, Rat'bone's cruel talk and Ryland's violence.

He showed me a roll of sticky tape and three sandwich bags. They were labelled. I read one – *Steve Petersen*. "Are you ready then?"

I didn't like it. "All right, let's get it over with."

The stewards and greasers had their cabins on one side of the ship, the deck crew on the other. A short alleyway connected them. We walked through.

Ossie halted and listened. No voices, no music disturbed the hum of the donkey engine. The bar was empty.

"You wait along there," he whispered. "That passage that leads to the g-gangway. Give me a signal if anyone comes."

"What sort of signal?" I asked. "Hoot like an owl?"

"Very funny. I don't know, call for Attila."

"How long are you going to be?"

"Depends what I can find." We stood by a blue and beige curtain. "This Steve's?"

"Yes."

"And Lenny's?"

I counted. "Three along."

"Right, off you go." He peeped through the curtain and vanished inside.

I walked to my lookout spot, wishing I had stayed ashore.

Two minutes, three minutes ticked by. Ossie emerged, fastening the top of a bag. He held it up for me to see, gave me a thumbs-up and hurried to Rat'bone's cabin.

I was certain, I *knew* we would be caught. A trickle of sweat ran from my hair.

Ossie did not appear.

There were footsteps on deck. I heard voices. The footsteps receded.

I relaxed.

Then someone appeared at the far end of the alleyway. It was Philip. I backed out of sight. There was a knock and questioning voice. "Ben?" I peeped round the corner and saw him looking into my cabin.

He went away.

Ossie emerged from Rat'bone's door. "Two down, one to go." He mopped his face with a handkerchief. "I d-don't fancy doing this again." He passed me two sandwich bags. Instinctively I took them. "Now, which is the b-bosun's cabin?"

I led him round the corner.

"Keep a good lookout." He slipped through the curtain.

With the bags in my hand, waiting was even worse. The minutes crawled by. I pushed the curtain aside. "Hurry up!"

He was bending over Ryland's pillow, dabbing it with a strip of sticky tape. "Just be a minute." He pulled a comb from his pocket and raked it through the bosun's hairbrush; a tangle of black hairs gathered in the teeth. He dropped them into his bag along with the sticky tape. I left him scraping whiskers from the washbasin and returned to my post.

Soon, to my intense relief, we were back in Ossie's cabin.

"Ohh!" He pushed the door shut. "Thank you, Ben. I'd never have dared do it on my own."

I sank onto the day bed. "What have you got?"

He dropped two bags on his bunk and examined the third: "A disgusting sock, b-broken specs, a used sticking plaster," he peered at the tape doubled back on itself, "and a few red hairs."

"No need to ask who that is. You took his glasses?"

"They'd had it, look, one of the arms is missing. Anyway, why should I care?" He picked up a second bag. "Steve Petersen."

It contained a strip of white towelling. "What's that?"

"Sweat band. And some long hairs and a bit of writing."

"What's the writing?"

"Start of a letter. Found it in the waste bin."

"Let's see." The paper was crumpled, the handwriting clumsy. I smoothed it out:

"*Dear Mats,*" I read aloud. "*I hope you and mum are well. I am well but all is not good on this ship. The bosun and the AB I told you about are – "* That was as far as it went. Are what, I wondered. What did Steve feel was not good?

I passed the paper back. "Tell me again what you do with all this stuff?"

"Mould it into the d-dolls so they're linked to the real people."

"Then what?"

"Just hope it works." Carefully he tore the excess paper from the letter and rolled the writing into a ball. With both hands he broke the doll in half, dug out some of the wax and pushed the writing and hairs into the space. Holding the body above a lighted candle he sealed it shut again. "I just c-can't stand up to them, Ben. Michael's told the chief steward and they've had a warning, but if they k-keep on at me I'm going to be ill again. Barbara told me I had to fight back. This is one way – trying to anyway." He removed the darning needle and smoothed over the hole.

It was madness. As Ossie went about his preparations, his big face like the moon outside, I could hardly believe what I was seeing.

"Do you expect it to work?"

He took Steve's sweat band and hung it round the doll's neck. Then he lowered his head and shut his eyes as if he was praying. His lips moved but I couldn't make out the words. The needle lay on the table. He warmed it in the candle flame. Slowly and deliberately he thrust it back through the doll's foot.

"Ossie," I said again to my troubled friend. "Do you *expect* it to work? I mean really?"

He raised his head but didn't see me for a moment and blinked to bring his eyes into focus. "Who can say, Ben. Prob'ly not. The devil looks after his own."

But when Steve Petersen returned to the ship after midnight it was by taxi and he was in pain. Two of the crew, drunk as himself, had to help him up the gangway. He had caught his foot in a drain and badly torn the ligaments in his ankle.

PART FOUR

THE GREAT OCEAN

The Praying Mantis

At five-thirty next morning the pilot came aboard. At six we cast off to begin our passage through the Panama Canal. At two in the afternoon, fifty miles and six locks later, we sailed out into the Pacific Ocean.

I'd been through Suez with dad and that was great too, but Suez was just a straight channel through the desert with sand tumbling to the edge. Panama was different. A series of locks, each over three hundred metres long, lifted *Pacific Trader* from the blue Caribbean. Locomotives called mules climbed slopes as steep as switchbacks to tow us through. The top gate swung open and we emerged into a chain of freshwater lakes fringed with jungle. Tropical birds flew about the trees. I saw a water snake and far away, through Aaron's binoculars, what I'm sure was an alligator. We sailed along a channel cut by hand through the solid rock of a mountain that towered above us: Samuel told me that over twenty-seven thousand labourers, mostly black, had died of yellow fever, dysentery and malaria during its construction. Then the tropical forest closed in and after a few more miles we descended the southern series of locks that led to the Pacific.

It was fantastic. I spent the entire morning peering from portholes and leaving my work to run out on deck.

Charlie enjoyed it less. In fact Charlie did not enjoy it at all, for like half the crew he was hung over from the night before. The new haircut was great but his head throbbed and his eyes were sick. "Oh, shut up, Ben!" he snapped when I joked about it. "It's not funny. I'm dying here!" He tottered back to the lavatory.

His return in the early hours was described by Brian, who came from Newcastle and had been on gangway duty:

"Him an' that stuck-up bastard of a cadet come back round the same time. Charlie's in a great mood, singin' like a lintie an' givin' us a bit dance. But the cadet, he's one o' them gets nasty drunk. Pickin' on everyone, askin' to get his face smashed in. Anyroad, turns out he can't stand Charlie, goes for him like a stoat after a rabbit. Catches him by the collar an' starts draggin' him round the deck. But yon Charlie – ye mightn't think it to look at him but he's strong as a horse – he knocks the cadet's hands off an' pushes him into the middle o' next week. So he falls an' hurts hissel' an' Charlie's standin' over him an' callin' him a thief an' an ignorant git. Tells him any more trouble he'll pull his effin' arms off. But yon Tony, he's so drunk an' stupid he gets up an' throws a punch, but he misses an' goes down again. It were great."

It gave me much to think about. Most of all, as we sailed placidly through the jungle-rimmed lakes and dropped down to the Pacific Ocean, I was glad I hadn't been drinking like Charlie and the rest. My head ached just to think about it. Smoky Crisp, to my surprise, who I would have expected to be worse than anyone after his hours ashore, was on the contrary as chirpy as a cricket, teasing the rest and working on a new painting.

But the crew were strong and healthy and the sufferers soon recovered. That evening and all next day, as we headed out into the Pacific, the ship rang with laughter at stories of the great night ashore.

This was the day, through no fault of my own, I got into more trouble with the mate.

After lunch the bosun had sent me to work round the officers' accommodation, up by number three hatch. My job was to paint the metal handrails. First I wrapped a heavy chain round the rail and pulled it back and forth. This removed the old paint and flakes of rust. The more resistant rust I chipped away with a chisel-edged hammer. Finally I scoured the metal with a wire brush. Later I would rub it with linseed oil, paint it with red lead and finish with a glossy coat of black.

The sun blazed down. I wore mesh goggles to protect my eyes, and my Panama cap, back to front to protect my neck. Dust clung to my sweating arms and legs. My shorts and T-shirt were filthy.

I was mopping my brow with a wrist when a shrill scream broke the stillness of the afternoon. It gave me such a shock I dropped the chipping hammer on my foot. A second later the mate's wife, Trish the Dish, wearing her famous bikini, came running out on deck.

Her face and arms were wet. "Help!" She stared around. I was the only person in sight and she ran to my side. "Oh, help! In there!" She pointed wildly.

"What!"

"Oh, please!" She was shaking. "Get rid of it!"

"Get rid of what?"

"Here." She grabbed my arm and pulled me towards the doorway.

I resisted but no one else appeared and her panic was so great that after a moment I followed. The officers' alleyway was cool, freshly painted a soft green. Through an open doorway I saw a cabin, larger than my own, with a bedspread, and pictures screwed to the bulkhead.

We stopped at the next along. "In there." A notice above the entrance read *First Officer*.

"Are you sure?" Where were the officers? I looked down at my filthy clothes.

"Yes, yes! Please!" She stood back, hand to her mouth. "Be careful."

Reluctantly I went into the mate's cabin. It smelled of perfume. Trish's clothes lay strewn on the double bed. I looked all round and saw nothing alarming.

"By the washbasin."

The cabin was en-suite. I stepped into the bathroom and jumped with fright. A huge praying mantis clung to the glass holder. I had never seen such an alarming insect, ten or twelve centimetres long with a triangular head, wings like leaves and powerful spiky forearms lifted to its chin. No wonder she had screamed. The washbasin was half-filled with water. I imagined Trish rinsing her face and finding those bulging green eyes and lethal limbs an inch from her nose.

Where had it come from? I assumed it had flown aboard as we sailed through the jungle. The truth, I discovered later, was that Michael, who couldn't stand the mate, had found it in the bar at

Madame Tamara's and smuggled it aboard in a box. I wondered if it was poisonous.

"What do you want me to do?"

"Kill it, what do you think?" Trish stood back by the bed.

"It's not doing any harm."

"Not doing any harm! Are you off your head? Do you want to wait until it bites me? Watch me die?"

I hesitated.

"Go on." She threw me a satin slipper. "Hit it with that."

I caught it clumsily and took it back. "Have you got a bag?"

"Anything, just get rid of it." She rummaged in the wardrobe and handed me a poly bag from Miss Dior.

I returned to the bathroom and lifted the tooth glass out the way. The mantis clung to the holder and rocked back and forth. I opened the bag around it and attempted to nudge the creature from its perch with a folded towel. Its grip was tenacious. The triangular head swivelled. A bead of brown saliva gathered at its jaws. Perhaps it could spit poison! Its front legs stirred as if preparing to strike. I wrapped the towel round my hand and prised it loose. But when I tried to drop it into the bag it clung to the towel. Gripping its hard, leggy body through the plastic, I pulled the towel free . The mantis jerked between my fingers and the two front legs slashed through the bag like knives. Uttering a cry of fright, I rolled the top shut.

"There you are." Returning to the cabin, I held up Miss Dior.

The mantis withdrew its legs and rattled to the bottom, scratching and scrabbling.

"Keep it away from me!" Trish drew back. She had the figure of a film star. "I can't stand things like that."

"It's safe now." I held the bag away from her. "I'll take it out on deck."

"Thank you," she said. "Thank goodness you were there. Oh!" She reached for a big pink comb. "What's your name?"

"Ben," I said. "Bennett."

"What do you do on the ship? I mean, what's your position?"

"Deck boy."

"My husband's the mate," she said. "Mr Rose."

"I know."

She crossed to the hospitality cabinet. "Can I offer you ... I don't know what deck boys drink."

"I'd better get back to work. Find somewhere to put ..." I raised the bag.

She looked round the cabin. "Have a chocolate at least." She opened the box.

"OK, thank you." I chose one with a filthy hand.

"What the bloody hell's going on here?" The mate stood in the doorway, his face furious. "What are you doing in my cabin?"

"Sorry, I was working – " I pointed through the window.

"Get out!"

"Don't be like that, Dunkie." Trish took his arm. "He's just saved my life. I was in the – "

He shook her off violently. "Are you deaf, Bennett? Get out! Out! What's in that bag?"

We spoke together: "It's this enormous – "

"Your wife wanted me to – "

"Oh, never mind. Take the damned thing with you. Just go. Go!"

I beat a retreat down the alleyway. At the entrance I caught my shin a crack on the metal sill. Later I found a track of blood to my shoe but at the time I scarcely noticed.

The mate's voice came from an open window: "Bloody deck boy! Both of you half dressed! Are you out of your mind? What do you think the crew are going to say? I'm the mate here, don't you understand that? This is a ship, not the tennis club. You can't just – "

She began to shout back: "... huge great insect! He got rid of it for me, that's all ... a sweet boy! And don't you dare raise your voice to me, Duncan Rose!"

"A sweet boy? He's one of those peeping Toms, remember ... a dirty tyke, that's what he is ... you saw him. They're all sex mad. He'll be telling ..."

I set the mantis in some shade and took up my chipping hammer. But instead of starting work I stood listening openly. The mate saw me.

"Bennett, leave that. Get yourself down to the bosun. Tell him to give you some other job. Anything, just so long as I don't have to clap eyes on you again today."

"Very good, sir." I nodded. "Right." I gathered up my gear.

"And I don't ever, *ever* want to see you hanging round this accommodation again. You understand?"

"Yes, sir."

The window slammed shut.

Although I only told Charlie, the mate was heard raging at me, and by evening the story was round the whole ship. Rough hands clapped me on the shoulder:

"Trish's toy-boy. Lucky beggar."

"Baby-snatching."

"What's so special about you?"

I gave the praying mantis to Smoky who thought it was beautiful and made a cage. He kept it in his cabin and fed it cockroaches and silverfish from the galley. The mantis, which turned out to be a female, snatched them like lightning in its fearsome front legs and ate them alive.

"They eat their mates too," he said. "Did you know that?"

He called it Dolores.

Black Bums

A SWIMMING pool was erected alongside number five hatch, on the port side of the afterdeck. It was made of heavy canvas inside a sturdy wooden frame supported by struts. If *Pacific Trader* had remained on an even keel it would have been about one metre sixty deep, but ships don't stay on an even keel, they pitch and roll, and in even a moderate sea the water swashed from side to side and end to end, cascading in torrents to the deck. A gushing hose, snaking from a seawater hydrant by the rail, kept it constantly replenished. Even though three strokes took you from one end to the other, it was the best pool I'd ever been in. After hard work on a hot day it felt wonderful.

Hours were set, sessions for the officers, sessions for the crew. A ladder led from the deck to a latticed diving platform. Charlie and I bombed in with explosions that sent the glittering water so high that it was still pattering down as we surfaced. When Aaron appeared, Charlie snatched the hose and sprayed him head to foot.

As we steamed west-sou-west we were accompanied by dolphins. I saw whales and sharks. Two days out from Panama I looked down into the glassy sea and saw a turtle. A blue smudge of land lay on the horizon. I was told it was the Galapagos Islands.

That evening, in the pool, there was a crossing the line ceremony. Tim Nettles, his eyes and forehead lined with eyebrow pencil, played old King Neptune. He wore a fine rigout: long hair and a long beard, crown, trident, flippers and a cape of artificial seaweed that went over one shoulder. Four of us were to be baptised: the galley boy, a young engineer, Trish and myself – for although the real Joey Bennett had been through Panama, he had not crossed the equator.

It was a popular event. At half past six spectators started gathering, Captain Bell and the officers up on the boat deck, the crew, who had a much better view, on the crew deck below. Those of us who were involved made our way to the pool.

King Neptune and four beefy attendants wearing trunks, gold eye masks, broad gold wrist bands and gold chains around their necks, climbed the ladder to the diving platform. Neptune blew his horn and made a brief speech, then two of his servants jumped into the water and one at a time the four of us were summoned from the deck.

Trish went first, looking like an entry for Miss World in a new bikini and silver sandals, her hair dressed and make-up immaculate. What she expected I have no idea. Gravely Tim Nettles addressed her:

"Patricia Lucinda Rose, better known to all aboard this ship as Trish the Dish and Luscious Lucy, do you wish to be admitted to the court of King Neptune, whales, albatrosses, sex-starved sailors and all who cross the burning equator?"

Trish giggled.

"Answer! Yes or no – not that it makes any difference."

"Yes," she squeaked.

"Very well." Neptune was no respecter of persons. "Servants, seize her!"

The two on the platform grabbed her arms. Trish screamed. From beneath his cloak Neptune produced an enormous dead fish. "I hereby pronounce you a member of the Royal Order of Neptune." He gave her a stately slap across the face, right and left, with the fish's tail. "Let her be ducked!" Trish could not resist. The masked sailors flung her headlong into the pool. The two who were waiting grabbed her by the arms and legs. Five times, in a tumult of shrieks and foam, she was plunged beneath the surface.

Coughing seawater, the mate's young wife clung to the neck of one of Neptune's attendants. Her hair trailed, her bikini was slipping, a ruined sandal floated nearby. The ceremony was complete. Laughing and rubbing her eyes, she looked for her husband up on the boat deck. The mate had gone.

Now the rest of us knew what was coming, or thought we did. My turn was next – the speech, the slap, the rough baptism – then the galley boy and lastly the fair-haired young engineer. It was great fun.

Neptune blew his horn a second time to show the ceremony was finished. It was a signal for half the crew to pile down to the afterdeck and jump into the pool, tight as sardines, larking and wrestling, blinded by spray. At the same time, unnoticed by the engineer, the galley boy and me, the ladies were led away and an old canvas was spread on deck in readiness.

The first I knew of this was when I was seized by a dozen hands, hoisted in the air and, though I struggled, stripped of my shorts. A shout went up as I was dragged from the pool and carried to the waiting canvas. There, with every hand on the ship taking part, it seemed, I was pinned down, flipped over and blacked from head to foot, even in the most intimate parts, from a bucket of engine sludge, graphite and liquefied shoe polish. My laughing attackers drew back. Stark naked and shining black, I stood alone in the middle of the canvas.

Flash! I turned round. *Flash! Flash!* Charlie was taking pictures.

"One for the girlfriend!" somebody shouted. *Flash!* "Good on you, deck boy!" Another shout went up and people clapped me on the back. "You put up a brave fight."

"Hey!" A cry came from nearby. "The galley boy's trying to escape!"

His name was Kevin and he came from Birmingham. Already he was halfway over the side of the pool. Strong hands grabbed his leg, his arm, the back of his trunks. Fighting like myself, he was hauled to the canvas. Still naked, I dug my hand into the bucket and joined in with the rest.

The engineer followed and soon it was all over. More cameras flashed. I wondered where the films would be developed.

"Good show! Great success! Get yourselves cleaned up and we'll see you in the bar." King Neptune, who had presided over the melee, strode away, trident in one hand, fish in the other.

We used the engineers' washroom where there was a giant tub of Swarfega. Rub by rub, hair and skin emerged from the black. We scrubbed each others' backs. The scummy water ran away down the plugholes. It took a long time to get clean. And when we were sure every cranny of our bodies must have been washed at least ten times, voices still said: "Behind your left ear ... back of your knee ... here, stand still a minute."

At last it was done. Dripping in my shorts, I padded back to the cabin.

Then Kevin – a skinny red-headed boy with acne who became my friend – and I went to the engineer's cabin and he took us to the officers' bar. Tim Nettles, back in his whites, with Trish and one or two others, gave us a warm welcome. Four large tots of rum stood on the bar and we drank them down.

I had to drink another in the crew bar.

They tasted terrible and that night I went to bed with my head spinning. The pleasures of alcohol, whatever they were, were not worth the pain and I resolved never, ever, to get drunk again.

Famous last words.

Afternoon on the Bridge

Sunday was my birthday. Mine, Ben Thomson's, not Joey Bennett's. I was fifteen.

There was no one I could tell except Charlie – and possibly Smoky. Charlie took a risk and sang *Happy Birthday to You*. After breakfast he ironed one of his shirts that I had always liked and gave it to me as a present.

Smoky gave me an uncle's hug. "Wish I was fifteen again." Cigarette in one hand and can in the other, he pointed my life in the right direction: "Shag all the lasses but keep off the fags and booze." I told him it sounded pretty good to me.

At ten-thirty that morning, as every Sunday at sea, Captain Bell conducted a short service. It was a peaceful half hour and always well attended. Michael and Barbara were there, Charlie, Luigi, Steve, Philip, Ossie, Tim Nettles and a few more. It took place in the Officers' Dining Room where there was a piano. There was a reading from the psalms; we prayed, remembering fellow sailors and families at home; the mate read a lesson for Advent, Samuel read another, and we sang two hymns.

Afterwards some of us went to the messroom for tea and tabnabs. The baker was having an off-day, melted flap-jacks and burned gingerbread men. On the day I turned fifteen, they were the closest I got to a birthday cake.

At two o'clock I had to go on the bridge. As part of their training, deck boys have to learn to steer the ship. It's not like driving a car, ships travel on rolling water, pushed this way and that by winds, waves and currents. Point a ship in the right direction, leave the wheel, and a minute later she's twenty degrees off course. Bring her back with the rudder, start twenty thousand tons swinging, and it keeps on swinging. In a moderate sea it takes skill to keep a ship within a few degrees of the intended course.

Today the sea was calm, the wind light. Tim Nettles – the second officer usually takes the twelve-to-four watch – switched from automatic pilot to manual steering and I took the big spoked wheel.

"Steering two-four-two," he told me formally, although it was written on a board.

"Two-four-two, sir."

"Taken the wheel before have you?"

"Yes, sir." Luckily I had, often, when I sailed with dad.

At the changeover the ship started swinging: two-four-seven, two-fifty, two-five-three. I spun the wheel to port and brought her back, countering the swing before we reached the intended course. *Trader* settled down. I lined up the stem post with a cloud.

"Very good." He stood at my back. "I can see you've got the hang. Leave you to it, can I?"

"I think so."

"Give me a shout if there's any problem." He moved away. "We'll have a look at the course recorder when the hour's up."

I had dressed in a clean shirt and jeans and stood on a wooden grating, slightly raised. Before me was the binnacle, the polished brass housing that contained the ship's magnetic compass. Although it was possible to steer by this it was difficult for the compass card swung constantly and registered magnetic north, a shifting location five hundred miles from the true north pole. True north was registered by a ticking gyro that stood alongside, with a repeater just above head height and forward of my right shoulder. I steered by this, all the time watching how the stem post swung against the white Pacific clouds.

On a Sunday afternoon it was peaceful on the bridge, and once I had settled into the routine my mind was free to wander: other birthdays, my gran, dad, fifteen, all those girls.

"Right, that's your hour up." Tim Nettles, his cap discarded and thinning ginger hair ruffled, switched back to automatic pilot. "Seem a long time?"

"Not really, I enjoyed it. Wouldn't mind doing a bit longer."

He seemed surprised. "We'll leave it there for now."

The bridge was in three parts. The wheelhouse occupied the middle fifty percent, with open deck to port and starboard. Immediately behind the wheelhouse was the chartroom, connected each side by a doorway. Between these doorways stood the long chart table with windows above it, so you could look directly from one navigating room into the other.

It is the most basic rule of the sea that at all times there should be someone on the bridge to keep a lookout, but crossing the vast Pacific we didn't see another ship for days at a time, let alone came close to any. The second mate scanned the horizon and led the way into the chartroom where the course recorder, an inked needle on a slowly revolving drum, was protected by a glass case.

"Very good, Bennett. Very good indeed."

The course line wavered across the paper, two and three degrees either side of two-four-two.

I was pleased. "Thank you, sir."

He looked at me. "You're not the usual run of deck boy, are you, Bennett?"

Again!

My heart lurched, my face burned – my wretched blushing. "How's that, sir?"

"Well," he led the way to the starboard wing of the bridge. "The way you speak for a start. And you seem very young. How old are you?"

"Sixteen," I said. "I get that from my dad, he only looks about twenty-five."

"Mm. And it seems you've struck up a friendship with Philip."

"Oh, we just ... You know, the shark and everything."

"It's all right, I don't mind. He tells me you're interested in navigation."

"Yes, all that about stars and great circles. I like maths."

"Understand it, do you – great circles, I mean?"

"As far as we went. It's not that difficult. Just like trig at school, except the sides are curved."

"That right? Did trig at your school?"

Another mistake.

He thought for a bit then crossed to the gyro repeater on the flying wing and lowered his eye to the prism. "Ever taken a bearing?"

I thought quickly. "Once or twice. One of the mates on my last ship showed me."

He spun the prism away. "What's the bearing of that little cloud, the one a bit like a dinosaur?"

I swung the prism to face the cloud. Then I lowered my eye and adjusted it delicately. The prism reflected the ticking compass card beneath. Quickly I read off the bearing: "Two-seven-nine, maybe two-eighty."

"Let me see." He took my place and adjusted the prism with stubby fingers. "Two-eighty. Excellent, Bennett. Very good." We returned to the bridge rail. My eyes roved the empty horizon.

"Know what an azimuth is?"

I knew perfectly. Dad had taught me. He had made me work one every day when I sailed with him, using the low sun or a star. "Is that where you take the bearing of the sun," I said uncertainly, "to check the accuracy of the gyro?"

"That's it. You *are* well-informed. Don't know how to work one though?"

"No, sir." I took a chance. "But I'd like to learn."

He looked me in the face. "I bet you could too."

I looked away.

He felt for a cigarette and realised he'd stopped smoking. Instead he pulled out a stick of chewing gum, tore it through and handed me half. "Ever handled a sextant?"

"Yes, sir. On my last ship, like I said."

The sun was on the port bow. "Go to the other side." I did so while the second mate went to the chartroom. He returned carrying two sextants. "Here, this is the ship's. Don't drop it for God's sake." He handed it to me. "See what you get." He flipped up the filters to protect his eye and pointed his own sextant at the sun.

I examined the instrument he had given me and did the same, putting my eye to the telescope and swinging the half-mirror to bring the sun's reflection down to the horizon. Pausing in my chewing, I turned the vernier screw to make the fine adjustment.

"Are you ready?"

A sextant is a very delicate instrument, measuring altitude to one sixtieth of a degree, which represents a mile in position. Since all morning the sun is rising and all afternoon it is sinking, altitudes have to be timed to the second.

"Just a tick." I turned the screw infinitely slowly, rocking the sextant and swinging the sun's reflection in little arcs above the sea. The bottom rim just kissed the horizon. I double checked. Already it was a fraction below. I hoisted it back. "Right, ready."

"OK – now!"

We lowered the sextants.

"What have you got?"

I read the brass scale and vernier. "Thirty-two degrees ... twelve minutes."

The second mate checked his own reading. "Thirty-two eleven." Again he looked at me with surprise. "That is *very good*, Bennett."

When I was with dad I had not only taken altitudes, I had worked out positions. It wasn't difficult, you only had to follow a few formulae – do this, do that. But here I was supposed to be a deck boy. "More like good luck." I looked down and swung the mirror.

"Not a bit of it. You knew exactly what you were doing."

I passed him the sextant.

He rubbed the peeling top of his head. "Come into the wheelhouse out the sun."

I waited by the window while he put the sextants away, cross with myself for showing off. As I stood there Tony Fanshott-Williams, wearing shorts and flip-flops, came trotting up the steps from the boat deck.

Down there with the Cockroaches

The second Tony saw me his face changed. "What the hell are you doing up here?"

"I had to do an hour on the wheel."

"Finished?"

"Yes."

"Then don't hang around sucking up to the officers." He stood aside. "Get yourself back down to the crew quarters."

"The second mate – "

"What about him?"

"He told me to – "

Tim Nettles emerged from the chartroom. "Hello, Tony. See you two having a chat. Know Bennett, do you?"

"Unfortunately." He didn't disguise his hostility. "Everybody knows Bennett."

"What do you mean?"

"Bloody deck boy, sticking his nose in all over the place."

"He was taking the wheel."

"So he told me."

"It's part of his training. What are you on about, Tony?"

"He shouldn't be hanging around up here on the bridge."

I was embarrassed and moved to the far end of the wheelhouse. They watched me go.

"He's not hanging around, I told him to wait. Not that it's any of your business. He's an able lad."

"That right? I wouldn't know."

"Then you'll just have to take my word for it."

"A fly hand with the patter, I know that much."

"Not at all. He's hardly said a word as a matter of fact, I've had to drag it out of him. But I do know he can steer a ship, handle an azimuth mirror and take an altitude."

"You've been teaching him to take an altitude?"

"No, he already knew how to do it."

"With the ship's sextant?"

"What else would he use?"

"Get it the right way up, did he, smarmy little bastard?"

"Use language like that about a rating and you'll find yourself up before the old man. But yes, he did, since you're asking. And better than some I could mention."

"What!" Tony's face flamed. "Are you talking about me?"

"Well, no one could have mistaken you for Christopher Columbus the last couple of mornings."

"Are you telling me the deck boy knows more about navigation than I do?"

"No, of course not. I didn't say that." He dropped his voice. "But his manners are a whole lot better and that's a fact. And remember who you're talking to."

Tony stared. " How dare you!" He turned abruptly and stormed away.

"Fanshott-Williams." The second mate called after him. "Come back here."

The cadet didn't falter. His flip-flops slapped down the bridge steps.

Tim Nettles was angry. He took a turn round the wheelhouse and summoned me across. "You'll not pass any of this on, Bennett, all right?"

I liked him, he was a good officer, but all the same ... "I'm sorry, sir, but I don't see why. I've done nothing wrong. Do you mean I should just stand here and let him swear at me whenever he wants?"

"No, of course not."

"It's not the first time he's picked on me. He's had it in for me the whole trip."

"That business with the hose, I suppose."

"And before that."

He drew a deep breath. "All right, Bennett, if that's how you feel about it. It's up to you." He pulled on his white cap. "Get on down now. See you next Sunday."

"Thanks, sir. It was a good afternoon until ..."

"There you go again," he said.

"What?"

Before he could answer there was a sound of quick footsteps and the mate appeared on the starboard wing. He strode into the wheelhouse.

"What the hell's going on here, Tim?"

"How do you mean?"

"Bloody cadet comes bursting into my cabin complaining about the deck boy there. Sunday afternoon, I want a bit of peace!"

"He came up to do his hour on the wheel, that's all."

"That's not what the cadet says. Something about you showing him how to take altitudes and God knows what."

"He already knew. Philip told me he's interested in navigation, so I was – "

"Listen, Two-oh, he's not one of the cadets, he's the deck boy. He comes up here to learn to steer the ship, end of story, not to learn navigation and fraternize with – "

"But if he's interested, Duncan. He's good, he's not like your average – "

"You can say that again. He's not like your average ... A pain in the bloody backside, that's what he is. Popping up here, popping up there. Spying on my wife. In my cabin. Giving the bosun hassle. Upsetting the cadets. Now swanning round up here with you." He turned to me. "Listen, Bennett. This is the third time you've got in my hair. And as far – "

The second mate laid a hand on his arm.

"Keep out of this, Second. And as far as I'm concerned, that's three times too often. Do you understand?"

"Yes," I said.

His eyes glittered beneath the dark bar of his brows. "Yes – *sir*."

"Yes, sir."

"Good. Now it's the last time I'm going to tell you this. On my ship, on any ship, there's nothing, *nothing*, lower than a deck boy. Deck boys are right down there with the cockroaches, scraping out the bilges with a teaspoon. Not even on the bottom rung of the ladder. Most deck boys accept that. And the sooner you can, the sooner you stop sticking your oar in and giving yourself airs, the sooner you get out of my sight and stay out of my sight, the better it'll be for everyone."

I was shaken and angry. I had done nothing to deserve this. Gran had taught me to be polite; dad had taught me to speak up for myself. "I'm sorry, sir, but that's not fair. I work hard, I do my job well, you can ask anybody. Tell me what I've done wrong. If you want to know who's – "

"Be quiet! How dare you, Bennett! One more word and I'll have you on a charge for insubordination. My God! A bloody deck boy! I've never heard … Get off this bridge! Go below! Now!"

Perhaps I should have shown contrition, slunk off with my tail between my legs. It might have defused the situation. But I didn't. There was nothing to apologise for. Head high I walked from the wheelhouse and descended the bridge steps. Whatever happened, as Charlie had said back in Westport, they couldn't hang me from the yardarm. And flogging was banned.

Star of Bengal

"He was your best friend," I said, "I know that. But is it OK to ask what happened? I mean I've heard – well, you know."

Every day the sun rose higher and beat on the decks. With a following wind the ship was like an oven.

In the evening we had gathered in Michael's cabin with the porthole wide and the air-vent blasting. Michael sat on the day bed in a David Essex T-shirt and a sarong. Barbara wore a new white boiler suit as a fashion statement, open to the waist. Luigi, hairy as a gorilla, sat next to Michael in his swimming shorts. Ossie, with his chubby chest and no body hair, sat on the bunk like an inflated baby.

We were talking about the *Star of Bengal* and the fateful trip when so much had happened, leading to the death of Michael's best friend and Ossie's mental breakdown.

I looked at the photo on Michael's locker, a young face with a wisp of blond whiskers, blue-eyed and smiling. "What was his name – apart from Curly?"

"Terry Wayman," Barbara said. "He came from Bristol."

"What was he?" I said. "What did he sail as?"

"Pantry b-boy," Ossie said.

"Usually a steward," said Michael. "Pantry boy was the only job he could get that trip – you know, so we could sail together."

"How old was he?"

"Eighteen," Barbara said. "Nicest guy in the world."

"Next week would have been his birthday," Michael said. "He'd have been nineteen next week."

Luigi put an arm round his shoulders.

Barbara hesitated. "Is it all right to tell Ben what happened?"

"Go ahead," Michael said. "I'd like Ben to know."

"Well," Barbara went to the door to see no one was listening. "It was one of Ryland's scams. Him and Rat'bone. Smuggling. And Curly got to hear about it."

"Tell him how," Ossie said.

"I'm just going to!" Barbara rolled his eyes. "We were anchored off Calcutta in the estuary of the River Hooghly – that's downstream from the Ganges. Coming back from Japan. The captain, I forget his name, put down one of the lifeboats so we could have some time ashore. Not Calcutta, of course, that's way upriver, but one of the little Indian towns – Diamond Harbour and that. It was good, the boat used to pick us up again about ten. Couldn't leave it alongside overnight, not without an armed watchman, so the hairies used to winch it up and lower it again next morning."

"Hairies?"

"Deck crew, your lot. Anyway, this day Curly had been ashore with Michael and some others, and when he got back he couldn't find his sunglasses. Bit later on, round eleven or midnight, he reckons he might have dropped them in the lifeboat. They cost a bit so he goes up to have a look. All the deck lights are on, ship lit up like Christmas. In those parts thieves throw up ropes and come swarming aboard, climb up the anchor chain. Stick a knife in you given half a chance. Anyway, Curly looks everywhere and finds his sunglasses fallen between slats of the bottom boards. Not jammed exactly but awkward to get out. So he's down there fiddling about when Ryland and his sidekick come to the rail just below him."

"Rat'bone?"

"The very same. 'Course Ryland wasn't bosun then, they were just a couple of ABs. Curly doesn't want to come out 'cause there's been trouble with the pair of them already. Don't have to tell you, couple of real nasty types, queer bashers. So he stays down out of sight and next minute they start talking about this job.

"They'd been ashore like the rest of us and met up with some Indian guy. Must've been arranged way back, when we were in Yokohama or Saigon, I don't know. Anyway, this chap's got everything lined up ready."

"Diamonds?" I said.

"Diamonds?"

"You said Diamond Harbour."

"No," Barbara laughed. "We'd all want a piece of that action. No, this was people. Indians, illegal immigrants. Life's hell where they are, poverty like you can't imagine. Do anything to get to a place like Britain. Sell everything they've got, put themselves in hock for the rest of their lives."

I'd seen a documentary about it on TV.

"And this Indian guy was one of the organisers. Fifty people waiting. All Ryland had to do, soon as we'd finished loading, was slip them aboard during the night and give them access to one of the holds."

"Fifty," I said. "There'd be no room."

"Always a space somewhere. We'd been to Japan, had a load of cars. Go down there, sleep on the back seat of a new Toyota. Or sacks of rice, wooden crates, whatever we were carrying."

"What about food?" I said. "And water? And going to the lavatory?"

"Don't think about it," Barbara said. "That was up to them. All Ryland had to do was smuggle them aboard, keep his trap shut, and smuggle them off again when we reached Cardiff. There'd be a lorry waiting.

"Well, Curly's in the lifeboat and he hears all this and he's scared witless. If Ryland knew he was there, God knows what he'd have done. So he stays where he is, quiet as a mouse, and as soon as the coast's clear he climbs out an' comes on down. White as a sheet. Tells Michael all about it."

"You were there," Michael said.

"I come in halfway through." Barbara lubricated his throat with gin. "If he hadn't overheard, or we'd all just ignored it, Curly would be here now."

"But that wasn't his way," Michael said. "People die down there in the holds, shut up in containers some of them, hidden away for weeks at a time."

"That's right, Curly reckons he can't just let it pass. But it's no good confronting Ryland directly, him just the pantry boy, so he goes to the Chief Steward. Makes him promise to keep his name out of it then tells him what he's heard."

"We all went with him," Michael said. "He was really scared."

"That's right. And the next thing, Curly's summoned to the bridge and has to repeat his story to the old man."

"Were the other two there?"

"No, but the Chief Steward was, lying rat. I reckon he's as much responsible for what happened to Curly as anyone. Anyway, after Curly had gone back down, one of the watch was sent to fetch them. First Ryland, then Lenny, one after the other."

"Must have put an end to their plan," I said. "Did they get into trouble, police and that?"

"You're right about the first part," Barbara said. "I reckon it cost them a packet. And the police came in a big launch and took them ashore for questioning – Curly, Ryland and Rat'bone. Kept them overnight. But what proof was there? Just the word of a pantry boy against two ABs. Naturally they denied it."

"When they came back," Michael said, "Curly was shaking like a leaf, terrified. Threw up in the washbasin."

"It wasn't the cells and the questioning," Barbara said, "though that was bad enough. He knew Ryland and Rat'bone would have it in for him now."

"I bet they did." I took a handful of crisps.

"Anyway, that night, what with the heat and everyone bored out of their skulls, there was a party on board. Crew bar, music, everyone getting plastered. After an hour or so Curly and one of the chefs, skinny chap called Squib, went to the galley to get the eats. You know, little kebabs, devils on horseback, that sort of thing. Chefs put themselves out a bit when it's for a party."

"The galley and the crew bar were right next to each other," Michael said, "just a few steps along the alleyway."

Barbara glanced at him. "But there was a door opposite that led out on deck."

"Starboard side," Ossie said. "Kept open to catch any breeze there was going."

"And that's the last we saw of him, heading off to the galley."

"I asked if they wanted a hand," Ossie said, "but they told me they could manage. Then Squib came back with his tray. He was only gone a couple of minutes, just long enough to take some stuff out the oven. Said Curly was right behind. But he never turned up."

"Never thought about it at first," Barbara went on. "Then after a bit we began to wonder where he'd got to, so Michael went to fetch him."

"There was no sign of him anywhere," Michael said. "Galley was empty, tray was gone. I looked in the fridge and saw the trifle and profiteroles for later, but not the tray Curly would have been carrying. I began to get scared. Then I spotted," he drew a deep breath, "fingers of pizza and quiche and stuff, kicked out of sight under the cookers. Something wasn't right and I began screaming, 'Curly! Curly!' and ran through the ship. He wasn't anywhere: not in the washroom, not in his cabin, not out on deck getting a breath of air – "

"When we heard him," Barbara said, "a whole lot of us ran out to see what was happening. Like Michael says, he'd just disappeared. Then somebody saw crumbs on the deck just by that door I told you about, and a smear of tomato sauce on the rail. We thought it was blood to begin with." He stopped. "You OK, Michael?"

His eyes were red. "It just brings everything back."

"I know, love. So anyway, we went up and saw the mate, and after what had happened with the police and everything, he organised a search. Every corner of the ship. When he was satisfied Curly wasn't lying drunk or hurt somewhere, he rang ashore. Police launches were out there in minutes, scanning the water with searchlights. There was no sign of anyone swimming or shouting for help, but what the police and some of the crew did see – "

"Don't!" Ossie cried. "Don't say it." He scrambled to the floor, spilling his drink down his chest. "I've got to have a pee." He ran from the room.

"That's what finished him off," Barbara said. "He went completely to pieces."

"We all did," Michael said. "If it wasn't for those Indian doctors, there'd have been two of us had a breakdown."

"Yes, but you're lucky, you got through it somehow, you've got your head screwed on tight." Barbara fanned the front of his boiler suit. "See what Ossie's like even now."

"Yes, yes," Luigi sat up impatiently. "But the river, the police'a with their searchlights. What you see?"

"Crocodiles," Barbara said. "Big estuary crocodiles. Low down in the water like logs. They come out scavenging at night."

"I hate them," Michael said.

"One swam right under the gangway light, remember? We saw it, big long snout, horrible thing." He hesitated. "People saw them fighting over something in the water."

Michael looked away.

"That's what happened anyway," Barbara said. "The crocodiles got him. He might have been dead before he went into the water. I hope so. No way of telling. But the river police knew where to look. A lot of bodies and dead cattle and stuff get chucked into the Ganges and come floating down the Hooghly on their way out to sea. They found him on a sandbank next morning."

"Or what'a was left of him," said Luigi.

"Yes, all right," Michael said. "That's enough."

"Except Ben doesn't understand it was Ossie who saw the body," Barbara said. "He really loved Curly."

"What do you mean?" Michael said. "We all loved Curly. What about me?"

"Yes, I know, but Ossie was the one on deck when the police launch came alongside to ask the old man for identification. Body covered by a tarpaulin. Pulled it back so he could have a proper look. Right below where Ossie was standing. Lying there in the sun. Black with flies. AB on the gangway said you couldn't hardly tell it was a man at all, except – "

"Stop it!" Michael was distressed. "Stop it!"

"Sure, sure," said Luigi. "But the police'a, they no question them? The bosun and this Rat'bone? First your Curly he accuse them, now he dead in the river. In my country we know this is revenge'a. We go one night when they no expect it, and we cut'a their throats."

"I wish you had been there, I'd have given you a hand," Barbara said. "But the Indian police did everything they could. Took statements from everybody. Handcuffed the two of them and took them back to headquarters. Four days in the cells but they couldn't break their story: said they didn't fancy the party so they'd spent the night in Ryland's cabin, playing crib and having a few drinks."

"Everyone knew it was a lie, everyone knew they'd done it, you could tell just by the look in their faces, but there wasn't any proof." Tears spilled from Michael's eyes. "Bastards!"

Luigi put an arm around his shoulders. "Sshhh. You OK now."

"What about Ossie though?" I said.

"That's what finally broke him," Barbara said. "Seeing Curly's body like that and the two of them winking at him every meal time. Knowing they'd killed him. On top of everything he'd had to put up with before. Completely went to pieces, couldn't stop crying and shaking. The mate had to sedate him. When we docked in Calcutta a few days later they took him off in an ambulance. Flew him home when he was fit enough to travel."

"And when we met him signing on, that was him just back?"

"Yes, I told you, after months in hospital and under the doctors. Then his mother died, remember, and left him alone in that horrible house. Would have driven *me* mental, never mind poor Ossie. No wonder he had to get away."

Right on cue Ossie appeared through the curtain, holding Attila in his arms. The ginger tom cat snuggled beneath his chin, purring like an engine.

"I think he likes me," Ossie said with pleasure.

"Course he does, you big daft brush." Michael wiped his eyes. "We all like you."

"You're my friends." Ossie regarded him with pale, protuberant eyes. "Have you been crying?"

"Yes, I've been crying."

"What for?"

"Why do you think, Ossie? We were talking about Curly, weren't we?"

He pondered Michael's words. "Are you all right?"

"Oh, for God's sake!" Michael pulled away from Luigi and drained his glass. "Here, somebody pour me another gin before I do something desperate."

Charlie looked in, a can of lager in his hand, then the cheerful Kevin and a couple of others.

Kevin had a new story.

Michael shrieked: "Kevin, you dirty, dirty boy! I'm disgusted! You'd never tell a story like that, would you, Ben?"

"Never," I assured him, and remembered a good one from school about some Girl Guides at summer camp.

Slowly the evening regained its gaiety.

But I had been frightened. Beyond the laughter I kept thinking of my own run-ins with the bosun and Lenny Rat'bone, not to mention their friend the senior cadet. After hearing about Curly, I did not wish to cross them again.

And I didn't, not for a whole twenty-eight hours.

Knife on the Funnel Deck

"Ben! Ben!" A hand was shaking my shoulder.

Slowly I surfaced from a sleep ten thousand metres deep.

"Ben!"

I pushed back the sheet. A figure loomed above me.

"They're away to get the whisky."

"Mm."

"Come on! Wake up!"

It was dark. I made an effort and my eyes swam into focus. "What is it?" My mouth tasted of sleep.

"Tony and some others," the voice was Philip's. "They're away down number five for the whisky."

I rubbed a hand over my face.

"Now?"

"Yes."

"Shut up!" A sleepy grunt from the top bunk.

"I thought you'd want to know. I got to get back." The shape vanished. There was a rattle of curtain rings, footsteps, silence.

I swung my feet to the deck. No light at the porthole. I looked out – black sea and a thick layer of cloud. My watch hung from a tack in the bunk post. Ten past one, "everyone in their pits", just as they'd planned. I didn't intend to go near the hatch, just see what was happening. Keep right back. All the same, I'd have to be very careful. What could I wear? Perhaps there'd be something dark in the drying room. I crossed the alleyway. The storm door leading to the crew deck, always hooked open, was shut as it had been the night I saw the senior cadet raid the cargo. The heat from the drying room hit me like a blast from an oven. Trailing clothes hung from the slats. No black T-shirt but plenty of blue boiler suits. I carried one back to the cabin.

"What's going on?" A glint of eyes from Charlie's pillow.

"Sshhh!" I pulled on the boiler suit. The legs trailed, the sleeves covered my hands. I turned them back and tugged my woollen hat to my eyebrows.

"What are you dressed like that for?"

"They've come for the whisky. Go back to sleep."

With the alleyway lights on, even though they were dimmed, I couldn't use the storm door and turned for'ard. The messroom smelled of toast. There were three to a night watch: one on the bridge, one keeping lookout on the fo'csle head, one on standby in the messroom. But the messroom was deserted. A small Stillson wrench lay on one of the tables. I slipped it into a pocket in case of trouble. A door led down to the engine room; another, directly opposite, led up to the engineers' cabins. I climbed the narrow stairs and stood in an entrance looking out on the night. A lifeboat overhead cast shadow. All was quiet. I emerged on to the boat deck.

Nothing moved but the waves and gently-rolling ship. I walked aft, avoiding the open deck and treading on the sides of my trainers. At the rail I halted. The stern of the ship lay spread before me. Directly below was number four hatch, astern of the crew accommodation. Below that again lay the afterdeck. I had a bird's-eye view of number five hatch with the swimming pool alongside, the mainmast housing, number six hatch and finally the poop. Our spreading wake gleamed in the darkness.

If I hadn't known there were men about I would never have spotted them. I fixed my eyes on the booby hatch which gave access to the hold, and at last detected movement. What was it, someone's head? a swinging block? I needed to get closer. Cautiously I descended a flight of steps to the crew deck and tiptoed the length of number four hatch to the after rail. A winch and samson post gave me cover. I crept into the space between the drum and the controls. I was terrified.

A spitting distance below me lay the canvas of number five hatch. At the far end, silhouetted against the white mast housing, I spotted a figure. Who it was I could not make out. He lifted the lid of the booby hatch. A second man emerged. With a soft grunt he passed something to the first man who set it on the deck. I heard a tiny bump. He descended again into the hold.

I waited, motionless. He returned. A second object was passed across. It was quite heavy. I heard a chink of glass. They were the crates of whisky.

A third crate emerged. And a fourth.

I was completely unprepared. I could have been knocked on the head and dumped over the side without knowing anything about it. All my attention was concentrated on the scene before me. But suddenly at my back there was a scuffle, a thud, a cry. I spun round. A few paces away a man fell to the deck. A baton of two-by-two rattled from his hand. Another man stood above him.

"Run!" he hissed.

I couldn't move.

"Go on, scarper! Quick!"

I may have been paralysed with fright but those on the afterdeck were not. There was a flurry of activity round the booby hatch. A single figure raced towards me. He reached the steps. I took to my heels. My saviour had vanished. The groaning man on the deck flung out a hand. I stumbled. He gripped the leg of my overalls. I kicked him and tore my leg free. Headlong I raced for the shadows. My pursuer was only metres behind. A dim-lit doorway was at my side. I dodged through, leaped up a staircase and ran out onto the boat deck.

The man on my heels was slower. Somewhere in the accommodation he fell. I sprinted round the corner. Beside me was a ladder to the funnel deck. I scrambled up and looked for a place to hide. The lifeboats, two at each side, were clamped in their davits and covered by tight canvas. The door to the funnel was locked. A narrow space between the funnel and a huge engine-room ventilator was black with shadow. I ran into it and froze.

My pursuer had lost me, but spotting the ladder he climbed to the funnel deck. My hiding place was so dark I could not see my fingers before my eyes. The man came into my field of vision. It was the bosun. He had something in his hand. From the angle he held it, I guessed it was his seaman's knife. Breathing heavily, he hunted the deck.

"I know you're there. Come on out."

He approached my hiding place. I could have backed out the far side and fled but he was too close. I was terrified to move. Only two metres distant he peered towards me. One metre. He stretched out his arm. If I had remembered the Stillson in my pocket I would have clubbed him with it. Instead, with all my strength, I hit him in the face with my fist and wriggled away backwards.

"Ah! Ah!" I could hear his gasps of pain.

A second man was on the funnel deck. "That you, Jumbo?" It was Rat'bone.

I circled the funnel and flitted aft. Someone was climbing towards me from the boat deck. Steve Petersen? The senior cadet? Shoes scraped on the iron rungs. I ran away between the lifeboats.

Rat'bone appeared from the shadows. In one hand he gripped the wooden baton. His other hand covered his mouth. "Who's that?" he said to the person who'd just arrived.

"Tony."

"Thought you was locking up."

"I have. What's wrong with your face."

"Someone give us a clout."

"You OK?"

"Not really, no. What about the crates?"

"Dumped them."

"The whole lot?"

"Hid one."

"Good on yer."

"Show you later. Any sign of …"

"He ran up here. Smacked Jumbo an' all."

"Who?"

"No idea. Wearing a boiler suit. Some greaser."

They spread out. I tried to squeeze behind one of the lifeboats but there was nowhere to go. Beyond the davits they hung in space. My back was against the safety rails. Fifteen metres beneath me the ocean swished past. There was no means of climbing to the deck below. I looked up. White hand lines were looped beneath the lifeboat's gunwales. They were for drowning sailors to cling to but gave me an idea. If I stayed where I was I would certainly be found. And if I were found – Rat'bone with his club, Ryland with his knife! I climbed the safety rail and reached for the nearest hand line.

My legs swung into space.

Saved by a Stranger

No sailor in a hurricane clung to a safety line more desperately. Face to the timbers, I swung hand over hand round the lifeboat's side. The rope hurt my fingers but I scarcely felt it. Somewhere near the middle I made a supreme effort, heaved myself up and after two failed attempts managed to hook a foot through one of the nearby loops. The second foot was easier. I hooked my elbow through the loop I was grasping and hung there panting.

If any of my pursuers saw me now I was a dead boy.

But they didn't see me.

"Not up here anyway." I recognised the bosun's voice.

They drifted away. I saw a hand on a rail. They descended to the boat deck.

For two more minutes I hung there, praying the lashings were strong and the rope had not deteriorated. Beneath me was nothing but the black Pacific. At last I lowered my legs and struggled back to the rail. Never had I felt so weak but there was no time to linger. I had to get back before they began searching the cabins.

I crept past the funnel to the for'ard end of the deck. Number three hatch, where we had watched Trish sunbathing, lay below me. I stopped in my tracks. A shadowy figure lurked in the officers' entrance. I backed behind a ventilator and tiptoed away. The after end of the boat deck seemed clear. I descended a ladder and headed for the steps to the crew deck. Abruptly Rat'bone appeared round a corner. He gave a shout. I fled back the way I had come and dived through the engineers' entrance, an alleyway that led directly from port to starboard.

The bosun, his back towards me, was descending a staircase. "Hey!" He spun round.

I shot past and out the doorway on the opposite side.

A voice hissed, "Down the steps. The way's clear."

"What?"

"Quick!"

I never saw him but did as he told me. In seconds I was on the crew deck and sprinting aft.

The alleyway door stood open again. I sprang over the sill and was just in time to see a back as someone disappeared into my cabin. He moved furtively. The curtain closed. It wasn't Charlie, I was sure of that. The washroom was right beside me. I darted inside. It was deserted. The washroom was spacious with doors to port and starboard – deck crew our side, greasers and catering crew the other. I headed for the door opposite then skidded to a halt. One of those who were hunting me might be in the alleyway. I stared all round, from the showers to the portholes and a wet towel hanging by the washbasins. Desperate for respite, I ran into a toilet cubicle and shut the door.

Silence, stillness. I sat on the lid and lifted my feet. White bulkheads, hanging paper, a flimsy bolt.

Then the squeak of a footstep on the tiles

The wet towel came flying over the door. "Gimme the boiler suit!"

I froze.

"For God's sake! Gimme your boiler suit – and the hat. Quick!"

Whoever it was, he was a friend. I tore open the buttons and tried to tug the legs over my trainers. They stuck. I pulled off the trainers too, threw down my hat and kicked everything under the door. They were snatched away. The footsteps receded.

I was alone.

The towel lay on the deck. I hung it on the back of the door.

There were voices in the alleyway:

"... not in his bunk. His mate's dead to the world."

"... that poofy greaser he knocks around with?"

"... always wears them white overalls. Smell his body rub anyway."

"... be that bloody deckboy."

"Where is he then? Have you tried the messroom?"

"... just looked."

"... about in here?"

Somebody entered the washroom. "Ah!" He addressed the cubicle door. "Who's in there?"

I didn't reply.

"Who is it?" Knuckles rapped sharply. "That you, Bennett?"

"Yes."

"Come on out."

"I haven't finished."

"Never mind that, come on out. It's the bosun here."

I took my time even though I was shaking: pulled some paper, lifted the lid, flushed the toilet. At last, wearing underpants and carrying the towel, I emerged.

Three men stood facing me: Ryland, Steve and Tony. Clearly they were taken aback. Tony pushed past and looked behind the cubicle door.

"What do you want?" I said.

The bosun said, "How long have you been in there?"

"What?"

"You heard. How long?"

"I don't know – a few minutes. I've got constipation. Why?"

"Never you mind." He looked at the others. A big red bruise was starting on the side of his face. His good eye was bloodshot.

"Not him anyway." Steve shook his head. "Guy was wearing overalls."

The bosun glanced in the cubicle. No water tank, no air trunk, no place I could have hidden them. He pressed the flush; the water ran away freely.

Rat'bone came in, holding a bottle of whisky. The club of two-by-two I had seen lying on the deck was thrust through his belt. Whoever had hit him, perhaps aided by my kick, had made a good job of it. His upper lip was split. Blood ran from his nose. "Good, you got the little bastard." He wiped off the blood and licked it from his hand. Tipping the bottle, he took a good swig. "What now, Jumbo?"

"Not him, looks like we got it wrong this time."

"What's he doin' here then?"

The bosun nodded towards the lavatory. "An' you can thank your lucky stars that's the only reason you're out your bunk this time o' night." He hitched the knife and marlinspike on his belt. "Never mind about us, that's none o' your business. Forget you seen us is my advice. An' put something on your feet when you come in here, you should know that."

They turned away.

"Whoever it was, we lost him now," Tony said. "What if he talks?"

"Better not if he knows what's good for him," said Ryland. "Anyway, Lenny says you got rid of ..."

"Yeah."

"Good lad. So where's the evidence? One man against four. You just make sure that key goes back sharpish." Ryland saw me listening. "You'll not be constipated if I have to come over there an' teach you some manners." He raised a fist. "Do what you come here for or get back to your cabin."

Just then Brian, AB on the middle watch with Rat'bone and Steve, appeared in the doorway. "Second mate's going ballistic! Wants you on the bridge, Lenny. Asking why you're not up there on the fo'csle, keeping lookout." He saw the bottle, smelled the whisky. "Man, you are *dead*!"

"How's he know?"

"Saw some people up on the funnel deck. Wanted you and me to check it out. Rang the fo'csle – nobody there."

"Oh, hell! Give us a minute." Rat'bone produced a filthy handkerchief. "Got any peppermints?"

Brian eyed the blood. "Been fighting?"

Rat'bone sneered. "Fell against the windlass, didn't I? Had to come aft an' clean myself up."

They drifted into the alleyway.

I returned to the cubicle and bolted the door. My stomach churned. Who, I wondered, had been my protector? Not Philip, it wasn't his voice. Nor Michael or Barbara. Definitely not Ossie. Aaron? – I didn't think so. Smoky? Charlie? – easy to find out. I flushed the toilet, rinsed my feet in the shower, dried them on the towel and returned to my cabin.

Was Charlie asleep or just pretending? The sheet was pulled to his throat. Perhaps he was dressed underneath. I eased it back and saw bare shoulders. Body heat wafted out at me. He shifted and pulled the sheet back. Charlie was definitely asleep.

So was Aaron, breathing deeply, snoring ever so softly.

"Aaron!" I whispered. "Aaron."

"Mmm." He turned on the pillow. "Julie."

I returned to the cabin and prepared to climb into bed then changed my mind.

"Charlie." I shook him gently. "Hey, Charlie!"

The Messman's Dolls

As I stood in the dinner queue three days later, I saw that Ossie was smiling. When it came to my turn he drew me aside.

"Isn't it great!"

"What do you mean?"

"The dolls, the juju – it's working."

For a moment I didn't know what he was talking about. "You mean Steve's foot?"

"And the others."

I hadn't thought about it, so much else had been happening. But surely his damaged ankle had been a coincidence. "You're not telling me – ?"

He nodded eagerly. "All three of them."

"You're kidding!"

"Come on, Ossie, mate." Angry voices intervened. "Stop faffing about!"

"Tell you later." He hurried back to the chops and vegetarian pie.

It gave me a lot to think about.

What had happened was this:

Following the struggle on the crew deck Rat'bone refused to have his lip stitched, he was frightened of needles, and it turned septic. I wasn't surprised, considering his habits and the dirty rag he was mopping it with. Inside and out, the wound turned into an abscess and the poison spread up into his nose and his cheekbone and the hinge of his jaw. His face was a mess and looked very painful. Eating and speaking became next to impossible. It gave many people a savage satisfaction.

Equally satisfactory, the bosun came off worse in an argument with my friend Kevin, the galley boy. I'm not sure what it was about, something to do with potatoes or a piece of fish. What I do know, because Kevin told me himself, is that Ryland flared up one lunchtime and stormed from the petty officers' messroom into the galley where he had no right to be. The chef at that moment was in the pantry but Kevin stood only a few paces away, his back to the door. The bosun, in a great rage, grabbed him by the back of his white jacket and spun him round. Kevin hadn't heard his approach and right then was paddling some battered fish in the deep fat fryer. He sprang back, startled by the sudden attack, and in so doing flung a ladle of seething fat over the bosun's bare arm.

Ryland screamed, he roared, he waved his arm in the air, he rushed to the sink and plunged it under a tap – the boiling hot tap! Too late the cold tap. The fat cooled to a white crust. But beneath it the bosun's arm was burned raw. He was taken to the sick bay and made to sit for half the afternoon with his arm in a basin of iced water.

Michael, who was constantly in and out of the galley, ran to tell me and gloat, so I was one of the first to know. That evening I saw the bosun, his arm swathed in bandages, reeling drunk from a cocktail of painkillers and alcohol.

Two of my tormentors laid low and Steve hobbling painfully as he went about his work. Only Tony to go. Time to celebrate – and later that evening with Charlie, Aaron and a few others, I drank a beer too many.

It was a merry occasion but my mind was in a whirl. Apart from myself Ossie had told no one – not Barbara, not Michael – about the voodoo dolls. He had only confided in me because he needed someone to keep a lookout in Panama, and had sworn me to secrecy. But now, it appeared, all the injuries he was conjuring upon people had come to pass. I had sat watching as he broke open the crude doll that represented Steve Petersen, pressed a scrap of his writing and some long hairs into the wax and wrapped his sweatband around its neck. I had heard him mutter some incantation and seen him thrust a hot needle through its foot. Just hours afterwards, Steve had returned to the ship with his ankle twisted so badly that a week later he still wore a tight bandage and walked with a limp. True, it was the wrong ankle, but all the same it was a coincidence. Now Ossie was claiming that the accidents involving Rat'bone and the bosun were also the result of his experiments. That night in Panama, before he added the scraps he had found in their cabins, I had seen the needles wedged in Rat'bone's mouth and Ryland's bulbous forearm. And now, spreading from his split lip, Rat'bone had this terrible abscess all over his face and the bosun's forearm was badly burned. But how could Ossie be responsible? Voodoo like that was all superstition, I told myself, it had to be. I had seen photographs of witch doctors in Haiti and Africa, and their terrified victims with rolling eyes. The dolls and needles were scary. But there was no way that sort of magic could work, not in the world I knew or among western people like the crew of the ship. Not with somebody like Ossie.

I had promised to tell no one but it was a promise I felt I could not keep. Huddled in a corner of the bar with Michael, I broke my word and told him everything. It was to have terrible consequences. All I can say in my defence is that I was fifteen years old, half drunk, and Michael was a much older friend of Ossie than I was.

"And now he's claiming to have supernatural powers?" Michael said.

"Sort of, I suppose."

And all this happened back in Panama?" He adjusted his colourful wrap-around to cover a bare leg. "What a secretive thing you are, Ben. Who'd guess it to look into that innocent face? I wonder what other surprises you've got tucked away up your sleeve."

"But now he's saying it's all three of them."

"Yes, I know, you just told me."

"You'll not tell anyone."

"Of course not. Well, Barbara, I'll have to tell Barbara."

"'Cause he made me promise."

"It's all right." Michael patted my arm. "All this occult stuff, we've seen it before."

"Raking through cabins for bits of hair? Sticking needles in dolls?"

"No, not the voodoo, that's new." He rose, taking his drink with him. "Come on, let's go and see what he's up to."

I wished my head did not feel so muzzy.

"You off then?" Charlie's shout rang across the bar. "If you meet the bosun give his arm a good thump from me."

Curtains drifted in every doorway but one. Ossie's door was locked. I smelled incense. Michael knocked.

"Who is it?"

"Me and Ben."

"Go away."

"That's not very nice."

"I can't see you right now."

"Yes you can. Open up."

"I'm busy. Come back in half an hour."

"Ossie!"

"Well you'll have to wait." There was a sound of bustle and drawers closing. Something fell. Ossie gave a little cry.

"Come on!" Michael rapped. "Just open the door."

More noises from within then a key turned. Ossie stood in the entrance looking flushed and guilty.

"What have you been up to now?"

"That's my business." Exotic smoke drifted into the alleyway.

We followed him into his cabin. He had opened the porthole but it would take some time for the air to clear. Joss sticks, one still smouldering, stood in a holder. A last candle flame guttered in the draught. The crimson cloth I had seen folded in his drawer turned out to be covered with gold and silver astrological signs and now hung above his bunk.

"Oh, Ossie!" Michael sat on the day bed. "We've been here before, haven't we?"

Ossie looked at his feet.

"You're not going to get ill again are you?"

"I'm all right." Surreptitiously he removed an ornate ring from his finger.

"Because your friends are worried."

Ossie glanced at me.

"Yes, Ben's told me," Michael said. "Don't look at him like that. You keep locking yourself away."

The fumes on top of the beer were making me dizzy. I sat in the chair. A glint of silver on the deck caught my eye. I picked it up, a triangular canvas needle.

"So what's it all about?" Michael said. "These dolls, you've been making, where are they?"

Ossie twisted his arms.

"Come on, love, this is Michael here. You can tell me anything, you know that. Where are they?"

Ossie mumbled, "In there."

"This drawer here?" Michael pulled it open. A variety of objects had been tumbled out of sight: tarot cards, candles, a black silk scarf, a freezer bag with a tight elastic band around the top. Michael picked it up and discovered the head, entrails and a few scattered feathers from a chicken. "Oh, Ossie!" He hesitated, holding it in the tips of his fingers, and threw it out the porthole. "You can't keep things like that in your drawer, it's disgusting."

"It's only been there a day. They use chicken blood and stuff in Jamaica – all over really."

"Not in the Merchant Navy, love. They'll have you off to the funny farm again if the old man finds out." He rinsed his fingers and returned to the drawer. Each of the dolls was now wrapped separately. Michael picked up the nearest and unfolded the bulky paper. "Oh, my goodness!"

It was Ryland. Ossie had worked on it since that night in Panama. Now the bosun doll had a straggle of real hair pushed into its head. Black specks, which I took to be the whiskers scraped from his washbasin, were stuck round its chin. A fragment of red underpants was knotted round its middle. And two needles, thick canvas needles like the one I'd found on the deck, were thrust into its body, one through the right arm, the other into its back.

It was a frightening object.

Michael gave the needles a little tug and push. They were rigid and must have been inserted hot. "Are you telling us you did this before the accident?"

"The one into his arm I did," Ossie said. "Honest! Ben seen it."

"Not that needle," I said.

"No, but the same place."

I nodded.

"What about the one in his back?"

"I done that after."

Michael turned the doll this way and that, set it back in the drawer and picked up another – Rat'bone. In a strange way the deformed lump of wax actually *looked* like the scruffy AB. Since I last saw it, Ossie had added the broken specs, a few straggly ginger hairs and a greasy comb. "I put all the other stuff inside the body," he told me.

"Where'd you get the comb?"

"He dropped it in the bar."

A thick needle had been pushed deep into its heart. A second needle, a darning needle, just as I had seen it in Panama, was thrust through the doll's mouth.

Ossie explained: "He was always saying filthy things."

"And you did it before Lenny got hurt?"

"The one in his mouth."

"But not this one?" With the tip of his finger Michael tested the needle fixed immovably into the doll's chest.

"No, I done that this afternoon."

It was the first time I'd seen Michael lost for words. "I don't know what to say, Ossie, love. I just don't believe in black magic. If what you're telling us is true, it's the most fantastic coincidence since – well, ever. Tell us again, on your word of honour, did you stick those needles in *before* the accidents – the ones where they've all been hurt?"

"Not much point doing it afterwards."

"Except I suppose it might feel like revenge. And make the rest of us believe in it a bit more."

"You'd never have known about them if Ben hadn't told you." His big round face was earnest. "I never expected it to work myself, not really, not just like that. But it did, and I'm glad. They deserved it."

Michael tried to digest it. "I can't believe I'm having this conversation." He drank off the last of his gin. "And what's this about a spell. Ben says heard you muttering something."

"I can't tell you that."

"Can't tell me?"

"It's forbidden."

"Forbidden? Who by?"

"Don't keep on at me, Michael. I knew you would, that's why I never told you."

"But Ossie, do you believe all this magic stuff, this voodoo, whatever you call it?

"It worked, didn't it? I've been studying."

I glanced up at his bookshelf. It held three or four paperbacks. A bigger book lay on the bunk, hastily hidden beneath a pile of washing. A corner protruded. Michael pulled it out, a tattered black volume with antique gold lettering on the cover: *Necromancy, a Dictionary of the Occult* by – the name was mostly worn away but something like Aydin Baghdatur. There was a second book, *Secrets of the Tarot*. I had not seen them before. If Ossie had a collection of such titles, he kept them well hidden.

"If you want to know what I done here, Michael," he said, "if you really want to know, I'll tell you. There's four things you need." He counted them on his fingers. "What they call the image: you've got to have a manikin or something to work on – it doesn't have to be wax, it could be cloth, or wood, anything really. Then some personal things to connect it to the victim. The punishment – like the needles or fire or something. And lastly the words – and the words are secret."

"What about the chicken innards?"

"That's more for divination, telling the future, like the tarot cards. But yes, you're right, sometimes you need something like that: pebbles, bones, salt." He took the books back and covered them with his washing. "I don't want to keep talking about it."

"So that's the three of them punished." Michael rocked the Ryland doll by the needle stuck in its back. "What about these? Do you want them dead?"

"They killed Curly. Luigi says he'd have cut their throats. Barbara says he'd have helped him. Back in India they'd have been hung."

There didn't seem any answer to that.

Ossie unwrapped the Steve doll. To my eyes, at least, it appeared unchanged from Panama, just the one darning needle stuck through its foot. Presumably he didn't think Steve Petersen deserved to be killed, or maybe he hadn't got round to it yet.

Steve was, I thought, the last of his enemies, but there was a fourth package in the drawer. Ossie handed it to me. Why me, I wondered, and opened it on my knee.

It was another wax figure, one I had not seen. Unlike the others, this was not pierced by needles but bound hand and foot with string. A crude gag covered its mouth.

"Who's that?" I said.

Ossie's weak eyes were watering. He mopped his cheeks and gave a little smile. "See if you can work it out."

Michael examined it. "I know."

He handed it back. Squiggles for curls, the scratched outline of a shirt and shorts.

"Tony?" I said.

Ossie beamed

"What's he done to you?"

"Nothing, except he's mates with the other three. I done that one for you, Ben."

"For me!"

"Everyone knows he's got it in for you. So I tied him up, tried to make him a bit helpless like. Only I can't get anything personal, him living up there with the officers."

"I can," Michael said.

"Not for me!" What with the beer, the fumes and now all this, my head was spinning. "Leave me out of it."

"Been a right pig, what I heard," Ossie said. "He deserves it."

"No way!"

I threw the doll back in the drawer. Bound and gagged, it stared up at me from the gouged hollows of its eyes.

Into the Candle Flame

When a secret is betrayed it's not long before everyone knows. I told no one except Michael, not even Charlie, but Michael's life-blood was gossip. There may have been other leaks too, because Barbara spent a whole evening with Ossie at the Ouija board and Kevin went to have his fortune told by the tarot.

However it came about, word of the voodoo reached Ryland and the next night, fuelled by rage, painkillers and whisky, he stormed through the ship to confront Ossie. I wasn't present but got a first-hand account from the pantry boy who shared a cabin with Kevin:

"You in there?" Ryland's face was crimson, his eye livid. "Open up!" He hammered on the door. "D'you hear! This is the bosun!"

Ossie didn't reply.

"Open this door! I want to talk to you."

A small crowd gathered. Ryland turned on them "What do you lot want?" He raised a fist but they didn't disperse.

"Bagot or whatever your name is, open this bloody door. I know you're in there." If Ossie thought the bosun would go away he was mistaken.

"This is your last chance. I'll count to three. If you don't open up, I'm going to kick it in."

Some thought he was bluffing.

"One ... two ... Right, I warned you. Stand back."

He raised his leg and gave the lock a tremendous blow with the flat of his foot. It burst open. The door crashed back.

Ossie was in his underwear. An alb, a long white robe worn by Catholic priests, lay on the deck. Feverishly he was tearing down the drapes from his bulkhead, tumbling everything into the drawer beneath his bunk. Candles flickered in the sudden draught, haloed by the smoke from joss sticks.

Ryland stepped into the cabin. "Dear God!" He looked around

and for a long time seemed struck dumb. "You're out of your mind."

Ossie cowered away.

"What a stink!" Ryland switched on the overhead light and opened the porthole. "This is what you were doing back there on the *Star of Bengal*. They come and took you away." He plucked at a corner of material and uncovered one of the dolls.

Some of the crew, the pantry boy among them, had followed him through the door. They gazed into the open drawer.

"So," Ryland said at last. "It's right what everyone's saying." He picked up the doll in a meaty paw. "Disgusting! You're sick! Who's this meant to be then?" He turned it over, using his bandaged arm with difficulty. "Steve? Big muscles an' a bloody great needle stuck through his foot?" He tore it out. "Another in his head. What you planning, hit 'im with a meat cleaver?"

He tossed the doll onto Ossie's bunk and threw the cloth aside. The next he picked up was Rat'bone, scraggy and dirty. The bosun gave a barking laugh. "Not hard to tell who that is. Poor sod!" His fingers were strong. He wrenched out the cruel needles, grimacing as if they were embedded in flesh, and gave Ossie a burning glance.

"Don't suppose you know who clocked him in the mouth?"

Ossie was terrified. He shook his head.

"No, I don't suppose you do."

The bosun picked up Tony, bound and gagged, a few personal items added since the day before. "God knows who that's meant to be." He threw it with the others. "And I suppose this is me." He examined the ugly doll – the tangled hairs, speckled whiskers, scarred eye, fragment of underpants, canvas needles through arm and back – and suddenly was consumed by anger. Dropping the doll in the drawer, he hit Ossie across the head, punched him in the stomach and hit him again. His nose began to bleed. "How dare you! Making this *thing*, this – puppet! Going into my cabin! Raking through my belongings!" He snatched the doll up again and tore out the needles. "Stabbing it with these bloody ... How'd you like it if I stuck 'em in you? How'd you like that, eh?" He shook them in Ossie's face. "For two pins I'd do it an' all. In your fat neck, in your eyes."

The pantry boy thought he was actually going to do it but Ryland threw the needles aside. He broke off the doll's head, pulled off the red cloth and everything that connected him with it, and thrust the pieces into his pocket. He did the same with Rat'bone and Steve and flung the remains out the porthole.

Abruptly he stopped. "What if I did do it to you? Yeah, how'd you like that?" He grabbed some candles and crushed the hot wax together, mingling it with what was left of the dolls.

"No!" Ossie covered his head with his arms. "No, please!"

Ryland tussled with him and pulled out a fistful of hairs. With a horny thumb he jammed them into the wax. "Couple o' buttons off that jacket." He wrenched them from the back of the door. "Yeah, and these?" He took Ossie's toothbrush and comb. "And your watch. And this picture, you and some ugly old tart."

"Not that!" Ossie struggled to get the photo back.

"Oh, means something to you does that? Good."

Squeezing and softening the wax, Ryland rolled everything into a misshapen ball. "That enough is it, mixture rich enough? I reckon so. Right, what we do now?" He looked round for inspiration. "How about this?" He recovered three of the canvas needles. "This is you now, right? Well, how does *that* feel!" He plunged one of the needles, eye-deep, into the ball of wax . "And that!" He added the others, pressing them until the needles disappeared.

"Ahhh!" Weeping with distress, Ossie sank to the deck.

"Now burn!" Ryland pulled the marlinspike from his belt, jabbed it into the studded ball, pushed a few last candles together and held it over the flames. "See how *you* like it." The wax smoked and melted, dripping to the chest of drawers. The photo caught fire. A corner of gold watch appeared. There was a smell of burning hair.

At length the bosun carried the fluttering ball of flame to the porthole and tossed it out. Bright for a moment, it arced towards the ocean and was extinguished. "I hope you drown!" He wiped the spike on Ossie's trousers which were lying on the bunk and returned it to its sheath. "Let that be a lesson not to play games with other people's lives." Contemptuously he looked down at the helpless messman. "You're fit to be locked up."

He turned to the group of seamen who blocked the entrance. "Out my way."

At the same moment Barbara, who had been in the messroom, came running down the alleyway. Through the crowd he saw Ossie huddled on the deck. The bosun shouldered him aside. Barbara grabbed him by the shirt. "What's been happening?"

The bosun turned. "Take your 'and off of me," he said dangerously, then saw that it was little Barbara. "Oh, it's you, ducky. Well, do your mate a favour and tell him to lay off the creepy stuff. Get himsel' a good shrink."

"He wouldn't be into 'the creepy stuff' if ignorant brutes like you left him alone."

"Don't give me that. Nutters like him shouldn't be at sea. Bloody poofs neither."

"How about animals that murder their shipmates?"

"Still on about that?" He sneered. "Let you into a secret. I wish it had been the lot o' you. Now out my way."

But Barbara was sturdy and wasn't going to be pushed aside. He bounced back off the bulkhead and spun the bosun round.

"I'm warning you." Ryland raised his fist. "Lay off me or I'll – "

He never got to say what he would do because Barbara grabbed his forearm, red-raw beneath the bandages, dug in his nails and gave it a vicious twist. The bosun screamed, staggered, slumped to one knee.

"Quits!" Barbara kicked him in the ribs and pushed through the crowd into Ossie's cabin.

Someone had helped him to the day bed. Ossie sat staring into space. Blood was smeared across his cheeks.

"All right, I'll look after him. Thanks." Barbara ushered out the onlookers, all but the pantry boy who was a friend, and wedged the door shut.

"Come on, Ossie love." He put an arm round the fat shoulders. "He's gone now, the nasty old Cyclops. Barbara's here. Nothing to be frightened about."

As Ossie gripped his fingers, Barbara felt a large cold ring. He looked down and saw a death's head, an iron skull and crossbones laughing up into his face. He shivered and moved his hand away.

"You're all right now," he said. "Ssshhh!"

Dump It

Ossie was badly shaken but little by little, with the help of friends and his medication, he became calmer and the trouble died down. Neither side wanted Captain Bell – 'Ding Dong' as he was affectionately known – or the mate involved: Ryland because it would resurrect the accusations from the *Star of Bengal*, and Ossie's friends because it might lead to his being sent home.

With the bosun hurt and Rat'bone sick, it was a good time aboard *Pacific Trader*. Freed from Rat'bone's influence, Steve was a changed man and tried to strike up a friendship with several of the crew, me among them. Lampie, good-hearted beneath his crabbed exterior, took charge of the work on deck and gave me better jobs. Under Samuel's guidance I learned to splice wire and overhaul the heavy blocks used in cargo work. Twice a week the engineers showed films on a big open-air screen rigged across number four hatch. Charlie and I won the deck tennis tournament. After work, as the sun sank on the starboard bow, we splashed in the pool and swapped stories on the warm deck. On Sunday I took the wheel again, the unpleasantness of last week not entirely forgotten. A couple of times a few of us carried our mattresses out on deck and slept restlessly beneath the stars.

One afternoon brought the idyll to an end.

"If you don't put them back I'm going straight to the mate."

"I bet you would too," Tony mocked. "That's just your style. Paki bloody two-shoes. You're jealous, that's your trouble."

"I've warned you about 'Paki' before," Charlie said. "How if I smash your face in first, then we'll go and see the mate? Suit yourself."

We had knocked off for smoko. Tony and Philip, taken off watches for the long haul across the Pacific, had been set the task of scrubbing out the lifeboats and checking the lifeboat stores – food, water, equipment – against a list. Tony, dishonest as ever, had stolen a Swiss Army knife and a jar of barley sugar. Aaron, working on the funnel deck, had seen him. When Charlie heard about it he was incensed:

"Have you got no wit? That's to keep men alive! When their ship's gone down and they're stuck out there in the middle of the Atlantic."

"I don't need a lecture from some bloody ordinary seaman. Anyway, who says I took them, where's the proof? It's a load of lies."

"Oh yeah? What's that in your pocket right now?" He grabbed for Tony's shorts. "Let's go have a look in your cabin, see if there's a nice jar of barley sugar."

Tony blustered. His face flushed.

"I'm going to check," Charlie said. "I'll get Lampie and I'm going to check, every single day that cover's off. If we find the knife's gone, or the hand compass, or any of the stores, I'm going to report you. You're not fit to wear the uniform!"

He came away but it was not the end of the incident.

Two mornings later, some time after smoko, I was mopping out the crew bar when there was a tap at the entrance. I looked round but there was no one there and the alleyway was empty. Some silly trick, I thought, but as I returned my eye fell on a scrap of paper. It lay on the table closest to the door. I knew it had not been there earlier because I'd wiped the tables before I started on the deck. I picked it up, a hastily-written note in thick pencil:

Ben,
Search your cabin. Now!
Things might be hidden there.
Be quick!

Who had left it? *Search the cabin? Things might be hidden there?* What did it mean? I abandoned my mop and ran the length of the alleyway. A half-eaten bar of chocolate, my own, lay melting in the heat. I popped a couple of squares in my mouth, sucked my fingers and pulled out one of the drawers. It contained my shirts, underwear and a few odds and ends. Nothing was hidden there. I turned to my jeans and sweaters in the drawer under the bunk. Nothing there either. I tipped up my mattress. To my astonishment a leather wallet lay underneath. What was that doing there? Whose was it? Terrified someone would see me, I turned my back to the door and opened it. Half a dozen five and ten pound notes were tucked into one pocket, a small wad of papers into another. It took only seconds to find a name I recognised: Timothy James Nettles – the second mate. I was holding the second mate's wallet!

Horrified, I stared around the cabin, looking for somewhere to put it. In the end I tucked it against my stomach under my T-shirt. Was there more? The note said *things*, plural.

I ran to fetch Charlie. He was working with Smoky on the foredeck, greasing cargo blocks in readiness for Fiji.

"You've got to come!" I pulled him by the arm.

He shook me off. "What is it?"

"Just come."

He looked round at Smoky.

"On you go, boy." Smoky threw him some cotton waste to scrub his hands. "Time for a fag anyway."

"Hurry!" I dragged Charlie to the steps and ran back to the cabin.

"Someone left this in the bar." I showed him the note. "So I started looking. Found this under the mattress." I pulled out the wallet.

"Whose is it?"

"Second mate's."

Charlie wore a filthy T-shirt and shorts. He stared at me then back at the note. "Who's it from?"

"No idea. We've been set up."

"Not hard to guess who by – that bloody senior cadet!"

"Or Rat'bone or the bosun."

"Second mate's wallet? Nah, not their style. It's because of the lifeboat."

"What do we do? There'll be somebody here in a minute."

Charlie was decisive. He drew a deep breath. "Dump it."

Dump it? Forty or fifty quid? The second mate's driving licence?

"An' search the cabin." He yanked open a drawer.

I stood uncertainly.

"Come on, Ben!"

I couldn't.

"Give it here." He flipped the wallet from the porthole. It flew open. For a split second I saw it against the sea. It was gone.

I was horrified.

"Now come *on*!"

Our course of action was fixed. I tugged open my locker and looked through the jackets – nothing. Dirty washing was thrown in the bottom. I pulled it out. Hidden beneath was a pair of binoculars. The word *Bridge* was printed neatly in white.

"Charlie!"

"Dump them."

"But they're the bridge binoculars. Zeiss."

"I don't care if they're the crown jewels, dump them!"

Half sick, half reckless, I threw them from the porthole.

"These yours?" He held out a new pair of swimming trunks.

"No."

"Recognise them?"

I shrugged.

They fluttered away.

We hunted through every drawer. I pulled them right out. Two books lay in the space beneath: *Nicholls's Seamanship* and *Principles of Navigation*.

"Whose are those?"

I looked in the front. "Philip's."

"Dump."

"But they're Philip's."

Charlie flung them out, one, two, pages fluttering. "Keep *nothing*."

I returned to the locker and pulled my clothes from the hangers.

"Here." Charlie had just finished. "Check mine again."

I scratched through fluff in the bottom of his pockets while he slid his hands inside the bunks.

"What's this?" Something pebble-like lay in the corner of an inside pocket. I raked for it with my fingernails and hooked it up.

"Oh, God!" Charlie stared at the ring in my hand, white gold with a large solitaire diamond surrounded by opals. "Whose is that?"

"Trish?"

"You are joking!"

"Who else? Heidi-hi? Not mine anyway."

He bit his lip. "Dump it."

"But it must be worth – "

"It'll be insured. Here, I'll do it." The precious ring flew through the porthole. I recalled the story of the ring found in the belly of a fish.

We hunted on in a fever but found nothing else. That was it, we were clean – we hoped. Every corner – under the mat, inside the pillow cases, the toes of shoes, the waste bin – had been thoroughly searched. Charlie's eyes roamed the cabin. "Did you check the bookshelf?" We shook the pages of our half-dozen thrillers. Private letters or twenty-pound notes could have been hidden in there.

Something fell to the deck. I picked it up and felt the blood drain from my face. It was a photo of Trish, the photo that had stood on the mate's dressing table. It had been taken from its frame and torn down the middle, the mate discarded. I showed it to Charlie.

"Boy, is that cadet an evil bastard!"

I crushed the photo in my fist and flung it after the rest.

We searched for a few minutes longer but could find nothing else.

"What's the time?"

I was shaking. "Half eleven – just after."

"I'd better get back to Smoky, he'll be wondering what's happened. What about you?"

"Finish mopping out the bar."

"See you in half an hour – if not before." He broke off some chocolate and was gone.

I straightened the bunks and got rid of the note. Wouldn't do to be found with that in my pocket! *Be quick,* it had said. As I headed back to work, I guessed it wouldn't be long before the thefts were discovered and accusing fingers were pointed in our direction.

I was right.

Our Cabin is Searched

"Bennett." The mate stood in the bar doorway. "Come with me."

I had barely resumed work and have no doubt I looked suitably startled because I was terrified. Pausing only to squeeze out the mop, I wiped my hands on my shorts and followed him down the alleyway. The second mate, wearing his official white cap, was standing by our door curtain.

"We're going to search your cabin," the mate said.

"Search the cabin?"

"That's right. Any idea where Sutherland's working?"

"Sutherland?" I said. "Do you mean Sunderland?"

"Yes, yes, Sunderland."

"On the – " I cleared my throat. "On the foredeck."

"Sir," he said.

"Sir."

"Fetch him. The second mate and I will wait here."

We were soon back, Charlie scrubbing his grease-black hands with fresh cotton waste. The mate led the way into our cabin. "Some things have gone missing," he said bluntly. "Your names have been mentioned and – "

"Who by?" Charlie said.

"That needn't concern you."

"What do you mean? Of course it concerns us, we're being accused of theft. Sir."

"You're not the only ones whose cabins are being searched," the mate said.

"Who else have you been to?"

"Again, that's none of your business," the mate said. "And frankly, Sutherland, I don't like your attitude. You want to consider your position on this ship."

"Sunderland, sir. And I know my position. I'm an ordinary

seaman and Ben here's the deck boy. We're honest and we work hard and we don't like being called thieves."

"All right, Sunderland." The second mate intervened. "All right. Look at it this way. Some valuable things have gone missing, and like it or not your names have been mentioned. Bennett here was in the mate's cabin a few days ago, he knows what's there, and he's spent upwards of two hours up on the bridge."

"Why me?" I said. "That's not fair, sir. It was Mrs Rose asked me to go into the mate's cabin to get rid of a big insect. And it was you invited me to stay on the bridge."

"Nevertheless, you have been up there."

"So have the watch," Charlie said. "And the stewards. And the cadets. Much more than Ben. What about them?"

"Fair enough. As the mate said, we *will* be searching other cabins. What we *don't* want to do is to stir up a lot of ill-feeling. So if we look through your cabin now and all's above board, that's you in the clear." He set his cap on Charlie's bunk. "It's not a nice thing but unfortunately we do have a thief on the ship. I'm sure you want him caught as much as we do."

"Yeah, OK." Charlie said. "Long as it's not just us. 'Cos if I thought Ben and me were being picked on I'd go straight to the Union, see what Brian has to say."

The mate's brow darkened.

"Maybe I should get him anyway."

"No need for that." The second mate was placating. "We'll just look through your things, if that's all right with you, and there's an end of it."

"And you'll do the same with the engineers and the third mate and the cadets after?" Charlie was enjoying this.

"By God, you're an impertinent young oik," the mate said. "What have the officers got to do with you?"

"Nothing," Charlie said. "Just as long as you're not suggesting officers don't steal and junior seamen do."

"He didn't say that." The second mate intervened quickly.

"'Cause there's no law says cadets are more honest than deck boys."

I took a chance. "Maybe they've checked the cadets' cabins already."

Charlie looked up. "Have you, sir?"

The mate finally blew his top. "Will you be quiet! My God! Ordinary seaman and deck boy talking like a couple of ship's lawyers. I've never heard anything like it. You, Sunderland. And you …"

"Bennett, sir," I said helpfully.

"That's right, Bennett! The pair of you, just shut up and stay shut up! Not another word! Sit down there," he jabbed a finger at the day bed. "I have heard enough, do you understand? Enough."

We did as he said.

"Bloody hell!" He lifted his cap and ran a hand through his hair. "Now the second mate and I are going to search your cabin."

Tim Nettles raised his eyebrows as if to ask permission.

I trusted him. "Yes, sir."

Charlie's nod was barely perceptible.

The mate started with Charlie's locker. Hanger at a time he searched jackets and trousers. Long hands probed into pockets.

"Nothing here." The second mate was checking drawers.

"Look underneath."

He pulled the drawers right out.

Having drawn a blank in Charlie's locker, the mate moved on to mine. Blankets were stored on a top shelf. He shook them out and dropped them on the deck.

"Nothing here." The second mate replaced the drawers.

"Did you search the pockets?"

"Pockets?"

"In their jeans and everything."

"No, but there's no way the – "

"Check them."

The mate pulled off pillowcases, threw back the sheets, tipped up the mattresses. Far from becoming calmer as he discovered the cabin was clean, his anger was increasing.

Meanwhile the second mate thrust his hands into the pockets of our shirts and jeans. He looked embarrassed. Carefully he refolded each garment and returned it to the drawer.

"Never mind all that," the mate said impatiently. "They can tidy up when we've gone." He shook each book by its cover. A card fell out. "Ah! What have we got here?"

My heart stopped.

He picked it up.

An old postcard someone had been using as a bookmark. Somehow it had got stuck. He returned the book to the shelf.

"Well," the mate stood scowling. "Nothing here. We seem to have been misinformed."

"Who by, sir?" Charlie asked again.

He did not reply.

The cabin was a shambles: bedding tumbled, clothes trailing, rug askew.

"It seems we owe you an apology, Bennett – and Sunderland," the second mate said.

"Nothing of the sort." The mate corrected him. "It was a perfectly proper search. Tidy your cabin up, the pair of you, then back to work." He turned away. "Come on, Second, we'll check next door."

They were gone. Charlie looked at me and gave a silent Wow! His eyes sparkled but he was angry.

The curtain was thrust aside and the mate's head reappeared. "Whose cabin is that?"

"Scott," Charlie said. "The other J.O.S."

"Sir!"

"Sir."

"Fetch him." The mate retreated.

"Please," Charlie said to the tossing curtain.

"What was that?" The mate was back.

"Nothing, sir. Just speaking to Ben."

"You sail very close to the wind don't you, Sutherland."

"My name's Sunderland, sir."

"Sunderland, Sutherland, bloody Newcastle-on-Tyne if you like, just fetch Scott! You should be halfway there already." Again he was gone.

Charlie winked. "Love it when they get like that." He hitched his greasy shorts. "I'll have a word with Brian, just to be on the safe side."

"You'll not tell him about – "

"Nah, nah. That's between you and me." He popped the last of the chocolate into his mouth and followed the mate into the alleyway.

Shaken by what had occurred, never mind what might have occurred, I picked up a shirt and began to fold it.

———•———

A River in Fiji

For fifteen days we crossed the Pacific, our only companions whales, dolphins, flying fish and a wandering albatross that accompanied us for a thousand miles. Then one morning there were seagulls flying round the masts, and the same afternoon we passed through a scatter of small uninhabited islands with white beaches and blue-green shallows. I longed to explore them and go swimming. As I worked on the hot decks, helping the ABs to prepare the cargo gear and hoist the long derricks ready for discharging, I could hardly tear my eyes away. That night I went to bed with Viti Levu, the main volcanic island of the Fiji group, a dark shape on the horizon.

Our days in Suva, the capital, apart from an event involving one of my friends, were among the happiest of my life. High mountains, shaggy with jungle, rose behind the city. On Saturday afternoon, with a sub in my pocket and the sun frying the back of my neck, I walked to the famous market. In a life spent mostly in Westport I had never imagined such smells and colour: exotic fruit and tropical flowers, multicoloured fish on slabs, strange-shaped vegetables, edible seaweed, ethnic carvings, crawling crabs and birds in cages, dazzling swathes of material, coral and seashells, Indian savouries that made my mouth water. Some of the men wore jeans or shorts but most wore sarongs; on these powerful south-sea islanders they looked terrific. At a jewellery stall I chose an earring and had it fitted to replace the sleeper. With Christmas only days away I bought cards for my friends aboard ship, and realised with a pang that I had sent none home.

For an hour, pressed round by tourists and Fijians with enormous hair, I wandered the market then headed into the city. Suva, according to Lampie and others, was the place to do my shopping and I was looking for a radio-cassette player. I soon found what I wanted, a state-of-the-art Sony at half the price I'd have had to pay at home. Half the price – but even so, including a few tapes, it left me broke. Carrying my parcel, I wandered the baking pavements and gazed through windows at the cameras, shirts, swimming trunks, binoculars and sunglasses I could no longer afford.

At length, hot and weary, I turned from the shops into a gracious square and found a café. Sitting in the shade beneath palm trees, I spent the last of my money on a coffee and pastry and watched the passing crowd. A grade-one girl of roughly my own age caught my eye and smiled as she walked past. I smiled back. There were lots of pretty girls. I smiled at another who ignored me. And then a third, but failed to notice that she was with her boyfriend, a massive Fijian heavyweight champion of the world who looked pretty angry. It seemed a good idea to stop.

When I got back to the ship in the late afternoon, I pulled on my black cotton football shorts – the shorts I had worn the whole trip, getting more and more covered in paint – and joined two ABs in the pool on the seaward side of the afterdeck. The cold seawater chased away my weariness.. After the heat of the city, I clung to the edge and gazed across Suva Bay to the mountains of the interior.

The next morning, which was Sunday, Aaron had news. He had, entirely by chance – *ho, hum* – met an Indian girl, a nurse, and ended up taking her to a disco. Lucky for him, I thought, but more than that, her father owned a tour bus company and she had volunteered to drive a crowd of us out to see the sights if we were ready by nine. We could if we wanted, she had said, drive up into the mountains where her uncle had a lodge, maybe go canoeing. If we wanted? I was three-quarters dressed before he left the cabin.

At nine o'clock a motley crowd stood waiting at the bottom of the gangway. Right on time Nadia drove up in a jolly minibus proclaiming *Ahmad's Safari Tours* in bold letters on the side. She was gorgeous!

"How does he do it?" Charlie said. "I'm as good-looking as him."

Aaron introduced us: Michael in cheeky shorts and a straw hat. Smoky with a tray of cans and a limp fag. Ossie all in white. Kevin with a black eye from his night ashore. Barbara in a tie-and-dye boiler suit. Philip, who had been to early communion, in a loose Polynesian shirt and sunglasses. Luigi in a glossy dark blue shirt and white jeans. Charlie munching a cold sausage. And me trying to look at least sixteen.

The tarmac roads were soon behind us. We drove on tracks through dairy farms and cane fields, up through plantations into the tropical forest. All about us were towering trees and giant ferns. Fruit bats, big as cats, hung high overhead. We saw parrots and bright finches. A wild pig crashed through the undergrowth. A mongoose dragged a lashing iguana across the track.

A sudden downpour, too heavy for the wipers to cope, forced us to stop. Lightning flashed, thunder rolled, the hairs on my arm stood on end. It passed and the clouds opened. The track and jungle steamed. Far beneath us lay the jade-green sea and distant islands.

The lodge, a fine colonial house, stood amid pastures between the river and the forest. Nadia's uncle came to greet us, accompanied by her cousins Sandeep, an athletic-looking boy of seventeen, and Kim, twelve and pretty. We sat at tables on the veranda. A servant, a huge Fijian man twice the size of his employer, brought tea and cake – and insect repellent to keep the vicious blackflies at bay.

Nadia said, "I suppose you can all swim, being sailors and everything?"

We looked round. I had seen nearly everyone in the pool.

"Ossie?"

"Mm?" He had hardly touched his tea and seemed preoccupied.

"Can you swim?"

"Yeah, course."

Nadia wasn't convinced. "You're sure?"

"I said so, didn't I?"

She glanced at Aaron. "If we go canoeing you'll have to wear lifejackets anyway."

Sandeep said, "We could take the rafts and go down the rapids. After the rain of the past few days it'll be white water."

White-water rafting! We finished tea and piled back into the minibus. Two miles upstream, the source of the river was revealed as a big mountain lake. Cataracts streamed down the jungle-covered hillsides. There were three two-man canoes so we took turns. It was brilliant, digging in the paddles and racing, or drifting along the edge of the forest where fish arrowed away from our shadow and parrots squawked at the intrusion. Another rainstorm swept the island. Drops the size of marbles lashed the lake and we were soaked to the skin. Back home we'd have run for cover but in Fiji the rain was warm and twenty minutes after the sun reappeared our shirts were dry.

When we gathered on shore Charlie said, "Can we still go down the rapids?"

A deep roar came from the foot of the lake. Nadia looked at her cousin.

"A bit more water than I expected," he said. "I think we'll be all right though."

We tightened our lifejackets.

There were two rafts. Nadia took charge of one, Sandeep the other. "Who's going where?"

"I'll go with Sandeep," Michael said at once.

"Oh, surprise, surprise!" Barbara patted Luigi's arm. "She's nothing but a little flirt. We're staying here on dry land, aren't we, dear."

Sandeep blushed, handsome and shy.

Smoky produced a battered notebook. "I'll stay an' all. Get down a couple of sketches. Makings of a great picture this."

We were soon sorted out. Charlie and I went with Nadia. So, to my surprise, did Ossie, whose idea of exercise was walking up the alleyway to make a cup of tea.

The rafts, orange inflatables with no outboards, were pulled ashore at the foot of the lake. We pumped up the pressure, tipped out the rainwater and launched them, wading out to step aboard. Nadia guided us into the current. Slowly at first and then faster, we were carried along. An outcrop of rocks drew closer, we turned the corner – and all at once were being swept downriver. I clung to a strap and trailed my free hand in the water. Nadia plied the paddle to keep our blunt nose pointing ahead. Charlie's black eyes danced. Ossie, who had hardly spoken a word all day, regarded me with eyes as dead as oysters.

"Come on!" I poked him with a foot. "Stop brooding."

He averted his big white face. I wondered why he had come at all, if he was determined to be so miserable.

A short distance ahead the hillsides were steeper, the jungle pressed closer. We speeded up. The roar of the river filled my ears. "Hold on tight!" Nadia fought to keep us midstream. We swung round a bend and I saw white water. A huge swell rose above some hidden sill of rock. The raft slid over and suddenly we were in the rapids. Giant boulders split the stream; leaping water was all about us; spray smacked me in the face. The raft bucked and slewed like a rodeo horse. I was flung into the air, hanging on to the strap. A second time I was soaked to the skin. As we reached the bottom, a ferocious narrows lay dead ahead. We sped through and were spat out the far end like an orange pip. It was *fantastic*!

The river levelled as it ran into a stretch about two hundred metres long. In the sudden stillness I heard a scream and looked back upriver. It was Michael, shrieking as he clung to Sandeep's arm.

"Look at him," I said. "He's not *that* scared."

Charlie grinned.

I took off my shirt, then pulled it back on as a big fly that looked as if it would sting, landed on my chest.

Nadia had got wetter than any of us. You could see her lacy bra and brown skin through the stuff of her blouse.

Charlie caught me looking and raised his eyebrows appreciatively.

Nadia caught us both looking and shifted her position. "You keep your eyes to yourselves," she said good-naturedly. "I've heard about you sailors. You're worse than the boys in Suva. Next time I go with Michael."

We laughed.

But not Ossie who sat gazing downstream, lost in a world of his own.

"Come on, mate, buck up," Charlie said. "It was brilliant!"

We waited for Sandeep then paddled ashore and pulled the rafts from the water.

"Do you want us to carry them back?" I said.

Sandeep shook his head. "We'll take them up on a trailer."

"Is that more rapids?" I nodded to smoke that rose above the rocks downriver.

"Yes, but not for the rafts, much wilder. Kayakers come up from town sometimes. People have been drowned there."

"Can we go and see?"

We walked down the riverbank. Dragonflies danced among reeds. Toads plopped into boggy pools. I found myself in the lead, clambering over roots, pushing through bushes and climbing up to a flat rock that looked down on a wild ravine. Grass and ferns grew in the crevices. The river was a tumult, surging between boulders and rebounding from rocky walls, sending a rainbow high into the air. How anyone could even think of tackling such a descent was beyond me.

"That Sandeep." Michael arrived beside me, vivid and blond and flushed with the sun. "Isn't he gorgeous!" He refreshed his insect repellent. "If it wasn't for Luigi I couldn't be responsible for myself."

I smiled and stepped to the brink.

"Oh, come away!" He plucked at my shirt. "It gives me the shivers."

"Yeah, but look at it. Wow!"

Ossie joined us, wheezing with effort.

"Look at the state of you," Michael told him. "No wonder, all that lard you carry around. You need to go on a diet."

Ossie craned his neck to look down at the crashing water.

"Why didn't you take off your lifejacket?"

He didn't seem to hear the question.

"You'll die of the heat. Come here." Michael loosened the tapes and left them hanging.

The toot-toot of the minibus recalled us to the track. Smoky had driven down from the lake. We pushed through the undergrowth and piled in. Soon we were back at the lodge. "What do you want to do now?" Nadia said as we stood in the shade.

It was after two and we hadn't had lunch. Her uncle could hardly be expected to feed ten of us.

"What about heading down to the coast?" she said. "We can get something to eat and go snorkelling. If you want to, that is. Maybe you've got to get back to the ship."

"Snorkelling," I cried.

"Food."

"Back to the ship? Are you mad?"
We gathered up our possessions.
But Michael was gazing around. "Where's Ossie?" he said.

The Rescue

We looked at one another. Where *was* Ossie?

"Prob'ly gone for a pee."

"Didn't head into the house," Sandeep said.

The only bushes he might have sheltered behind were in the garden. Kevin checked. There was an awful silence.

"Anyone see him in the minibus?"

"Didn't sit beside me."

"Well, when did you last see him?"

No one was sure.

"He was up on that rock," Michael said. "With Ben and me."

"Oh, God! D'you think he's fallen in?"

Michael and Barbara shared glances.

An icy feeling gripped me in the stomach.

Nadia drove back up the track. I jumped out with some others at the foot of the lower ravine and she headed on to the top with the rest. We forced our way through vegetation. Creeping vines cut my legs. Something bit me behind the ear and drew blood. I reached the water's edge. A hundred metres upstream, at the bottom of the perilous descent, the river boiled between rocks. At my feet it swirled and levelled, flowing on through dense undergrowth until a mile downstream it reached the clearing around the lodge.

There was no sign of Ossie. I half walked, half waded a short distance upriver and climbed a boulder to get a better view. A corner of something orange caught my eye. The current swept it out then carried it back again. It was a lifejacket, trapped in a backwater on the opposite bank, half hidden by a fallen tree, stripped of its bark and bleached by years in the sun.

I shouted and pointed. A little below me Michael also was shouting. "There! There!" Fully dressed, he waded into the water. "Behind that rock! Those bushes! See?"

"No! Wait!" Sandeep tried to stop him.

But Michael was too far out, splashing and calling. He flung himself full length and struck out for the opposite bank.

The current was too strong. For every metre he swam across, the river carried him down two. In a minute he was no longer trying to rescue Ossie but struggling to reach the bank before he drowned.

Philip stood a short distance downstream. He pulled off his shirt and trousers and dived headlong. I had forgotten he was a schoolboy swimming champion. With powerful strokes he cut across the current and caught the flailing Michael beneath the arms. Soon they reached the far side and floundered ashore.

Michael fell back, coughing water. "My hero!" He struggled for breath. "I think I need ... the kiss of life."

"In your dreams."

"Oh, well!" He coughed some more. "Worth a try. Can you ... reach Ossie?"

Meanwhile Sandeep, too, had stripped to his underpants and crossed the swirling river. As I returned to my earlier position, I could see Ossie better. His hands were knotted in branches and at first I thought he was trying to crawl from the water but it was only the river moving his legs. By the time Sandeep had manoeuvred him to a place where he could be taken ashore, Philip had joined him. Together they hauled Ossie up the bank. Sandeep put an ear to his chest and listened intently.

How Ossie had survived the descent of that wild ravine I have no idea, but survive he did, unconscious and badly beaten, but still breathing. His shoes were missing, his shirt survived by a single button. Neither Sandeep nor Philip was expert in first aid though they knew a little. They laid Ossie on his side in the recovery position with his head down the slope and checked for broken bones. There seemed to be none though three injuries were obvious: a badly grazed arm, a gash in his side and missing teeth. Uncertain what else to do, Philip rocked him to empty the water from his lungs and stomach.

A minute passed. And another minute. Ossie's hand moved. His leg twitched. He lay still again then suddenly was racked by a spasm and water gushed from his mouth. More water. An arm stirred as if to wipe his lips.

Philip rose. "He'll live."

Michael joined them, kneeling alongside. As Ossie came round he gave him a push. "Oh, you silly, stupid ...!" he said, and burst into tears.

Nadia's uncle kept a small boat with an outboard engine at the lodge. The Fijian servant motored upstream and ferried Michael and Ossie to a little landing stage. Sandeep and Philip swam back and the bus picked us up a few minutes later.

Ossie was in pain. Nadia cleaned his wounds and put a dressing on the cut which would need stitching. We helped him aboard the minibus and accompanied him to the hospital in Suva where Nadia worked as a nurse. For two hours, when we might have been snorkelling in the blue Pacific, we sat in a waiting room while Ossie was examined. In addition to the visible injuries, he was found to have a broken rib and extensive bruising but hopefully nothing more serious. They kept him in for observation and further tests. Unless there were complications, a doctor told us, he should be fit to rejoin the ship in a couple of days, though it would be a week or longer before he could resume duties.

Barbara took Michael's hand as we drove back through the city. "Poor Ossie!"

Michael squeezed his fingers.

"But how the hell did he fall?" Kevin demanded. "That story about feeling dizzy and tripping over a root or something. I mean, he didn't even let out a yell. No one heard him or anything."

"For God's sake, boy!" Smoky said. "Are you daft as well as blind? What do you expect him to say?"

Kevin was silent.

I looked from the window. A group of children in ragged shorts were playing football. Their shouts rang on the afternoon air.

Christmas at Sea

On Wednesday, with Ossie back aboard, we left Fiji and headed south to New Zealand. Thursday was Christmas Eve. We worked until midday then showered, changed and gave ourselves up to leisure and parties.

Some of the crew, even rough tough ABs, had decorated their cabins with streamers and red-cheeked Santas bought at the market in Suva. I delivered my Christmas cards and hung those I received over a string on the bulkhead. Laughter, music and the smell of booze drifted down the alleyways. I wandered from cabin to cabin but couldn't settle: I didn't want to read, didn't want to drink, didn't want music, didn't want to sit, didn't want to lie on my bunk, didn't want to sunbathe, I don't know what I wanted. At least, I do know what I wanted but I couldn't have it. What I wanted was Christmas the way it had been all my life: Christmas with my gran; Christmas with my dad when he could get home; Christmas with my friends in Westport.

A bit before ten I was thinking of going to bed when I heard singing – not tapes, people. Christmas carols. I went to investigate. The source was Samuel's cabin. I knocked and pushed back the curtain.

His cabin was different from others in the alleyway. The only illumination came from his bunk light with a handkerchief thrown over it, and some flickering tea-candles around a nativity scene on the chest of drawers. Philip and Brian were there. So, to my surprise, were Smoky and Barbara, of whom Samuel disapproved, and Steve Petersen. As I entered they were singing *Once in Royal David's City*, accompanied by Smoky on a mouth organ. Samuel had got some carol sheets from a church in Suva and handed me one as I entered. Philip made room on the bunk but just as I found the place the carol ended.

"That was lovely, folk," Samuel said in his deep voice. "What next? Come on, Ben, you just arrived. You choose."

Others threw in their suggestions: "*The First Nowell ... O Little Town of Bethlehem ... Away in a Manger.*"

"*Good King Wenceslas,*" I said.

Smoky cupped his hands and practised a few notes then nodded:

> *Good King Wenceslas looked out*, we sang,
> *On the Feast of Stephen,*
> *When the snow lay round about,*
> *Deep and crisp and even ...*

It was Christmas turned on its head but I loved it: seamen in vests and T-shirts, brown with the sun, singing carols about shepherds and snow in Samuel's cabin with the ship rolling to the long Pacific swell, the porthole open, and fat southern constellations dancing overhead. Very different from school assemblies back in Westport, the Midnight Service at St Matthew's with a glittering tree beside the altar, and *Carols from Kings*, which was gran's favourite programme ever. For as long as I could remember, we had watched it with a cup of tea and a slice of fruit cake every Christmas Eve. Before my voice broke, she had always asked me to sing *Once in Royal David's City*, like the boy in the choir.

Others joined us, many smelling of drink, until the cabin could hold no more and the overflow sat in the alleyway with the curtain thrown back over the door. Samuel, it turned out, was a lay preacher, and he read the Christmas story from the Bible and asked if we would like to say a private prayer for friends and families back home, and people like us all over the world who could not be with their loved ones at this time.

It was the part of Christmas I liked best.

Then it was Christmas Day with the sun high above the mast, pinning us to the ocean. Despite the occasion, someone had to clean the bar and mop out the washroom. Who else but the deck boy? I whizzed through my tasks and well before eleven was finished for the day. As I returned to the cabin, I saw that Christmas messages had been Blu-tacked to the bulkhead outside a dozen or so cabins.

They were from Barbara who had been on the vodka. I read those that were nearest:

To Aaron, Best wishes for a very Happy Xmas. If you can't be good be careful. Love – Mother.

To the Divine Charlie, Lots of love and Christmas hugs, from – Mother.

For our lovely Ben, I hope your first Christmas at sea will be the best ever, Lots of love – Mother.

It was the first Christmas greeting I'd received from any 'mother' and I carried it into the cabin.

Charlie sat hunched over a jigsaw.

"Where'd you get that?" I said.

"Present from Michael and the rest of them. They've got something for you an' all. Said to go round to the cabin when you come back from work."

"A present! I never got them anything."

"Me neither."

"I thought we weren't giving presents."

"That's all right, when we get to New Zealand we can take them out for a drink or something."

"I'm fifteen!"

"Pictures then, milkshake and sandwiches. Whatever. Don't worry about it."

I tried to make out the jigsaw. "What is it?"

He passed me the lid. A girl in tight shorts and no top sitting astride a Harley-Davidson. "Very sexy," I said. "More your taste than theirs."

"Yeah, she can give me a lift any time." He laughed. "Oh, you've got another present too. On the bunk."

It was a pound box of chocolates, the same silvery-blue selection we had been given when we left Westport. A handwritten card was Sellotaped to the top: *Deck Boy Bennett : With all good wishes for Christmas, J. J. Bell, Captain.*

I was surprised. "Did you get one?"

"Yeah, so did Aaron. Everyone, I suppose."

"Captains always do that?"

"You must be joking."

I tore off the cellophane. "Want one?"

"Thanks." He took two.

Everyone knew, even the lowliest greaser down in the bowels of the engine room, that Captain Bell, 'the old man', as captains are known, did as little as possible and left the running of the ship in the hands of his first mate. At the same time, he had a kind word for everyone and was popular.

I squashed a caramel with my tongue, took a Turkish delight and threw the box back on the bunk. "I'll go along to Michael's then."

"Drink before lunch?"

"Yeah, OK. We need to dress?"

"Well I wouldn't go like that. Most people tidy themselves up a bit."

As I was walking round, Ossie emerged from his cabin. The official story, the story put about by his friends – though I don't know how many believed it – was that he had stumbled into the ravine, it was an accident. Now, four days later, the bruising was at its height. Most was hidden by his clothes but he had shown Barbara and me the day before. Ugly patches of purple, green and yellow, some big as a spread hand, covered his body. The gash in his side was a long black scab fuzzy with stitches. More scabs covered the scrape on his arm and lesser wounds. The captain had radioed ahead for dental treatment when we reached New Zealand.

"Hello, Ben." He smiled painfully. "Happy Christmas."

His broken teeth made me wince. "Happy Christmas, Ossie. How are you feeling today?"

"Not too bad, thanks." He was carrying the urn containing his mother's ashes. "Thought I'd just, you know … Christmas Day. The decks will be quieter."

I said, "Are you coming to the lunch?"

"Michael and Barbara said to go with them. You going with Charlie?"

"And Aaron," I said.

"Will you come and sit with us? I want to keep away from that Rat'bone and the others."

"Yeah, sure, if we can. I'm just going to Michael's now."

"See you later then." He could hardly walk. I watched him hobble down the alleyway, one hand against the bulkhead.

A smell of cologne or springtime body rub met me at Michael's curtain. Shirley Bassey was singing her heart out. I tapped and went in. "Ben! Darling! Happy Christmas." He kissed me on the cheek. The cabin was gay with streamers. Bright stars and a Christmas fairy swung from the deckhead. Two bottles of champagne, one open, stood in a red fire bucket. "Luigi! Barbara!" He yelled down the alleyway. "Ben's here."

Luigi arrived looking like a pirate with a big gold earring and a scarf round his hair. Barbara carried a glass and was a wreck.

"For goodness sake!" Michael said impatiently. "Look at the state of you." He took the glass and tipped it down the sink. "Sit down there and I'll make you a coffee."

Barbara resisted. "No, I wan' give Ben his present." A parcel wrapped in Christmas paper and tied with ribbon lay on the bunk. He pushed Michael aside and gave it to me with stubby hands, his nails bitten and fingers ingrained with engine oil. Not many people called Barbara had hands like that. "Hap' Christmas, Ben. You're our frien'. I hope you like it." The ship rolled and he clung to Luigi for support.

"It's from all of us," Michael explained.

"I didn't realise we were going to ... I'm afraid I haven't ..."

"Oh, that doesn't matter. Don't be so *bourgeois*! Anyway, you gave each of us a gorgeous card."

"Go on," Barbara said. "Open it."

I read the Santa gift tag, untied the ribbon and opened the wrapping paper. It was a black shirt. I had never owned a black shirt.

"Try it on then. Let's see if it fits."

I pulled off my crumpled T-shirt. The shirt was silk with mother-of-pearl buttons. I fastened them and pulled it straight.

"Oh, yes," Michael said. "Very Rudolph Valentino."

"Who?" I said.

"It was either that or the red," said Barbara.

"No, it's great," I said, secretly wishing they had chosen red.

Luigi stood back critically. "You look'a good. You remind me of my brother. He wears'a black. Only his hairs'a dark like me."

"I didn't know you had a brother," I said. "What's he called?"

"Giuseppe," he said. "He's eleven."

"Eleven! I hope I look more than eleven."

"Mm ... Twelve maybe."

"I'm sixteen!" My age was a subject I tried to avoid. "Anyway, I love it. Thanks very much." I stroked the shiny material. "OK if I wear it for the Christmas lunch?"

"Of course! Now," Michael pirouetted and struck a pose "Christmas comes but once a year, You've *got* to have some shampoo, my dear!" He screamed with laughter and pulled a bottle from the ice.

Unwisely I accepted.

Fishnet Tights and a Party

FOR THREE hundred and sixty-four days of the year, the crew of a ship do the officers' bidding. Just once the roles are reversed; the officers serve Christmas dinner.

At one o'clock I was sitting between Charlie and Aaron with a third glass of champagne before me and a can of lager waiting to be poured. Michael, Barbara and Luigi sat opposite with Ossie safely among them. We pulled the crackers and put on paper hats, read out the jokes and told better jokes of our own.

The first course was prawn cocktails with avocado, served by the mate in Santa Claus whiskers and Philip in a stetson with a toy gun belt round his hips. Barney, the chef, had made a special effort for Christmas and they were delicious.

There was to be a second starter and Tim Nettles, wearing a Westport Wanderers' strip with American football shoulders, emerged to serve the soup – according to the menu, cream of asparagus. Word had reached us that he would be assisted by Tony Fanshott-Williams. But where was the senior cadet? My friend Kevin, the galley-boy, sweating in his white jacket and hat, emerged from the galley and beat a saucepan with a large wooden spoon. Everyone turned. Kevin retired. We waited. Seconds passed. Then the galley doors burst open and Tony appeared.

"Ta-ra!" He struck a pose.

A shock ran through me. My skin crawled.

Tony had planned to be the star of the occasion but he was unpopular and had gone too far. Like a student on rag day, he had dressed in drag: a shimmery top with a padded bra, a tight skirt, blond wig, bangles, make-up, false eyelashes. With a sexy wiggle he crossed to the soup tureen.

"What a prat!" The air filled with catcalls: "You fancy yoursel' don't yer? ... Get 'em off! ... Anyone gorra sick bag? ... Rather kiss my old woman than you! ... Boo, boo!" Bread rolls rattled about his head.

The second mate turned his back to hide a smile.

"What a Mary!" Charlie said. "He's blown it."

"Great!" It was a moment to savour. I reached for my champagne.

The second mate started at the far side of the messroom. It was Tony, hot-eyed and sweating with humiliation, who served our table. His lips were shocking red, his mascara was melting. Deliberately he slopped the soup into my bowl, letting it splash the table. As he withdrew the ladle it dribbled across my new shirt.

I jumped back, mopping and rubbing, but the damage was done. "You did that on purpose!"

"Little accident," he sneered, venting his anger on me. "I'm more used to the bridge than this sort of work."

"Do that to me," Charlie said, full of the Christmas spirit, "I'll knock your teeth down your throat."

Tony didn't spill a drop.

But Michael, who cleaned the officers' cabins and served them at table, was incensed. "Hey, Second," he called loudly. "I never use bad language but this bastard here deliberately slopped soup all over the place. Will you get him to mop it up please."

"It was an accident!" Tony protested.

"Liar," everyone shouted.

The second mate came to mediate. Tony was told to fetch a cloth from the galley. With hate in his eyes he wiped the table and brought me a clean plate.

The main course – freshly-carved turkey, stuffing, chipolatas and all the trimmings – needed every officer to lend a hand. Like the rest of Christmas dinner, it was excellent.

Then it was time for the pudding. Kevin appeared a second time and rattled his saucepan. "Not that bloody cadet again," somebody said. Conversation died. We waited. The galley doors opened a slit. A slim leg appeared, clad in fishnet tights. Then an arm with a silver glove to the elbow and glittering bangles. This wasn't drag, it was the real thing. A blast of *Big Spender* came from the loudspeakers. The crew whistled and shouted. The door opened wider. A bare shoulder appeared. A sequined hip. A second glove. Then the doors were flung wide and Trish stood in the entrance. She had dressed as a bunny girl and looked sensational. The whistling and shouts rose to a crescendo.

"Hello, darlings!" She had to say it four times before she was heard. "Now it's time for something – sweet!" Her voice was husky, seductive. I wondered if she had been an actress.

Some of the crew jumped to their feet, others sat back laughing.

"Silly cow." Smoky sat at the next table. "It's pathetic. Showing off to a bunch of sex-starved sailors. What's she think she's doing?"

I looked round for the mate. He had gone, just as he had disappeared when his wife was being ducked on the equator.

Charlie half sang, "There's going to be trou – ble."

"Now, all you lovely sailors. What would you like next?" She wriggled her shoulders. "Christmas pudding with dee-liciously smooo-th *spicy* sauce?" Kevin passed it to her on a dish and she held it aloft like a beauty queen. "Or succulent, crea-my trifle?"

The messroom erupted:

"Whatever you like, darlin'! ... Who cares? ... What're you doin' this afternoon? ... I'd rather 'ave an 'elping o' you!"

Trish had wanted to make an impact but not like this. She looked round anxiously.

Tim Nettles moved to her side. "OK everyone, settle down." He waved quietening hands. "I'll do the Christmas pud, Mrs Rose will serve the trifle."

"I want trifle!"

"We want trifle!" Spoons and fists thudded on the tables.

"All right, all right." The second mate stepped forward. "Mrs Rose wants you all to have a good time. Give her a chance."

"I'll give her a chance all right."

"What's a bunny girl got to do with Christmas? That's Easter."

"Any time suits me."

Another cheer.

Tim Nettles murmured in her ear. They began to serve pudding. He started at the back, football shoulders moving between the tables. Trish started at the front.

It was never going to work. As she bent to serve the trifle, rough hands grabbed at her fishnet tights.

"Don't!" She straightened.

Someone caught her pompom tail and wouldn't let go. A strong arm circled her waist.

"What about a Christmas kiss?" A mouth was raised.

"No!" She backed away. "Please!"

"What about my puddin'? I bin waiting hours!"

"Sorry, I – " She snagged a heel and stumbled. Someone caught her. The big bowl of trifle smashed to the deck. Her tights were covered in cream and jelly. Somehow she was sitting on Rat'bone's knee. She tried to rise. He held her tight.

"Leave her alone." Samuel stood above him.

With a laugh Rat'bone opened his arms.

Trish's heel was broken, her hair tumbled from its clasp. She was crying. Samuel tried to help. She pulled from his kindly support and ran away to the galley. Kevin emerged to see what was happening. Her trifle-covered foot skidded. She crashed into the door and fell. With a final sob she pushed past and was gone.

"Poor Trish," I said.

"Silly bitch, more like." Charlie was unsympathetic. "What's she expect, flaunting herself like that to a roomful of half-drunk sailors?"

The mess was cleared up. Philip appeared with a second bowl of trifle. It was followed by fresh coffee with cream, marzipan fruits and chocolate mints.

The memorable lunch was concluded.

"Three cheers for the chef! Three cheers for Barney!"

The wizened chef, who had been labouring for days and was now helplessly drunk, appeared from the galley.

"Hip-hip, hooray! Hip-hip – "

Smoky presented him with a tumbler of whisky.

"Thanks … boys." He clung to the side of the door. "Enjoy … your meal?"

"Fantastic! Best ever!"

"Good." He raised the glass. "Cheers!" He drank it down. "Just what the doctor …" His eyes glazed and he slid to the deck.

"Hooray!"

*

There was plenty of company and no shortage of things to do: deck golf, sunbathing, cooling off in the pool, films on video, reading, music, sailors' yarns and Christmas cake for smoko.

I spent the afternoon sobering up and by seven o'clock, my black shirt washed and ironed, I was lying on the day bed, killing time before the party that was planned for that evening.

Abruptly the curtains swished back and Barbara appeared, ready for the fray, glass in one hand, green nail varnish drying on the other. "What do you think?" He spun round on the rug. "Your honest opinion. I want to hear it from you because you're my friends."

I was startled but Charlie was more laid back. "Very nice," he said. "Turn round again."

Barbara turned his back.

"Yeah, fine."

"You don't think it's too – well, you know what people are like."

"Absolutely not," Charlie said decisively.

Barbara turned to me. "You're very quiet, Ben. And if I may say so you look absolutely dishy, those trousers with the shirt. And your hair done like that."

I didn't know what to say, for Barbara was wearing a little black dress with a sequined skirt, black tights, a tumbling auburn wig and green accessories. The top of the dress cut into shoulders that looked as if they humped sacks of coal. His muscular legs were those of a wrestler, bleeding where he had cut himself shaving. His eye shadow was opal green above a broken nose.

"You look great," I said.

"You think so, really?"

"Only one thing," Charlie suggested. "If you don't mind my saying. Your boobs are a bit lopsided."

"Oh, tell me about it, I've been trying for half an hour. They keep slipping." Barbara dived into his cleavage and rearranged the scrunched-up paper towels that served for the real thing. He wriggled his shoulders. "There, is that any better?"

"Much."

"Oh, thanks. You boys have no idea what us girls have to put up with."

*

There's an old story: Two sailors are walking down the road and see a man lying in the gutter outside a pub. "Look at that," says one. "It's disgusting, he's drunk!" "No he's not," says the other. "I saw him move."

I tell this story because that's more or less what happened to me at the party. I got drunk. Really drunk. For the first time in my life and the only time that trip – in fact, the only time until I was much older. How it came about and why I kept on drinking I've no idea, because getting drunk was the last thing I intended, especially since I'd spent the afternoon sobering up. Maybe it had to happen sometime, I don't know. Maybe if I'd had any idea how truly awful the hangover was going to be I might have exercised some self control. But I didn't, it was a kind of madness, and when people tried to restrain me I brushed them aside.

I remember the first hour well enough: the karaoke, the music, the cheers as Michael and Barbara made their entrance, the first two lagers with Charlie and Aaron. After that things get increasingly blurred. At one stage, I know, I tried and failed to do some breakdancing with Charlie who was brilliant. Another time I danced cheek to cheek with the delectable Trish and got into trouble for clutching her bottom. During a lull in the music I picked up one of those chrome ashtrays on a stand, overflowing with cigarette stubs, and having missed out on the karaoke, I sang into it like a microphone while everyone laughed and Michael tried to get me to put it down. Then I think I must have dozed off in a corner because someone buried me in empty cans and when I struggled to my feet they crashed around me like a dozen suits of armour. At some stage too, I jived with Barbara, his wig lopsided, teeth red with lipstick and one boob missing. And there's a half-memory of leaning on the stern rail, looking down at the wash and eating a slab of Christmas cake while Charlie and Michael ran through the ship in a panic, shouting my name. Michael, no doubt remembering Curly, was so upset that he burst into tears and smacked me across the face.

I must have returned to the party after that because I clearly remember Barbara getting into a fight with the bosun and kicking him in the crotch, which earned him a cheer.

By this time I was wearing shorts because my shirt and trousers had gone missing. The next morning, when I felt so terrible I wouldn't have minded if I *had* been tipped over the side, the four-to-eight watch found them fluttering like flags from the mainmast. I think I hoisted them up there myself because I have a dim memory of giggling as I slotted the halyard through the belt loops. But I could be wrong.

Anyway, that was Christmas. And two days later, in the early morning of December the twenty-seventh, we arrived in New Zealand.

PART FIVE

NEW ZEALAND

Volcanic Springs

"I'm going to like it here." Charlie sipped from his mug of tea. "Look at those beaches."

"And the water," I said. Crystal clear and every blue from ultramarine to palest turquoise. A big fish, not a shark, swam in the depths. "Different from the mucky brown in Westport."

It was afternoon smoko and we idled offshore to allow a container vessel to clear the narrows before heading in around the mountain. 'Mountain' is an exaggeration, but Mount Maunganui, the extinct volcano after which the town was named, rose seven hundred feet straight from the sea. As soon as the channel was clear, we turned into the vast Tauranga Bay, took the pilot aboard, and an hour later were tied up alongside.

To my delight there was a letter from home. Joey had only written half a page, most was from Fizz, but there was plenty of news. They were getting engaged at Christmas, she had written in mid-December. In the new year she was starting a computer course at Westport Tech. Joey had found a job stacking shelves at Sainsbury's, but he was training with the Wanderers' youth team and expected to get a game soon. They hoped I was having a great time and sent their love. Happy to be remembered, I found fresh tea and chocolate cake in the messroom and took them to the cabin to re-read my letter and play some tapes.

My days in Maunganui, a town in the Bay of Plenty on New Zealand's east coast, were among the happiest of the trip. The happiest, that is, apart from an incident on the very first evening.

The mountain towered above us. There must be, I was sure, a terrific view from the summit and I tried to persuade some of the others to climb it with me. No one was interested, at least not right then, so shortly after dinner I set out by myself.

There were tracks but much of the way I found myself ploughing through heather and shrubs. It was hot work but that did not trouble me. What did trouble me were the clouds of black flies, minute and vicious, that rose from the ground and every single twig. My legs were savaged, they stuck to my sweating neck, crawled up my shorts, swarmed in my hair and sank their teeth into every morsel of flesh within their reach. I broke into a run, a panting uphill scramble, hoping to leave them behind. It didn't work; the second I slowed down there they were again, intent, it seemed, on driving me crazy so they could feast at their leisure on my remains.

At last I reached the summit where thankfully a land breeze cleared the air. It had been worth the effort: beneath me lay the great sandy sweep of the Bay of Plenty, the darkening Pacific, and westward, towards the setting sun, a wilderness from which dinosaurs might have emerged. I wished Charlie had been there to share it.

The town of Maunganui was spread at my feet. I looked down on the great ships tied up at the jetties, *Pacific Trader* among them. Closer at hand, amid the shadowy streets, a cluster of blue, open-air swimming pools steamed gently into the air. I had heard about them on the ship, salt-water pools heated by thermal vents in the earth. They looked very inviting.

I couldn't stay long on the summit because daylight was fading fast and it would have been easy to turn my ankle on the treacherous ground. As I descended, the black flies resumed their attack. Directly below me, at the foot of the mountain, the turquoise pools glowed in the dusk. The thought of rinsing the flies from my hair and sweaty skin was too tempting to resist and so, when I reached the bottom, I made my way through lamplit streets to the entrance. I had no shorts except the work shorts I was wearing but the ticket attendant lent me a pair someone had left behind. Minutes later I was changed, showered and luxuriating in the warm salt water.

There were, I discovered, four temperatures: gently warm, medium warm, hot, and a smaller ice-cold pool for cooling off. It was a new experience, swimming in water as cosy as a bath, floating easily, like bathers in the Dead Sea, and looking up through wreaths of steam at the New Zealand stars. Shading my eyes I searched for

Rigel and Canopus, and turning south saw the Southern Cross, halfway up the sky.

This was the medium pool. After a while I wanted to cool off and jumped up to the side. While the warm pools had a scattering of bathers, the cold pool was deserted. I swished my fingers. It was arctic – or antarctic. Should I or shouldn't I? For a minute I dithered then took a determined breath – and dived. The water hit me like an electric shock but after the first few seconds it felt great, icy clean and freezing away the itch of my bites. I swam a few short breadths – it was enough. I sprang out, my whole body tingling, and now the night air felt warm. Briefly I looked around, wondering where to go next, and made my way to the hot pool. The bathers here were lethargic, ducking to their shoulders, holding the edge and passing hands across faces that might have been scarlet, but in the floodlights it was difficult to tell. I jumped down.

This was a second shock to my system. The water was burning hot. After a few seconds I was sure I couldn't stand it – then thought that perhaps I could. In very little time I stood like the rest, surrendering to the pleasure. The steam drifted, swept by a gentle night breeze. I watched it for shapes, little pictures there for a second.

After a while I set out for the far side, swimming a few strokes then walking. The water wasn't deep in the hot pool, about up to my armpits or maybe a little higher. I wasn't aware of anyone approaching, but suddenly there was a voice at my shoulder:

"Hello there, deck boy."

I spun round. It was the bosun. He was grinning, his birthmark livid in the heat. His bandaged arm was covered by a rubber sleeve I had seen in the POs' washroom.

"Havin' a bit swim then?"

Rat'bone was with him, hollow-chested, the thin hair plastered across his skull. And Tony, thick-lipped and fleshy.

"Not got your pals with you this time?" The senior cadet pushed the black curls from his eyes. "Let's see what you're really made of."

Without warning, he sprang at me. Instantly I lost my footing and went under. I struggled desperately and managed to snatch a lungful of air then went down again. All was confusion. Though I fought and kicked out, Tony was not the only one holding me under. The hot salt burned my eyes, forced its way up my nose and into my throat. I was swallowing it, choking. Still I struggled. Still they held me down. I was drowning. My senses began to slip. I couldn't stand the pain, the pressure. I had to breathe.

There was no shortage of guards and I am sure they were doing their job properly. Ryland and the others had been laughing. We must have looked like friends larking about.

In such panic and fear I did not feel a new hand grasp my arm. All I could tell was that my head was above water and there was air and I was able to fill my lungs. The next second, I was sure, I would be ducked again and clung round someone's neck, wrapped my legs round his waist and hit out blindly. But there was no return blow, no attempt to force me back under. The attack had stopped. I opened my eyes and tried to blink away the salt.

The first thing I saw was Tony holding his face and blood running through his fingers. I coughed, still choking. My stomach heaved. There too were the bosun and Rat'bone. Had I hurt Tony, bloodied his nose? I hoped so. But who was I clinging to? Whose hand was under my arm?

I looked down – Steve Petersen!

My stomach heaved again. I was going to be sick. I struggled free and ploughed a path to the side. With an effort I managed to drag myself from the water then threw up spectacularly all over the tiles.

The management was not sympathetic. "You off one of the ships?"

I nodded and was sick some more.

"Pigs! Get yourself dressed and get out of here."

"But it wasn't my – " I belched.

"Disgusting! This is a place for decent people. Fighting like that then throwing your dinner up all over the place."

"I'm really sorry." I wiped my lips. "I swallowed a lot of the salt. Would you like me to – ?"

"I know what you swallowed, sonny. Too much beer, that's what you swallowed. This isn't one of your grotty Pommy dumps, you know. If you want to fight and vomit, do it back home. We're not accustomed to your type here. And what I'd *like* is for you to get dressed an' sling your hook, that's what I'd *like*. And never come back. Understand?"

My stomach heaved again but it was empty. Nothing came up but a sort of stringy yellow spit.

Other bathers stood watching and listening.

Steve was one, still standing where he had rescued me. His companions were climbing out the far side of the pool, taking no notice, as if whatever was going on had nothing to do with them.

An assistant arrived with a shovel of sawdust and scattered it over the mess. I remembered my dad's words, speak up for yourself.

"I haven't been drinking." My mouth tasted vile. "I was – "

"Look, son, I've got no more to say to you. Just – "

"Well I've got something to say to you," I said, "if you'd just shut up for a minute!" I was fed up with people in authority talking down at me. "I haven't been drinking, I've just been up the hill, not that it's any of your business. And I've just been attacked in this pool, right there!" I pointed. "And where were *you* when you were needed? I thought I was going to die. If it had been left to the guards I could be dead. And I've just swallowed pints of very hot, very salt water and it made me throw up. That's what happened, all right? You want to listen!"

He stared at me. I was quite impressed with myself.

"And as regards coming back, you need have no fears about that!"

But I was sorry because it was a great place. I'd have liked to come back with Charlie and some of the others.

Apart from this incident and the bites from the black flies which came up in lumps and drove me crazy with itching until I got some cream, I had a great time in Maunganui. A couple of times a crowd of us body-surfed in the tremendous waves that rolled in from the Pacific. Charlie and I took a tour by boat and swam with dolphins. And on Sunday we joined some engineers who had hired a minibus and drove to the volcanic springs of Rotorua where the air smelled of sulphur, the earth was orange, yellow and white, mud boiled and geysers shot a hundred feet over our heads. We ate fish caught in the nearby lakes and cooked in the thermal waters. And in the evening we attended a Maori concert at the meeting house, two hours of story-songs and whirling Polynesian dances in full costume, where a ferocious warrior in war paint taught us to dance a haka.

All I remember of the journey back is thick vegetation and swerving to avoid possums, because within minutes of setting off I was asleep, slumped in a corner against the window. By the time we reached the ship it was midnight. Charlie woke me just long enough to reach my bunk.

Next thing I knew it was Monday morning. And as I stood yawning and rubbing my eyes, I saw that the radio cassette player I had bought in Fiji was missing.

The Cassette Player and a Girl with Dark Hair

I ASKED round the cabins but no one had seen anything.

"Sorry, mate."

"That new Sony?"

"Likely one o' the dockers, thieving gits."

But when it came to smoko and we sat in the messroom, Kevin remembered: "I saw yon cadet with a cassette player, that smarmy one. Port side, heading for'ard. Bit after lunch, 'cause we'd been busy an' I went out to have a quick drag."

"You sure?"

"Yeah, definite. Black an' silver, 'bout this big."

"Bastard!"

"After lunch?" Smoky sat up. "'Bout two o'clock?"

"Something like that, why?"

"'Cause I'd just gone out on deck, getting' a bit of bronzie like, an' I heard this splash. Went to have a look an' here's his nibs along by the lifeboats lookin' down over the rail. Water settling. He'd dumped something, that's for sure. Don't know what it was mind."

People looked at me. My stomach churned with anger.

"Sort of thing he'd do," Charlie said. "Hates the two of us."

Rat'bone and Steve sat at another table but they heard what we said. Rat'bone's face was healing, the abscess scabbed, purple fading from the side of his nose. Steve, wearing jeans and a dirty singlet, looked unhappy. His eyes caught mine and he gave a nod, so slight it might have been my imagination.

As I jumped up Samuel caught my arm. "Don't do anything hasty."

"Hasty! I'm going to kill him!" I stormed from the messroom.

Philip sat on number three hatch eating a pastry. Tony wasn't there, he told me. The mate had sent him ashore with some papers.

I told him what had happened.

"Know nothing about it." He shook his head. "I never saw anything."

"Well the others did," I said. "Saw him carrying it. Saw him drop something over the side." I went to the rail. "Just along there."

Philip joined me. "Well, if you like …" He chewed a lip.

"What?"

"I could maybe go down and have a look."

"How do you mean?"

"Well, dive."

"Dive?" I stared at him. "It's fifteen metres."

"Bit less at low water" He looked down. "It's very clear, not like the docks back home. You can almost see the bottom. I've done it before."

"You're joking!"

"Not here, I mean, not in New Zealand, not off a ship. Swimming team used to go to summer camp in Cornwall. There was a platform out in the bay. We used to dive off that. Grab a stone and jump."

"Without air tanks?"

"Like pearl divers."

"Are you sure?"

"Well I've done it."

"No, I mean could you go down and have a look? Really?"

"Don't see why not."

"That would be fantastic! Sure it's not too dangerous?"

"Slack water, low tide. It's not like it's really deep. I'll tie a rope round my waist to be on the safe side. Need it anyway if I find the radio."

"It'll be ruined," I said. "I realise that."

"But you'd like to know. I would anyway."

I thought about it. "What about Tony?"

"None of his business." The Christmas fiasco had destroyed Tony's authority. Philip was more confident. "Don't need to ask Miss Fanshott-Williams' permission to go diving."

Michael's name for the senior cadet was catching. I laughed. "When then?"

Several criteria had to be satisfied: low tide, as Philip had said, out of work hours, not too many people about, good sunlight on that side of the ship. The only time these coincided, as far as we could tell, was three o'clock the next afternoon, New Year's Day.

"I'll get Smoky to show us the exact spot," I said.

"And bring a heaving line and some old shackles for weights," Philip said. "Can you rig a stage?"

That night, New Year's Eve, we had a party aboard the *Trader* – I mean a party with girls. It wasn't planned, it just sort of happened. So many brand-new girlfriends and old pals from other ships turned up that it overflowed from the bar onto the deck and into cabins up and down the alleyways. Michael and Barbara were in their element, resplendent in wigs and war paint, popular with everyone. Wherever the action was, there they were, drinking and dancing the night away. The visiting girls loved them. One even deserted her boyfriend for Michael, sure he would find *her* sexy and fascinating.

"Get off!" he said crossly as she sat on his lap and wound arms around his neck. "Stupid slag! Go and squeeze your spots!"

Midnight came with shouting and hugs and *Auld Lang Syne*. We partied on into the New Year. Voices grew louder. Somehow I got involved in a snogging session with – well, I was never sure what she was called or where she came from, but a terrific girl with a slim waist and dark hair. Michael spotted us across the crowded room.

"Ben! Stop it, you'll go blind! Put her down."

I ignored him.

"Oh, you sailors are all alike. Fickle! Anything in a skirt." Clutching a bottle of gin he fought a path through the crush. "Jezebel!" He pulled the girl's arm from my shoulders. "Baby snatcher!"

"Baby!" She looked up. "You've got to be joking."

Which made me feel good but it broke us up. I could have killed him.

She looked around vaguely. "Anybody seen the guy I came with? Alistair something."

She moved away.

"Not your type at all, darling," Michael said.

My heart was hammering. I collected my breath. "How do you know what my type is?"

"Common as muck!" he said dismissively and waved the bottle. "Come on, everyone's looking for you."

But I steered clear of the booze that night. Instead I went searching for the dark-haired girl, more than ready to resume where we had left off. Ten minutes later I found her out on deck, mouth-to-mouth in a passionate clinch with Kevin.

By one o'clock the party was breaking up, moving on to other ships, other cabins, all-night clubs in the town. I took a shower to rinse the smoke from my hair and the sweat from my skin. I don't know where Charlie had got to but before two I was in my bunk with the cabin door shut against drunken shouts and intruders. If I had thought there was any chance the intruder might be a girl with dark hair – or fair hair, or ginger hair, in fact any girl at all – I would certainly have left it wide open.

The Diver

I wore the black cotton football shorts I'd bought back in Westport, which doubled as my swimming shorts, my paint-covered work shorts, my climbing-the-hill shorts, my canoeing-in-Fiji shorts, my knocking-around-on-deck shorts, and on occasion my sleeping shorts also. I had to buy some new ones.

Philip wore blue-and-white Speedo trunks. By a nice touch of irony he had borrowed Tony's flippers and face mask which had been left drying in the officers' washroom.

With Charlie's help I'd rigged a stage and hung it just above the water. Philip and I descended a long rope ladder lashed to the rails. Smoky and a few others came along to watch and lend a hand.

The sun was high. At my feet the water sparkled down and down, five metres, ten metres, until I could see no further. Philip looped a heaving line round his waist and fastened it with a quick-release clip. He pulled on the flippers and dipped the face mask.

"Are you right?" I handed him the heavy shackle that would carry him down.

He nodded, eyes watchful behind the mask and called up to Smoky: "Going now. Let the line run then take up the slack."

"I know." Smoky threw the butt of his limp fag over the side. "Take care."

Philip took a few deep breaths and launched himself into the water. It was a splashy entry. As the water cleared I saw him, pale and shapeless, sinking out of view. Then he was gone. The line slid through Smoky's fingers. We waited. I imagined Philip deep down among the harbour eels and fish, swimming above the sand, hunting through the debris, the vast flat bottom of *Pacific Trader* turning day into night. A scatter of bubbles danced from the depths. I saw him returning. In a rush of water, gasping for breath, he surfaced a dozen metres away.

"Oohhh!" He swam to the stage and hauled himself up. "It's cold down there."

"What'd you see?"

"Bit of a jumble but if it's there I think I'll find it. Ohh!" He rubbed his shoulders and turned to the sun.

His skin was icy. "D'you want a T-shirt?"

"Wouldn't mind, yeah."

Charlie's T-shirt was buttercup yellow. He threw it down.

"Thanks." Philip tugged it over his head. "You wouldn't believe the stuff down there: electric wheelchair, one of those dummies you see in fashion shops – gave me a hell of a fright – wheelbarrow, artificial leg. How's an artificial leg get down there?"

"Maybe a shark sicked it up."

"Oh, shut up. I saw one."

"What!"

"Yeah, came out the dark under the ship. Thought I'd had my chips but it was a sand shark, they're harmless."

"You sure?"

"I'm not going down again if they're not. Pum-pum-pum-pum. Aarrgghh!" He sang the track from *Jaws*.

Slowly he recovered his breath. Someone lowered another old shackle.

"Well, here we go. Wish me luck." With a clumsy leap he was gone again. The yellow T-shirt sank into the depths.

We waited

Half a minute passed. A minute.

The safety-line jerked, and jerked again. Was something wrong? I looked up. Hand over hand, Smoky was hauling it in. A rush of bubbles jostled to the surface. Beneath them, five metres under water, Philip was kicking upwards. He burst into the sunlight and gasped for a lungful of air.

Something black was following him up. The shark? I couldn't make it out. The next second a cassette player, the Sony I had bankrupted myself to buy in Fiji, broke surface and skittered across the water to crash into the ship's side. Philip had released himself from the safety line and clipped it to the handle. Smoky pulled it up, water streaming from the inside.

"Good on yer, cadet." A scatter of shouts and applause from the rail. "Like the bloody telly." The reputation of the soft-spoken Philip had gone through the roof.

He caught hold of the stage and pulled off his face mask.

"Thanks." I gripped his icy arm. "I couldn't have done that in a million years."

"Yeah, you could, just never tried it." He was grinning. "Bit scary but it was good fun."

"Ben ...!"

I looked up.

Barbara nodded along the rail.

Tony was looking down.

I was surprised he dared appear. Then I realised he hadn't seen the player heaved aboard.

"Them my flippers you're using?" His voice was hostile, aggressive.

"They were in the washroom."

"I know where they were. Bloody cheek. If you want to use other people's things you're supposed to ask."

"He's unbelievable," I said. "I told you he nicked them from the cargo?"

"Yeah." Philip shook water from his ears.

"And the whisky. And that stuff from the lifeboat."

"Come on up," Tony called. "You and that toerag of a deck boy you pal around with."

My anger boiled over. "I'll come up all right," I shouted. "What about my cassette player? Grab a hold of him."

The ship's side rose above us like a cliff. I grasped the rope ladder and began to climb, knuckles and toes scraping against the black plates. Philip hooked the flippers and face mask over his arm and followed at my heels. Overhead there were raised voices, a scuffle, a cry, a sound of running feet.

"Aye, go on, run away!" This was Smoky. "I'll kill you, you bastard!"

There were other voices then all at once the group fell silent. I looked up again. The rail was deserted apart from a scatter of hands. The mate's head appeared.

"You again, Bennett. And you, Hare." He was angry. "What the hell's going on? What's this stage rigged for? On deck, the pair of you. Right now."

The order was superfluous. In less than a minute we swung our legs over the rail and stood before him.

"Right, now what's this all about? Fanshott-Williams nearly knocks me off my feet, then you're what – swimming over the side?"

Philip was silent. I couldn't blame him, it wasn't his quarrel and the sea was his career. He was shivering.

"Take off that wet T-shirt." The mate looked round. "Goldie, fetch him a towel."

Michael ran off.

"Now, who's going to explain?"

"It's that bastard of a senior cadet." Smoky's eye was watering. I guessed he had tried to stop Tony running off and Tony had hit out. "Two days back he nicked Ben's – "

"Not you," the mate cut him off. "One of this pair."

I glanced at Philip then pushed through the others and grabbed my cassette player, still fastened to the line. "It's the senior cadet. He's had it in for me since Westport, before we joined the ship. He tried to pick a fight at the disco. Then that business with the hose pipe. Tipped soup all over me at the Christmas dinner. Now my cassette player's gone missing. Kevin, there, saw him with it on deck. Smoky saw him drop it over the side. Philip's a great swimmer, said he'd go down and see if he could find it. An' he did. Look at it, ruined!"

The mate fixed Philip with black, unblinking eyes. "You've been to the bottom of the harbour? Here, just now?"

Philip couldn't hold the stare. "Yes, sir."

"Bloody fool! Have you got no sense at all? I'll speak to you later." He turned back to the rest of us. "Right, you all heard Bennett. Who hasn't heard Bennett? The whole world's heard Bennett. So, anyone got anything to add?"

No one had, it seemed, and he was about to continue when Barbara intervened:

"I'll speak up for him if nobody else does. Ben's our mate, a lovely lad, I'd trust him with my life. Everybody likes him. If he tells you something, you know you can believe it. Which is more than you can say for some people – like Miss Fanshott-Williams up there for a start."

This was followed by a scatter of agreement, a few handclaps.

"Well, that's not my impression," the mate said. "Or the bosun's."

"The bosun!" Michael was back with a big towel striped with the company's name. "That ugly old Cyclops! I can tell you a few home truths about – "

"Oh, no you can't." The mate cut him off. "We're not going to stand here attacking the characters of people on this ship, people who aren't here to speak for themselves. I've heard what you have to say, Bennett, and I'm sorry about your loss but these things happen. I'll speak to my senior cadet though I'll be very surprised if there's any foundation to – "

"What do you mean, these things happen … if there's any foundation?" I was furious. "He took my new cassette player and threw it over the side. We've got the proof, here it – "

"Be quiet!" The mate's voice would have split a rock. "By God, Bennett, I've never met a deck boy like you in all my years at sea. Open your mouth just once more and I'll have you on a charge. D'you understand?"

"Yes, sir." I stared back insolently.

"And you can take that look off your face right now." For a moment the veneer of an officer cracked and I'm sure he'd have liked to hit me. "Dear heaven!" With difficulty he controlled himself. "As I was saying, I'll have a word with Fanshott-Williams, but I shall be very surprised if things turn out the way you've presented them. I can't say more for the moment. Now, it's New Year's Day, so I suggest you dismantle the stage and stow it away then go about your business. All of you. Enjoy the rest of your holiday."

He turned away.

The next afternoon I was chipping paint on the afterdeck when I was summoned to the mate's cabin. "Just go as you are," Lampie said. So I did, in a filthy T-shirt, covered in sweat and rust.

Kevin and Smoky were leaving as I arrived. Smoky shrugged silently and raised his eyebrows.

"What's he say?" I asked softly.

"Doesn't want to know. Big cover up."

I watched them go and tapped at the mate's door.

"Ah, Bennett. Come in." Immaculate in whites, three gold stripes on his shoulder, he set down a cigarette. His gold Rolex lay beside the ashtray. I didn't think my dad could afford a watch like that. "About this business with your cassette player. I've just spoken to the two you saw leaving and I interviewed my senior cadet this morning. This seems to be the nub of the matter: he doesn't deny carrying a player through the ship but it was his own. He'd been sunbathing and listening to some music. I've seen the two machines and they're not dissimilar. The galley boy can't swear it was yours. And like your friend the AB, Fanshott-Williams heard the splash as he was passing and stopped to look over the side. Until yesterday he wasn't even aware that you owned a cassette player. So, it's very unfortunate and it appears someone bears a grudge against you, but in the absence of any further evidence there's no more I can do. I'm certainly not going to instigate a major investigation."

Tony was lying all the way but I had no proof.

The mate was satisfied with my silence. "Now, concerning another matter." He regarded me with those deep-set eyes. "Fanshott-Williams has accused you of mounting a malicious campaign against him among the crew. I've noticed something of it myself and it is not – *not* – something I am prepared to tolerate aboard this ship. Do I make myself clear?"

After my bolshie attitude the day before I stood straight, the way we had been taught at *Frankie's*, my feet apart and hands behind. "Yes, sir."

As I stood facing the mate that afternoon I realised there was something about him that I didn't like. Not that he was giving me a dressing-down, that was to be expected. Nor that he simply wasn't a nice person. No, it was something else, something I'd felt unconsciously for a while. Something dark. I couldn't put my finger on it.

"And one final thing, Bennett. I don't approve of friendships developing between my cadets and members of the crew. I've told Hare that he is not to visit your cabin again. You are not to go ashore together. All fraternisation between you is to stop forthwith. Do you understand what that means?"

"Do you mean fraternisation, sir?"

He looked at me narrowly. "You're not getting smart with me are you, Bennett?"

"No, sir."

"Because I wouldn't advise it." He toyed with his wedding ring, pulled it over the knuckle and pushed it back. "Right, back to work with you."

I dipped my head. "Thank you, sir."

As I left the cabin he crushed the stub of his cigarette into the ashtray.

Claire

Two days after the diving incident we left Mount Maunganui and sailed round the East Cape to continue discharging. I hadn't been able to afford a new cassette player, but I'd bought sunglasses and a pair of shorts for going ashore.

Following the mate's intervention life on board was more peaceful. Tony kept out of my way. Steroid Steve Petersen seemed eager to make up for past unpleasantness. Even the bosun and Rat'bone were preoccupied and forgot to give me a hard time.

As we sailed south, the blue Pacific to port and the headlands of New Zealand far off to starboard, I went about my work happily. We carried cargo for three more ports: Napier in Hawke's Bay, Lyttelton in the South Island and finally Port Chalmers, the port for Dunedin, which lay further south again.

The weather was beautiful and whenever there was a chance I went ashore with Charlie or some of the others. We swam from the beaches, bought souvenirs, drank ice-cold beer and malted milk shakes, and went exploring. In Napier, which had been rebuilt following an earthquake, we wandered round the beautiful buildings, visited Marineland and drove out to the gannet colony at Cape Kidnappers. There wasn't much to do in Lyttelton, built in the leafy green core of a collapsed volcano, but a tunnel took us through the mountains to Christchurch where we visited a famous wildlife park and went mountain biking in hills above the city. And in Port Chalmers we took a bus to the Royal Albatross colony at the end of the Otago peninsula, where the gentle birds, cousins to the wandering albatross which had accompanied us across the Pacific, passing the ship at the speed of a train, were sitting on eggs, feeding their chicks and landing right beside us on three-metre wings.

They were days I would never forget, but two events which occurred at this time were particularly memorable to me.

*

The first took place in Lyttelton where one evening the engineers, desperate for some female company, had invited a crowd of nurses from the local hospital to come aboard for a film show and a party. There were about eight, accompanied by a couple of male nurses, and they arrived in one of the hospital minibuses.

The youngest and prettiest was a girl called Claire and quite by chance I met her on deck where she had come to escape the crowd and get some fresh air. For a while we chatted, leaning on the rail, and I offered to show her round the ship. One of the junior engineers, who had drunk a bit too much beer, came looking for her and didn't like it:

"Bloody deck boy! Go on, get lost." He took her arm. "Come on, darling, they're waiting for us inside."

"Let go." She pulled away. "Ben's going to give me a tour of the ship. Tell them I'll be back in a while."

He was furious but I felt pretty good, especially when she took my hand as we crossed the tumbled foredeck and climbed to the fo'csle head. Leaning against the windlass, with my heart hammering, I plucked up my courage and gave her a kiss. She seemed to like it so I did it again up by the lifeboats, and a third time as we stood at the stern with the moon shining across Lyttelton Bay.

"How old are you, Ben?" she said.

"Seventeen."

"You sure?"

"Well, nearly."

"How nearly?"

"Next month."

"You don't look seventeen."

"Oh, I get that from my dad," I said. It was a line I'd used before. "He's forty but he only looks about twenty five."

"Mm," she said, so I kissed her again to stop the questions.

And somehow, though I'd only met her an hour earlier and such a thing had never entered my head except as a dream, we ended up in my cabin, and in my bunk, with the lights switched off and the door to the alleyway bolted.

At some point the handle was rattled. "Ben?" It was Charlie. "That you in there?"

"Go away," I said.

"You OK?"

Claire giggled.

There was a pause. "Bloody hell, he's got a girl with him." Charlie wasn't alone and there was scattered laughter.

"Lucky beggar!" I think that was Kevin.

Someone rapped loudly. "Don't do anything I wouldn't."

"Hey, whoever you are. You got a mate?"

"Come on, leave him alone." The voices receded.

I was scared they would frighten Claire back to her friends but she giggled again and curled into my shoulder.

It was my first time and I felt stupendous. She didn't want to go back to the party so I made a pot of tea and found some cake in the messroom. Which was where Michael found us a few minutes later.

"Well, darlings, it's no secret what *you've* been up to. The whole *ship's* talking about it." He put his head on one side to look at Claire and evidently approved. "Come on, you can't stay skulking away in here. If ever there was a time for a sin and frolic, this is it."

So we left the tea and followed him to his crowded cabin where Kevin shifted to the deck and Charlie bunked along the day bed to make room. Barbara, who had been a hospital orderly before he joined the Merchant Navy, had struck up a friendship with one of the male nurses and they sat together on the bunk.

Everyone was great and we had a couple of drinks, but I was so jazzed up I wanted Claire to come back to my own cabin. I whispered in her ear and she squeezed my hand, but before we could make a move her friends arrived in force to carry her back to the minibus.

I tried to persuade her to stay a while and I'd call a taxi but she said she couldn't, everyone would talk, and anyway she started early the next morning. I didn't think that was a very good reason, I started early as well and wouldn't have minded if I didn't get any sleep at all.

Regretfully I stood on the gangway and watched her go, but before she got on the minibus she looked back and blew me a kiss.

It was the best night of my entire life.

I had arranged to meet her the next evening and thought about nothing else all day, but she wouldn't come down to the ship again, not by herself. So we went to the pictures instead and sat cuddling in the dark.

There had been a chance we'd stay another night in Lyttelton. I longed to see her and if she still wouldn't come back to the ship I was going to suggest a walk in the scenic reserve on the edge of town. In a wild place such as that, I imagined, there must be many quiet spots. Alas discharging finished ahead of schedule, and at four o'clock in the afternoon we were summoned to stations. Bitterly disappointed, I helped to throw off the mooring lines and watched the little town slip astern as we sailed out between the headlands.

"Aye, you're not the first sailor to feel like that," Smoky told me when at last I came off deck. "It's the way things are if you're mad enough to go to sea."

I was sure he was right but it didn't seem to help.

For a couple of months we wrote and swapped photos but I never saw her again.

The second incident occurred on our second day in Port Chalmers. For some reason, perhaps not unconnected with my experience in Lyttelton, I had woken early and took a mug of tea out on deck. It was a beautiful morning, not yet seven o'clock. A light breeze, funnelled between the hills, blew down the many miles of Otago Harbour. I leaned on the rail and watched an elegant black cargo ship with eau de nil superstructure and an orange funnel come sailing in from the sea. Tugs took tow lines in mid-harbour and turned her towards a berth at the next-but-one jetty. As the ship came close enough for me to read the name it was obscured by the tug at the bow. Then the tug swung aside and I saw it plainly:

London Pride

The mug slipped in my fingers and spilled hot tea down my leg. I scarcely felt it. Rarely have I had such a shock.

It was my father's ship.

London Pride

I DODGED out of sight although we were so far off there was no way anyone aboard *London Pride* could have recognised me, at least not without binoculars. The officer on the fo'csle head didn't look like my dad but I couldn't be sure. Maybe on that ship the mate didn't go to stations for'ard anyway, maybe he stayed on the bridge with the captain and the pilot. I ran down the alleyway to borrow Aaron's binoculars but by the time I got back the bows and bridge of *London Pride* were disappearing behind the ship that lay between.

What was I to do? I pulled my woollen hat down to my eyes, turned up the collar of my denim work jacket and ran along the quay. By the time I reached the berth the crew were leaving stations. Only a cadet remained on the bridge. For half an hour I lurked among containers and portacabins, torn between fear and a longing for a glimpse of my father, although what I would do if I saw him I had no idea. The gangway was lowered, officials went aboard, seamen crossed the decks, but I never saw an officer. Probably they were at breakfast or opening their mail. Was my dad up there by the bridge, I wondered. Was he opening a letter from me?

I couldn't stay any longer and ran back to *Pacific Trader*, ducking behind trucks and pallets of cargo as I went. It was high tide and now that most of her cargo had been discharged the ship rode high above the jetty. The gangway was steep.

I found Charlie in the messroom. Over breakfast I told him what had happened. Afterwards Smoky, the only other person on board who knew my secret, joined us in the cabin.

"Bit of a coincidence," he said, "but not enough to make you believe in fate. Freezer ship like us, yeah? Freezer ships come here from all over the world."

"I suppose so," I said.

"Well think about it. What does the bloody country produce –

lamb, isn't it? Beef, mutton, butter, cheese, wool, skins – stuff like that. Stuff everybody wants. Bit of a fluke your dad turning up in Port Chalmers, I suppose, but not New Zealand – or Oz, of course."

I hadn't thought about it that way.

"So, if he is on board – what?" He examined a new-made fag and nipped off some loose strands of tobacco.

"Dunno." I shrugged. "I haven't got that far. Just want to know if he's on board, that's all."

Charlie said, "You an' me could go over tonight, Smoky. Take a few cans. See what we can pick up."

"If you like, yeah." He felt for his lighter. "Prob'ly somebody I know, all the years I been at sea keepin' out the road of the old woman."

"Dolores," Charlie said.

"That's right. I forgot, you've met her." He looked across, clouded in smoke. "You know what I mean then."

As it turned out, Smoky knew three of the crew, one a great pal, and the visit turned into a session. Charlie, half-blitzed before he arrived, saw the way things were heading and made an early escape. Smoky, who had been well behaved all trip, went on a bender and didn't turn up until midday the next day.

Charlie brought back the news that my dad wasn't on board. I made him a mug of coffee and we sat in the empty messroom. According to the crowd in the bar, he told me, my dad had been a great mate, one of the best, popular with the crew and always ready for a joke, but there'd been some trouble back in the UK and he'd had to fly home. Nobody knew what the trouble was, something to do with his son. Anyway, he'd been replaced. According to the captain's steward, who kept his ears open and knew about most things, he'd got a job as skipper on one of the North Sea ferries so he could stay close to home until the trouble was sorted out.

I traced a pattern in a spill on the table. "Don't suppose he knew what ferry it was."

"Matter of fact he did 'cause he heard the old man talking about it and he'd sailed on her as bar steward for a couple of years. The *Maid of Rotterdam*, sailing out of Harwich. Says she's a smart ship."

"Thanks," I said. It gave me a lot to think about.

Charlie belched and took a mouthful of coffee. For a couple of minutes neither of us spoke.

"You OK?"

"Not really," I said and took a shaky breath. "Back in a minute." I pushed back my seat and hurried out on deck because it very much felt as if I might be going to cry.

When I returned Charlie had made a plateful of toast. He pushed it towards me. "What're you going to do then?" he said.

"Not much I can do, not if I want to stay here. I'll send him a letter to the new address. Write it today. Let him know I'm OK."

"Care of our Bill."

"I've been writing every couple of weeks."

"I know." He spread a slice with thick butter. "Incidentally, Bill says he'll be in Catterick till we get back. Started a mechanic's course."

"Sounds good."

"Yeah, he loves it." Charlie furrowed his brow. "What about you though? When we get back to the UK." When I didn't answer he went on, "I've been thinking about it. I mean it's great the two of us, sharing a cabin and all, but you can't stay at sea for ever can you? Not with a false name and everything, not right now. You'll have to tell your dad some time an' he'll want you back at school."

"S'pose so." I didn't like to think about it.

"So where'll you go? Can't see they'll have you back at that posh place, not after running away and everything. What's its name again?"

"*Frankie's*. You're prob'ly right."

"What then?"

"You tell me."

"You liked *Westport High*, didn't you?"

"Yeah, it was a good school. But that's when I stayed with gran. Can't go back there now, can I?"

"Well," he hesitated, "that's what I was going to say. Mum often mentions you in her letters, wonders how you're getting along and everything. You and her got on great – an' dad, of course. You never saw it, but a few years back the house was bursting at the seams:

mum, dad, us five kids – an' grampa when I was little. Now we've all moved away and they're missing us – not that she goes on about it. Frank was at home but he's just moved out to live with his girlfriend and the place feels empty. Five bedrooms and just the two of them, as she says, rattling round like peas in a tin kettle. Penny calls in with the baby but it's not the same, not like the rest of us coming and going all the time, sitting down to meals, having a laugh. And I was thinking, if you'd like to go and stay there, mum would love it. Least I think so. Remember what she said: it's a treat to have lads about the house again. And you've told me your auntie doesn't want you there full time – you don't want to go anyway. So if you think you'd be happy staying back in Westport with mum and dad, go back to the old school, I'll ask her. It would be good, you'd be there when I go home on leave."

Lying in my bunk at night I had sometimes wondered about it.

"'Course I'd have to tell her what we done, you being here on the ship an' everything, forging Joey's Discharge Book."

"What'll she'll say?"

He thought for a moment. "She'll be surprised, got you marked down for a good lad. But after bringing up us four boys, the things we got up to, she'll not be too hard on you. It's not like you've done anything bad. Have to talk to your dad, of course." He took a mouthful of cold coffee. "What do you think?"

> Dear Dad,
>
> I hope you are well. Everything is going great up here although it's cold. The boss has given me a rise.
>
> My best friend here comes from Westport. I know you would like him. His mum and dad have got a big house. I might be able to stay with them and go back to the comp like when I lived with Gran. I liked it there. That's if you agree.
>
> I've got a girlfriend. Her name is Claire. We go about together. She's got brown eyes and brown hair.
>
> I have just found out that you left the last ship so maybe you have not received my letters. But now you are captain of the Maid of Rotterdam so I can write to you there. I am very proud to have a dad who is a captain. And I was proud when you were a mate too.

I know you have taken the new job because of me and I am very sorry to give you so much trouble. I hope you are not angry. I'm having a great adventure and in two or three months I'll come and tell you all about it. I promise.

Please don't worry.

Your loving son,

Ben

A Mystery in Wellington

Port Chalmers was our last port of discharge. Gangs of carpenters, known as chippies, came aboard, and as each hold was emptied they started battening out.

A freezer ship like *Pacific Trader* carries general cargo from Britain to meat-producing countries such as New Zealand, and frozen cargo back home again. To do this the whole ship, except a few spaces that will carry wool and skins, has to be transformed into a giant refrigerator. Miles of pipes, only a few centimetres apart, carry super-chilled brine around the bulkheads. Fans blow cold air from vents. The temperature is lowered to minus twelve or minus fourteen degrees centigrade. Plainly foodstuffs such as lamb and beef wrapped in muslin cannot be carried on decks that previously were loaded with sacks of phosphates and drums of chemicals. So before loading can begin it is necessary to clean the holds thoroughly and flush out the bilges, cover the decks with a deep layer of sawdust and line the whole cargo space with battens of new timber. It is called battening out.

This takes several days and needs many chippies. Charlie spoke to the foreman and got us a job as labourers when our work for the day was finished. The pay was good: time and a half in the evening, double time on a Saturday and triple time on a Sunday. Compared with my deck boy's wages, I was a millionaire.

We started with the biggest holds and worked our way through the ship. As each cargo space was made ready, the refrigeration engineers dropped the temperature and the wharfies swarmed aboard in their warm jackets, hats and gloves to load the pallets of deep-frozen lamb, butter and the rest that swung in from the quay.

We began loading in Port Chalmers and continued in Timaru, a pretty seaside town twelve hours to the north. I saw little of it because again Charlie worked his charm on the foreman and all our spare time was spent shovelling sawdust, carrying planks and nailing them to the deck.

After a busy week we sailed on to Wellington, the capital of New Zealand. As we passed Lyttelton at dusk, I stood on deck and watched an apricot sunset above the mountains, remembering the hours I had spent with Claire and regretting there was no chance of seeing her again.

In Wellington, which lies at the southern tip of North Island, we moored starboard side to the quay. Refrigerated lorries and rail wagons stood waiting. Cheerful gangs of wharfies streamed up the gangway, stripped off the hatches and at once resumed loading. In Port Chalmers and Timaru they had knocked off at six; here they worked on until nine and right through the weekend to keep to schedule.

Battening out was complete, there was no longer a chance of earning some extra money, so on Saturday afternoon, our second day in the capital, I walked into the city.

That morning, Captain Bell had hailed me on deck. "Here a minute, Bennett. Got your jacket ripped that day we left Westport, didn't you?"

"Yes, sir."

"Broken wire – bloody lucky. Anyway, bought yourself a new one yet?"

I shook my head.

"Well, now's your chance. Get yourself away into town. Don't worry about the cost, just bring the receipt. Company'll pay. Good God, could've taken off your arm."

I showed him both arms were complete.

He laughed. "Good lad, that's the spirit. On you go."

Ossie came with me. He wasn't my regular going-ashore companion but Charlie and Aaron had gone off to check out the talent at the university; Michael, Barbara and Luigi had taken a taxi somewhere; Kevin had an upset stomach; and Smoky was hitting the bottle again.

Ossie's friends, of whom I was one, were anxious about him because the pills he had been prescribed after his suicide attempt in

Fiji – if he was still taking them – seemed to be losing their effect. He had started locking his door again and a whiff of incense hung about his clothes. The casket containing his mother's ashes, by this time two-thirds empty, stood on a beaded mat on his chest of drawers with a fresh candle at each corner. He had shaved his pumpkin head. And now some evenings, during our brief periods at sea, he wore his white priest's alb for the scattering ceremony at the stern.

It was not surprising that Rat'bone and the bosun – though not Steve who seemed to regret his early behaviour – had started picking on him again. They were the same old taunts that had followed him from the *Star of Bengal*: 'Ossie Maggot ... Ossie Faggot ... the white worm ... mad Mary ... the dotty druid'. Although Captain Bell had warned them off, with the passage of time they delighted in returning to their sadistic ways. Wherever Ossie encountered them, in the messroom or out on deck, the insults were flung and they were having the old effect.

So I didn't mind in the least, on that Saturday afternoon, when he said he would like to come ashore with me. I was glad of the company.

He wore his customary white: white shirt, white trousers and scuffed white shoes. A straw hat protected his head from the sun and a rosary of fat wooden beads with a ten centimetre cross hung on his chest. "Thanks, B-Ben," he said as we walked down the quay. "I'll enjoy g-going into town. I've got a b-bit of shopping to do but there's no hurry." Like a child, this shapeless man with the voice of a girl, nearly old enough to be my father, caught my arm and gave a skip. His teeth, so badly broken by that descent down the rapids in Fiji, had been repaired in a series of visits to a dental hospital and he gave a big, white, porcelain smile.

After a couple of arguments with bartenders we abandoned plans for beer and had milkshakes instead which we both liked better, served in big metal containers with long spoons and noisy straws.

We went up in a cable-car and looked across the blue Cook Strait to South Island; walked back through the exotic blossoms of the botanic gardens; sat on a wall to eat ice-cream; and nearly got into a fight with some teenagers who shouted after Ossie.

Back in the streets we went our separate ways. The money I'd earned labouring was burning a hole in my pocket. In addition to the jacket, I wanted a new cassette player, swimming trunks and trainers – Charlie kept complaining that my old ones stank out the cabin.

"Bye, Ben. You're s-such a friend. It's been a lovely afternoon. Apart from – you know."

"I've enjoyed it too, Ossie."

He smiled. "See you b-back on board then. God bless."

"You too, Ossie."

I watched him dodge the traffic, a fat eccentric figure. The crowds swallowed him up.

I had enjoyed his company but it was a relief to be alone. Taking Captain Bell at his word, I bought a black zipper jacket that cost three times the price of the original. In a huge sports emporium I bought blue and gold swimming trunks, and trainers with a dolphin motif on the side. I wandered on, looking for an electronics shop which had a sale. The sun was hot and I turned from the busy street into a boulevard where trees spread shade above a broad pavement. Seats were set back off the road and I was just about to flop down when a short distance ahead I spotted a figure I recognised.

It was Jumbo Ryland, dressed in his best and standing at the foot of a broad flight of steps with an ornamental balustrade that led to the entrance of a very smart hotel. Luckily his back was towards me. Wondering what he was doing there but not wishing to be seen, I stepped over a low railing into the hotel garden. A shrub and fluted pillar provided a perfect hiding place.

Plainly Ryland was waiting for someone, and someone important, dressed as he was in a suit and tie, freshly shaved, his hair flattened with gel. But though he was tidy, nothing could disguise that coarse face and apelike posture. Even if his suit had been hand-stitched Armani instead of old-fashioned Oxfam, and his aftershave Georgio, the bosun was one of nature's thugs.

In marked contrast, the man who stepped from a black limousine five minutes later might well have been wearing Georgio and Armani. He was erect, muscular, immaculate, jet black hair brushed to a gloss. The limousine, long and discreet with smoked windows, stood by as he verified that Ryland was the person he had come to meet. He signalled to the driver who emerged carrying a black holdall. The driver handed it to Ryland and returned to the vehicle. With an engine note so soft it was barely audible, the limousine drew away.

The two on the pavement spoke briefly then Ryland led the way up the steps to the hotel. At the top the stranger turned, removed his expensive sunglasses and looked all round. He appeared about thirty years old and was not European or Maori. Indonesian perhaps, with taut skin and high cheekbones. Was it my imagination or did that keen gaze pick me out among the bushes?

The next moment the entrance had swallowed him up.

The Man with Tiger Eyes

I was intrigued. What was the bosun doing there? Who was the stranger? What was in the holdall?

I looked down at my clothes. Though I only wore shorts and an open-necked shirt, so did many men, some carrying briefcases. I decided I was presentable and ran a comb through my hair. Then, returning to the pavement, I walked to the hotel entrance and mounted the steps.

It was called the Ascot and was perhaps the best hotel in the city: small palms and an elegant fountain in the foyer, bright handrails, polished oak furniture, beautiful paintings, staff in dark green uniforms with scarlet trimming. I did not register this all at once for I entered slowly, my eyes darting to every corner, ready to beat a retreat. Ryland was not there, nor was the Armani man with golden-brown skin who travelled in a limousine with smoked windows.

A middle-aged porter approached and asked in a snooty manner if he could assist me. I had been to enough hotels with dad not to be troubled by people like that. Thank you, I told him, no he couldn't. Instead, seeing tables and easy chairs set around the foyer with newspapers behind which I could hide, I approached a kindly-looking waitress and asked for coffee and biscuits.

While it was being prepared, I went exploring. One door led to a music room where elderly ladies were taking tea and being entertained by a harpist in a long green dress. A corridor was set with glittering showcases of jewellery, expensive handbags and other desirable objects to tempt the wealthy guests. Carpeted staircases led up to bedrooms and down to cloakrooms. A double door with decorative glass panels revealed the sparkling silver and wine glasses of the dining room. But it was in the Albatross Lounge Bar that I found what I was seeking.

It was a large, bright room with a horseshoe-shaped bar behind which the barman was mixing a cocktail. Cool curtains moved in the breeze. Wood and glass partitions divided the walls into a number of shallow bays.

Sitting at a table in one of these bays was the man I had seen enter with the bosun. He was, I think, the most powerful man I had ever seen. I don't mean his shoulders and chest, though these were broad enough, it was the energy he radiated. I couldn't say where he came from, Malaya or the Philippines, perhaps, somewhere down that way. Dad once sailed with a crew from Burma, he looked a bit like some of them. It was his face that caught the attention. He was clean-shaven, his skin slightly pocked. His blue-black hair grew thick and low on the forehead. His mouth, strongly-etched, had the high cupid's bow of his race and gave him a sensual look. But it was his eyes, slanted by the high, strong cheekbones, that were the dominant feature. They were an animal's eyes, tawny as a big cat beneath black brows. He was a man too wild and untamed for the suit he was wearing, no matter how beautiful the tailoring.

Jumbo Ryland, who sat beside him, looked the clumsy thug he was. This man could have batted him aside, permanently, with scarcely a thought.

A third man was with them, hidden from where I was standing by a tub of New Zealand ferns. All I could see was a long hand holding a cigarette. He flicked it with a thumb nail. As he raised his whisky tumbler, cigarette protruding, a signet ring on his little finger flashed in a stray beam of sunshine.

All this I saw in a matter of seconds. I hadn't dared go into the Albatross Bar but stood at the entrance, peeping round the doorpost. I would have stayed longer but there was an intrusion:

"That's your coffee, sir." The waitress stood at my elbow.

I jumped with fright.

"I've left it on the table."

"Thank you," I said and came away quickly.

They may have heard but I don't think they saw me. At least, no one came raging from the bar to confront me.

The coffee was delicious and the motherly waitress had brought a double helping of shortbread. I'd have enjoyed it more if I hadn't been hiding behind the *New Zealand Herald*, every second fearing to have it snatched from my hand and the bosun or the scary stranger staring down at me.

I finished my first cup and poured a second. Then, being still unmolested, I put on my sunglasses and returned to the door of the Albatross Bar. The three men sat as I had left them. The only difference was that their glasses had been refilled. The powerful Filipino, if I may call him that – though he could have come from anywhere in southeast Asia or even the Pacific islands for all I know – was drinking cocktails, Ryland beer, the hidden man another whisky.

As I stood watching, Ryland unzipped the holdall at his feet and took out a box of chocolates. Chocolates? He set it on the table. I couldn't read the lettering but it looked like those we had been given by Captain Bell. Identical in fact. He bent to the holdall again and rooted beneath a number of similar boxes. But it wasn't chocolates he was seeking this time, and he emerged holding what appeared to be a sturdy portable radio. What was it all about? I was so intrigued that I failed to pay proper attention to the others at the table.

Sensing something, perhaps, the Filipino turned towards me. Just in time I ducked back and hid for a minute but no one appeared. I returned to my seat. Sheltering behind the *Herald* again, I added cream and sugar to my coffee and ate another shortbread. No matter how I puzzled my brain I couldn't make sense of what I had seen. Then, needing the toilet, I checked the coast was clear and headed down some broad carpeted stairs.

They led to an elegant basement lobby with a waxed floor and rugs. The gents, or *Gentlemen's Cloakroom*, was situated at one side. Like the rest of the hotel, the cloakroom was spacious and spotless. A row of ornate washbasins stood apart. Perfumed soap scented the air. I was drying my hands on a luxurious paper towel when the door opened and the Filipino stranger walked in. For a split second our eyes met in the mirror then I looked down and continued what I was doing.

"I saw you outside," he checked the cloakroom was empty. "In the hotel garden. You were hiding behind some bushes."

I was so frightened I could hardly breathe.

He joined me at the washbasins. "Now I see you inside, spying at the door."

"I'm sorry?" I pretended puzzlement. "I don't know what you're talking about."

"Don't lie to me, I saw your reflection in a mirror."

"I just came in to get out of the heat, have a coffee."

"An unusual place for a boy your age to come for coffee." Those tiger eyes bored into me. "Expensive, no?"

"I can afford it. Anyway," my heart thudded, "what's it got to do with you?" I dropped the towel into a wicker basket and turned away.

He gripped my wrist, his fingers so strong I cried out. "It has everything to do with me. I do not like people who spy on me."

I tried to pull away.

"Who are you?"

"That's," I struggled, "none of your business."

He threw me backwards and the next moment a knife was in his hand. Where it had been hidden in that thousand dollar suit I have no idea.

"I will ask you again." The knife was very sharp. He pressed the blade against my forearm. "Your name."

"Billy Wilson."

"And where do you live – Billy Wilson?"

"Out ... out the edge of town."

"Oh, I believe you. So tell me, Billy Wilson from the edge of town, how is it you've got an English accent? Why are your nails broken with hard work? What's this paint on your wrist?"

"I ... I was just ..." The knife had me hypnotised.

"Let me tell you what I think." He pressed the blade harder. "I think you're not spying on me at all – at least you weren't to start with. I think you saw that gorilla who met me in the street. I think you recognised him and became curious. Which probably means you're off the same ship."

"What ship?" I blustered. "I don't know what you're talking about."

It was a clumsy lie.

"Yes." He slid the knife sideways, just a centimetre. A red-hot pain made me cry out. A ten-centimetre cut opened in my arm. Blood ran towards my wrist. I snatched up a towel to staunch it.

"Call it a little reminder," he said and wiped the blade. "Now, Billy Wilson or whatever your name is, let me give you a piece of advice. You snagged that arm on a wire. You were never here. You never saw me. You never saw your ugly shipmate on the pavement." He returned the knife to some sheath inside his jacket. "Tell no one about this afternoon and it is finished. Open your mouth – and I assure you a lot more blood will be spilled than that. If the need arises, I will cut your throat. You would not be the first."

I was shaking.

"Now go," he smiled. "Perhaps we will meet again, who knows?"

I lifted the towel and saw my blood, vivid against the snowy paper.

"Here," he handed me another. "It's not deep, the bleeding will soon stop."

I looked him in the face, a face I would never forget, and made my way across the cloakroom. As I reached the door it opened and an elderly guest came in. He held it for me to pass. Scarcely knowing what I did, I crossed the downstairs lobby and climbed the staircase. The remains of my coffee and shortbread lay on the table. I collected my small bags of shopping and left the hotel.

"Hey! Hey!" The porter ran after me. "You paid for that coffee?"

"What? Oh!" I returned to the foyer. "Sorry, I went to the toilet."

"And forgot, I suppose. Well, we'll see what the manager has to say. Rowena," he called to the waitress. "This lad you were serving. Tried to slip off without paying."

She hurried across. "Let go of him, Eddie. It's only a cup of coffee."

I didn't feel too good.

"You all right, dear? You're white as a sheet. What's wrong with your arm?"

"Nothing, just a bit of a cut. It's opened up again."

"Let me see. Come on, sit down over here." She took my elbow. "I'll fetch a plaster."

"No, it'll stop in a minute. Thanks."

"Are you sure?" The red had soaked through. "Looks nasty to me."

"No, really." I turned away and doubled the towel. "How much do I owe?" Awkwardly I pulled out a small wad of notes.

"I'll get your bill."

Just at this time there was an influx of guests and amid all the activity I lost sight of the Albatross Bar. By the time they had dispersed and I'd paid my bill – *eight dollars* for a coffee – the three I had been watching had gone. I looked through the door and the barman was wiping their table. They hadn't crossed the foyer and gone out through the main entrance, I was pretty sure of that, they had left by a different route.

I returned into the sunshine and stood wondering: what was Ryland up to? I had met the Filipino but who was the third man? Was he off the ship? A New Zealander? Perhaps another Asian – certainly his hand was brown. But then my own hand was brown. Although I had been badly frightened, I was curious.

I ran down the steps to the pavement, still pressing the towel to my arm and feeling a bit sick, and along a leafy side street to the back of the hotel. They were nowhere to be seen. Somewhere an expensive car engine coughed into life. I looked towards the sound and the black limousine emerged from an entrance between vine-covered pillars. It turned towards me. Hastily I pushed through a gate into someone's back garden. The limousine purred past. Had I been seen? Were three pairs of eyes turned in my direction? I stared through branches but the person or people inside were invisible behind the smoked windows.

Cargo Lights

"Singapore, Colombo, Naples and Liverpool," Charlie said.

"Sounds good," I said. "Have you been there before?"

"Liverpool, not the others though. I like the sound of Naples."

"Oh, Naples is gorgeous," Michael said. "Pavement cafes, lovely wine, all those scrumptious dark-eyed boys."

"Hey!" Luigi turned on him. "I thought I your scrumptious dark-eyed boy. We go Napoli, I show you Napoli."

They were our ports of discharge. I had seen them chalked on the side of freezer wagons.

"You from round there then, Luigi?" Aaron said.

"My village in the mountains, fifteen kilometres. I go to school'a Napoli."

"Family still there?" I said.

"Si, my mother, my father, my brothers, my – "

"Sisters?" Aaron said. "Got any sisters, yeah? Dusky Marias, figures like – " he sketched them with his hands.

"You think I introduce you to my sisters?" Luigi said. "A dirty Don Juan like you? You touch'a my sisters, my brothers they kill you. They chop you into little pieces and send you home to mama."

It was a joke but only half a joke.

"All that Latin blood," Barbara said. "It's just like an opera."

"Come on, Luigi," Aaron persisted. "You've been around a bit, you're not like that are you?"

"Me? No, I stab you in the heart, cut out'a your eyes, chop off your – "

"All right, all right," Aaron said. "I get the picture. Dear, oh dear! … How about cousins?"

Loading continued full steam ahead throughout the weekend and well into the evenings, but because of some dock dispute there was to be a strike on Wednesday. The bosun waylaid me as we knocked off at teatime the day before. Covered in paint, my gloves black and hair streaked, I waited for a blast of ill-humour or some filthy task to stop me going ashore. To my surprise the blast never came and the task was easy enough.

"It'll count as overtime so put it on your sheet." He nodded amicably. "The cargo lights are bashed to buggery, mate wants the whole lot bringing up on deck. This strike tomorrow, gives the leckies a chance to get them serviced. I want you to fetch 'em up out of four and five holds, cadets are doing the rest. Obviously the wharfies need 'em while they're still loading so you'll have to wait till knocking-off time. Shouldn't take long."

I was pleased at the chance to earn some extra. "Thanks, Bosun."

"Put down a couple of hours." He patted my shoulder. "I'll OK it with the mate."

He never mentioned the pad of lint and sticking plaster on my arm. I'd bought some first-aid stuff in a chemist's on the way back to the ship and Charlie helped me with the dressing. I had told him about my frightening encounter the moment I got back, but stopped short of telling the mate, who was responsible for the well-being of the crew. The memory of that knife against my arm and the threat of what might happen if I reported it were more than enough to ensure my silence. Unlike the bosun, the mate spotted the dressing when I was working on deck and enquired in a concerned way, which surprised me. I told him, as I had told everyone except Charlie, that I had scratched myself on a wire as I walked into the city. He took me to the sick bay to examine it, but since by that time the cut was scabbed over and there was no sign of infection, there the matter rested.

And so, a bit after seven on that Tuesday evening, I pulled my working gear back on, collected a heavy-duty torch and headed down the hatches. Loading was still in progress but I could make a start with the cargo lights that were obviously broken. The bosun was right, they were in a bad state.

A working hold contained about eight. The wharfies shifted them from deck to deck and port to starboard, wherever light was needed. Each consisted of a domed metal shade about fifty centimetres across with a 150 watt bulb protected by steel mesh. They had handles but were normally lugged about by long electric cables that plugged into sockets in the holds. At every level I found at least one damaged, either hanging useless or kicked into a corner.

The cold was intense. Like the dockers, I had to wear gloves or my hands would stick to the metal rungs of the ladders. Number five hold, situated on the afterdeck, had three levels: starting at the bottom these were the lower hold, which was by far the biggest, the lower 'tween deck and the upper 'tween deck, in all about fifteen or twenty metres from top to bottom. Number four hold, situated at the after end of the crew deck, had a non-refrigerated shelter deck in addition.

I began my work, unplugging the broken lights, unhooking them, carrying them to the ladders, heaving them up by the cables – deck by deck, one at a time, clattering against the manholes – finally depositing them in a corner of the afterdeck ready for the electricians.

A klaxon sounded. Eight o'clock, they were knocking off early. Time for the wharfies to start plugging up, closing the holds so they could be frozen down during the strike day. I hauled out the lights they had been using but though I worked like a slave, it wasn't possible to keep up. Before I could finish, the working holds were plugged, the hatches were covered, the canvases were heaved on top, and the wharfies were streaming across the quay on their way home, or to the nearest pub.

Still, my work was more than half done. I descended into the lamplit darkness. It was spooky down there, pillars all about me, thousands of carcasses, shadows leaping as I carried the lights from hook to ladder. It grew colder. Fans which could not be turned on when the wharfies were working, filled the holds with arctic blasts.

I heaved the last light from number four hold, dropped the refrigeration plug in place and closed the lid of the booby hatch. Daylight was almost gone, the last streaks of sunset darkened above the city. Orange lights illuminated the quay. Deck lights shone from the mast and bulkheads.

Only number five hold to finish. I grasped the sides of the booby hatch where so long ago I had watched Tony Fanshott-Williams emerge with the snorkelling gear, and descended the ladder into the shadows.

The lower hold is a single, enormous space, seven or eight metres high. The 'tween decks are much lower and may be a single space extending the full width of the ship, or may be divided into two huge lockers, port and starboard, with an open section between. This was the case with number five hold.

The wharfies, knowing my task, had left the manholes open. I descended to the upper 'tween deck and continued down to the lower 'tween deck. They had been loading the starboard locker, lamb above butter, destined for Liverpool. I was surprised to see the insulated door stood ajar, emitting a shaft of light from a cargo light that had been left inside. I put down my torch to leave both hands free and heaved the door wide. The 'tween deck was bitterly cold, the locker even colder, sparkling and smoking with frost. As I laboured, my breath condensed in white clouds.

The walls of the locker were permanent wood, the deck covered in deep sawdust beneath wide-spaced battens – five-inch planking. The cargo light had been hung from a frame that protected the overhead refrigeration pipes. I could not untangle it wearing my clumsy gloves and set them aside on a carcass of lamb. As I picked at the wire it stuck to my fingers.

It was while I was engaged in this that I heard a little sound, and looking round saw the locker door swing shut.

"Hey!" I shouted. "Who's that?"

It was a joke, I thought, Charlie was having a bit of fun at my expense.

"Hey!"

There was no reply.

"Hey!" I stumbled across the awkward battens. "Charlie? Philip?"

Still no one replied. I felt a twinge of fear .

"Come on! Open the door!"

Then I saw that, far from opening, the thirty-centimetre-thick door was squeezing shut, nipping the electric cable. Whoever was outside was tightening the clamps, big screws turned by an iron lever. It was necessary to have an air-tight seal when the temperature would be dropped to minus fourteen.

I hammered on the metal-strapped wood. "Open up!"

Another centimetre. A squeak of wood on wood. The door was almost flush with the bulkhead.

"Come on! Come on, who is it?"

The movement stopped. The door was screwed fast shut.

"Hey!" Again I hammered, kicked it with the toe of my trainers.

From the far side there was a mocking tap.

"Open up!" Twice I beat on the wood with the flat of my hand.

Tap – tap!

Then silence.

I gazed around my smoking, frosted, half-loaded prison. Ice crystals glittered in the cargo light.

Now truly frightened, I almost broke my fist beating on the door. "Hey-y-y-y!" The walls and carcasses deadened my shout.

The cold air bit my neck. I turned up my collar.

"Hello-o-o-o!"

Silence.

I looked around for something with which to batter the door and saw only the icicle-fringed refrigeration pipes, boxes of butter, carcasses of lamb and the swinging cargo light. There was nothing else.

Then the light went out

The Freezer Locker

I don't know what more I could have done.

As the light was extinguished and silence clamped about me I was sure I was going to die. I had left my torch outside the locker, the darkness was absolute. Freezing gusts blew about my head. For a while I panicked, shouting at the top of my voice and beating my hands against that solid door. My wrist struck a projecting bolt.

The shocking pain brought me to my senses. I licked the wound clean, my blood tasting like metal, and located my gloves. How long, in such conditions, could I survive? An hour – maybe two? Certainly, unless I were rescued, I would be dead long before the wharfies returned at eight o'clock on Thursday morning. I recalled a scene from television where a character was locked in a butcher's freezer and found white-faced and lifeless. What could I do to prevent this happening to me?

I think I was seized again by a kind of madness. Perhaps, I thought, I could build a kind of igloo, using butter boxes instead of blocks of ice. I groped in the darkness, stumbling and falling. There had been butter, I remembered, under carcasses of lamb a short distance from the door. I heaved the hard-frozen carcasses aside and pulled a box into the open. It was heavy. I made a line of three and set three more on top. Another three and it was high enough. Then I started on a side.

The cold made my head ache. My ears were numb. I pulled off my gloves and rubbed them hard. How could I protect them? Like all the deck crew, I carried a working knife on my belt and kept it sharp. The carcasses of lamb were wrapped in muslin. I dragged one down and sliced it from neck to tail. The cold muslin stuck to the grease and snagged on legs and bones but in a minute I had torn it free and wrapped it around my head. I groped for another, then another, slashing away the material until my head was swathed like a mummy with just enough space for my eyes.

Despite the energy I was expending, in such conditions it did not bring me warmth, or not enough warmth. Clad only in working jeans, my legs were frozen. I thrust a rag of muslin down my trouser leg then thought of the thick sawdust that covered the deck. The planks which covered it were not nailed down hard, as I knew from my time with the chippies, just enough to hold them in place. I felt for an end, set my legs and heaved. With a squeak of three-inch nails, the plank parted from the batons below. The sawdust was there for the taking. I tucked my jeans into my socks, loosened my belt and flies and stuffed my trousers. Then I tucked my jersey into my belt and stuffed that too, above my shirt, ignoring the scratchy sawdust that fell inside.

When I had done everything I could, I returned to the igloo – though not properly an igloo because it had no roof. Soon it was completed, each side three boxes long and three boxes high, not enough to keep out the cold but a little shelter from the subzero gales that blew from the fans.

I groped for the plank I had lifted, holding it like a ram, and battered it against the locker door. BANG! BANG! BANG! BANG! If anyone came looking for me, surely they must hear.

The butter boxes were made of corrugated cardboard and glued shut. I ripped two open, tipped out the blocks of butter and made a floor for the igloo. Then I tore open some more, climbed inside the igloo and pulled the cardboard over my head. Curled up, collar high, hands in my armpits and knees to my chest – or as near as I could get them with my jeans packed tight with sawdust – I nurtured what warmth remained.

There wasn't much. My jaws were chattering. Icy shivers like burns ran across my back. I pulled my sweater this way and that, trying to close every chink, and rearranged the muslin that tasted of ice-cold grease against my lips.

I'm not sure how long I remained in that position. Not many minutes, I think, because I had to leave the shelter and lose any warmth I might have gained to batter the door again.

BANG! BANG! BANG!

Silence beyond. No sound but the remorseless rush of air from the vents.

BANG! BANG! BANG! BANG!

I stumbled back to the igloo, pulled the frozen cardboard over my head and huddled into my clothes.

Slowly, although I didn't register it, my temperature dropped. I began to feel sleepy.

BANG! BANG! BANG!

Sleep was dangerous, I knew that. While I was standing I punched the air for exercise, ran on the spot, jumped up and down, yelled aloud, anything to coax a little warmth into my muscles.

Perhaps it worked a bit because certainly I didn't feel so cold. I retreated again to the igloo and hid away beneath the cardboard. The gouge on my wrist had stopped bleeding. I licked it again, cleaning the crusty edges.

But slowly, slowly, as time passed, the sleepiness gained strength. Twice more I battered the door. A protruding nail pierced the glove and cut my hand. What time was it? How long had I been imprisoned here? What were my friends doing? Eyes closed, eyes open, the darkness was the same. My thoughts drifted to gran, and Westport, and dad, and the tiger-eyed stranger who had assaulted me. I wondered if my imprisonment had anything to do with that meeting in the Ascot Hotel. For some reason the old song from Boys' Brigade came into my mind and I began to sing softly:

> *"Will your anchor hold in the storms of life*
> *When the clouds unfold their wings of strife,*
> *When the strong tides lift and the cables strain ..."*

My fingers crept to the dressing on my arm. I couldn't feel it through the glove and though I pressed quite hard it didn't hurt at all. In fact it felt quite nice, warm and curled up there in my little igloo.

My Life is Saved

"Ben!"

"Mm?"

"Wake up."

"Nnn."

"Come on, wake up!"

A million miles deep. "Leave me al …"

"No. Wake up!"

My eyes wouldn't open.

Voices above me. "That's a boy. Come on, you're doing fine."

I struggled towards the surface. My eyes cracked open, shut, and cracked open again. Dazzling lights. Silhouettes. Green uniforms. A man I didn't recognise. Then Charlie.

"Hello, Charlie."

"Hello, Ben, mate."

My gaze slipped sideways. What was I doing on deck? Wrapped in a soft, peach-coloured blanket. Two blankets, in fact.

The man in green said, "Can you hear me, son?"

I blinked yes.

"How many fingers am I holding up?"

What a silly question. "Fourteen."

"*How* many?"

I think I smiled. "Twenty-two."

The answer was three but I couldn't be bothered. And now I saw there was quite a crowd, a couple bare-chested for the night was warm. Faces stood out, people I liked: Philip, Smoky, Samuel – and Michael, awash with tears.

A second man in green said, "He'll be OK now. Another few minutes then we'll take him in." He turned to someone I couldn't see. "Got that warm drink?"

Barbara stepped forward with a mug.

The man tested it. "That's fine." He crouched beside me and lifted my head. "Here, see if you can take a drop of this."

It was tea but somehow I couldn't swallow properly and it spilled onto the blanket. "Sorry."

"That's all right." He put a mask over my face and I breathed warm oxygen.

There were clothes on the deck, my clothes, and torn cottony stuff, and scattered sawdust. It reminded me of something.

The men in green lifted me onto a stretcher. The mate was in attendance. The crowd followed as I was carried to the gangway and down to a waiting ambulance.

"No! Charlie!" As they were shutting the door I put out a hand. "I want Charlie to come."

He sat on the bunk opposite. "This is another fine mess you've gotten us into."

His shirt and hair were speckled with sawdust. As we bumped over cobbles and turned into the road I began to remember: the locker, the cold, the nightmare.

"Who got me out?"

"Me and the second mate." He put a hand on my chest. "Tell you later."

I closed my eyes "Yeah."

The next morning Captain Bell and his wife paid me a visit in hospital. They brought magazines, a bunch of grapes and a box of those excellent chocolates. "You're a resourceful lad," he said. "A credit to your family and your ship. Good to see you pulling round so quickly."

In the late afternoon, when I was discharged, he sent the second mate in a taxi to collect me.

I felt a bit weak but not too bad, though the tips of my ears were blistered with frostbite. They would soon heal, I'd been told. They had cleaned up the wounds on my hand and wrist, put a light dressing on the scab on my arm, done a lot of tests and given me a jab. "Couple of days' rest," the doctor said as I came away. "Don't get upset, one capsule twice a day, then you can go back to work. Take it easy to start with. You've had a lucky escape, young man. Another hour in that freezer, you wouldn't be here today."

Charlie and I went round to Barbara's cabin. "Ben!" He threw down a magazine and hugged me tight. "Oh, Ben! Here, have a brandy."

"They said no alcohol."

"Pooh, what do the doctors know? Just the one, a thimbleful to celebrate. Aid the healing process. Then a coffee. Michael made a fruitcake. He'll be back in a minute."

"Sounds great." I sat on the day bed while Barbara, woolly-shouldered and wearing nothing but a wrap-around, busied himself with the drinks. "Charlie says it's you I've got you to thank for my life."

"Not me. Well, maybe a bit at the end. He's the one got you out. The way he raged on at the mate, I thought he was going to hit him."

"Tell me."

"Well, we were all waiting for you an' you didn't show up," Charlie said. "Last seen going down the freezer holds an' all the holds locked up. Still in your working gear, your other clothes lying on the bunk where you'd left them. All that had been happening it wasn't right, so some of us went to the mate up in his cabin but he wouldn't do anything. Kept saying you must have gone ashore; he wasn't going to start opening all the holds up just 'cause a deck boy had gone missing for an hour."

"That's right," Barbara said. "He was really horrible: you know, all official and I'm the Chief Officer, how dare you argue with me. Then Charlie began shouting and saying he didn't care if he was the sodding mate, because he knew you hadn't gone ashore and if the mate wouldn't give him the keys right then he was going to the old man."

"And the police," Charlie said. "Bastard!"

"So did he hand them over?"

"No, he still wouldn't," Barbara said, "but there was such a barney that people came to see what was going on: second mate, cadets, the old man. So the old man told everyone to shut up and asked the mate what the trouble was. Then he spoke to Charlie here, and when he heard you were missing he said, right in front of us all: 'If there's any chance one of my crew is trapped down there in the freezers, Mr Rose, we don't wait to find out, we go and have a look.' Mate was so angry he went white. Then the old man told the second: 'Take charge of it, Mr Nettles. And take this young man with you,' meaning Charlie. 'And one of the cadets.' Well, Miss Fanshott-Williams jumps in, doesn't she, and says she'll go. But the old man says: 'Not you, there was that trouble with you and Bennett a while back. Hare, you go with the second mate – and get a move on.' Then he tells me to run and tell the fridge engineers to switch off the fans."

"Bunny was ever so upset," Charlie said. "It was him locked up. He never checked down the holds, didn't need to, just saw the plugs were in place and locked the booby hatches."

I knew the routine, I'd done it myself when I sailed with dad.

"It wasn't just the three of us," Charlie said, "some of the others joined in: Smoky, Kevin, Samuel, anyone with a torch. Pitch dark down there. You could have been anywhere. All those decks, acres of space, thousands of tons of bloody beef and mutton. But it was Bunny found you. Knew you'd been collecting the cargo lights and saw the locker screwed up tight with the cable running under the door. Give us a shout and we got the door open, plugged the light back in. Place looked a hell of a mess and there you were under the cardboard in your wee shelter, wrapped up like a mummy. Still breathing but only just. Samuel lifted you out and wrapped you in his jacket, hugged you tight against him. Give you the kiss of life while the second went up with the others to get the hatches off."

"Well, doesn't Samuel have all the luck!" Michael swept in bearing his fruitcake aloft.

I laughed.

"Ben, darling, we've missed you." He set his cake on the table and gave me a kiss then pulled out a box of matches. "I've iced it and put in seventeen candles because – well, here you are back from the dead so it's a sort of birthday isn't it. And you've got to be at least seventeen 'cause you had that birthday – though honestly, with skin like that you look more like twelve sometimes. Still, maybe that Claire wouldn't agree with me. Baby snatcher, I could scratch her eyes out."

A crowd joined us and the candles were lit. Then Barbara and a few others sang *Happy Birthday* to welcome me back and I blew them out.

A cup of tea and two slices of cake later I said to Charlie, "If you and everyone got me out the locker, how come it was Barbara saved my life?"

"That was a bit later, up on deck. You were still unconscious."

"It was the mate," Barbara said. "He wanted you put in a hot bath to bring your temperature up."

I was puzzled. "What's wrong with that?"

"Are you joking? A hot bath! It could have killed you. And him in charge of the sick bay. I said to him: Are you out of your mind? A couple of blankets, that's all he needs, got to warm him up gradual."

"Mate was livid," Charlie said.

"Well, I know about these things," Barbara said. "Before I come to sea I was a medical orderly. Mate says: Are you questioning my orders on this ship, Tanner? Dead right I am, I said. Threatened to put me on a charge. You can put me on the Charge of the Light Brigade for all I care, I said. The only way Ben's going in a hot bath is over my dead body. Have a look in your first-aid book. You don't know your arse from your elbow."

"I thought he was going to have you arrested," Charlie said.

"So let him arrest me, just as long as he didn't put Ben in a hot bath. And I was right, wasn't I, sweetheart?" He squeezed my hand. "Here you are, back among your friends."

"Alive and kicking," somebody said.

Michael raised his glass. "Here's to Ben, our favourite deck boy."

"Not the mate's favourite deck boy."

"Who cares about the rotten mate. Cheers!"

Then I had to tell my side of the story.

I had already told half a dozen people, including the Wellington police, and later Captain Bell made me write a full account for the ship's log. The facts were as I've described them. Everyone had a theory. I personally thought the senior cadet was responsible although there wasn't a shred of proof. The police interviewed every member of the crew, some more than once, and uncovered a complex web of friendships and hostilities, but were unable to reach a conclusion. Yes, the mate said, he'd instructed the bosun to get the cargo lights up for repair, they were in a terrible state. Yes, the bosun said, he had given me the job, a chance for the young deck boy to earn a bit of overtime. But who had set the trap and shut me in the locker? Who had extinguished the cargo light? Who had dropped the insulation plug in the booby hatch and shut the lid? Who couldn't account for his movements around eight o'clock that evening? Nobody knew anything. Everyone had an alibi. Could it somehow have been one of the wharfies? If there had been more time perhaps they would have uncovered the truth, but loading in Wellington was almost complete and ships sail on. In the absence of any answers from the police, Captain Bell instructed the mate to conduct a shipboard enquiry in the course of which we were interviewed all over again and put our names to statements, but nothing came of it.

"Better phone your parents," Captain Bell told me. "We're responsible for your well-being on board the ship. Can't hush up a thing like this."

"I will, sir, but I can't just yet," I told him. "They're off on a caravanning holiday. I'll write though, and I'll phone as soon as they get back."

"All right, son. But be sure you do."

He was a nice man. "Yes, sir, I will."

After a great deal of thought I had decided to say nothing about the events at the Ascot Hotel. I should have done, of course, but my reasons were these: first, I was pretty sure that if the police were to be informed that a few days earlier I had been assaulted with a knife in a gents' cloakroom, the freezer incident would become a major investigation. Within an hour they would be in touch with the police in Westport, who would contact Joey's parents and discover that far from working on a ship in New Zealand, their son was living with his girlfriend around the corner and stacking shelves in Sainsbury's. My secret would be out. They would discover I was fifteen years old and had run away from school. Charlie and Joey would get into trouble. My dad would be informed. I'd be kicked off the ship and put on the first flight home. I would never see my friends again.

My second reason, assuming I remained aboard, was that I feared it would make a bad situation even worse. If I said nothing now, perhaps the bosun and whoever else was involved would realise I was so badly frightened that I would never report it, and leave me alone. After all, that was what the Filipino, if that was his nationality, had promised: 'You were never in this hotel; you never saw me; you never saw your ugly shipmate. Tell no one and it is finished, you will not be harmed.' Well, someone *had* tried to harm me – though possibly it had nothing to do with the Ascot Hotel at all. They hadn't succeeded but perhaps that was it over now. I certainly hoped so.

That night, asleep in my bunk, I was troubled by nightmares: dreams about freezing, and blindness, and imprisonment, and men with knives, and the mate inviting me into a steaming bath, and the sea thrashing with crocodiles and sharks as I was tipped over the side.

My cries disturbed Charlie. In the middle of the night he called down to wake me.

As I crossed to the washbasin for a glass of water, I was running with sweat.

Ossie Tears his Clothes

THE NIGHTMARES continued and I stopped going out on deck at night, at least by myself, and I tried to stay close to friends. Physically I quickly recovered and two days later joined the second mate's crew at stations as we set sail from the capital.

New Plymouth, our last port of call in New Zealand, was a short journey to the north-west: through the Cook Strait, across the bight and round the Taranaki peninsula. There was a full moon that night. Hour after hour the Cape Egmont lighthouse flashed to starboard. In the darkness between the flashes a ghostly mountain peak, capped with snow and perfect as Mount Fuji, hung in the sky.

A group of us stood watching.

"Mount Egmont," Aaron said. "Extinct volcano. Wouldn't mind climbing that if I can get a day off. Anyone fancy coming?"

We docked at dawn and an hour later the slings and pallets of cargo began swinging aboard: mutton and lamb, butter and cheese, beef, sheepskins and wool. I returned to my peggy routine: tidying the petty officers' cabins, mopping the alleyway, cleaning the crew bar and washroom.

I felt fine but Charlie, for the first time since we'd met back in Westport, was complaining:

"Oohh!" He held his stomach. "Hurts like hell. That curry last night. You OK, are you?"

"Yeah."

"Not like me this. Give us a plate of rusty nails an' I'll digest 'em like baby rice." He made a face. "Think I'm going to be sick."

By evening it had eased off. We went to the pictures with Kevin and a few others, and the following morning his pain was no more than a distant grumbling.

This was the day that Rat'bone, who had resumed his cruel teasing of Ossie, got a taste of his own medicine.

It started at dinner time, six in the evening. Loading would continue for another three hours but for us work was finished for the day. I was standing in the queue, thinking of nothing in particular, when suddenly there was a cry of outrage:

"No! No! Aahh! Take them off!" It was Ossie, serving the meal in his white cap and apron. "You horrible, disgusting – !" He threw over a tray of food. Haddock hit us where we were standing. Next moment he was gone and we were left staring.

"Bloody nutcase!" Aaron was dressed for going ashore. Angrily he examined a grease mark on his shirt. "What was all that about?"

I looked around. The reason was not hard to find. A figure dressed in priest's garb had joined the queue. Beneath one arm he carried Ossie's ouija board. In his other hand was a coffee scoop, held daintily as if offering sugar. He tipped it over and dust filtered to the deck. It was Rat'bone, unshaved and smirking, the abscess faded to a purple scar. Finding Ossie's cabin unlocked, he had gone in and rooted through the drawers. There lay his medication, his books and other personal possessions. Opening the casket containing his mother's ashes, he had dug out a scoopful.

I left the queue and ran down the stewards' alleyway. Ossie had shut himself in his cabin and refused to open the door.

"No, Ben. I'm all right." His voice was choked. "Leave me alone."

I heard rustlings and bumps. "Ossie!"

No reply.

"Come on."

"Go away."

"No." I was scared he might harm himself.

Barbara joined me and rattled the handle.

"Ossie? It's Barbara."

Again, no reply.

"Come on, let us in. Ben and me are worried ... If you don't open up I'm going to kick the door in like the bosun. You'll not be able to lock it again."

There was a long silence. The key turned.

Ossie was unharmed. No knives or cords were in evidence, nor were any pills, though I had seen enough in his drawer to polish off a dozen men. But he was naked, or almost, an enormous pink grub, clutching a handful of ragged white material. More lay on the deck. He had torn his clothes to shreds.

"What are you doing? Oh, Ossie, love!" Barbara, barely up to the big man's shoulder, hugged him tight.

Ossie was frozen then broke down in tears.

"Off you go and get your dinner, Ben," Barbara said. "You'll be all right now, won't you, darling."

Ossie nodded and rubbed snot from under his nose.

"Tell Kevin to put something in the hot plate for me," Barbara said.

I was getting more used to this high emotion but still found it a bit embarrassing. "See you, Ossie." I rested a hand on his arm.

He covered it with his bear-like paw and sniffed soggily. "Thaks, Bed."

Serving was almost finished. I took over from Aaron whose shirt was now spattered with beans and gravy. "All right, is he?" he asked unsympathetically. "Going to live?"

Rat'bone sat alone, ostracised by the rest of the crew and sneering to show he didn't care. He wiped his lips with Ossie's robe and mopped the dew from a can of lager.

And that, I thought, apart from the memory, was that – until about eleven the same evening when I lay reading in my bunk. Charlie lay overhead. The ship was at peace. Feet padded past, voices murmured, a few cabins away someone was playing Elton John. Comfortable sounds.

The peace was shattered by a bellow of rage. I let the book fall. Angry shouts.

I pulled on shorts and ran up the alleyway to see what was happening.

The disturbance came from Rat'bone's cabin. Others were before me. The story went round: he had been ashore for a few beers and returned to find his clothes and possessions heaped on the deck. A tin of condensed milk, a jar of coffee, Rat'bone's own whisky, a six-pack of Foster's and the contents of several ashtrays had been tipped over the top. His bunk, drawers and the bulkheads were similarly fouled. It was a thorough job.

A scrap of paper was being passed round. I read the scrawled message:

> *Rat'bone the sadist!*
> *This is for Ossie Bagot.*
> *He is not responsible.*

"Not responsible?" Rat'bone was murderous. "Who else would do it? I'll kill the bastard! Get out the way."

But Ossie had friends, lots of them. I could think of several people who might have done it: Michael, Barbara, the chef, Kevin, me. I was delighted someone had given Rat'bone a taste of his own medicine.

Savagely he stormed down the alleyway. "Maggot! Maggot!" He beat on Ossie's door. "I know you're in there. Open up!"

There was silence then a high tremulous voice: "Go away. What do you want?"

"I want to break your fat neck, that's what I want. I'm going to murder you. Open this sodding door."

"What's all this noise?" A calm voice at the back made us turn. Captain Bell, in flowery shorts and a jersey, had come up unnoticed. "I go for a stroll round the deck and it's mayhem down here. Like a damned prize fight."

Men stood aside to let him through.

"Now what's going on?"

Rat'bone is Put on a Charge

"It's that mad bloody messman!" Rat'bone was raging. "He should be locked – "

"Not you, Rathbone. And don't swear in my presence." Captain Bell looked around. "Jones, you tell me."

Samuel, in boxer shorts and a white singlet, explained what had happened. I passed Samuel the note and the captain read it.

"And what makes you think Bagot did this," he asked Rat'bone, "when the note specifically states he did not?"

"'Cause he's a nutter!" Rat'bone said. "Who else would be bloody mad enough to pull a stunt like that?"

"I told you, watch your language. And why should Bagot, this night of all nights, suddenly decide to make a heap of your clothes and cover them with condensed milk?"

Rat'bone shrugged.

"You didn't, for example, ransack his cabin before dinner? Dress in his personal clothes to make a fool of him in front of the others?"

"Well ... yeah." Rat'bone was taken aback – how did he know? "But not to make a fool of him, just as a joke like."

"Rathbone, what do you take me for? Do you think I don't know what's going on aboard my own ship?" He tried the handle on Ossie's door then knocked. "Bagot? This is the captain. Open your door."

"That right? An' I'm the Queen of Sheba. Go away!"

The hint of a smile showed on Captain Bell's face. He knocked again. "It *is* the captain, Bagot."

"Leave me alone. I'm telling you, if you kick the door in, I've got a big knife."

"Excuse me, sir." Barbara was having a night aboard. He wore red matador pants and a white angora sweater. Captain Bell, a little surprised but unfazed, stood back. "Ossie, love. You know who this is."

"Barbara?"

"That's right, dear. It is the old man, honestly. He's standing right here beside me."

Something from inside.

"Yes, really. And he's ever so nice, you know that. A real sweetie. So open up, love, and let's get all this cleared up. ... Yes, Michael's here as well. And Ben, and Samuel, a whole lot of people. It's quite safe." He stood aside. "I think he'll come out now."

"A real sweetie?" The captain's twinkle had become a smile. "I'll show you, Tanner."

There was movement in the cabin, the scrape of a key.

Captain Bell turned. "All right, back to your cabins, the lot of you." His eye sought out Michael, the officers' steward. "Goldie, ask the duty officer to step down for a moment please. I'll either be here or in Rathbone's cabin."

We dispersed, though in my case only two doors along to Michael's cabin. Barbara joined me. We listened at the curtain.

"Bagot, just wait inside, I'll speak to you in a moment. Shut the door." We heard the click. "Now, Rathbone. Do you remember what I said after that little incident in Fiji?" There was silence. "Straighten up when I'm talking to you. Off the bulkhead! Do you remember? You do? Well, let me remind you anyway. I told you to leave Bagot alone. He's been ill but he's doing a good job. No complaints from anyone about his work. He's got good friends on this ship and if it wasn't for the likes of you picking on him he'd be fine. Now I don't know if you're stupid, sick or just plain evil, but I'll tell you one last time: leave Bagot alone! Do you understand? Leave him alone and he'll leave you alone, or if he doesn't, let me know and I shall deal with it."

"But he's a loonie. Do you know about his mother's ashes, the way he dresses up, his queer voice an' – ?"

"Yes, I do know. But none of that affects you, not since that voodoo business – which you brought on yourselves as I seem to remember, and I spoke to him then. Now, shall we go and see this mess you're complaining about?" He tapped on Ossie's door. "All right, Bagot, let's have you out now."

The second mate arrived and Michael joined Barbara and me in his cabin. "Dressed like this up there, I nearly died." He wore mascara and lipstick, a shirt knotted across his ribs, chopped-off jeans and flip-flops.

Ossie emerged from his cabin.

Captain Bell spoke more gently. "There's no need to distress yourself, Bagot, but I have to know. The absolute truth mind. Did you go into Rathbone's cabin and make a mess of his clothes?"

"I d-don't know what you're t-talking …"

"Dump them on the floor and pour beer over them."

"Over his c-clothes? I'm sorry, I d-don't understand."

"You lying bastard!" There was a scuffle and raised voices.

"Enough! That's enough!" Captain Bell's voice rose above the rest. "Right, Rathbone, that's it. I'm putting you on a charge. Make a note in the log, Second. I want you in my cabin tomorrow morning, Rathbone, properly dressed, half past nine. Have a shave and get yourself cleaned up, you're a scruff."

"I'll see the union about this!" Rat'bone's voice was a snarl. "Hardly needs open his mouth an' you believe his side of the story."

"If you know what's good for you, you'll be quiet. Speak to me like that again and I'll have you locked up."

Figures emerged into the alleyway, Michael, Barbara and me among them.

"This ship!" Captain Bell shook his head. "I never knew anything like it."

The second mate, in full uniform with his white cap, took Rat'bone's arm.

"Take your 'and off of me!" He jerked his arm away and looked down the alleyway. "Had a good look, have you? Bastards! An' you three," he jabbed a finger, "if it wasn't 'im it was one o' you. Bloody poofs! I'll see you tomorrow."

"Come on!" Tim Nettles urged him along.

"Touch me again an' I'll land you one. You're not allowed to lay a finger on me, officer or no."

"I am when you're on a charge. And when I write it up I'll add these little threats. Right now you're on a loser, Rathbone, so do yourself a favour. The rest of you," he looked back, "into your cabins. Now."

And that was it. We never discovered who had carried out that act of revenge on Ossie's behalf. Although his friends in the catering department were the most likely, my guess is that it was Smoky, who couldn't stand Rat'bone. Somewhere between his scraggy exterior and his alcohol and nicotine-fuelled interior, Smoky Crisp was one of the kindest men on the ship. There was a recklessness about him, something about the way he said, "Me? Why pick on me?" that marked him out as my chief suspect.

But soon, dramatic as these events had been, they were swallowed up in the greater drama that was to follow.

Mount Egmont

But not just yet.

Two days after the events I've just described, there was a local holiday. The mate saw it as a chance to get some much-needed maintenance work done, but Captain Bell announced that we were to have the day off too.

Aaron got a group of us together to climb Mount Egmont, the beautiful snow-capped volcano which rose from the surrounding plain.

"I've been reading up about it." He produced a leaflet. "I thought it was extinct but it's not, blows off every few hundred years. Come on, it'll be great. Bit of bad luck we get our arses singed tomorrow. Ben can go first, just in case."

Brian, who was about the same age as my dad, hired a minibus. We planned to take it as far as a lodge, four thousand feet up a twisting track through rhododendron forests, and climb the remainder of the way.

Charlie was looking forward to it but his bellyache had returned. "I shouldn't have had that pizza," he said as we came back from town the same evening. "Giving me gyp."

He spent a disturbed night and in the morning was no better. "Sorry, Ben, mate. Don't want to let you down. But there's absolutely no – aahh! – no way I'd be able to climb a mountain today. Sorry, I think I'm going to be – " He lurched towards the washroom but didn't make it and threw up in the alleyway. I said I would clear it up but he wouldn't let me.

"Will you be OK?"

"Yeah." He mopped his mouth with a wrist. "I'll go to the sick bay. Mate'll give me something."

I was disappointed but Kevin joined us at the last minute, so in the end there were six of us: Brian, Aaron, Philip, who met us round the corner, Kevin, Michael and me. I was surprised that Michael wanted to come.

"I didn't think it would be your sort of thing."

"Just because I'm gay doesn't mean I'm a limp-wristed Mary-Ann," he said reprovingly, and I remembered how he had attacked the brawny Ryland in the dock office.

It was a great day. At half past nine we reached the lodge, a large wooden chalet, and ate a packed breakfast. Then, tightening laces and in high spirits, we set off climbing. It was a beautiful morning, the summer sun high in the north-east, but not too hot for there was a steady sea-breeze and we were high above the surrounding plain. Far above us the twin peaks were white with snow.

It was a hard slog. For two hours we struggled uphill. Aaron, to my surprise, was the first to drop out.

"Too many women," Michael said sagely. "That's your trouble. Sapped your strength."

"You're just jealous." He sat on the scree. "It's my feet."

I wore my heavy work shoes but Aaron had borrowed boots. He unlaced one and tugged it off. An enormous blister covered his heel. There was a smaller, vicious-looking one on the knuckle of his big toe. The nail of his little toe was bleeding. He turned to his second foot and looked up at the summit. We were barely halfway. "Damn," he said, "and I was looking forward to it. I'll go back to the chalet, wait for you there."

"Will it be open?"

"Yeah, opens at eleven."

"I'll go with him" Kevin had been wheezing from the start. Climbing Mount Egmont was harder than he had expected. "Too much fags and booze."

"You said it." Michael hooked his thumbs under the straps of his borrowed rucksack.

"You need talk. Never see you without a gin in one hand an' a fag in the other."

"Ah, but gin's mother's milk to me. And I smoke," he dropped his voice, "Macho Fags, made from the dung of mountain lions. Macho Fags, for macho men!"

"Go on, you great fairy," Kevin said.

We set off again, leaving Kevin and Aaron to make their way back down.

I thought I wasn't going to reach the top myself. The grey slopes of volcanic rock, sparse with vegetation, went up and up, up and up and up. My knees strained, my muscles ached. Philip halted, panting, to wait for me. Michael, who was in the lead and by all the rules should have been back with Kevin, saw that I was struggling and sat on a rock until we caught up with him. He unwrapped a few squares of chocolate and passed them across.

At last, as the air grew colder and the glacier that lies between the peaks came close, I realised I was going to make it. My legs found new energy. We negotiated the ice. Drank from streams of crystal water. Climbed the topmost rocks. And at length stood upon the snowy summit.

I felt terrific. Eight thousand, two hundred and sixty feet, nearly twice the height of Ben Nevis. Far off to the east, halfway across North Island, other snow-capped volcanoes rose from the New Zealand plain. Below us lay the grey volcanic scree, the forest of rhododendrons, miles of green farmland, and finally the patched Tasman Sea, stretching for ever to a misty horizon.

The wind blew more strongly on the summit. It was bitterly cold. For fifteen minutes we explored and took photographs, then started the long descent.

By the time we reached the lodge my knees had turned to rubber. We fished out money and collapsed into chairs while Michael, still the freshest of us all, bought drinks and Danish pastries.

Kevin, in the hours he had been waiting, had drunk a beer too many and was telling a middle-aged Kiwi couple how effing marvellous it was to live in Birmingham. Aaron was nowhere to be seen. Once we had recovered a little we went searching and found him on a broken settee in the back premises where an off-duty waitress was dropping morsels of caramel shortbread into his open mouth.

So, in our different ways, it was a successful day all round.

By the time we reached the ship dinner was over. Charlie said he was feeling better although he didn't look too good. He had been sick again and spent most of the morning in his bunk feeling rotten. A violent attack of diarrhoea seemed to have settled him.

"What did the mate say?"

"He didn't have much time, there were two others as well as me. Thought I'd got a touch of food poisoning or maybe some stomach infection. Just asked a couple of questions an' give me some antibiotics and a bottle of pink stuff. Said to go back tomorrow if it's not any better. Comes and goes, it's been hanging around for days." He winced and sat up. "Anyway, enough of that. What about you?"

So I told him about the mountain.

After a long shower and comparison of blisters, a few of us limped ashore for a curry. Charlie wouldn't come, not even for a coffee or some chips, although he hadn't eaten all day. "Maybe tomorrow. Give the old guts a chance to settle down. Couple of spoonfuls of that pink jollop and an early night."

"Like me to stay?"

"Don't be daft," he said, but his eyes were puffy and I could see he was still in quite a bit of pain "Get my head down, see if I can't sleep it off."

The others were waiting at the gangway, so off I went.

Emergency

It was after ten when we returned, four weary sailors trailing up the quay.

At once I looked in on Charlie. He muttered in his sleep and his pillow was wet with perspiration. His forehead radiated heat.

I went to fetch Barbara, who knew a lot more about sickness than I did.

He turned down the bedclothes. "Got a touch of fever," he said.

"He's been in terrible pain."

"Look at him," said Michael who had come with us. "Bless him."

"Never mind all that," I said, "what are we going to do?"

"Change his sheets anyway," said Barbara. "Get him out of those wet clothes."

Michael, who had keys to the linen store, hurried away.

"Charlie, love. Charlie! It's Barbara." He shook his shoulder gently. "Come on, sweetheart, wake up. We need to get you changed."

Slowly Charlie came round. It hurt to clamber down. Dizzily he stripped off his T-shirt and boxer shorts. I fetched a fresh set from the drawer while Barbara handed him a towel to rub himself dry and Michael changed the sheets. Though it was warm, Charlie began to shiver. He pulled on his clean underwear but was unable to climb back to the top bunk where he had slept all trip. There was a ladder but he never used it and we'd put it away in storage.

"Take mine," I said.

Without a word he crawled into the bottom bunk and collapsed on his back, waiting for the pain to ease.

I was scared.

Barbara covered his legs with the sheet. "Where exactly does it hurt?"

Charlie gestured to the bottom of his belly.

"Right hand side?" Barbara glanced at Michael. "Mate checked for appendicitis, I suppose."

Charlie didn't seem to care. "Just asked some questions and give me the medicine." His eyes were closing.

"This is Barbara, love, all right? Just tell me if it's sore." Like a doctor, he eased down the waist of Charlie's shorts and rested two fingers on his skin. Gently he pressed. Charlie didn't stir. He moved his fingers and pressed again.

"Aahhh! Aahhh!" Charlie tried to stifle his cry.

"All right, love. All right. That's it. All over. You can go to sleep now." He pulled the sheet to Charlie's chin.

"Hard as a rock," he said. "Clearest case of appendicitis you'll ever see. Every symptom and now this. He needs to get to hospital."

"Who'll tell the mate?" I shrank from another tongue-lashing. "Will you come with me?"

"You stay here with Charlie," Barbara said. "I'll go."

"I'll come with you," Michael said.

They told me what happened. The mate came to his door wearing a silk Paisley dressing-gown, and was far from pleased to be disturbed at that time of night. "Who says he's got appendicitis?"

"Me," Barbara said.

"And you know, do you?"

"I should do, I've seen enough."

"He used to be a hospital orderly," Michael explained.

"So I believe, but not a doctor." He turned to Barbara. "Then you were a steward, if I remember correctly. Blotted your copybook there and now you're a greaser. And I'm the mate. I've seen Sunderland, I've given him a course of antibiotics. He'll live until the morning. If he gets any worse, come and see me again. In the meantime," he disappeared into the cabin and they saw Trish, a towel round her hair, sitting with a magazine. She waggled her fingers and made a rueful face. The mate returned and tipped four tablets into Barbara's palm. "Paracetamol. Give him a couple now. He can take the others if he needs them."

"But he's really quite – "

The mate stepped back. "Goodnight." The curtain closed behind him.

"He should be in hospital," Barbara said again as they returned to the cabin. "All right, we'll give him the pills. They'll help the pain, anyway, help him to sleep. But if he gets any worse we're phoning for an ambulance."

Charlie seemed to settle down after that and when I climbed into the top bunk some time before twelve, he was sleeping quietly. I thought I might lie awake but after spending most of the day on the slopes of Mount Egmont, I was so tired I crashed out the minute my head hit the pillow.

"Ben! Ben!" A voice reached me in the deepest fathoms of sleep. A hand was shaking me by the shoulder. I struggled awake.

The cabin was dark but it was Charlie. I heard him being sick.

I switched on the bunk light and jumped down, dazed with sleep and trying to avoid the mess.

"It hurts!" He was doubled up with pain. "I can't stand it."

"OK, Charlie. OK! Hang on!" I ran from the cabin and up through the ship. A shore telephone was hooked up by the gangway. I snatched the receiver and rang the operator.

"Emergency! Emergency!"

She put me straight through.

"Ambulance! Down at the docks. *Pacific Trader.* Hurry!"

"What berth, caller?"

"Berth? I don't – "

"Five." Steve Petersen was night watchman.

"Five," I almost shouted. "Berth five."

"The ambulance will be with you right away. What's your name, caller?"

"Eh? Oh, Benjamin Thomson."

"Is that Thompson with a 'p', caller?"

"What?" I realised what I had said and glanced at Steve. "Sorry, Joseph Bennett. I wasn't thinking. My name's Joseph Bennett."

"And what's the problem, Mr Bennett?"

"Charlie. Charles Sunderland. He's got appendicitis. He's in terrible pain. Being sick. Everything. Hurry!"

"Leave directions at the gangway, Mr Bennett, and return to the patient. The ambulance is on its way."

"Could you fetch Barbara?" I clattered down the receiver and turned to Steve. "He knows all about it."

"Barbara? Yeah, sure. Charlie bad, is he?"

"Yes, very."

"You smell of sick."

I realised my bare foot felt slippery and looked down. My stomach gave a lurch. "It'll wash off."

"Poor Charlie." Steve was a changed man. "Anything else I can do?"

I hesitated. "Would you tell the mate? After the ambulance gets here."

"Shouldn't I tell him straight away?" He pushed back his blond hair.

"He'll be furious. Told us to leave it till the morning. Got to go."

I couldn't stand the sick on my foot and rinsed it in the shower then hurried back to the cabin. To my astonishment Charlie was calm and sitting on the day bed.

"It's gone."

"What?"

"Yeah, hurt like hell, I never felt anything like it. Then suddenly, I don't know, it was like something shifted inside and the pain just sort of ebbed away."

"Completely gone?"

"No, it's still sore, like somebody give me a kick in the guts, but not like before."

"I phoned for an ambulance." I began to wonder if I'd done the right thing.

"Maybe it was some sort of blockage. Perhaps that's it away now." He shut his eyes. "I do feel a bit queer though."

He certainly didn't look well.

Barbara joined us. He had grabbed the first garment that came to hand, a crumpled boiler suit. "Here, out the way." Most of the sick was on the rug. He rolled it up and mopped the deck with a wet towel. "Wish I had a quid for every time I've done that." He dumped them in the alleyway and rinsed his hands.

"He says the pain's – "

"He can tell me himself. Come on, love. Got another T-shirt and pants?"

Soon Charlie looked more comfortable and a few minutes later a doctor arrived with two paramedics.

The doctor was young. "Smart ship you've got here." He smiled to put us at ease. "Now, what's the problem?"

We told him.

"Right." He looked down at Charlie. "How you feeling, mate? Bit rough, eh?" He felt his brow, looked into his eyes. "Now, let's see what the problem is." He made Charlie lie on the day bed and eased down the waist of his boxers. Gently he probed his belly. "There?"

"Yeah. Ow!"

The doctor looked anxious. "Look, mate, afraid I'm going to have to hurt you a bit more. Little poke around. Only take a minute."

He was good. Stubby fingers moved over Charlie's brown skin.

Charlie winced. Barbara and I stood watching.

The doctor was soon finished. He pulled up Charlie's shorts and popped a thermometer into his mouth. "Which of you rang the ambulance?"

"Me. I share a cabin with him. I didn't know what to do. I hope – "

The mate burst through the curtain. "Bennett! Just who the hell do you think you are, phoning the ambulance without consulting me? I told you I'd see Sunderland first thing in the morning." He turned to the doctor and held out a hand. "I'm the mate. I'm sorry, this bloody deck boy's been a pain in the – well, right from the start of the trip. He had no right to call you out without my permission."

"Just as well he did, it seems to me. You've got a sick boy here, Mr Mate. I'm taking him right into hospital."

"Into hospital. Are you sure?"

"Let me put it this way. You're the mate and I'm the doctor. Yes, I'm sure. He should have been there days ago. Acute appendicitis and now it's burst. Get him into the operating theatre soon as we get there. Leave it till the morning would *not* be a good idea."

The mate was silenced.

"Who's in charge of the sick boy here?"

"I am."

"As in medical?"

"Yes."

The doctor had taken a strong dislike to the mate. "Well, I don't want to speak out of turn but it seems to me there's one or two things you might brush up on."

The mate flushed darkly.

"OK, Tommy." The doctor spoke to a middle-aged paramedic. "I'll give him a shot then we'll take him in." He smiled down at Charlie. "You'll be all right, mate. Have you chasing the sheilas round the ward in no time."

He opened his bag and prepared the hypodermic.

PART SIX

HOMEWARD BOUND

I Receive a Letter

THEY OPERATED in the early hours of the morning and that evening I went to the hospital with Aaron. We found Charlie in a single ward. A drip led into his arm and two tubes emerged from the sheet that covered his lower half. Watery red stuff slithered down one. He was sleeping, his face yellow. Every so often some little stab made his forehead twitch. I thought he looked terrible.

"No, he's fine." A motherly nurse smiled. "That's just the after-effects of the op. Handsome young chap. The nurses'll enjoy nursing him back to health. Not just the young ones either. Wouldn't mind a toy boy like him myself."

"Is he going to be OK?" I asked. "It's serious when an appendix bursts, isn't it?"

"It certainly is, but Mr Dawkins is an excellent surgeon and he's a strong young man. No need to worry, your friend will come through fine."

She cheered us up and we had a beer on the way back to the ship. I was having less trouble getting served because my whiskers were growing thicker and three months on deck had given me the look of a regular young seaman. But I was worried. Charlie had been my guide from the start. In fact the whole trip had been his idea. I had done the deck boy's work but that was the easy bit. Without Charlie in the cabin to keep me right, I wondered how I would get on.

I didn't get a chance to see him again because loading was almost complete and we set sail for home the next day. Aaron found a card and got it signed, every corner crammed with messages, kisses in pink and gold from some, more manly 'Miss you mate', 'See you in Singapore' and 'Give the nurses one from me' from the rest.

Charlie was seventeen and I wondered if his mother had been told about the operation. I held back from asking the mate but spotting Captain Bell on deck, I went across. Yes, he told me, he had spoken to Mrs Sunderland on the phone, a nice woman. When Charlie recovered he would be flown back to the UK. Possibly, if he recovered in time, he might rejoin us in Singapore or Sri Lanka when we called there on the way home. He hoped so because he didn't want to lose such a likable young seaman and there was no chance of finding a replacement at a day's notice.

Charlie and I had talked several times since he first mentioned it about the possibility of staying with his mum and dad when the trip was over. On the day we sailed I received an unexpected letter:

Dear Ben,

I hope all is going well and you are enjoying the trip!!! Charlie has written and told me the trick you played, taking Joey Bennett's place on the ship. You are two very naughty and unthinking boys. What your poor dad must have suffered I can't imagine. I have not told him – yet. But once you are well and truly on the way home I shall certainly do so. Charlie tells me you settled well into life on board and have had no trouble with the work. I am not surprised, you seemed a very sensible lad the days you were staying here. Fourteen years old, I can't believe it! I wondered how I'd seen Joey's name in the papers when he should have been at sea, scoring all those goals for Westport Juniors.

Anyway, as regards you coming to live with Dad and me when you come back. It all depends on your dad, of course, and whether the headmaster at Westport Comprehensive can find you a place. If the answer to both of these things is yes, and you would like to come here, we'd both be delighted. The house is far too big for just the two of us and it would be lovely to have some young life about the place again.

I have written to Charlie telling him that I am very cross with him – not that it will make any difference. Boys will be boys and I suppose you can't change human nature. He's a good lad at heart.

Looking forward to seeing you both when you come back safe and sound.

With love,
Meg Sunderland

At smoko I wrote to Charlie telling him how great his mum was and put the note with his belongings when they were taken away to the hospital. I wanted to get in to see him at lunchtime but we weren't allowed ashore. Michael phoned from the gangway instead. A few of us gathered round to listen:

"Hello? Can I speak to Charlie Sunderland, please ... Ward 14 ... Thanks ... Hello? ... Yes, Charlie Sunderland ... He's sleeping? ... But he's OK yes? ... Who am I speaking to? ... Sister Mackay? Well will you give him a message? ... His friends on the ship ... Yes, sailing this afternoon. But listen, you're to tell him we all love him madly and lots of hugs and kisses ... Pardon? ... This is Michael ... You'll kiss him for us? Lucky old you! ... Ooh, cheeky! ... And tell him if he doesn't come and join us in Singapore we're all going to kill ourselves ... Well come down and find out for yourself ... I've got a friend here beside me, he's very keen on nurses ... Ask him about Lyttelton ... What happened? If I told you the half of it the receiver would melt ... Next trip? I'll tell him ... Thanks, you're a pal ... Byeee!"

We sailed at seven in the evening, straight out into the Tasman Sea. Our route led north-west through the Coral Sea and past the Great Barrier Reef; through the Torres Strait between Papua New Guinea and Cape York at the north-east tip of Australia; then west by Borneo and the myriad islands of Indonesia to Singapore.

The summit of Mount Egmont, lit by the setting sun, sank behind us. The stars appeared. I left some others on deck and went down to see Aaron.

"Would it be OK if I moved in with you? After what happened down there in the freezer locker and everything."

"Of course. I'll just shift – " Aaron used the spare bunk as a dump.

"I don't want to be next door by myself."

"Me neither, if that happened to me."

"You can keep your extra stuff in there. There's an empty locker."

"Don't worry." He slotted a Dylan tape into his player. "I'll enjoy the company."

I had never bought the cassette player I wanted myself, even though it was top of my list of priorities. That day in Wellington the events at the Ascot Hotel put it right out of my mind. And afterwards, even though I had plenty of money, somehow I'd never got round to it. People told me it would be cheaper in Singapore anyway. In the meantime Aaron let me use his, and in the light of what happened not many days later, it made little difference

I took the bottom bunk again. Aaron slept in the top, where he could see the photos of his girlfriends on the bulkhead. He'd stuck them up for the voyage home. As he told me, it wouldn't have been a good idea to let them see the competition when we were in port. I counted, there were eleven.

I'd only had one and hadn't got over it yet.

After six weeks on the coast the ship was filthy. The bosun put us to work sweeping up the debris, hosing down, holystoning the decks, suji-ing the paintwork, polishing the brass, and by the end of our second day at sea all was shipshape again. Trish returned to her sunbathing on the monkey island. The pool was rigged on the port side of the afterdeck. As we sailed north into the tropics the sun climbed higher, the days grew hotter. Except that we were heading home and the cargo space was now a series of giant refrigerators, it was little different from the voyage out.

Ossie, too, settled into his routine. Following the incident with Rat'bone, he had shredded all his white clothes and now, except when he was at work, dressed head to foot in black: black shirt, black trousers, black cassock and a black stole when he went aft for the ceremony of scattering his mother's ashes – how ever much remained. As Michael observed, there seemed an awful lot of her. With a needle and ink from a squashed ballpoint he tattooed the Devil's mark, 6-6-6, on his forearm. "It's always been my number," he explained in that strange high voice. "My mother was a sixth child, I was born on the sixth of June, I weighed six pounds and we lived at number six Station Terrace. It should be 6-6-6-6-6 really."

It took no time for Rat'bone to ignore the captain's warning. Within days he was back to his tricks, new tricks, harder to pin down. It was as if he was determined to exact revenge for the turmoil in his cabin and drive poor Ossie to a breakdown – or worse. Every mealtime, every time they passed in the alleyway, there was something: a wink, a hand on his knife, a blown kiss, fingers on his stubbly throat, a hanging gesture, a swimming movement, a handful of pills into his mouth, the face of a simpering madman. When he collected his food he smiled with exaggerated politeness: "Thank you very much, that looks delicious." Ossie had no defence. It got beneath his skin as surely as a burrowing worm.

The bosun joined in the game. So, like a parrot, did the senior cadet. Steroid Steve Petersen, who had rescued me from the thermal pool and shown several little kindnesses since, seemed to have cut himself off from them.

Their mockery, although cruelty is a better word, started in New Plymouth and got worse after we sailed. Ossie was trapped. There was no escape. If the doctors he attended in New Zealand had not renewed his supply of medication for the voyage home – that drawer half full of pills, bottles, inhalers and the rest – he might not have lasted as long as he did.

Then one evening, when we were three days out, the unthinkable happened.

A Crash of Water

ACTUALLY TWO things happened that evening. The first might easily have caused the death of three people. The second, which involved Ossie, occurred later, when everyone except the watch was in bed and the ship was quiet.

There was to be a film on deck and the engineers had rigged the screen by number four hatch. Some of us thought it would be good to have a swim then shower off and take a drink and some biscuits to the hatch cover for the show. I pulled on the swimming trunks I'd bought in Wellington and joined Kevin and Aaron in the swashing water. As I arrived they sprayed me with the gushing deck hose. I yelled and jumped on them from the board. Daylight was fading. It was great fun, diving and splashing, floating on my back to look up at the first stars and the towering mainmast with its navigation light cutting slow arcs across the sky.

What happened then was not an accident. I think I realised that, even amid the turmoil. Anyway, one second we were laughing in the pool, next second the seaward side of the pool collapsed and we were swept away in a forty-ton tidal wave that crashed through the ship's rails and down into the ocean.

At that moment, by good luck, I was clinging to the pool's inboard edge. As the water surged away I tried to hold on but the torrent was too strong and my grip was broken. That split second may have saved my life. My hip and then my head hit something hard, my back wrenched, my shoulder twisted.

Then it was over. Dazed and battered, I lay jammed in a corner between one of the mainmast stays and a side plate where the rails began.

What of the others? I looked along the brimming scupper. Aaron was groaning. Where was Kevin? The ocean sped past beneath.

"Where's Kevin?" I dragged myself to my knees. "Kevin!"

"Give us a hand." The voice was muffled.

"Where are you?"

"Under here." Planks and canvas were jammed against the rail. I hauled them back. Kevin was trapped beneath. One leg and half his body hung in space. The other leg and both arms were clamped around the rails. He struggled inboard. I grabbed the back of his swim shorts and heaved. "Ow! Hey, careful!"

Aaron sat by the rail, nursing his arm. One look was enough. I felt sick. His left forearm had a kink in the middle.

Others were arriving. "Bloody hell! ... You two OK? ... Oh, man, Aaron! Here, come away from the rail."

We sat on the hatch cover. I was bruised and bleeding from a small cut in my scalp. Kevin, apart from a bad fright which he seemed determined not to admit, was unhurt. Aaron needed treatment, but when the mate arrived he swore at him: "Don't you touch me! Charlie could have died! Eff off!"

Since he was in such pain there was nothing the mate could do.

Captain Bell and his wife, Heidi-hi as she was known among the crew, came to see us. "Bit of a knock, son?" he said kindly to Aaron. "Here, let my wife look at it."

She was thick-waisted, motherly, her teeth worn stumpy. "Hello." She smiled. "I vas nurse. Long years ago but broken arms I know."

Aaron allowed her to examine him.

"Oohh!" She drew in her breath. "Poor you. Look sore."

"It is a bit."

"Sure." She thought. "I tell you vhat ve do. My husband give you jab, ja? Then ve go inside, have a cup of tea, rest your arm on a table. Ve see it better there."

Captain Bell gave Aaron a big shot of morphine and I accompanied them to the messroom. Michael, Barbara and a couple of others were already there. Though the break was nasty it was clean, a single fracture of the two bones in his forearm. As Heidi moved the limb gently and I heard the ends of bone grate, I almost needed treatment myself.

"Ja, I set that no trouble. You hear?"

Aaron was half out of it with the drug. He nodded.

"Ve go the sick bay."

"I used to work in a hospital." Barbara wore shorts and a headscarf like a pirate. "Often give a hand with fractures. Mind if I come along?"

"Yeah, I want him to come." Aaron blinked sleepily. "Barbara's my mate. Knows what it's all about."

"Barbara?" She looked at her husband.

He smiled. "Come along if he wants you, Tanner. You can lend a hand."

"Ja, need strong man to pull."

They rose.

"Will he be all right?"

"Don't vorry." Heidi patted my shoulder. "Your friend, he vill be fine. Ve make him like new. Better."

"Will he be back tonight?"

"No, tonight ve keep him in sick bay. Tomorrow he back vith you in cabin. I think so."

They left. I imagined what lay ahead for Aaron: more injections, Barbara pulling on the broken arm, the ends of bone grinding together, the splints and plaster. What if it wasn't straight?

"They'll check him out in Singapore," Michael said. "Give him an x-ray. If it's not right they'll fix it there."

Not an hour had passed since the crash and again I felt the water carry me off and crush me against the rail. Then I remembered the igloo and my struggle in the freezer locker. Who could hate me so much – and why? What might they do next? With Charlie in hospital and Aaron in the sick bay, I was going to be alone again.

"Can I ask you a favour?" I said to Michael. "Will you sleep in our cabin tonight?"

"I thought you were never going to ask," he said. "Which cabin is that? Do I get to sleep in the bunk of the divine Charlie? Or hunky Aaron?"

"Whichever you want. It's just with everything that's happened – "

"Oh, come on, Ben," he said more practically, "this is Michael, you don't have to explain. Of course I will. I was going to suggest it anyway."

The tea had gone cold. He made a pot of coffee and raided the galley for some gingerbread.

Afterwards I went to the sick bay but they were still busy so I joined Smoky on deck. The film had been cancelled. He was sitting on number four hatch with a tumbler that looked suspiciously like juice.

"On the wagon," he explained. "Half vodka, half orange juice, that thick stuff they give to kids."

I looked down at the ruined swimming pool.

"Dangerous stuff, water." He sipped his drink, fag in the same hand.

Where had I seen that gesture recently?

"You were lucky. The lot of you, even Aaron."

"Guess so." I raised my eyes to the black sea. "Could be out there somewhere."

"Not an accident, you know."

"There's a surprise," I said.

He looked at me. "You mean after the freezer locker and everything?"

I shrugged.

"Bloody hell! Anyway, I spoke to Chippy. Some of the bolts were missing." He rested an elbow on his knee. "Mate asked him if they couldn't have worked loose. Chippy says no, he put it up same as always. Checked it over. No way it could have just collapsed."

"Nope."

"Any idea who it might have been?"

"Somebody who didn't care if three people went over the side."

"Who's that then?"

"One or two people spring to mind. You tell me."

He blew out his cheeks. "Turning into a bit of a hairy trip."

"You could say."

A movement at the stern caught my eye. "Who's that?"

"Who d'you think?"

It was Ossie, all in black, his head a pale blob in the shadows. As I stared, the wind blew his cassock. He stood at the rail and raised his arms like a prophet. He may have been praying, he probably was, but I heard nothing. Nor did I see the swirl of dust as he tossed a measure of his mother's remains into the Coral Sea.

In a couple of minutes his small act of commitment was over.

"Hello there, Ben. Smoky." He waved as he reached the crew deck but didn't stop.

"Poor bugger," Smoky said. "Carrying her ashes round like that."

"You want to see his cabin."

"Yeah, I heard." He watched him go. "Not keen on all that supernatural stuff. Gives me the creeps."

"Surprised he goes wandering down there in the dark though," I said. "Lenny Rat'bone hating him the way he does."

"Never thought of that."

"Him and the others. The foul foursome, Michael calls them."

"Who's that then?"

"You know, Lenny, bosun, Steve Petersen, senior cadet."

Smoky considered. "Steve's all right."

"Yeah, he's changed."

"Started out in the wrong company, that's all. Not too bright upstairs."

"I gathered that. All brawn and no – "

"He reads the *Dandy*, for God's sake. Asked me the other day if there really was a planet Krypton. Did I think Marilyn Monroe was being kept frozen somewhere and was going to make a comeback?" He picked a shred of tobacco from his tongue. "You're right about the others though. Bad lot. Got a feeling they're up to something."

After a while he went in to feed Dolores a fat cockroach and I made my way to the bar seeking company. For an hour I played draughts and dominoes then returned to the cabin to wait for Michael.

He had promised to come about nine and arrived right on time. Michael liked to make an impression and tonight was too good an opportunity to miss. He arrived looking like a schoolboy fresh from the shower, wearing blue-striped pyjamas, his blond hair parted on the left and brushed across.

"Never fear, Michael's here," he cried as he burst through the curtain and set down a tray containing thick wedges of cherry cake and two mugs of cocoa. "What an adventure! It's like being on holiday. I thought we'd have a dorm feast."

I pulled up my chair. "Looks good."

"Kenny's on the wagon, he made it specially. Only the best for my little brother."

As ever, Michael rose to the occasion and did his best to cheer me up, but the collapse of the pool had affected me more than I realised. My eyes were closing and after we'd played a couple of tapes and chatted for a while I was ready for bed. Michael took Aaron's bunk.

"Ben?" His voice drifted down.

"Yeah?"

"It's nice up here." Then a minute later, "Got a lot of girlfriends, hasn't he?"

"Lucky devil." I guessed he was looking at the photos. "Ten more than me."

"Pooh, what's ten between friends. Once you get into your stride you're going to leave him standing."

"I hope so."

"I'm telling you, trust Michael." He switched off his reading light and I heard him settling down. "I wonder how Charlie and Aaron are getting on." There was silence. "You don't think we're going to be visited by some mad, axe-wielding AB do you?"

I smiled. "I hope not."

"Me too." He thought for a moment. "Do you think I should have fetched along one of the galley knives?"

Michael in his schoolboy pyjamas brandishing a bloody butcher's knife! "I guess we'll just have to take a chance."

We fell silent again. No sounds but the creaks of the ship and soothing throb of the engines.

I turned on my side and was on the verge of sleep when a high-pitched cry rang through the accommodation and startled me wide awake again. I sat up. Michael, unused to double bunks, cracked his head on the ceiling.

"What's that?"

"No!" The cry came again. "No-o-o-o!"

"It's Ossie." We sprang to the deck and ran up the alleyway.

The Missing Pills

His cabin was a blaze of light. Candles everywhere. The reek of incense.

Ossie himself, limp as a puppet and ugly with sobs, slumped against his locker. Barbara was there before us. Luigi and one or two others hurried up the alleyway.

"What's happened?" Michael said.

Ossie turned swollen, frightened eyes towards him. "My pills have gone," he said.

For a second I almost laughed. All this drama over a few pills.

But Michael wasn't laughing. "Are you sure?"

Ossie gestured to an open drawer. One end was empty. "Must have been when I was down with mum's ashes."

An astringent dispensary smell clung to the wood. I remembered the array of boxes and bottles I had seen. And Ossie's sickness: his black clothes, the panic attacks, the river in Fiji, his acts of desperation.

"You didn't move them somewhere else?" Michael said.

"No."

"Have you searched?"

"Yes."

Barbara slipped a comforting arm around his waist.

Ossie whispered, "What if we don't get them back?"

"We will, love. We will."

"But if we don't? What's going to happen to me? You can't just stop taking them, the doctors said. There's withdrawal symptoms."

"Yes, I know, Ossie. But you're going to be all right, will you listen to me. Don't get yourself upset. You've got Michael and me."

"And'a Luigi."

"That's right, and Luigi. And Ben, and oh, lots of people."

"Maybe they'll have something in the sick bay," I said. "Just till we get to Singapore. It's only a week."

"I shouldn't think so." Ossie wiped his eyes: pale eyes, pumpkin head, little mouth, curls shorn to a stubble. "Ships don't cater for nutcases. Athlete's foot but not nutcases."

"Stop it, Ossie!" Michael spoke sharply. "We're all doing our best, you've got to try. So for a start tell us exactly – "

A face caught my eye. Rat'bone and the senior cadet were among the crowd that had gathered in the alleyway. Both were grinning. When they saw they had been observed they came forward.

"You bastards!" Luigi said.

The grins broadened. "That's not very nice," Tony said.

"Heard the voices, come to see what's up."

"As if you didn't know," Michael said. "Where are they?"

"Oh, dear!" Tony had been drinking. "Somebody lost something?"

"Mebbe we can help you look."

"What is it, dear, your new lipstick?"

"Don't tell me." Rat'bone raised his skinny hand. "It's the Maggot, he's lost his marbles."

Tony laughed too loudly.

"Look at them," Rat'bone said. "What a load of rubbish. Makes you ashamed to be a British seaman."

"You watch your mouth," Luigi said. "I smash your face in."

"I'll ask you again," Michael said. "His pills, what have you done with them?"

"Pills? What pills?" Rat'bone bared his awful teeth. "I know about clothes heaped on cabin floors, covered in muck. Don't know nothing about no pills."

"I know a bit." Tony's red lips shone. "Pills got to be washed down with water."

"Shut up, you fool," Rat'bone said.

But Tony was too drunk to listen. "Lots of water round a ship." He made a bowling action. "Splash! Plop-plop!"

"What!" Michael exploded.

"His old mum's down there somewhere, in't she?" He grinned. "Old cow was prob'ly as mad as he is. Who knows, might do her a bit o' good."

There was a shocked silence then Ossie gave a cry of outrage and hurled himself through the doorway. Although he was one of life's victims with a weak head and big soft body, Ossie was enormously strong. Left alone he might have killed the skinny Rat'bone, but it was two to one and there were other men there. Punching and clawing and kicking, Ossie fought like a wildcat. Rat'bone quailed before the onslaught until Tony, coming up behind, delivered one, two, three vicious blows to Ossie's neck and kidneys. He went down, a huddled figure in black. There was just time for both to put the boot in, then Michael and Luigi were upon them. Shouting and swearing, they took to their heels. I snatched up the first weapon I could find, a heavy coat hanger, and followed.

No one knew that Captain Bell and his wife were in the sick bay, visiting Aaron before settling down for the night. The captain stepped out into the alleyway and stopped us in our tracks:

"In heaven's name, what is happening? The whole ship's turning into a donnybrook. You," he addressed Luigi, "take your hands off his throat. Fanshott-Williams, what are you doing down here? You've been drinking. I'll speak to you later. Right," he surveyed us in our various attire. "Goldie, start with you. You're a sensible chap, most of the time anyway." Michael rolled his eyes. "What's all this about?"

So we all, except Tony, told our stories.

Rat'bone, who couldn't possibly admit to stealing the pills, denied all knowledge of them. "Accused us, so we was just stringing 'em along like," he said. "Poor old Ossie, he needs them pills. Stop him goin' doolally. Might kid him a bit sometimes, but wouldn't touch his pills. No way."

"My God!" The captain was angry. "It's not a week since I put you on a charge, told you to steer clear of him."

"I know, sir." Rat'bone tried to fawn. "But this wasn't nothin' nasty, we was just – "

"Don't give me that." Captain Bell was having none of it. "I know your type. Lies and bloody insubordination, that's what it is. Half past nine, my cabin – again! And you, Fanshott-Williams, ten o'clock. Now back to your quarters, the lot of you. I don't want to hear another whisper."

We stood aside as he headed up the alleyway to see how Ossie was faring. He had risen from the deck and leaned against the bulkhead. One eye was watering and he held his ribs.

"I'll be all right, sir, thank you," he said.

"Is there anything you're needing?" the captain asked. "Right now, I mean."

"No thank you, sir." His cassock was ripped, the neck hung open. "Maybe Michael can give me a couple of aspirin. Then I just want to go to bed."

"That's right, see if you can get some sleep." Captain Bell peered into his cabin. "Better blow the candles out first, eh, don't want a fire. Report to the mate in the morning, see if we can get something sorted out." He turned to those of us who stood nearby. "Didn't you hear what I said? Back to your cabins, now! And stay there."

We did as we were ordered but he called me back. "Scott's your cabin-mate, isn't he?"

"Yes, sir."

"Just thought you'd like to know everything went fine. Couple of weeks his arm will be good as new." For the first time he appeared to notice the coat-hanger which I held like a club. "What's that for?"

I shrugged.

"For God's sake!" He seemed at a loss for words. "Anyway, do you want to come along for a couple of minutes? He'll be glad to see you."

"I'll just go and – " I indicated my bare legs.

"No need, three boys of our own, my wife's seen enough lads in their underwear. She was a nurse."

I pulled down my T-shirt and followed him to the sick bay. Heidi was there, checking the plaster cast. Also Barbara who was staying the night.

Aaron lay on the pillow, drugged for the pain.

"He a very brave boy." Heidi rumpled his hair fondly. Aaron seemed to attract women even when he was semi-conscious.

"Hello, Ben." He smiled sleepily. "How's it going? What was all the row?"

"Tell you tomorrow," I said.

*

Ossie went downhill rapidly. I don't know what medication they found for him but it didn't seem to be working. His mood changes were extreme. For periods he was cheerful, hectic, singing as he went about his work in the messroom. An hour later he was brooding, depressed, his mood so black that even Barbara could not lift him out of it and he locked himself away in his cabin. Other times he was angry and swearing which sounded worse coming from Ossie because he had always been so polite and well spoken; one evening, while he was serving dinner, his mood was so violent that he smashed his ladle down on a pile of plates and shattered the top six. And sometimes at night, when we knew he was alone in the cabin, we heard him talking, arguing, whispering – who to? His mother seemed the most likely person, though perhaps they were people on the ship, or creatures conjured up from his imagination.

Barbara, who loved him the most, told us he had descended into a state of full schizophrenia. No one knew what to do. The best we could hope was that with our support he would reach Singapore safely where doctors and psychiatrists could give him the treatment he needed.

In the meantime our attention was distracted and the ship was thrown into disarray by another event.

Rat'bone had disappeared.

The Hunt for Rat'bone

THE FIRST I knew something was wrong was when Brian shook me awake at sunrise on Sunday morning.

"Come on, wakey-wakey."

"Gerroff."

"Up you get, no falling back to sleep again."

"What?"

"Mate wants everyone up in the officers' dining room, right away."

"Officers' dining room?" I heaved myself onto an elbow. "You sure? What time is it?"

"Quarter to six."

"Quarter to what?"

"Six." He shook Aaron in the bunk above me.

Dazed with sleep, I pulled on clean jeans and a T-shirt and made my way out on deck. It was a beautiful morning, the sun just clear of the horizon. At that time of day it was roughly in the east. Heading north-west as we were doing, it should have been on the starboard quarter. Instead it was on the port bow.

"We're heading the wrong way," I said to Lampie who had followed me out.

"Yeah, we've turned back," he said. "Haven't you heard? Lenny Rathbone's gone missing."

The dining room was crowded. Captain Bell, flanked by the deck officers and senior engineers, all in full uniform, sat at a table facing us. The mate rose:

"By now most of you will know why you're here. One of the ABs, Leonard Rathbone, has gone missing. We've searched the ship from stem to stern, all the cabins, all the deck lockers, every corner we can think of. There isn't a sign, so regrettably we've come to the conclusion that somehow he's gone over the side. His friends tell us he's not a strong swimmer but as you can see, we've put back to make a search. From what we can make out he went to his cabin at around half past nine last night. Petersen, who's on the same watch, spoke to him in the washroom. Following that, all we know for certain is that when Mitchell, who's on the middle watch, went to call him at quarter to four, he wasn't in his bunk, and when he went searching he was nowhere to be found. One odd detail, make of it what you will, his bunk had been stripped to the mattress."

He paused to take a sip of water.

"We're fully aware that Rathbone wasn't one of – sorry, I should say *isn't* – one of the most popular members of the crew. His manner worked against him. As a matter of fact, in the last few days he's twice been up on a charge, but we don't think that's depressed him to the point where – well, he might have done something desperate. If humanly possible we need to find him. That's principally why you're here, to see if anyone can shed any light on what might have happened – or when. And to organise a rota of lookouts." He paused. "Don't worry, you'll be paid overtime."

Brian spoke up: "Is that what you think of us, worried about overtime when someone's gone over the side?"

Another voice called: "I do, any rate, keep a lookout for that scumbag."

There was a scatter of laughter.

Lampie said: "He's been persecuting that messman. Bad blood between them. You should talk to him."

"The captain's already spoken to the messman," the mate said. "We're aware of the problem. He can't help us in any way."

I looked round for Ossie. He was in one of his hectic, excited phases, a figure in black among the tropical whites and colours. A smile chased a frown across his face. Catching my eye, he wiggled his fingers.

The mate spotted it. His glance darted between us. "This is hardly a matter for levity, Bennett. A man may be drowning here."

"I realise that, sir." My wretched blushing. Why should I feel guilty?

"You say his bedding's missing?" Samuel said. "You suggesting some kind of violence here?"

"We simply don't know at this stage. Yes, it's a possibility."

The deafening roar of an engine distracted our attention. Several men, myself among them, scrambled to the window. A helicopter hovered at eye level, just beyond the rail. The down-draught flattened the waves. For a minute it remained, making speech impossible, then lifted away.

"We've called out the Air Sea Rescue," the mate said. "If he is in the water – well, we're doing all we can. Now about these rotas ..."

Kevin and I asked to be teamed together. We stood on the port wing of the bridge with the sun at our left shoulders. The vast expanse of the Coral Sea spread around us. Did I care that Lenny Rathbone – Rat'bone with his mean face, stained teeth, skinny chest – had gone missing? Not really, although it was terrible to think about. He could have been anywhere: right alongside, ten miles off where the sea dipped below the horizon, behind any of a million waves. The chance of spotting one tiny head in that thousand square miles of rolling, splashing, black-and-silver water seemed nil. By this time he must have drowned anyway. We were sailing just east of the Great Barrier Reef where the sea was shallow and I pictured him lying on the coral sand with crabs and shoals of coloured fish for company.

Kevin nudged my arm and nodded. I looked down into the glassy waves and saw a shark – then another, and a third. I don't know what kind they were but they reminded me of my experience in Curaçao. We left those three behind but there were more, many more. There seemed no shortage of sharks to sweep up the debris near the Barrier Reef.

Every few minutes a search plane or helicopter flew past but like ourselves they spotted nothing. Eventually Captain Bell gave the order to return to our original course. Lookouts remained on station. Astern of us the search and rescue aircraft continued quartering the ocean until daylight faded. It was a vain hope. What little chance there had been of finding him, alive or dead, was gone.

Nearly half a day had been lost and the engineers put on speed to keep to schedule. Rat'bone's cabin was sealed for police investigation. Interviews were conducted. Statements signed.

Reports written. Work on deck returned to normal, or as near normal as possible with Charlie back in New Plymouth, Aaron injured and Rat'bone missing.

Aaron had been released from sick bay, his plastered arm in a sling. For three days he was excused duties. As I passed him, sprawled in a deckchair with a magazine, a tape deck and a glass of iced orange by his side, the accident seemed almost worth it.

To raise our spirits, Chippy and the day watch were set to work to repair the damaged pool, Chippy sobered by accusations that he was an alcoholic and had not erected it properly when we left New Zealand. By knocking-off time it was finished, the hose throbbing as it filled the canvas from the sparkling sea. It had been a hot day and I couldn't wait to leap into the cooling water, even though parts of me were multicoloured with bruising.

After I'd read some new messages on Aaron's plaster, I pulled on my trunks and joined Barbara on the diving platform, waiting for the pool to become deep enough. While we were chatting, I noticed that a corner of the canvas covering number five hatch – number five hatch again – had come loose. Though not exactly loose, more as if it had been bundled up and tucked behind the locking bar. I knew it hadn't been like that when we sailed because I'd helped Chippy and Smoky to batten down. I've no idea why it should have captured my attention – or why, without even considering the alternatives, it suggested a terrible possibility to me.

I told Barbara.

"Come on!" he said. "Who'd have the strength for that? Pull back the tarpaulins, OK. But lift the hatch board? It's too heavy."

"I'm going to tell the second mate."

"Ben, don't."

"But I've got this feeling."

"Just leave well alone." He pulled me to my feet. "Come on, the pool's deep enough now."

I resisted. "But what if I'm right?"

"You're not. Who'd stick a body down there when they could just drop it over the side? It's crazy, he'd have to be nuts."

I stared at him.

"Please, Ben," he said. "Let it go."

"Come on, Barbara," I said. "You know better than I do, there's only one person might do a thing like that and he's very strong. If he was desperate he could easily – "

"I'm just asking you, that's all. I can't bear it!" Holding his nose, Barbara jumped into the water and splashed to the far end.

"You can't ignore it," I called. "If I'm right they're going to find out sometime. I mean, it's not like throwing your mother's ashes over the stern. This is murder."

I pulled a shirt and jeans over my trunks and went up to the officers' quarters. The second mate, a bright gin and lemon in his hand, came out to speak to me.

"Well spotted the hatch cover," he said. "I'll get Chippy to fix it in the morning. But Rathbone's body being down there ... Have you thought about it? Who in his right mind would – " The penny dropped. He stared at me just as I had stared at Barbara. "My God, Bennett, if you're right. You really are ... I'll speak to the old man. You go on back to your cabin."

But how could I wait in the cabin? Dinner wouldn't be for another twenty minutes. I threw my clothes on the bunk and went back out in my trunks. Wet footprints crossed the deck. Barbara had gone. The pool was deserted. I sat on the board with my feet in the water. *My God, Bennett,* the second mate had said. *You really are* ... I was what? Ordinary would suit me fine. I wanted to fit in. I thought I did fit in.

There were voices behind me. Captain Bell had come down with the mate, the second mate and a scattering of others. I slipped into the water and stayed under for a few seconds to avoid attention, then swam to the far end. My little ploy did not escape the captain:

"Well, Bennett. You again."

"Yes, sir. I'm sorry, sir." I made as if to climb from the pool and go away.

"No, no. Stay where you are until we see if this is some fantasy or a remarkable bit of deduction."

Water cascaded from the pool and swilled about the officers' shoes as the ship rolled. The second mate said, "Turn off the hydrant would you, Philip."

The bosun appeared with Lampie and Chippy.

Michael and Barbara, looking very nervous, watched from the crew deck.

"Definitely been tampered with." Chippy examined the canvas. "Along here, see? Bit of rough weather, seas breaking over the afterdeck, could have washed off."

Aided by a couple of ABs, he removed the chocks and locking bar and pulled back the canvas. The big hatch board lay before them. They looped a rope through the iron ringbolts and heaved. The board slid aside. Beneath lay the heavy beams and insulation plugs.

"Oh, my God!" Tim Nettles stared down. "Someone *has* been here. Look."

To ensure an airtight seal between the insulation plugs, broad strips of brown paper had been pasted across the joins. They were torn away at the corner.

"All right," he said grimly. "Let's have 'em out."

Each plug had a central ringbolt. The ABs led the rope through the one in the corner and heaved again. With a small crack the heavy plug broke free. They lifted it aside. Then the one next to it. A swirl of fog rose above head height as the warm sea air encountered the icy temperature of the hold.

I had been watching from the diving board. Barefoot I descended to the deck and pushed through the crowd.

The Red Singlet

Rat'bone's body straggled among the carcasses of mutton. I could have leaned down into the hatch and touched him.

In life Rat'bone had been mean and ugly; in death he looked worse. After fourteen or eighteen hours in a fan-assisted deep-freeze, he was crusted with ice. His face was stubbled with ice crystals. His frosted eyes gazed into space. His lips had shrunk back from teeth that snarled at death. Still dressed for bed, he wore frayed pyjama bottoms cut off at the knee and a grubby singlet that once had been white.

And he had been stabbed.

Ragged holes in the singlet revealed where the knife had gone in. From the breast to the waist it was red with frozen blood. He had bled from the mouth and nose also.

Word had gone round and the crew came running to see the grisly sight.

"Stand back. Stand back. Right," Captain Bell addressed the ABs who had opened the hatch. "Let's have him out of there."

They waited while the mate took photographs for the police.

There was room in the hold for only two men. One took his head, the other his ankles and they lifted their shipmate, stiff as a board and so cold that he burned their fingers. The man holding the head stumbled on a carcass of mutton and fell backwards with Rat'bone on top of him. Briefly he was trapped.

He screamed: "Aahh! Aahh! Get him off me!"

Samuel jumped to his rescue and the appalled man scrambled from the hold.

"Ohhh!" He shuddered, scrubbing at his hands. "I couldn't stand him even when he was alive."

The body was hoisted to the hatch cover. I thought, this is what they'd have done with me if I'd been left down there in the locker.

One arm had frozen at right angles as if he was pointing. I was glad he wasn't pointing at me.

"Stand back," Captain Bell said again. "Give us a bit of space."

He tried to lift Rat'bone's singlet to see the wounds but blood had frozen it to the skin.

"We'll have to leave him to thaw for a couple of minutes."

"Like picking the wrapper off a packet of sausages," somebody said.

A strand of hair, warmed by the sun, fell to one side. His eyelashes defrosted. Ice crystals melted and trickled down his cheek like tears.

Where was Ossie? I had scanned the crowd a couple of times but he wasn't there, conspicuous by his absence. Perhaps, with dinner interrupted, he had remained at the serving counter or gone to his cabin. Since the loss of his pills he had taken to sitting on sacks of potatoes in the store-room where it was cool and dark and no one disturbed him.

Not that evening:

"I see you there! You wicked, black, son of Satan!"

The shrill scream made everyone turn. Ossie stood at the rail, two decks above, looking down on the proceedings. He wore his black cassock, a big wooden cross resting on his chest. In his right hand he carried a staff of two-by-two like an Old Testament prophet. He had cut a series of blue sixes across his forehead with some sort of pen, so savagely that blood trickled down to his eyes.

"Your sins have found you out now, haven't they? No more plotting and planning now, spreading your evil through the ship. The Maggot's put a stop to you."

He drew back his arm and flung the staff. It missed the body and rebounded from the hatch coaming. People ducked as it rattled about their heads.

"Bosun." The mate spoke quietly. "Take two seamen and arrest that man."

Captain Bell said, "Don't hurt him, he's sick."

"Take care," the mate said. "He might have a knife."

"Poor beggar." Captain Bell shook his head. He looked down at the dead Rat'bone and repressed a swear.

The bosun's party detached itself from the crowd.

Ossie spotted them. "Your turn next, Ryland. I know about you, what you and that cadet done to our Ben. I've got your measure."

I had not spotted a bag at his feet. He rooted inside and produced something with a gesture of triumph. I could not make it out then saw it was a wax manikin, the same as the ones he had made in Panama. He grasped it with his left hand. In his right hand, though I could not see it, he held a thick sailmaker's needle.

"See, this is you, Lenny Rat'bone! There! There!"

One, two, three – six times he plunged the needle into the doll's chest and flung it at the dead man on the hatch cover. Like the two-by-two it missed, struck the metal beam with a crack and shattered into fragments. They fell among the frozen mutton.

The bosun hurried from deck to deck.

"Now you – Cyclops!" Ossie produced a second doll and threw the bag aside. "Hair, see, got it from your cabin. An' a ring. Missed a snotrag recently?" A scrap of cloth was knotted round its middle. "Got you that burn last time, remember? This time – " He jammed the needle into the doll's back and screwed it round.

The bosun was upon him. Ossie dodged behind a winch. The seamen cut him off. It was over in seconds. One got an arm round his neck. Unseen by the captain, Ryland thumped a fist into his stomach, clubbed him across the head. They dragged him out, choking and screaming and struggling.

"Shut up!" Ryland called down to the mate: "What you want doing with him?"

"Lock him in the fo'csle."

Captain Bell murmured in his ear.

"No, take him to the sick bay," the mate said. "Inner cabin where the bunks are. There's bars on the porthole."

The captain scanned the crew and found Barbara. "Stay with him, Tanner, see he's all right; you should be safe enough. Jones, you're a strong reliable chap, wait by the door just in case. I'll come along when I've finished here."

Barbara and Samuel departed. Slowly the buzz died down.

Captain Bell gave a deep sigh, the sigh of a man who had been at sea too long. He looked down at the thawing body. Trickles crossed the canvas. With the tips of his fingers he hooked up Rat'bone's singlet. Stab wounds showed black through the sticky red. I craned my neck and counted six. He held it while the mate took more photographs.

"Any sign of a knife, Two-oh?" he said. "One of those big galley jobs by the look of it."

The second mate and Philip searched among the carcasses. "Could have fallen through."

"Over the side more likely," the captain said. "Leave it for now, police job anyway." He pulled down the singlet and stepped back, wiping his fingers on a handkerchief. "Better get him back in the cold."

Returning Rat'bone to his resting place was less respectful than it might have been. Kevin was sent for a sheet of polythene in which to wrap the body. He returned with two plastic sacks, one stencilled 'carrots', the other 'baking potatoes'.

"Taters! That's very nice!" Lampie commented.

"It's all I could find," Kevin protested. "They are clean."

"They'll do fine, son," said Captain Bell. "Just to keep off the frost."

"Like freezer bags."

"That's right, like freezer bags."

"Sick bags would be too good for him," Michael said, "what he did to Ossie."

The projecting arm posed a problem. Either it had to be broken and forced down to his side, or a sack had to be slit and the arm left sticking out like a signpost. So one bag was cut and pulled over Rat'bone's snarling head, the other over his feet, and they were bound like a clumsy parcel with one bare arm protruding. Then two sailors grasped the bags and slid him to the brink of the hold. Unnoticed by one, the arm swung upright and Rat'bone's fingers clawed up the leg of his shorts. He gave a yell and jumped back.

"Ooh! I hate bodies." He rubbed his leg as if the chill of death had got right into his bones. "Give me the creeps."

Another AB took his place. Carefully they lowered their shipmate into the smoking hold. But the plastic was slippery and pulled from their hands. The body slewed and fell. With a noise like a coconut, Rat'bone's head bounced off the frozen mutton.

Michael gave a shriek of laughter and clamped a hand over his mouth.

"Come on there, show a bit of respect." There was a twinkle in the second mate's eye. "Philip, straighten him up. Put him on his back."

Michael said, "Once defrosted do not re-freeze."

The hold was sealed and covered. Beneath the plugs the cold tightened its grip on Rat'bone's thawing body.

The pantry boy turned on the seawater hydrant and sprang into the pool with one of the greasers. The crowd dispersed.

I joined Michael and we leaned on a rail, catching the last rays of the sun. The sea was gold, so bright it hurt my eyes. I turned my back.

"Deserves everything he got." Michael was unforgiving. "Poor Ossie."

I had been thinking about it. "How much do *you* know about all this?"

"What do you mean?"

"You know perfectly well, you and Barbara."

"What about me and Barbara?"

"He tried to stop me reporting the loose canvas."

"Well, he'd just come down for a swim, probably wasn't very interested."

"Oh, come on, Michael."

"What?"

"Hiding the body like that, it's too big a job for one man."

"I'm sure I don't know what you're talking about." He looked me in the eye. The look was too direct, his face was too honest. With a jolt I realised that my suspicions were correct. Michael and Barbara, having met Ossie sometime during the night, had helped him to get rid of the body. Whether he had gone to their cabins or they had met by chance, there was no way of knowing. In either case, it made them accessories to murder. What a nightmare for my two gay friends, finding Rat'bone covered in blood then carrying him about the ship! Small wonder Michael was unwilling to admit it.

He hid his face by turning to the sunset. Neither of us spoke and after a while he pushed himself from the rail. "Well, see you later. This girl needs a shower and a few stiff gins."

I changed the subject: "Captain handled it well, didn't he?"

"Who, Daddy Bell? He's an old darling. Got class. Not many of his sort around. Incidentally," Michael took refuge behind his camp manner, "I don't think I've told you, I just *love* those trunks. With your eyes and colouring. Like those gorgeous Australian boys you see at the Olympics."

"They're just trunks," I said. "Ten dollars."

"Don't give me that. Don't pretend to be all macho and innocent with Michael. He can see through you."

He was right, I did quite fancy myself in them.

"You're nothing but a tease. If Luigi was here he'd give you such a slap."

"Michael, stop it."

He laughed. "Anyway, if you want any dinner you'd better get along now."

"Kevin's put it in the hot cupboard," I said. "Going to have a dip first."

He went below and I returned to the diving platform. With a tremendous *per-lunk* I joined the others in the pool then stood, ducking and ducking again, scrubbing my chest and hair as if the clean ocean water could wash away the proximity of death.

The Fatal Snack

"It's just wicked," Michael said. "When you think what he was like that day we signed on, remember? We went to *Chez Marilyn*. He was so happy, so pleased to see us all. I know his mother had died but that was a blessing really."

"Fat old cow," Barbara said. "Sitting there like the potato witch, sucking the life out of him."

Michael nodded. "The hospital had got his medication sorted out. It was a fresh start. And now this, it's too awful to think about. And it's all the fault of that ugly scrag out there in the deep freeze."

"And the bosun," Barbara added.

"That's right, and the bosun. And the sooner someone does the same to him the better it'll be for all of us."

It was three days later, nine in the evening, and we sat in Michael's cabin. By that time we had travelled north beyond the Great Barrier Reef, turned west through the Torres Strait at the north-eastern tip of Australia, and now were sailing through the jewelled seas of Indonesia. At midday the sun stood right above the mainmast and although twice we had been assaulted by torrential rain squalls, most of the time the skies were hot and clear. Occasionally we passed close to an island and lined the rails to see the jungle-covered slopes and white shores lined with palm trees and villages.

But while the rest of us enjoyed our days in this tropical paradise, Ossie, locked in the sick bay with a guard for his own protection, grew steadily worse. His friends called it schizophrenia; the rest, more simply, said he was barking mad. His mood changed by the hour. Barbara had done his best to scrub out the line of blue sixes on his forehead. The cuts had scabbed over but some of the ink had got beneath his skin and it would take a surgeon to remove it.

That evening, when I had called before dinner, I could get little sense out of him:

"See that island this afternoon, Ossie? Great smoking volcano."

He wasn't interested. "Look, Ben, it's snowing." He had picked a cushion to pieces and threw a cloud of feathers into the air, laughing as they floated to the deck. He did it again. Little white feathers clung to his hair and shoulders.

"That's nice," I said, wondering how it was all going to be cleared up. "A bit hot for snow though."

"This is hot snow." He had taken out his dental plate and gave me a broad smile, revealing the gaps where his teeth had been broken in the rapids.

"How are you feeling anyway?" I said.

The smile faded. "All right, I suppose, but I can't find the lizards. And they won't let me have mum's ashes."

"Lizards, Ossie?"

"You know, those green ones, long as this." He held his hands out. "Forky tongues. They were here yesterday but now they've gone. I've looked everywhere."

There were two bunks in the sick bay; a scatter of clothes and magazines lay on one. He lifted them aside but found no lizards hiding underneath. "Maybe Tiger saw them off. You know Tiger. What's his name?"

"Do you mean Attila?"

"That's him, Attila." His brow creased and I thought he was going to cry. "Where's Attila, Ben? My little Attila." He looked around his hospital cabin, grasped the bars on the open porthole. "Puss-puss. Come on, my lovely."

I could not tell him that Attila, showing complete disregard for the man who loved him, had immediately moved in with Aaron and me. Of the two of us he favoured Aaron and sprang up to sleep on his bunk.

Back in Michael's cabin I told them about my visit. "But why is he talking about lizards – on a ship?"

Barbara explained: "One of the greasers brought him a jigsaw, an old Indian temple or something, you know, sinking back into the jungle. There were lizards on the rocks. Somebody must have taken it away."

Now he told me it made a sort of sense. "And all those feathers,"

I said.

Michael laughed. "I'll take the Hoover along later."

I pictured it. "He's got a lot of friends."

"Well, I should hope so. He's a nice man and he's been very badly treated. Life's given him a raw deal. People like you and me, we don't know how lucky we are."

There didn't seem any answer to that.

I ran my finger down a dewed can of orange. "But that other," I said. "You know, about Rat'bone. Tell me again. I don't quite follow what happened."

"We could end up in jail," Barbara said, "you do realise that. For years likely. Maybe in Singapore. That would be lovely, wouldn't it? For murder – manslaughter anyway. Helping to conceal a body. Accessories after the fact."

"But I'm not going to tell anybody."

"What about Charlie if he comes back?"

I hesitated. "Not if you don't want me to."

For three months Charlie and Smoky had kept my own secret. They'd been terrific about it: one silly joke, one careless word and I'd have been on the first flight home. If they could do it, so could I.

"All right." Michael was back in his schoolboy mode: no make-up, hair parted at the side. A decadent schoolboy with a large gin and a cigarette. "Where do you want to start?"

"Why you don't give up smoking?"

"I have," he said shortly. "This one's just to remind me what a disgusting habit it is."

It wasn't worth pursuing. "That night," I said. "Start at the beginning."

"Right." He sat up and tucked his feet beneath him. "Rat'bone had been on the lager – with me so far?

"No need to be sarky."

"And about one o'clock he wakes up and goes for a pee. On the way back he must have seen a light in the galley – "

"So he goes to look," Barbara said, "and he finds Ossie in there, helping himself from the fridge."

"That's right, he couldn't sleep so he'd gone to the messroom for something to eat but there's only these curled-up sandwiches.

Galley's locked, of course, so he goes to get the keys from the chef, finds him snoring like a pig and takes the keys off his locker. You probably don't remember but we'd had beautiful roast silverside that night, so he takes it out the fridge and cuts himself a beef sandwich. Half a gateau in there too, so he cuts a good slice of that and makes himself up a nice tray. All it needs now's a cup of tea. So he's boiling the kettle and tidying things away when who turns up but Rat'bone in his chopped-off jambies and droopy vest."

"Starts in right away," Barbara continued. "You know the kind of thing: 'That's how Maggots get so fat; I'll have that or I'll report you to the chief steward; how'd you fancy a good thumping, getting me in trouble with the old man?' Then he sees the knife Ossie's been using to cut the beef. 'What if I stuck this right in your fat belly?' he says, and he goes to pick it up."

"One of those big butcher's knives," Michael said. "Nine-inch blade, sharp as a razor."

"That's right. Anyway, Ossie grabs up the knife before he can get it and he points it at him. Scared out of his wits. Threatens him with it. Tells him to get out the galley, leave him alone."

"Yes, I can follow all that," I said, "but it's what happened next. That's the bit I can't understand."

"Me neither, not exactly. Take a psychologist, I reckon. Anyway, Rat'bone's so used to Ossie being his victim, backing off like a rabbit, he's sure he'll never use it and he stands there tempting him. 'Go on then,' he says. 'You got the knife, use it. I dare you.' But Ossie's terrified. 'Come on, right here,' he taps his skinny chest. It's like Ossie's hypnotised, he can't move. 'See,' Rat'bone says, 'you haven't got the bottle. You're chicken. You and all your poof mates, you're just pathetic!' And Ossie doesn't know what happened next. Really he doesn't. All he can remember is how easy the knife went in. He couldn't believe it, right to the handle. And the surprised expression on Rat'bone's face. And when he falls over backwards, Ossie stabs him five more times to make six, his lucky six. And this is the bit that gets me, then he just leaves him lying there and boils up the kettle again and makes his mug of tea – like nothing's happened."

"And he puts it on the tray," Michael said, "and he goes to take it back to his cabin. Then he looks down and sees Rat'bone lying on the tiles. Means nothing to him at first, might have been a sack of turnips. Then in a rush it comes to him what he's done and he goes all to pieces."

"Doesn't know what to do."

"All he does know is that he can't let anyone see. So he switches off the light and locks up the galley and goes wandering out on deck."

"Thought about jumping," Barbara said. "Then he realises maybe he can get rid of the body. He'd like to do it himself but there's all this blood. So he wakes me up in the middle of the night."

"And Barbara comes to me." Michael refreshed his drink. "Eyes like the Bride of Frankenstein. So I get dressed and we all go along to the galley. There he is, great knife handle sticking up from his chest. Blood everywhere, run all over the deck."

"Cut a long story short," Barbara said, "we took the sheets off his bed to wrap the body, stop it dripping, and carried him aft. I thought just dump him but Ossie wouldn't have it."

"Me neither," Michael said. "Deserved everything he got, bastard! Excuse the language, Ben, I just hated him. But everyone's got to have a funeral."

"Give him to the sharks, far as I'm concerned," Barbara said. "But Michael's a Catholic. Used to be an altar boy, swinging the incense and all that, everybody watching him. I reckon that's what gave him the taste for dressing up."

"Hark who's talking!" Michael said. "At least when I was eight I didn't ask Santa for a dress like the fairy on the Christmas tree. Anyway, it's not a joke, we're talking about immortal souls here."

I was surprised. "I didn't know you were a Catholic."

"Why should you? Lots of things you don't know about me."

"Never mind all that," Barbara said. "If he wasn't going over the side, the only place we could think of – "

"Where he wouldn't start to rot – "

"Was down the hold, in with the cargo. So we took a chance no one would catch us, shut the alleyway door like that cadet you saw thieving, and stashed him in with the mutton."

"Threw the bloody sheets over the side then went back and mopped out the galley."

"Cleaned the knife, dumped his snack in the bin."

"Slipped the keys back to the chef – and that was it."

"Then we all came along here to Michael's for a much-needed drop of mother's ruin."

"A drop? Couple of bottles more like. I was shaking like a leaf."

"And everything would have been fine," Barbara said, "nobody would have known a thing, if it hadn't been for you. I tried to warn you but no, you wouldn't listen."

"You can't blame Ben just because he's got sharp eyes," Michael said.

"And too much imagination."

"If you like, but *he* didn't kill Rat'bone. He didn't know anything about it. Why didn't you just tell him?"

"I couldn't."

Michael nodded. "Anyway, who could have guessed Ossie was going to break up like that?"

What he said was true but I felt terrible, as if I personally was responsible for Ossie's situation, locked up in the sick bay with a guard on the door.

Some others joined us. Voices grew louder. At one point Michael went off for half an hour to Hoover the feathers from the sick bay. Barbara entertained us with outrageous tales about his life as a hospital orderly. The lager flowed. It was after eleven when I came away.

The next morning Barbara was summoned to see the captain.

The Bucket and the Oil Drum

He told us what happened:

An engineer brought the message, shouting above the noise of the engines. "Captain wants to see you. Up in his cabin, right now."

Barbara was mopping up an oil spill in the starboard bilge. His heart stopped. "What for?"

"Didn't say."

He climbed out, scrubbing black hands on a wad of cotton waste. "I'd better go and change."

"Just go as you are, they said."

He looked down at his filthy boiler suit, his engine room boots. A smudged mirror above the control table showed streaks down his face. Barbara detested being dirty, it made him ill. Reluctantly he mounted the long engine-room ladders and made his way to the captain's quarters behind the bridge.

Three officers – Captain Bell, the chief engineer and the chief steward – wearing immaculate whites with lots of gold braid, sat waiting to interview him. Barbara, bedraggled as a seabird plucked from an oil spill, stood on sheets of newspaper in the middle of the carpet and prepared to hear the worst.

"Thank you for coming up so promptly," said the captain. "Let's get straight down to it. We want to speak to you about Oswald Bagot."

Barbara's knees turned to water.

"The messman who killed that AB a couple of days ago," explained the chief engineer in case Barbara needed reminding.

"He's a friend of yours," said the captain.

Barbara swallowed.

"That's right, isn't it?"

"Yes, sir."

"Well, we've been looking at your discharge book, Tanner," said Captain Bell. "For some years you sailed as a steward."

Barbara was puzzled. "That's right, sir."

"Until some unfortunate occurrence involving a bucket of water."

"Yes, sir, I'm sorry, sir. But it was one of the engineers, he provoked me to it."

I knew the story, Michael had told me long ago. Following his years as a hospital orderly, Barbara had undergone a period of training and joined the Merchant Navy as a sea-going steward. He loved it, it enabled him to live the life he wanted, and all went well until three years earlier when he had signed on as engineers' steward. The third engineer, a bully and a brute, took delight in tormenting the gay and sprightly Barbara, much in the same way as Rat'bone had enjoyed tormenting Ossie. But Barbara, only half the size of Ossie, was a very different character. He wasn't going to put up with it and decided to teach the man a lesson. So one evening when he had drunk rather too much, he filled a two-gallon bucket with ice and water. It was his intention to fling it over the third engineer as he lay sleeping in his bunk, and run away before he had a chance to recover. Unfortunately, as he approached the third engineer's cabin, there were voices in the alleyway and he had to dodge into a cupboard until the road was clear. When he emerged, his brain befuddled by gin, he mistook the cabin for the one next door where the second engineer, recently married, was sleeping with his pretty wife. In the darkness he failed to see his error and somehow, as he flung the iced water, the bucket slipped from his hand and hit the young couple where they lay on the pillow. The second engineer received a nasty cut on the forehead and his wife lost two of her front teeth. In the ensuing screams and confusion, Barbara stumbled and was seized before he could make his escape. The injured couple were very nice about it and he was not charged by the police, but it marked the end of Barbara's life as a sea-going steward. Some months later, after further training, he was allowed to return to sea as a greaser. And it was as a greaser and an accessory to murder that he stood now before Captain Bell and tried to calm his shaking.

"It says here," the captain referred to the document before him, "that for a time you served as a messman."

"Messman?"

"That's right, isn't it? Got a good report."

"Yes, sir."

"And the chief steward here tells me that some years ago you sailed together when he was a chef. You know each other from the past."

"That's right, sir. On the old *North Star*." Barbara's heart surged. Was that what this was all about?

"He speaks well of you," the captain said, "and the thing is, we were wondering, in the present unfortunate circumstances, if you might be persuaded to – "

"Oh, yes, sir. I can, easily. Right away. I'll start tonight. Thank you, sir." He bobbed. "Thank you."

"You seem to have got there before me. I was going to say take over for the rest of this trip."

"Rest of the trip? Oh, yes, sir, yes. If I make a good job of it, will you recommend I'm reinstated as a steward? Put in a good word like?"

Captain Bell glanced at the others. "I don't see why not – on condition you don't kill too many of us with buckets while we're asleep."

"Let's get this straight," the chief engineer said. "Your past experience isn't the only reason you're being offered the job. You're such a bloody awful greaser."

"Oh, yes, sir. I know. You're quite right."

"Tell me," said the chief engineer, "what is it about being a greaser that you dislike so much?"

"I'm just not cut out, sir. You know what they say, oil and water? Well, oil and cup cakes, it's the same thing. I mean, just look at the state of me!" He held his arms out. "I can't make head nor tail of it. You know them big things down the engine room with all them bolts, you have to take them apart. And them little jiggly ones. It's all a mystery to me. And I keep jamming my fingers. Look at these hands – and that nail. That's going to come off, you know."

He never returned to the engine room and that lunchtime, to my relief, Barbara replaced me at the serving counter. He was on top form, swapping backchat, giving cheek, and somehow the whole messroom began to sparkle in a way it had not done since I joined the ship.

*

Not once did I think 'poor Lenny' but many times I thought 'poor Ossie', and when work was finished for the day I called to see him again.

"He's got a visitor," said Brian who sat outside with a paperback.

I knew who it was before I went in because her perfume filtered round the door. Trish came regularly to sit with Ossie. The fact that she was a woman and very pretty seemed to comfort him. Sick of being told what to do by her self-righteous husband, Trish saw no reason why, if the captain's wife could set the arm of an ordinary seaman, the mate's wife couldn't comfort a crazed messman. Everyone liked her for it, though she was still Trish the Dish in skimpy tops and tight shorts, and followed by many lustful eyes as she walked about the ship. "Cor, I wish she'd come an' sit with me," Kevin said more than once. "I need comforting an' all."

"Is that right?" I said, mimicking his Birmingham accent. "Well we could all do with a bit o' that."

"Here, watch yourself," he said good-naturedly. "Good Brummie, that is. But what about the mate though? She's really nice an' he's horrible to her."

Ossie was calmer than the last time I had called. "Hello, Ben." He wrapped me in a bear-like hug. "You're my friend, I like it when you come to see me."

"I like it too, Ossie," I said.

"This is Patricia." Ossie introduced us. "Everybody calls her Trish but I call her Patricia. Have you met her?"

"Yes," I said.

"She's nice. She comes and sits with me. When *she's* here, the others stay away."

"The others?"

"The ones who come and sit on the bed and won't stop talking. Sometimes there's hardly room for me."

"But you like it when your mum comes," Trish said.

"Yes, I like that," he said. "I tell her my stories. Michael brings me tea and sometimes I share it with her."

"Did you know Barbara's messman now?" I said. "Just for a while until you get better."

"Yes, he came and told me. He'd better look out for that bad one." He looked towards the porthole. "I can't remember what he's called but I think something happened to him."

"He doesn't come and see you in here does he?" I asked.

"Sometimes," he said. "But not when Patricia's here. Or my friends."

That evening there was an impromptu party on the afterdeck. An empty oil drum, punched full of holes, was set on chocks and a fire was lit in the bottom. Barbara appeared, wearing his dirtiest engine-room boiler suit. In one hand he carried a bulging bin bag, in the other a can of paraffin. He set them aside and chose a spot near the leaping flames. A small crowd had gathered. Barbara struck a pose. Then, to the thumping notes of *The Stripper* from Michael's tape-deck, he performed the striptease of a lifetime. The boiler suit went first, slipped from one shoulder, then an arm, peeled to his waist, past his bottom, off altogether and whirled round his head while he danced and wriggled and stamped his work boots to the rhythm. He doused it in paraffin and set fire to it, whirled the roaring flames until they reached his fingers and dropped the blazing boiler suit into the oil drum. By this time the rest of us were shouting and clapping and stamping in time to the music. Barbara had put on several layers of underwear. He pulled off one dirty shirt, then another, three T-shirts, his boots and socks, three pairs of underpants. A single, oily, saggy pair of Y-fronts remained.

"Get 'em off!" Aaron shouted.

"All in good time. Control yourself." He opened the bin bag, filled with his remaining boiler suits, engine-room shirts and underwear. All went into the inferno.

"Get 'em off!" The shout was universal and at last Barbara obliged, soaked them in paraffin and whirled the blazing Y-fronts around his head. Like a torch, they sailed over the rail and were extinguished by the waves.

Then he ran to the pool and leaped in. Cheered by the occasion the rest of us followed, fully-dressed, and for ten minutes we splashed and clowned in the cold water, lit on one side by the dusky flames of the oil drum, and on the other by the rising moon which cast an orange track across the sea.

Coral Island

OUR COURSE, as the second mate had shown me on the chart when I took the wheel on Sunday afternoon, lay roughly west through the sparkling seas of Indonesia, then north-west between Sumatra and Borneo to Singapore. Captain Bell and Tim Nettles, the navigating officer, wanted to keep as far from land as possible to avoid the local fishing boats – small, unlit and careless of the rules of the sea – which swarmed in the coastal waters. It was difficult, for the seas of Indonesia are thronged with islands and in places we had to thread a passage between them. For those of us not engaged in navigation and keeping a lookout these were good times, waving to the cheerful fishermen and exploring their jewelled islands through binoculars.

We passed the southern tip of Sulawesi and all seemed to be going well as we altered course from the Flores Sea into the Java Sea heading towards Borneo. It was another perfect morning and I was leaning on the rail looking down at the water when I realised that our speed had dropped.

Philip was passing. "What's up?" I asked him.

"Some problem with the engines," he said. "Bearing running hot. Might have to stop for repairs."

"Before Singapore?"

"They say it's quite serious. Two – three days yet to Singapore, maybe more, even at sixteen knots."

I was following our progress: every day the noon position was plotted on a chart in the crew alleyway. "Where will we put in?"

"You mean what port?" he said. "Don't need to, just drop anchor off some little atoll. The engineers can do the repairs themselves."

"How long for?"

"Maybe a day."

"Sounds good. Think we'll get ashore?"

"I hope so." Philip was eating a Mars Bar from the fridge. He offered it and I bit off an end.

"I haven't seen Tony for days," I said. "How's he doing?"

"Miss Fanshott-Williams?" Michael's manner was catching. "Oh, charming as ever. Spends most of his time with the bosun. Smells of drink. I reckon they're up to something again – don't know what. Goes about with a little smile on his face. Can't be the cargo, who's going to nick carcasses of lamb in this heat? Or boxes of butter?"

The mate appeared on the deck above.

"See you." I shot back inside.

Philip was right; an hour later we altered course to starboard and the engine note dropped still further. Crew gathered along the rails to see a coral atoll which lay dead ahead. While we were eating lunch the engines went astern and brought us to a halt. With a loud rattle, the starboard anchor was dropped. An eerie quiet fell over the ship. For weeks, months, we had grown so used to the roar and vibration of the engines that we never noticed them. Even when we berthed in New Zealand there was the buzz of the harbour and clatter of winches. Now there was no sound but the soft slap of waves against the ship's plates. Men talked, some loudly, to fill the silence.

I hurried to finish my pudding and went out on deck. Without the benefit of a breeze the ship baked in the midday heat. Beneath our keel the water was emerald green. The atoll lay a mile distant, maybe a little more, with dazzling white beaches, rich green vegetation, and the water above the coral so clear it had no colour at all. Like many of the tiny islands in the archipelago, it was uninhabited.

To avoid speculation, Captain Bell called the crew on deck and explained what had happened. A bearing on one of the main propeller shafts had overheated. The engine had to be stopped to prevent further damage. It was not a difficult repair, just time-consuming. We expected to be anchored off the atoll, which was unnamed on the chart, for approximately thirty-six hours.

"Why not continue on one engine?" someone called out. "Fix it when we get to Singapore."

"Yes, indeed we could," he answered. "But it would mean less power and these aren't the safest seas in the world, all the islands and little native boats and what not. If bad weather blew up as it might any time, I'd prefer to have the use of both engines."

"Any chance of putting the boats down and going ashore?" came another voice.

"I've been speaking to the chief officer about that. It seems the perfect opportunity for a full lifeboat drill. I'm sure many of you will be glad to explore such a beautiful island, I know I will. For the moment work will continue as normal. We'll let you know when everything's been arranged."

At four o'clock, orange life-jackets securely tied, we gathered at lifeboat stations. There were four lifeboats. I had been assigned to Captain Bell's boat, the for'ard boat on the starboard side. The canvas cover was removed, the boat swung out on its davits and lowered to the water. We descended long ladders. The heavily-laden boat pushed off and four seamen, myself among them, fitted oars. To the captain's command we pulled away. It was great, like rowing on the lake at Westport, only a thousand times better.

For half an hour we rowed to orders, erected the mast and sail, though there was not enough wind to fill it, and motored around the ship with the black plates towering above us and the anchor cable descending into the depths, down and down, rusty brown in the clear green water. Then all four boats lined up, we took the oars again and, at a signal from Captain Bell, we raced each other to the shore.

The island was a paradise: white coral sand, shoals of coloured fish thronging the lagoon, lizards, land crabs, tropical birds, the sun slanting through palm trees, not a sign that man had set foot there since the beginning of time. I had never been anywhere like it and never will again. Yet this Garden of Eden was not without its dangers, for in the depths of the lagoon I saw a sea snake, and one of the engineers trod on a spiny fish hidden in the shallows that caused him agony and made his foot swell until it was scarcely recognisable.

All too soon the excitement was over and we returned to the ship. But afterwards, since there were few currents, we were allowed to swim over the side. Rope ladders were hung from the rails. It was scary, all that water beneath us with who knew what sharks and octopuses, electric eels and boxfish waiting to strike. A shark watch had been set so it wasn't really dangerous but it felt it was. Philip and some of the others dived from the foredeck, a couple even from the deck above. They were brilliant. I wanted to dive as well and stood clinging to the rail for ages. But it was such a height that I didn't dare, so I jumped, holding my nose, the other arm straight by my side. The impact was so great it knocked my arm high above my head.

Smoky, to my surprise, was one of the divers. On his second dive he hit the water so fast he shot out of his shorts and never saw them again. Stark naked, to raucous shouts from everyone in the water, he climbed the long ladder and stepped over the rails.

Floating on my back, I saw Ossie up on the crew deck. I waved and he waved back. Most of the time he spent locked in the sick bay with a guard on his door. It was a prison but no great hardship, for he had many visitors. They played dominoes, draughts and crib for pennies; more jigsaws appeared; and the captain thought it could do no harm to let him have the tarot cards and one or two of his books if they helped to keep him happy. Three times a day he was allowed out for exercise. He had been at Barbara's party and seen his striptease and the blazing overalls. He had watched us in the lifeboats, and now stood laughing delightedly as we sprang from the foredeck into the deep green sea.

Captain Bell was the kindest of sea captains but he was not a psychologist and knew little about the cunning of confused minds. None of us did and as Ossie walked about the ship with whichever sturdy seaman was guarding him, we had no idea that he was spotting a detail here, a detail there, and filing them away for future use. In themselves they were nothing, the lashings on a ladder, a couple of cans, but when they were all brought together they enabled him to carry out a plan that those of us who were there will never forget.

That afternoon Samuel had been splicing a thimble into a new shroud for the foremast. Coiled wire and pieces of equipment were scattered nearby. A heavy shackle lay on a bitts close to where we were diving. I set it on the deck and sat down. The hot bitts scorched my legs. I spread my towel on top.

An engineer had come up for a breather. Enviously he watched the swimmers: "I could do with a bit o' that. Hot as the furnaces of hell down there." He mopped his face with a rag.

I didn't know much about engines and asked him about the damaged bearing. It was, he told me, on the port propeller shaft. The two enormous shafts, polished steel and turning like silk, are supported throughout their length by a series of bearings. These are lubricated by pressurised oil pipes. Each bearing has its own valve to control the flow and somehow the valve which controlled the flow to this particular bearing had been shut off. As a result the bearing had overheated and become badly burned. If it were not repaired it could cause damage to the propeller shaft, possibly even seize up, a major disaster. Each propeller shaft runs down a long tunnel from the engine room. In the general course of work there is little reason to enter these tunnels, and since the valve was situated far down towards the propeller, it was some time before the problem was discovered.

It would have been perfectly possible, as Captain Bell had told us, to stop the port engine and continue to Singapore using the starboard engine alone – but he'd been guilty of a little deception. We hadn't stopped because of the possibility of bad weather – at least, not principally that; a valve had been shut off on the starboard propeller shaft also. Luckily it was discovered before the damage became so acute, but like the damaged port bearing it needed to be dismantled for inspection.

It was hard to imagine how one valve might have been shut off, the engineer told me, two could not be accidental. The chief engineer was conducting an enquiry.

Sitting in the bar that evening I said, "Who on earth would sabotage the engines?"

Luigi shrugged. "What for you ask'a me?"

"I'm not asking you," I said. "I was just wondering."

"Well, I don'a know."

Aaron and I had been joined by a few others. He eased his broken arm. As the bones knitted they gave him little stabs of pain. "Can't help you, I'm afraid. Not really mates with the engine room crowd. Most of the people I know are deck crew."

"Saw you talking to Trish this afternoon," Barbara said.

"Hey, yeah, down on the foredeck." Aaron widened his eyes. "Not just on the foredeck neither, ever since I'm off work. Keeps coming round for a chat, checking me out. I'm not kidding. I reckon she's giving me the old come-on."

"No, she just'a lonely," Luigi said. "That peeg of a husband. She talk to me also."

"That's OK then. Phew! Didn't know what to do, invite her down for a coffee or act cool like, tell her I'm a married man." He supped his export. "Mate don't like it anyway. One time he comes an' almost drags her away."

"This afternoon she was in her bikini."

"That's right. Smashing little figure an' all." A distant look came into his eyes. "Lucky her old man weren't there."

"He was," Barbara said. "Looking down from the bridge. Saw you give her a hand over the rail. Bit more than a helping hand, what I could make out."

"You're joking."

"I'm not."

Aaron thought about it. "Ah, well, there you go. Some of us have got it, some haven't."

"And some husbands are the mates of ships," Michael said. "But going back to what Ben was saying, there's got to be *somebody*, Luigi. Somebody down there in the thundering bowels might be a bit bent."

"No, I tell you already." Luigi spoke crossly. "I got no idea. Why not you ask Barbara?"

"No good asking me," Barbara said. "When I was down there all I ever thought about was surviving long enough to get back up alive."

"Back in your court then, Luigi," Michael said. "Come on, everybody down there can't be pure as the driven whatsit."

"How often I have to say?" Luigi crashed his can on the table. "You make'a me sick. Just because I work down the engine room, you think I know something. How often I have to tell you? I know nobody wan'a sabotage the engines. The engineer? The donkeyman? The electrician? The fridge engineer? Nobody, I know nobody. All right?"

We stared at him. His handsome brow was dark.

"Come on, mate," Aaron said. "Dear, oh dear!"

"You keep asking. Perhaps you think I do it, eh?"

"No we don't," Michael said. "Come on, Luigi, this isn't like – "

"I go to my cabin." He rose. "I thought you my friends. Maybe I come back later."

We watched him leave.

"Well," Barbara raised his eyebrows. "What was all that about?"

Fire on the Sea

KEVIN AND I carried up our mattresses and slept on the funnel deck that night. Rocking at anchor off the island with scarcely a breeze, the little sounds of the ship for company and the moon rising, it was magical.

But less perfect in other ways. In that part of the world, although the risk was slight, there was a chance that robbers or opportunist fishermen might attempt to board us during the hours of darkness. Because of this the lower decks and the anchor cable had been floodlit. The watch were told to be vigilant and went round to ensure that no ladders or ropes had been left hanging. Three of the four lifeboats were lifted from the sea and returned to their cradles. Only the for'ard starboard lifeboat, my lifeboat, which might be used the next day, remained in the water alongside the foredeck. One of the watch was detailed to remain on the foredeck and keep guard directly above it. A spotlight had been rigged on the bridge. Two rifles, Philip told me, stood in a corner of the chartroom. If there should be any attempt to board us, we were well prepared.

None of this affected Kevin and me. Snug beneath our blankets, we talked softly and told outrageous jokes. My book lay unopened, my torch unlit. But we were tired, certainly I was, and little by little we fell silent. Above our heads the equatorial sky was spattered with fat stars. Little creaks and slaps of water came to our ears; an occasional murmur of voices from the bridge. Soon we were fast asleep.

A couple of times during the night I woke and lay for a while, gazing at the moon and hearing Kevin's soft breathing before drifting back to sleep again.

No place in the world, it seemed, could have been more at peace when a sudden outbreak of shouting, alarm and running feet wrenched me out of a dream. Kevin pulled his head down into the bedclothes but I sat bolt upright. The footsteps approached the bridge. More shouting. I tugged on trainers and ran to the for'ard rail.

It was dawn, maybe ten minutes to sunrise. The decks were deserted. Then the second mate, who was on anchor watch, closely followed by Brian, appeared on the wing of the bridge and ran down the steps to the boat deck beneath me.

"What is it?" I shouted.

"Fire," Brian shouted back. "On the afterdeck."

I scrambled down a ladder and followed them. Although the ship was floodlit and the sky grew brighter by the minute, I saw the flickering light of the flames before the blaze came into view. What I had expected I don't know, certainly not the sight that greeted me. Someone had tied a bundle of bed linen to the flag rope, set fire to it and hoisted it halfway up the mast. Orange flames and smoke billowed in the light morning breeze. I was surprised it burned so fiercely, then I spotted the can of paraffin with which Barbara had drenched his engine-room clothes for the striptease. It had never been put away and lay empty on its side, a last dribble spilling into the scupper. As I watched, the flag rope burned through and the ball of fire crashed to the steel deck. Brian pulled the hose from the swimming pool, turned on the hydrant and soon the flames were extinguished.

The second mate stood looking around, uncertain what to do. He wore a loose green polo shirt, football shorts and sandals.

Steve Petersen, who had been detailed to guard the lifeboat, saw the smoke and came running. He joined me on the afterdeck. "Who'd play a stupid bloody trick like that?"

I had been wondering the same thing myself. The answer came a moment later and after that things moved pretty fast.

One of the watch ran from the accommodation. "Bagot's gone, sir."

"What?" The second mate swung to face him.

"Yes, sir. Overpowered Smoky Crisp and tied him up."

As if to confirm it, Smoky appeared behind him, mopping blood from his hair.

"What the hell happened?" the second mate wanted to know.

Smoky examined his wad of bloody tissues. "Said he wanted to go to the bog so I let him out but he'd pulled a rail off the bunk. Never heard a sound. Next thing he's clocked me over the head, stuffed a sock in my mouth and tied my hands and feet with his shoelaces. Tight an' all." He showed his wrists. "Said he was sorry, locked me in there and scarpered."

"For God's sake!" Tim Nettles looked at the scorched mast and blackened bedding. "You mean Bagot did this?"

"Yeah, I guess. He took some sheets an' stuff with him."

"What for?"

"Well that, I s'pose."

"Right, start a search, that's everyone. Bennett, get the bosun out his pit and tell him to get it organised. Petersen, I left you guarding the lifeboat. Get yourself back there. I'll be up on the bridge. Let me know as soon as there's any news."

But the news he was looking for came even before we'd started. "It's Bagot, sir." Philip arrived at the rail above us. "He's taken the lifeboat."

"The lifeboat!"

"Threw over one of the ladders on the foredeck."

The second mate looked at Steve.

"I've only been away a couple of minutes," he protested. "There's no fishing boats or anything, nothing in sight. I thought I might be needed."

"Yes, all right." He turned back to Philip. "What's Bagot doing?"

"He's cast off and he's rowing away."

"Towards the island?"

"No, out to sea."

"Out to sea! What's he think he's playing at?"

We hurried to find out, jostling on the steps, and ran for'ard.

Ossie was a hundred metres from the ship, heading out into the opal dawn. He wore pyjamas and was pulling on the oars with much splashing.

"Ossie! O-o-ossie!" Our shouts rang across the water. "Come ba-ack!"

He took no notice.

"Better get after him," the second mate said. "What's the state of the boats?"

"All in their chocks," Brian said. "Mate said put the covers on 'case we get another downpour."

The second mate sighed. "All right, fast as you can. Take the port for'ard, it's got an engine. You two go with him. No, not you, Crisp, better get that head seen to."

The boat crew ran off.

"What's all this noise?" The mate appeared in his Paisley dressing gown. Tim Nettles told him what had happened. "Bloody messman!" the mate said under his breath, not caring that we could hear him. "Mad as a hatter. Should have left the bugger to drown back there in Fiji."

"That's nice," Smoky said.

I hurried to fetch Michael and Barbara. They ran out in their night clothes.

Aaron met us in the alleyway. He was carrying his binoculars. "That right Ossie's done a runner?" he said.

"'Fraid so."

"Poor sod."

When we returned Ossie had stopped rowing. Quarter or half a mile distant, the lifeboat rocked on the waves. Beyond it, just to the right, the sun was on the point of rising.

Leaning over the side, Ossie rinsed his face and hands in the bright seawater and scooped it over his bristly head. At the time I thought he was washing off sweat or refreshing himself; later I realised it was a kind of ritual cleansing. Still dripping, he took something from a plastic bag. It was his surplice, the only white religious garment he had retained. He pulled it over his pyjamas and hung the big wooden cross around his neck.

"Ossie!" Barbara shouted. "Ossie, love!"

Perhaps he did not hear. Standing, he turned to the east where at that very moment, by good luck or extraordinary timing, the first burning dot of sun tipped the horizon. Looking, from that distance at least, like some ancient priest or druid, Ossie threw back his head and raised his arms in a gesture of adoration. For a full minute he remained like that, silhouetted against the sunrise, his surplice billowing, staggering a little as the lifeboat rocked on the waves.

Then he bent, balancing with one hand on a seat, and lifted something from the deck. "What's he got there?" I asked Aaron.

He struggled to take his binoculars from the case. It was awkward with one hand: the straps were tangled, he dropped a lens cap. "Oh, here, you have them."

I turned the milled knob and Ossie sprang into sharp focus. He was holding the bronze plastic urn. "It's his mother's ashes." I could see his lips moving – was he praying or talking to her?

He pulled off the lid and threw it into the sea. The alarm bells inside my head grew louder. Carefully he withdrew a scoop of ash, threw it into the air and watched it blow away down the breeze. He threw a second, and a third, then tossed the scoop after the lid. Grasping the urn in both hands, he set his feet and swung it in a wide arc. The last of his mother's ash billowed forth. Some fell heavily and was swallowed up by the sea but the finer particles hung in the air, enveloping him in a golden haze as they were caught by the rising sun. They drifted away.

Casually, as if it no longer mattered, he threw the urn aside. I saw a little splash as it hit the waves. At the same moment the second lifeboat came into view. For some reason, instead of using the engine, the crew of four – the bosun, Brian and two others – were rowing. But my eyes were not on them because Ossie had sat down and lifted a foot to the seat in front of him. He appeared to be fiddling with his shoe.

"What's he doing now?"

"It's a shackle." Aaron had reclaimed his binoculars. "He's fastening a big shackle round his ankle."

A shackle! I ran to the rail above the foredeck. Directly beneath me stood the bitts where I had sat the previous day when we were swimming. A heavy shackle had lain upon them, part of Samuel's work on the foremast shroud. I had set it down on the deck and spread my towel on the bitts because they were too hot. Ossie had stood where I was standing now. The shackle was gone. The ladder he had thrown over to reach the lifeboat hung close by.

"Ossie!" I shouted at the top of my voice. "Ossie!"

"Poor devil," Smoky said.

But it was not his intention to end his life by drowning, nothing so simple. Now Ossie grasped one of the oars and rose to his feet. Holding the oar vertically with the blade in the air, he drove it with all his strength against the bottom planking. The thuds reached us across the sea. Six, seven, eight times he smashed it down and at length broke through to the ocean beneath. The lifeboat gave a lurch and began to settle.

Having achieved what he wanted, he laid the oar aside and reached for another object, hidden until that moment. It was a red plastic container. Even at that distance I recognised the petrol can with which an engineer had topped up the tank when we went to the island. He unscrewed the cap and sniffed at the liquid inside. It was a ten-litre can, quite heavy. To the horror of everyone who saw it, Ossie steadied himself and upended the can above his head. The bright fuel splashed to his shoulders and saturated the surplice and pyjamas, making them cling to his body. He flung more about the lifeboat and tipped what remained into the sea.

"Ossie!" Everyone was shouting. "Ossie! No!"

At last he took notice of us and turned to face the ship where twenty or thirty fellow seamen had gathered along the rails. He raised a hand.

"Ossie!"

The men in the lifeboat were rowing hard. I grabbed back the binoculars. Ossie was smiling. In the brightening daylight I could even see the scabs on his forehead. He turned again to face the sun, by this time almost clear of the water, and raised his arms like white wings or a sacrifice.

Then he struck a match.

A blinding ball of fire erupted from the lifeboat, filling my vision. I cried aloud. All along the rail others did the same. The binoculars fell, dangling against my chest. Across the water whatever was happening was hidden by the blaze. A pillar of flame rose high above the lifeboat. The sea was on fire.

The petrol burned out but now that part of the boat that was not flooded was ablaze, the many layers of paint, the tar, the wood, the oars and sail. The sun lifted above the sea. Thick smoke fouled the beauty of the morning.

Of Ossie there was no sign, either then or when the rowers could draw near enough to peer into the glowing, flaming shell. Nothing remained to bear witness of my clumsy friend. He had gone into the sea. The shackle had carried him beyond our reach. A fragment of charred, white cotton floated several metres away and that was all.

Out Like a Light

I FOUND Michael and Barbara in Ossie's cabin. It was a couple of hours later. The cabin had been stripped. Nothing of our friend remained: boards, candles, clothes, shoes, books, vestments, everything had gone. The locker door hung open revealing empty rails and hooks. The drawers were bare. Ossie had got rid of it all. It was as if he had never existed. Except …

Except for a few playing cards and a scrap of paper on the coffee table. I picked up the paper:

> Dear Barbara,
>   I am so sorry! I do love you. Thank you for being my friend. And Michael. And Ben and the others. You've all been so kind.   Ossie B
>   x x x

I looked at the cards. They were from the tarot: the Fool, the Tower, the Moon and one or two more.

Barbara was watching me, his face wet with tears.

After a while I said, "Why did he do it?"

"He couldn't bear it any longer, I suppose. He was ill."

"Yes, but why – you know, the petrol and – "

"I expect it was the dolls."

"The dolls?"

He smiled faintly. "Perhaps you don't remember."

"Don't remember? How could I forget? I helped him collect the stuff. That night in Panama. I kept watch outside the cabins while he went raking through their hairbrushes and everything."

"No, not then, later. That time the bosun kicked his door in."

"And they had the fight? Yeah, I remember that, but what's it got to do with – ?"

"How everything seemed to come true: Steve with his twisted

ankle, Rat'bone's horrible abscess, the bosun's arm red raw with the chip fat. Then the bosun burst into his cabin all bandaged up and blazing drunk, remember, and found him with the dolls lying there on his bunk and went mad. Pulled out all the needles and made this big ball of wax with a tuft of Ossie's hair in it – and his watch and comb and that picture of him with his mother and whatever else. Turned the voodoo back on him. Stuck it on the end of his marlinspike and melted it in the candle flames, everything on fire and smoking and dripping on the dresser? *Go on, burn!* he said, remember? *Burn!* Then he threw it out the porthole into the sea. *I hope you drown!* he said. And Ossie screaming and going out of his mind."

I hadn't been there but everyone had told me about it. "So do you think that's why he ...?"

"Well, it was Rat'bone and the others drove him to it, but it's what he did, isn't it, set fire to himself and – " His voice choked. "Can you think of any other reason?"

Michael comforted him.

"Not really," I said when he had calmed down a little "It's just, well ..." I picked the cards from the table.

"The tarot, you mean? I don't know anything about that. Not more than messing around and having a few laughs." Barbara sniffed noisily. "Ossie did though, you're right, it was important to him. Could have had something to do with it."

"I'm sure it did," Michael said. "It's all tied in together: the voodoo, the tarot, his mother's ashes, those clothes he wore ... Then after they threw his pills over the side ..."

I had seen it all – the dolls, the candles, the incense, the needles. I had played with his tarot cards and he had been going to tell my fortune but somehow we'd never got round to it. Some were scary: *Death, the Devil, the Hanged Man*. One was *the Fool*, another was *the High Priestess*. Was that how he saw his mother and himself?

"I don't like it," I said, "all that black magic and stuff. Not when it gets serious."

"Didn't do Ossie much good," Michael said, "that's for sure."

Which made us remember the petrol, the match, the exploding lifeboat, and we were silent for a long time.

Later that morning, after photos had been taken from every angle, the blackened lifeboat, which had remained afloat and been brought alongside to prevent it drifting, was towed to the island and dragged far up the shore. It was a pity to defile so beautiful a spot but in time the rainstorms and typhoons that swept the Java Sea would strip it bare and it would become a home for crabs and a nesting spot for seabirds.

The engine repairs were taking longer than expected. A message came down from the bridge that we could expect to weigh anchor around breakfast time the next day. In the meantime, work would continue as normal but finish at three so that anyone who wished to visit the island again or swim from the foredeck would be free to do so.

To take my mind off the terrible events of the morning, I did both.

My mattress had lain on the funnel deck all day, baking in the sun, and that evening, taking my seaman's knife and a metre-long cudgel of two-by-two in case of intruders, I went to bed early. It was dark up there by the lifeboats and engine-room ventilators. Covered by my blanket, I gazed up at the stars. It was impossible to stop thinking about Ossie and for a time I came close to tears. Those who had been there coped in different ways: a few stayed in their cabins. Others sat drinking. Most appeared to have got over it very quickly and gusts of laughter reached me from the bar.

There were snatches of music too, carried intermittently on the breeze. The bosun, possibly missing the company of Rat'bone, had taken his radio to the poop and settled himself in a deckchair with a beer and a paperback. I had seen him there at lunchtime and again when we finished for the day. Now he sat with fresh cans, reading by floodlight. Perhaps even beasts like the bosun liked solitude sometimes. Yet something felt wrong. Although he was half a ship away, I didn't like it and made sure my cudgel was ready to hand.

I had taken a chance on a few minutes but there was no way I could risk spending the whole night up there by myself. I had tried to persuade Aaron to join me but he reckoned he wouldn't sleep very well and preferred to stay in the cabin. Kevin, however, who had been my companion the night before, had enjoyed it and promised to join me as soon as he'd finished his drink and a game of darts.

"You'll not be long?"

"Ten minutes tops," he said. "See you up there."

A loud belch announced his arrival. "God, look at those stars!" He threw down his bedding and flopped beside me. "Brought us these." He set down a couple of cans and offered me something wrapped in a screw of paper torn from a magazine.

"What is it?"

"Chocolates."

"Where'd they come from?"

He shrugged. "Box in the messroom. Want one?"

"No thanks."

"Come on." He urged me.

"No, really, just brushed my teeth. Still taste the toothpaste."

"You should, they're good."

"Only got one filling, want to keep my teeth."

"Always get falsers." He shone his torch and chose another. His breath smelled of beer and chocolate.

"Whose are they anyway?"

"No idea. There's boxes all over the place. Another one in the bar. Engineers' rest room. Saw Tony Fanny Whatsit taking one up to the bridge. Reckon the old man sent 'em down to cheer us all up a bit after what happened."

He spread his blankets and slipped beneath. For a while we talked. The smell of chocolate was very tempting.

"I'm tired. Been a long day." He yawned. "Hey, hear the one about the woman teacher and the trapeze artist?"

It was very smutty but a good joke. I laughed. "Charlie tell you the one about the elephant in the Garden of Eden?"

He didn't reply.

"Kevin?"

He was sound asleep, out like a light. Too much beer.

The ship grew quiet. I lay for a while then turned on my side. My thoughts returned to Ossie. Where was he now? Had octopuses found his body? The Garden of Eden – was there a heaven? Gran said there was. But I was tired too. Little by little the day slipped away.

If I'd known what lay ahead I would never have closed my eyes.

Ka'tang

ONE SECOND I was asleep, the next I was wide awake. My skin prickled. I gazed across the moonlit deck, stared into the shadows. Nothing moved.

What had wakened me? I listened. Silence. Then a patter of feet on the deck below. Whispers.

I pushed down the blanket. "Kevin."

He did not stir.

I reached across and shook his arm. "Kevin!"

Still nothing.

"Kevin! Wake up!"

He lay like one dead. I crawled across. "Come on! Wake up!" I shook his shoulders. Shook him till his head wobbled.

No response. A wet snore. A slobbery intake of breath.

What was wrong? Was he drunk?

More running. In T-shirt and underpants I crept to the for'ard rail where a lifetime ago we had peeped down on Trish in her bikini. The funnel deck was at the same level as the bridge. Between them and one deck lower lay number three hatch with open wooden deck at either side. I could see as clear as day because apart from the bridge and the funnel deck – the two topmost decks – the ship was lit like Christmas from stem to stern, deck lights as well as floodlights, in case of any attempt to board us.

A man appeared below me. He was not one of the crew. I shrank back and watched. He was Asian and thin with a bare chest and bare feet, a dark red sarong, his wild black hair bound up in a scarf. He carried a rifle, worn and businesslike. The light caught the whites of his eyes. He terrified me.

A second man appeared, also Asian, at the opposite side of the hatch. He had a long face and a glint of gold in his teeth. This man wore jeans and a loose shirt. He carried a machete.

One signalled to the other. Agile as cats, they flitted up the steps to the bridge, one port, one starboard, and vanished into the shadows. A sudden scuffle, a cry, a thud. Then silence. I glanced at my watch. It was after midnight.

A light went on in the chartroom, another in the wheelhouse, flooding out through the open doors. It illuminated a figure lying on the deck. It looked like Philip. The man in the sarong prodded him with a foot. He did not stir. Was he dead?

Directly beneath the bridge lay the deck officers' quarters. More lights were switched on: the rest room, the cabins, the radio room. I heard voices, one loud and complaining. It was Tony, the senior cadet. Wearing boxer shorts, he appeared in the doorway, driven backwards, gesticulating. The man in jeans slapped him across the head, struck him with the flat of his machete, knocked him down.

Now a third man appeared, accompanied by a boy. I recognised the man at once, even though he was dressed very differently from the last time I had seen him. It was the man I had met in Wellington, the educated native, if I can call him that, with a high cupid's bow, high cheekbones and animal eyes; the man who had cut my arm and threatened to cut my throat. The beautiful suit was gone, now he wore a sarong and a loose native shirt. They suited him better. He carried two weapons: an ornate dagger on a cord round his neck and a Kalashnikov rifle slung across his shoulders. It was plain that he was the leader.

Though he looked no more than thirty, I took the twelve or thirteen-year-old boy beside him to be his son. He had his father's broad face, golden-brown skin and blue-black hair, only where the man's thick hair was brushed straight back, the boy's hair hung in a fringe. Like his father he wore native dress but his weapons were different: on one hip he carried a sheath knife, on his other hip a worn and empty holster. The pistol was in his hand, not a shiny plaything but a battered, military-type weapon that looked as if he shot things with it.

"Ka'tang." The man in jeans dragged Tony to his feet. "Ka'tang!"

The leader looked towards him. They exchanged words in some foreign tongue. Tony was flung back down and threatened with the machete.

I crawled back to Kevin and shook him again. He did not wake. I slapped his face. He swallowed, gave a little moan and slept on.

A screw of paper fell from his blanket. The remaining chocolates scattered across the deck. Without thinking, I popped one into my mouth and crunched down. Cherry creme. The flavour flooded my mouth. Then – *chocolates*! Instantly I spat it out, a chewed lump. I sucked the saliva from my cheeks and drooled it on to the deck. Sucked it from around my teeth. Hawked softly and spat again.

How could I have been so slow, so stupid? Jumbo Ryland and this man called Ka'tang meeting by appointment at the Ascot Hotel; boxes of chocolates, identical to those Captain Bell had given us, lying on the table; the black holdall full of them; suddenly the whole ship awash with chocolates; and Kevin lying unconscious at my feet with chocolates by his trailing hand. No wonder there had been no alarm. No wonder these raiders, pirates, whatever they should be called, had met no resistance as they boarded us. No wonder they went about the ship unchallenged. The chocolates had been spiked with some powerful drug, and heavily spiked it seemed. Who wouldn't help himself to a chocolate or two if a box was left open invitingly and they were there for the taking? Perhaps not everyone but nearly everyone. The watch and lookouts, I guessed, were out cold, dead to the world. Even if the alarm had been raised, how could the remaining sailors have resisted these armed brigands? Ka'tang was free to do whatever he wanted, take the whole ship if he felt like it, once the engines had been fixed.

Once the engines had been fixed! That explained the sabotage.

In a second the whole plan became clear. It was so simple, so audacious. All it required were a few boxes of chocolates, a seaman to scatter them around, an engineer who would take a bribe – and the ship's position.

But how could they know the position? It was impossible to know in advance where the overheated bearings would bring us to a standstill. And even if *Pacific Trader* was lit up like a beacon, that didn't help the raiders if she was ninety miles away, hidden below the horizon. They needed a D.F. radio bearing. I remembered the second object I had seen in the Albatross Bar – a portable radio. But not principally a radio for entertainment, I guessed, a compact and powerful transmitter. As Ryland had sat at the stern listening to music, he had not been missing his friend, the abominable Rat'bone, as I too generously thought. Far from it, he had been signalling to these cutthroats who had come aboard while the crew lay in a drugged sleep, and now swarmed about the ship.

I looked down at my tangled bed. There wasn't much I could do about the mattress, but I threw my blankets on top of Kevin and arranged the pillows to look as if he was alone up there, then crawled back to the rail.

Ka'tang and his son had gone. So had the man with the rifle and a scarf round his head. Tony had crawled to his knees. He was trying to explain something to the pirate who stood above him. The man took little notice, perhaps he did not speak English. When Tony tried to stand, he kicked him back with a bare foot and raised the machete. I saw the metallic glint of his smile.

Voices came from aft. There was a shuffle of feet. I pressed deeper into the shadows. A number of the crew – I counted nine – had been rounded up and were herded on to the open deck alongside the hatch. These men, I guessed, had not eaten the chocolates. I saw Michael, Smoky, Steve Petersen, the alcoholic Chippy, some engineers, the donkeyman and Jumbo Ryland. Tony was beaten along to join them.

Seven of Ka'tang's men stood round. All were armed. They were a mixed bunch in jeans, shorts, sarongs, some bare-chested, some in ragged-T-shirts, some with cloths twisted round their brows. They lounged or stood easily, weight on one foot. Except for one, yellow-haired and restless, who seemed in the grip of some drug or illness, constantly touching his face, his chest, plucking at his clothes. If any of the crew attempted to escape, I had little doubt they would be hacked down or stopped in some other terrible way before they had gone a dozen paces. These men, particularly the twenty or twenty-five-year-old with tight yellow curls, might enjoy it.

They stood waiting. Beyond the hatch, the deck officers' cabins were illuminated. The radio room was in the same accommodation. I could see a figure moving about inside. There was a deafening, staccato burst of machine gun fire, then a second burst. Gunsmoke drifted from the window. There was a noise of smashing, splintering, a shower of electric sparks. It continued for some time. The radio room was being comprehensively destroyed.

It ceased and the figure went from sight. Shortly afterwards, Ka'tang emerged from the officers' entrance. He was followed by the mate and Ka'tang's son, his pistol still in hand. Ka'tang approached the assembled crew. Lightly he patted the barrel of his Kalashnikov and found it too hot to sling across his shoulders.

"Good evening. Do please sit down."

I was startled. The crew did as he suggested.

"I'm sorry to disturb your evening like this but we won't keep you long. If everyone does exactly what he's told, nobody will be hurt and you can all be back in your beds or getting on with the engine repair in," he glanced at his watch, "say three hours. If you don't ... Well, let's not think about that."

"What about all them blitzed out?" said one of the engineers.

"It depends how greedy they were. Six hours, twelve, it shouldn't last much longer." He looked around the listening faces. "I don't see the boy I met in Wellington. Stuffed full of chocolate, I suppose. Snoring his head off.

"Now, why the engines broke down. Why I'm here, in fact. What we're looking for is stowed away down there." He glanced at the hatch cover. "Strong room in number three hold. Boxes of currency and registered mail. I want none of your personal possessions. My men feel differently, I'm afraid, they're very fond of watches and tape recorders, that sort of thing; I leave that to them. But first things first. The hatch needs to be opened, and if my copy of the cargo plan is accurate, twenty tons of wool have to be hauled out to give us access to the strong room. That's where you come in. Once we get down there," he turned to the mate, "I hope one of the officers might be persuaded to hand over the keys."

The crowd on deck were silent.

"Right. Gilolo." Ka'tang addressed an older man whom I took to be his second-in-command. They exchanged a few words and Gilolo took over. He had little English but made up for it by gestures and violence.

"Come! You work!" He brandished a thick end of rope. "You! Yes, you."

The chocks were knocked from the hatch coaming, the canvases were pulled back, the hatch boards were dragged aside. Beneath lay the trunk, a non-refrigerated shaft that led down to the hold. It was packed with bales of wool. They were large and heavy, wrapped in sackcloth and strapped with metal bands. Two pirates went off with the bosun and returned with ropes and hooks. One jumped into the trunk and jammed hooks behind the metal bands. Three men to a rope, the crew hauled the bales up on deck and tumbled them aside.

They had come from their bunks and the engine room. Some wore pyjamas, some their underwear, some their boiler suits. Fat and thin, young and middle-aged, they heaved on the ropes. A few of Ka'tang's men, eager to get the job finished, lent a hand.

"Aah! Aah!" A metal band sliced Tony's fingers. He clenched his fist and slowly opened it. I saw his palm red.

Gilolo shouted and lashed him with his end of rope. Angrily he made pulling motions. Tony shouted back and showed him his hand. Gilolo beat him about the head. He raised the butt of his rifle. Tony resumed heaving.

There was no need to empty the whole trunk, just the for'ard end which gave access to the strong room. Steadily they burrowed down. On all sides, like building blocks discarded by a petulant giant, enormous bales of New Zealand wool littered the deck.

It was at this moment something occurred that was to give me nightmares for a long time. One of the engineers, the fair-haired junior who had gone through the crossing-the-line ceremony with me, tried to make a run for it. Where he expected to hide on a ship, I have no idea. Perhaps in the engine room there was some locker or store with strong metal doors. Whatever his thoughts may have been, he did not get far. Before he reached the corner, the pirate with yellow hair threw up his rifle, took quick aim and fired. The bullet hit the engineer squarely in the back and kicked him forward. He gave a gasping cry, flung up both arms and crashed headlong among the bales of wool. I could just see him, a red stain appearing through the cotton of his boiler suit.

He was dead, of that I had no doubt. All in a couple of seconds. There was a stunned silence.

The man who had fired the shot made his leisurely way across the deck. As he reached the young engineer he worked the bolt of his rifle, lowered the muzzle and shot him again.

Just to make sure.

The Black *Ishtar*

THE BANG, shockingly loud, echoed in my head for weeks.

Ka'tang said something. The yellow-haired man put down his rifle and dragged the body to the rail. With a little grunt he heaved it over. I heard the heavy splash as it hit the water. The young engineer, who had become something of a friend, was gone.

His killer, twitchy and half smiling, touched his hair, cracked his neck, plucked at his clothes, blew his nose on his fingers. He pulled something from a pocket, unscrewed a cap and tapped it onto the back of his hand. He sniffed it up.

Ka'tang sighed. "I did warn you," he said to the crew. "Why do you not listen? Let me say it again. Do exactly what you are told and no one will be hurt."

Gilolo lashed Michael across the back. The work continued.

As the men in the trunk burrowed down, clearing the for'ard end only, the bales of wool at the after end rose above them like a ragged cliff. I feared it might collapse and bury them, but it didn't and after a long time the top of the door to the strong room appeared.

"Sulu!" Ka'tang summoned his son.

They spoke briefly. Sulu checked the safety catch on his pistol. Ka'tang, followed by the mate with Sulu bringing up the rear, mounted the steps to the bridge.

The guards sat smoking, rifles on their knees. After the fate of the young engineer, no one seemed likely to make a break for freedom.

A score of bales still needed to be shifted. Chippy, drunk from the start, had no strength left; an hour's heaving had reduced his arms and legs to rubber As he tried to pull again, his knees gave way and he collapsed, clinging to the rope for support. One of the engineers, a tubby bald man, was nearly in the same state. Michael, standing up to it better than most, looked down at his hands.

Up on the bridge, meanwhile, Philip lay motionless. Light spilled from the door of the wheelhouse. From my position on the funnel deck I could see shadows and occasionally movement within the wheelhouse and chartroom. It was impossible to tell who this was but presumably Ka'tang, Sulu and the mate. They moved in unhurried fashion, there seemed no urgency, then all at once there were shots: *Crack! Crack – crack!* Sulu's pistol, I guessed, not loud enough for a rifle. I saw the flashes. What was happening? Had the mate been killed?

He had not, for a moment later he emerged, followed by Ka'tang, and they stood talking by the wheelhouse door. What about, I wondered; was the mate bargaining for our safety? No one working round the hatch took any notice and I realised the two on the bridge could not be seen from the deck below. The mate looked away from his captor. This seemed to enrage Ka'tang for his drew back his fist and hit him on the side of the face. It was a wicked blow and the mate dropped from sight. Ka'tang drew the dagger at his chest, a heavier weapon than he had carried in Wellington, and leaned forward. I froze, was he about to cut the mate's throat? Seconds later he rose, wiped the blade between thumb and forefinger, and returned the dagger to its sheath.

What had he done? What had taken place up there on the bridge, just out of my field of vision? I could see a section of deck and stared at it, dreading to see a slow tide of blood.

But killing the mate had not been Ka'tang's intention. He stooped again and this time, by some perverse quirk of humanity, he appeared to be helping him to his feet. Perhaps he felt he had been punished enough. The mate was doubled up and clung to the wheelhouse door for support. When he had recovered sufficiently, he limped painfully past Philip and began to descend the bridge steps. At his back came Ka'tang. Then Sulu, carrying a large cloth bag which I learned later contained the contents of the ship's safe.

They reached the cluttered deck and the mate sank onto a bale of wool. He looked dazed and lifted a hand to his injured face. His arrogance was gone. The front of his shirt was red.

Ka'tang crossed to the open hatch and tossed something down. I saw a glint of silver. They were the keys to the strong room.

Sulu handed his bag to a pirate who carried it away aft. With the muzzle of his pistol he motioned Michael, Smoky and one of the engineers to step over the hatch coaming and climb down the unstable wall of wool to join those at the bottom. Two pirates, armed with rifle and machete, followed at their heels. It was strange to think that back in Westport the alarming Sulu would be in his first or second year at high school.

By this time the entrance to the strong room had been cleared. The locks were complex: first the top, then the bottom with a different key, then the top again. The heavy metal door swung wide. The locker was packed to the roof.

Discharging resumed, only now the cargo was sealed mail bags, red and buff, with the word REGISTERED stencilled on the side in big black capitals. One and two at a time, they skidded up the trunk. Among them were sturdy cardboard boxes whose lettering I could not make out. Ka'tang sliced one open. He pulled aside the packing paper and rooted beneath. A thick wad of banknotes appeared in his hand. Laughing, he held it high to show his followers. With shouts they ran across. One fired a volley of shots into the air. Ka'tang ripped off a paper band and tossed the notes high overhead. The wad disintegrated, fluttering in the breeze like autumn leaves. Some blew over the side, some into the hold. The pirates scrambled to gather them up and tucked them away into ragged pockets.

The discharging had ground to a halt. Gilolo shouted and laid about him with the end of rope.

Ka'tang slit open one of the mailbags and pulled out a padded envelope. He tore it open and tipped the contents into his palm. A fiery necklace glittered in the deck lights. He held it up, diamond and ruby, and smiled with satisfaction. A second envelope contained documents: bonds, deeds, certificates, I could not tell. A third was full of money. A box contained an exquisite ornament. Ka'tang thrust them back and handed the mailbag to the youth with yellow hair.

In under an hour the locker was emptied and the men down the hold were summoned back on deck. Twelve-year-old Sulu, shouting and brandishing his pistol, forced the mate to join them. In a long file, guarded like slaves or convicts, the crew carried the booty aft. I backed out of my hiding place and ran barefoot to the after rail of the funnel deck.

For the first time I saw the pirate vessel, a two-masted cutter with brown sails and a strongly raked bow, illuminated by our floodlights. Fifty feet long and built for speed with, I guessed, a very powerful engine, an engine capable of thirty knots or more. She was black with dark masts and superstructure, a bit shabby-looking. In a vessel like that, Ka'tang could tie up at some remote berth without attracting attention, lie innocently at anchor, or slip away in the night unnoticed. The name painted on her bow, whether permanently or just for a few hours, was *Ishtar*.

She was lashed to the starboard quarter. Our crew, negotiating the steep metal steps with difficulty, deposited their burdens on the afterdeck of *Pacific Trader*. Ka'tang's men passed them from one ship to the other. Smoky stumbled and dropped his load. Before he could rise, the flat of a machete struck him on the back, a foot thudded into his ribs. The pirate shouted, threatened.

"All right! All right! I only tripped." Smoky picked up his mailbag and continued. "Dear, oh dear."

It took several journeys.

The last box, the last bag, were handed aboard the black cutter and carried below. Then all our crew, those who had been working, were herded to the port quarter opposite the *Ishtar*, and made to sit on deck. Ka'tang and Sulu, weapons in their laps, sat on the canvas of number six hatch to guard them.

It was the moment the pirate crew had been waiting for. With whoops and shouts and a slap of feet they ran through the ship. Stereos and leather jackets, wallets and binoculars, gold chains and credit cards, sextants and chronometers were gathered into personal heaps on deck and carried aboard the *Ishtar*. I saw, or thought I saw, Aaron's cassette player. Certainly it was gone when he returned to the cabin. They seemed fated.

Two of the pirates went among the crew on deck, relieving them of watches and neck chains. Those who lay unconscious elsewhere in the ship were robbed as they slept. One had a gold ring torn from his ear. Another, for some reason, was hacked in the upper arm and nearly died from loss of blood. Captain Bell's cabin was ransacked while he and his wife lay sleeping in chairs; her jewellery box, which had been locked in the safe, was gone.

At last they were finished. The ship had been stripped of its personal possessions and most valuable items of cargo. The radio room and transmitters in the lifeboats had been destroyed; the radar had been shot and imploded; the navigation equipment had been stolen; the distress flares were gone; pipes and chains and cables in the engine room and on the bridge had been chopped through. The pirates had got what they came for and now they could leave, secure in the knowledge that for several hours, at least, we could neither report them nor weigh anchor.

Their work was not quite finished however:

Several had been drinking and carried bottles. Gilolo, an angry and violent man at the best of times, kicked a path through the crew and dragged Tony to his feet. Tony resisted, then allowed himself to be led forward. Looking down from my vantage point, I wondered why he had been singled out. Did Ka'tang know of him? As a friend of Ryland, did he expect to be treated differently from the rest of us? Whatever he may have presumed, that was not what happened. As they reached the open deck, Gilolo thrust him towards a group who knocked him down and bound him hand and foot. Tony struggled but it was futile. A fist struck him on the ear. "What are you doing?" he shouted. "Let go of me! You've got it wrong, I'm the one that – " A ball of rag was thrust into his mouth, a gag tied across. His eyes rolled. His body bucked. Two of the pirates dragged him across the hatch to the starboard rail. What were they going to do? Drop him over the side? Let the sharks, gathering for the engineer, have him too? But no, swinging Tony like a sack, they flung him down to the deck of the *Ishtar*.

Another of the pirates, bare-chested and with a flower in his hair, had been sent back through the ship. He reappeared above the swimming pool. He was grinning, white teeth in the brown face. Over his shoulder was slung the unconscious body of Trish.

Michael jumped to his feet. "No! No!" He rushed towards Ka'tang. Two men blocked his way.

"You do well but she will come to no harm." Ka'tang raised a reassuring hand. "We are not savages, we take her for ransom, that is all." He glanced towards the mate. "She will be safe."

"That's what you say." Michael was reckless. "Him," he pointed to the yellow-haired raider, "he just shot a man. I don't believe you."

"Listen to me," Ka'tang said quietly. "The man, that was different. The girl, I tell you she will be unharmed. Now, I am being very patient. Sit down please."

Michael retreated.

"She's my wife," the mate said belatedly.

"Yes, I know. And …?"

"How much money do you think I've got?"

Ka'tang smiled. "Well, perhaps her parents."

The pirate carried Trish aboard the *Ishtar*.

"And the boy," Ka'tang said, "that very unpleasant boy, we take him for ransom too. My sources tell me his father is rich: big house, land, Rolls Royce. Tell him five million. Dollars US."

"Five million," Smoky was unsympathetic. "Give you five million to keep him more like."

Ka'tang shrugged. "His father won't pay, we sell him to work in the mines."

I had been unobserved for so long and strained so hard to hear that I became careless. My head emerged from my hiding place. The floodlights on the mainmast caught my sun-bleached hair. Although three decks above them I was spotted, not by the pirates but by the bosun. At once he betrayed me:

"There's somebody up there."

Flight

"There's somebody up there."

Ka'tang swung round. "Where?"

"Up on the funnel deck." The bosun pointed, unshaven, squinting in the floodlights.

I had ducked back but it was too late. Beneath me there was a hubbub of voices. Shouts. Commands. Running feet.

Dressed only in the T-shirt and underpants I'd worn for sleeping, I raced past the lifeboats and engine-room ventilators and slid down the ladder to the boat deck. Bales of wool were heaped around me. I clambered through them. My hand was sticky – the engineer's blood. I reached the steps that led to the bridge and ran up them. My feet were bare. One foot slipped and I wrenched the nail of my big toe. Behind me there was a shout, the crack of a rifle. A wooden rail exploded into splinters. I ran into the wheelhouse. Broken radar screen crunched underfoot. The second mate lay dead or unconscious on the chartroom floor. The rifles Philip had told me about were gone. Where now? A door stood open. I raced through, slammed it behind me and leaped down the stairs to the officers' cabins. Where could I hide? Which cabin? More stairs descended to the officers' dining room and galley. I ran on down. Somewhere behind me there were voices. Shouting. Not English. Vaguely I was aware I had done something terrible to my toenail. The dining room and galley were locked. I sped through a fire door. The alleyway branched. Directly in front of me lay the stewards' alleyway. A man with a machete was heading towards me. I cut past the petty officers' cabins into the deck-crew alleyway. It was deserted. I sprinted aft. The man with the machete had not yet turned the corner. Ahead lay the open crew deck with Ka'tang and his cutthroats immediately below on the afterdeck and the *Ishtar* tied up alongside. The cabin I shared with Aaron was right beside me. I pushed through the curtain. Aaron lay drugged and unconscious. Since the swimming-pool incident he had slept in the bottom bunk. His plastered arm trailed on the edge. I heard footsteps. Seconds later I had leaped to the top bunk and pulled the sheet to my throat.

Someone entered the cabin. The light was switched on. A long silence. I struggled to stay still, not to pant. The curtain rings rattled. Again silence. Then voices in the alleyway. I risked a half peep through closed lashes. The cabin was empty. I shifted my position. My foot hurt. The nail of my big toe wobbled. It was hanging off. I felt sick. And terrified.

More voices. Closer at hand. Whispers. The faintest brush of the door curtain. I held my breath. A hand pulled down the sheet. Fingers wiped sweat from my forehead.

"Ahh!" Glistening faces. A jabber of foreign voices. The stink of sweat and breath. Hands dragging me down to the deck. Blood from my toenail all over the sheet. Fists beating me about the head.

Helpless, I was dragged from the cabin, down the alleyway and out to number four hatch. Three men gripped me by the arms, the T-shirt, my hair. They shouted to Ka'tang. Followed by some of his men and our captive crew, he came to the steps to meet us.

"Ah, we meet again." He called to me on the deck above. "My young friend from Wellington. The boy with the English accent." He eased the rifle on his shoulder. "Despite the warning I give you, you spy on me even ..."

I heard no more. I was too frightened. They were going to kill me like the engineer. How would it be? A bullet? A knife? The sea? A machete that could hack off an arm with a single blow?

They dragged me, fighting, to the top of the steps. Savage faces looked up. I struggled back. They forced me forward. Something struck the back of my neck. My senses reeled. I gripped the handrail and tried not to let go. Blows rained down upon my arms, my shoulders, my head. I was driven over halfway down. The man with yellow hair seized a machete and ran forward. Sulu was in his way. The man pushed him aside and reached the foot of the steps. His eyes were crazed. He raised the machete.

"No-o-o-o!" Someone charged forward.

I was kicked in the back and lost my footing. My grip was broken. I was falling through bodies. A roar of noise. My head struck the metal deck: a crack like death, like a baking bowl on the back step. A stunning flash of red, white, black, and bigger black and …

The Pilot's Cabin

The light hurt my eyes.

Where was I? In bed but I'd never seen this cabin before. I had a splitting headache. My whole body felt heavy as lead. What had happened to me? For a minute I lay still then turned my head a fraction. Somewhere in my neck a bone cracked and rearranged itself.

The curtains were drawn. It was night. Aaron was sitting with me, reading a magazine. I was absurdly grateful. It was like being ill when I was little and waking in the dark to find gran at my bedside.

"Hello." My voice was a croak.

Aaron looked up. His eyes brightened. "Ben! Mate! Back in the land of the living."

I smiled, weak as a kitten. "What time is it?"

He pulled his watch round. "Bit after two. How d'you feel?"

"OK. My head hurts."

"Not surprised."

I put up a hand and winced as I encountered something hard in my hair. It made me feel a bit sick. I investigated with my fingertips. A scab, four or five centimetres long. The prickly ends of stitches.

"What happened?" My mind was a blank.

"I wasn't there. Say you gave your head a hell of a crack."

"Who says?"

"Michael, Smoky, a few others."

I let this sink in.

Aaron crossed to the bunk. "Anything you want?"

"A pee. In a minute." I shut my eyes. "Where are we?"

"Somewhere south of Borneo."

"No, I mean here."

"Oh, pilot's cabin."

"Pilot's cabin?"

"Up with the officers."

"What am I doing in the pilot's cabin?"

"Mate wanted you up here. Sick bay's full."

It was too much to take in. "How long?"

"'Bout a day."

"A day!"

"Don't ask me, I was out of it. Michael an' somebody carried you up last night."

Did I care? Did I want to know? I thought my head was going to burst. "Start at the beginning."

"The beginning? Well you know more about that than I do, you were there."

"No, I don't. I was where?"

"When they come aboard."

"When who came aboard?"

"The pirates, mate."

I was dazed but with that one word it came surging back: the raiders; the guns and machetes; the dead engineer; my flight through the ship; being dragged across the deck. My stomach rose into my throat. "I can remember them – forcing me down some steps."

"To the afterdeck. Everyone's been talking about it. Steve saved you from some maniac."

"With a machete." Like a nightmare, I remembered the man with yellow hair coming at me.

"Reckon he was going to chop your head off; anything he could reach. Steve dragged him back. Guy turned on him. Saved your life."

I shut my eyes but it didn't go away. "What happened?"

"Head honcho shot him."

"Shot Steve?"

"No, his own guy. Hophead, snowed out of his mind. Boss had a Kalashnikov. *Pa-pa-pa!* Bullets went straight through him. See the marks on the bulkhead. Blood everywhere."

"Why? I mean, why not me?"

"Took a shine to you, apparently."

"Took a *shine* to me?"

"Said he met you in Wellington. That right?"

"Yeah."

"You never said."

"Never told anyone 'cept Charlie. He cut my arm as a reminder." I showed him the fading scar, a pink line in the sunburn. "Said he'd cut my throat if I didn't keep my mouth shut."

"God! I'm glad he didn't take a shine to me." Aaron eased his arm in the sling. You could hardly see the plaster for messages.

"Tell you about it later," I said.

"He left you something."

"What do you mean?"

"A keepsake."

"A keepsake! You're joking. He's left me a keepsake? What is it?"

"I think Michael's got it, let him show you. It's cool."

I tried to take it in. "What about Steve?"

"Got cut up pretty bad. Old man had to stitch him up. No more body beautiful. Wasn't for Steve, you'd be – well."

I'd be what: dinner for the sharks? In the freezer next to Rat'bone? In a body bag with my head down there between my ankles? And Steve risking himself to save me. Steroid Steve – all those nasty things I had said about him! I looked down at my hands, limp on the sheet, fingers all there.

"Thanks for sitting up. Are you going to bed now?"

He glanced at his watch. "Hour and a bit. We've been taking turns, don't want to leave you alone up here."

"I'll be OK."

"Yeah, well."

"Who else?"

"Smoky, Michael, Barbara, Kevin. You're one of the good guys, got a lot of friends."

My eyes blurred. "Sorry." I rubbed them with the heel of my hand. "What a Mary-Ann!"

"Could have fooled me."

Cautiously I swung my feet to the rug and discovered I was still wearing my T-shirt and underpants, grubby after the events of the night. A burning pain shot through my toenail – or more precisely, the raw place where my toenail had been. It was swathed in bandages. I stood, taking my weight on my heel, and grasped the locker.

The ship rolled heavily. I realised we were under way again.

"Got the engines going yes'day teatime." Aaron lay back on the day bed. "Just as well, this sea getting up."

As if in response, the ship gave a lurch and spray spattered the window, high above the foredeck.

Right and left I staggered against the bulkheads as I made my way to the officers' washroom. The accommodation lights were on. Outside all was dark. The wind whistled in the rigging.

I don't like two o'clock in the morning at the best of times but after visiting the lavatory I felt a bit better and examined my face in a mirror above the washbasins. I looked dead beat, dark around the eyes. The wound in my scalp was too high up to examine. All I could see was an iodine stain, a patch of cropped hair, the blood-stiffened ends of stitches and a centimetre of black scab. Still, better than a machete-chop all the way down to my Adam's apple. My hands were dirty and when I washed them the water turned pink. I couldn't think why, then I realised it was the blood of my friend the engineer. I rinsed my face, scooped up a drink of water in my palm and lurched back to the pilot's cabin.

Aaron had straightened the bedclothes. "Fancy a cup o' tea? Couple of digestives? Got a little galley next door."

"That would be great." I pulled the sheet to my chin. "Thanks."

"Don't let the mate give you any jabs."

"What?"

But Aaron was gone. Don't let the mate – ? It was the middle of the night. What did he mean?

His head reappeared round the curtain. "You just think about that sexy wee nurse in Lyttelton."

"Sexy wee nurse in – ? Oh!"

He was gone again.

Aaron was right, it seemed an excellent thing to think about "But hey," I called after him. "What's that you said about not – ?"

I heard the rattle of the kettle. He'd be back in a minute. In the meantime ... I shut my eyes. I was so *tired*.

———•———

The Dagger

I never got that cup of tea. Or the biscuits. When my eyes opened again it was daylight, Aaron was gone and Michael sat in his place eating fingers of buttered toast and drinking what looked suspiciously like orange juice. He saw my eyes open.

"Ben, you're back."

"Mm."

In a second he was at my bedside. "How d'you feel now?"

My scalp hurt, so did my toe, but the headache was nearly gone. "OK. A lot better than last night."

"Aaron told us." He tidied my hair. "It was such a relief. There's all those murderous pirates and you just lying there. We thought you were dead." Abruptly his eyes filled and tears spilled down both cheeks. "Silly me." He wiped them away.

I caught his arm. "Thanks."

"Oh, Ben!"

Outside the storm had increased. *Pacific Trader* pitched and rolled. Heavy spray smacked the window.

As always, Michael rose to the occasion. "You're not the only one that suffered, you know," he said. "Look at these hands – ruined!" He spread them towards me. "Look, blisters! Calluses! How can I put *Coral Blush* on nails like that?"

I smiled.

"Ah, well. Best tit forward. Don't let the baskets grind you down." He blew his nose. "Fancy a bit of breakfast?"

I thought about it. "Lovely. Breakfast in bed."

"Tea and toast?"

"Coffee. Any chance of a bacon butty?"

"Have to go down to the galley. I'll get it when someone takes over. Don't want to leave you alone up here."

"That's what Aaron said. Why?"

"It's the mate again. When Barbara was up before."

"What about him?"

"Well," he checked there was no one listening at the door and perched on the end of the bunk. "Here's Barbara sitting with you and the mate comes in to give you this injection. You lying there dead to the world and Barbara says, 'What's that for?' 'What business is that of yours?' the mate says. 'I'm his friend,' she says. 'Well, it's just to keep him quiet.' 'Keep him quiet!' Barbara says. 'Look at him! How quiet do you want him to be?' 'It's for his own good,' the mate says. 'Keep him sedated until he's had a chance to recover.' 'He doesn't need sedating,' Barbara says, 'he needs to regain consciousness.' 'You trying to teach me my job?' the mate says. 'No,' she says, 'but he's not having that injection.' 'I think you ought to go back to your quarters,' the mate says. 'I think you ought to get back to navigating the ship,' Barbara says. 'Go near him with that hypodermic an' I'll bash your head in.'" Michael screamed with laughter.

"To the mate?"

"Oh, she's fierce, Barbara, sometimes."

"What happened?"

"Well, the mate gets on his high horse but there's nothing he can do about it, is there, 'cept have Barbara arrested. And she knows more about sick people than he does. Blew it with Charlie, didn't he? And Aaron wouldn't let the mate touch him. So he can't do much but go away again."

The curtain swished back and Philip came into the cabin. He wore oilskins and was streaming with water.

"Just looked in to see how you're doing."

"Oh, he's much better," Michael said.

"Last time I saw you," I said, "you were out cold on the wing of the bridge."

"Yeah, I'd eaten a couple of those chocolates. Just about zonked out then someone must have hit me round the back of the head. Knew nothing about it." He put up a hand. "Big lump. OK now though." He turned to go. "Can't stop. Old man sent me down to make some tea. Bottom's dropped out of the barometer. Hell of a storm coming up."

He left with Michael and I heard them clattering in the little kitchen. Michael brought in a tray with coffee and toast.

"Instant rubbish, I'm afraid, it's all they've got. Make you a decent cup with the bacon sarnie."

"What time is it?"

He checked. "Quarter to ten."

I propped myself against the pillows. "Tell me again what happened – that guy with the machete. Aaron says the leader shot him."

"Well, he did. You never saw anything like it. Guy's stoned out of his skull, gone mad crazy, slashing out and Steve's struggling with him, then suddenly this blast of machine-gun fire: *Tat-tat-tat-tat-tat!* About bursts your eardrums. Kicks him back like a horse and he crashes to the deck there beside the steps, blood leaking out all over him. And Steve's cut to ribbons. And you're lying there like you're dead. It was horrible."

I stopped chewing. "What happened then?"

"Well, the leader – "

"Ka'tang," I said.

"Pardon?"

"Someone called him Ka'tang."

"That right? Dead scary but ever so dishy, isn't he?"

"Is he?"

"Of course he is. How can you be so straight? Back at the clubs in Westport they'd be calling for oxygen." He laughed. "Anyway, the rest, they don't seem that surprised. So he tells them to take the dead one, him with the bleached hair, back aboard the boat. Seems more concerned about you. Bends to see if you're still alive. Tells Smoky, he was nearest, to look after you. Said some pretty nice things considering."

"Like what?"

"About you being a fighter, stuff like that. And he was sorry about the engineer and all, he didn't want anyone to get hurt."

"Funny thing to say when you come on board armed with machetes and machine guns."

"That's what we all thought." Michael picked up something from the day bed and staggered as the ship lurched. I slopped my coffee on the blanket.

"Anyway, he left this for you. Told Smoky to see that you got it."

It was a knife, not the knife he kept hidden inside his suit, but the dagger he was carrying when he boarded the ship. The cord was greasy, the sheath stained with what could have been blood. I pulled it free, a savage weapon that made my skin prickle. The blade was carbon steel, about twelve centimetres long and nicked in a couple of places, slightly curved, both edges razor-sharp. It had a steel guard and a handle of hard black wood inlaid with red and silver wires. A chipped red stone, possibly a garnet, was set in the pommel. It was a frightening gift. I tested the edge against my thumb and wondered if it had killed anyone.

Why had he left it for me? It was a question I was to ask myself many times. Aaron said he had taken a liking to me though I couldn't think why. Something in Wellington? Because I'd spied on them? Because I was only a bit older than his son? Because I'd fought back when they caught me? It was only later, when everything was over, I wondered if he'd guessed that sometime I might need a weapon to defend myself.

"Horrible, isn't it?" Michael said.

"Yeah, I suppose." I swished the blade in the air. "Great knife though."

"Oh, Ben! How can you say that?"

"I dunno, just feels good. I like knives."

"Well I don't, so put it away, murderous thing. I wish I'd never given it to you now."

I returned it to the sheath and threw it towards the day bed. It bounced to the deck. Michael picked it up and scrubbed the taint from his fingers.

"So I'm lying there," I bit into my second slice of toast. "What happened after that?"

"Nothing really. They carried everything aboard, that awful dead man and the stuff they'd taken from the crew, and just took off. Fired a last burst of the machine gun to remind us to stay where we were, used the engines to get clear then hoisted the sails."

I pictured the black *Ishtar* against the streak of moonlight on the sea, vanishing into the darkness. "What about the chocolates?"

"I went round and gathered them up, all the ones I could find anyway. Ten boxes – they were evidence. Except – you won't believe this – one of those thick engineers and the donkey-man, they only went and ate some, didn't they? After all that." His eyes opened wide in disbelief. "Ones that were bombed-out before, they started to come round a couple of hours later. Wicked headaches, hung over. I reckon they were the lucky ones."

"Wish I'd been one of them." I sucked marmalade off my fingers. "I wouldn't be lying here with my head stitched up and my toenail torn off."

"That leader, the one with the machine gun – "

"Kalashnikov," I said.

"If you say so. Anyway him, he called you 'the boy I met in Wellington, the boy with the English accent'. What did he mean?"

"I never told anyone except Charlie," I said. "He threatened to kill me. Said if I went blabbing he'd cut my throat."

"What!"

"It was pretty hairy."

"So you did meet him?"

"Only by accident. I'd gone shopping – with Ossie actually but we went our own ways after a bit. There was this big hotel in a square, the Ascot, and I saw the bosun standing outside. He's got on his suit and he's waiting for someone so …"

I told him everything: Ka'tang arriving, the scene in the Albatross Bar, what happened in the cloakroom, the way they slipped out the back to avoid passing me in the foyer.

Michael was horrified. "And you didn't tell anyone?"

I shook my head. "Except Charlie."

"You could have told *me*," Michael said. "Secretive thing! I always knew there was something funny about that cut on your arm. It didn't look a bit like a scratch."

"Well, now you know," I said.

"And it was definitely the bosun you saw with him? You're sure?"

"Come on," I said, "I'm not going to get something like that wrong, am I? He called him a gorilla."

Michael smiled. "I've been thinking: if it's the bosun took the chocolates out the holdall like you said and put them on the bar table, his fingerprints will be all over them – all over the cellophane anyway. And everyone saw the transmitter, if that's what it was. Looked like a pretty good radio to me. Maybe he's still got it in his cabin. Too thick to sling it over the side."

"Unless the pirates took it."

"Of course they would, that's a pity." He sat forward. "Anyway, what are you going to do?"

"Give us a chance," I said, "I've only just come round. What do you think?"

"Tell Daddy Bell," he said at once. "You've got to. All those accidents you've had, you're lucky to be alive. And now we've all been drugged and beaten up and robbed by this terrible gang – and the bosun's been helping them. There's an engineer dead! People are badly hurt. The engines have been scuppered, all the registered cargo's gone, we've got no navigation equipment. And now there's a storm coming up. What's going to happen next?"

I couldn't think of anything to say.

Michael helped me out. "It's enough to make a girl reach for the gin bottle, I'll tell you that for nothing."

Interview with the Mate

CAPTAIN BELL was on the bridge and hadn't left it for twenty-four hours. The tropical storm, which bore every sign of developing into a full typhoon, was strengthening by the minute. Our speed had been reduced, just enough to hold headway into the wind, and our course altered to meet the sea head-on. Visibility was less than a mile. *Pacific Trader* had no radar and no radio. All the captain's efforts were concentrated in nursing his ship safely through the atoll-studded waters of the Java Sea; one mistake and we could end up fighting for our lives in the towering waves that bore down from the north-west. At that moment he had no time for a deck boy with a tale to tell, no matter how important.

"See the mate," advised Tim Nettles who met me at the chartroom door. "There's nothing the captain can do right now."

As if to confirm his words, the ship lurched with the impact of a wave and solid spray smacked the windows of the wheelhouse.

I limped back down the stairs that led from the chartroom to the officers' alleyway. One foot was bare, my heavily-bandaged toe made it impossible to put on a shoe. Michael waited at the bottom.

"I suppose you've got no option," he said when I reported what Tim Nettles had told me. "Either that or wait until the storm dies down."

I thought about it. "Will you come with me?"

"Of course I will, try to stop me. You're not going by yourself, that's for sure."

The mate's cabin held unhappy memories for me. I had been given a spectacular bawling-out there for helping Trish with the praying mantis. His curtain swung far out as the ship rolled heavily. I tidied my clothes and knocked.

"Come in." A relaxed voice came from within.

I made a face at Michael and pushed the curtain aside.

"Oh! It's you, Bennett." The pleasantness evaporated. "Always you, the ubiquitous deck boy. What is it this time? If you've got any business that needs my attention, tell the bosun, you know that. You are not, repeat *not*, to come bothering me in my quarters."

"It's about the bosun we've come to see you, sir." I stepped into the cabin with Michael at my heels.

"Oh, you've got Goldie with you. So it's *we* this time, is it?"

"Well, it's mostly me, sir." I staggered, trying to save my foot as the ship rolled far over. "But Michael knows all about it."

"Oh, he does? Well bully for him." The mate sat in a wooden armchair. His cheek was bruised from the punch Ka'tang had given him on the bridge. He wore patterned swimming shorts and a blue shirt unbuttoned to the waist. He had been drinking. "Well, soon I'll know all about it too, so we don't need him here, do we?"

I looked at Michael. "No, I suppose – well, not really but he can corroborate everything if – "

"Corroborate, no less. My goodness, deck boys do use big words. Well, if we need corroboration we'll send for him. But right now I'm tired, I've got a headache and the weather's bloody awful. So get out, Goldie, sling your hook. You're not needed."

Michael hesitated.

"Did you hear what I said?"

Michael gave him a blue stare and turned away. "Wait for you outside," he said softly and retreated through the curtain.

The mate sipped from his whisky glass. "Right, Bennett, something you want to tell me about the bosun."

"Yes, sir."

"You do realise that Mr Ryland might be annoyed, you going over his head like this."

"Yes, sir, but I don't see what else I can do." I staggered again and knocked my toe. The sudden pain made me gasp.

The mate watched me coolly; he didn't invite me to sit down.

"All right, what is this *vital* piece of information?" He reached for a cigarette and stretched out his legs. His shirt fell open and I saw a thin red line across his chest. I realised this was the wound he had received up on the bridge when Ka'tang draw his knife and I had thought he was going to be killed; the wound that had bloodied the front of his shirt. To my surprise it was nothing, barely skin-deep, little more than the cut on my arm. Already, in less than two days, it was healing over.

The mate saw me looking and pulled his shirt across. "You were saying, about Mr Ryland."

So I told him, just as I had told Charlie, Aaron and Michael: all about the Ascot Hotel, and Ka'tang in his Armani suit, and the bosun, and the third man, and the chocolates, and the senior cadet distributing them around the ship, and the radio, and what had happened in the hotel cloakroom, and Ka'tang's remark about *the boy I met in Wellington*. And going back to the start of the trip I told him about Tony stealing the snorkelling gear from number five hold, and the bosun taking the whisky. But I didn't tell him about the sextant, binoculars and other things hidden in my cabin and how Charlie and I had dumped them over the side.

The mate listened attentively. "Well," he said as I finished, "full marks for imagination. I never heard such a farrago of lies and ridiculous accusations in my life. You've really gone to town this time, Bennett."

"I beg your pardon?"

"You don't expect me to believe all that?"

"But it's true, sir. Every word."

"Oh, yes? And what's your verification? Where's the proof? Who, apart from you, can vouch for any of it?"

"Well, Charlie Sunderland that had the appendicitis, Michael Goldie, Aaron Scott, they know."

"And who told them?"

"Well, I did. But it was right when it happened. I was the only one there so it had to be – "

"Precisely, you were the only one there. At the – what did you call the hotel?"

"The Ascot."

"Sir."

"Sir."

"So, the only one who saw Mr Ryland at the Ascot Hotel, the only one who saw Fanshott-Williams raid the cargo, the only one – "

"But it's true!" I said again. "Sir."

"Repetition doesn't alter facts, Bennett. Shouting isn't proof. You've got a grudge against the bosun, had it from the first day you stepped aboard this ship. And it's a bit underhand, not to say convenient, to start accusing the senior cadet the second he's been abducted by those damned savages."

I heard footsteps in the passage. Someone, Philip I think, stopped to speak to Michael.

"You've got a tip about yourself, Bennett," the mate went on, "got a chip on your shoulder. You see yourself as different from the rest of this crew – seem to think you're somehow superior. So you come up on the bridge and try to ingratiate yourself with the second officer, I've seen it myself. Pal up with one of the cadets. And when the bosun cuts you down to size you don't like it. First chance you get, you invent this tissue of lies."

"That's not right," I said. "It's not fair. And they're *not* lies."

He drew on his cigarette. Smoke stung his eyes. He assessed me through it.

"I don't like you, Bennett, I can't speak more plainly than that. You're a bloody nuisance. I think you wouldn't know the truth if it jumped up and bit you on the arse."

There was no point in arguing, no point repeating myself, plainly I was getting nowhere. "I'm sorry if you don't believe me, sir. All I can do is tell you what I saw and I came to report it." Struck by a thought I added, "And when the captain asks for statements and the police come aboard, I'll tell them exactly the same thing."

"What?"

"There's bound to be an enquiry, sir, surely. There's a man dead, people kidnapped. All the crew have been – "

"My God! Who the hell d'you think you are? D'you think I don't realise all that?"

Angrily the mate sprang from his seat and crossed to a little sideboard that doubled as a bar. The bottle clashed against the tumbler as he replenished his whisky. The water in a jug was warm and he went through to the bathroom. I glimpsed an enamel kidney dish beside the washbasin. A hypodermic syringe lay on a cloth. Was this the shot Barbara had stopped him from giving me? It sent a shiver down my spine. The mate saw me watching and pulled the curtain across.

I checked in the alleyway. Michael stood by the door. I beckoned him in.

For a couple of minutes the mate was gone. I told Michael what he had said and looked around the cabin. To me it appeared much the same as the last time I had been there but Michael, who was the officers' steward, said:

"Do you see his wife's picture's gone?"

"What?"

He explained: the photo torn in half and planted in my cabin had been replaced by another. It was no longer there. Nor, when I thought about it, were her gold sandals, her hairbrush, her lipsticks, her bottles of lotion and underwear that had littered the mate's cabin. Within two days every trace of silly, sexy, kindly Trish had been removed. Even the bed now had a plain blue cover and the air, which had been fresh and perfumed, was heavy with the male odours of whisky and cigars.

"Nothing to do with me," Michael said. "He stuffed it all into a bin bag and dumped it in the bottom of the wardrobe."

The mate returned, glass in hand, leaving the bathroom curtain open. The kidney dish and its contents had been removed.

"Oh, you're back, Goldie." He wasn't pleased. "Very well, I've been thinking about what you told me, Bennett, and I think we'll have Mr Ryland up here. See what he has to say about these accusations of yours."

"He'll deny it, sir," I said, emboldened by Michael's presence. "What else can he do? But it makes no difference, he was there. I know what I saw."

"Yes, yes, so you keep saying. Incidentally, that knife the leader – what did you say his name was – ?"

"Ka'tang."

"That's right, what was that about some knife he dropped?"

"He didn't drop it, sir, he gave it to me, told Barry Crisp to pass it on. It's in the cabin."

"Dropped, gave, whatever. We'll need that for evidence. When you come back bring it with you. Now go down and tell the bosun

I want to see him." I turned to leave but he called me back. "You still in the pilot's cabin?"

"Yes, sir, but now I'm feeling better I thought I'd go back to – "

"Stay where you are for the time being. I'll send for you when I want you. Goldie, we'll not be needing you, I'm sure there's work you should be getting on with." He sipped from his glass. "Right, on you go."

As we left the cabin Michael said at once, "Did you see? His wedding ring's gone as well."

I hadn't noticed.

"It's as if he couldn't wait to be shot of her."

"When he says he'll not be needing you – you're not going to leave me alone up here?"

"Course not. I've got to get Daddy's tea and tabnabs but one of the others will come up instead. You'll not be on your own, I promise you that."

There were two staircases in the officers' quarters, the narrow flight leading up to the chartroom, and a broad flight leading down to the dining room and crew accommodation. I descended to fetch the bosun, clinging to the rail to save my toe, and found him in the petty officers' mess.

"Oh, it's you." He had been laughing, a can of lager in his massive paw. The laughter turned to a snarl. "Not dead then, more's the pity."

"Thank you, Bosun. It's nice to know you care." I'd never have dared say it if Lampie hadn't been there as well and Michael at my back.

"Why, you cheeky – " He tried to rise, gripping the arms of his chair as the ship heeled far over.

Lampie bared his gums. "You asked for that, Jumbo. Lad's got spirit. Look at him, head split open, toe wrapped up like a mummy. How's it going, Ben boy?"

"Fine, thanks." I looked at the unshaven Ryland. "The mate wants to see you, Bosun. In his cabin. Sent me down to tell you."

"Right, now you've told me. So get out."

I did as I was told.

"Bloody deck boys," I hard him say to Lampie. "I can't stand 'em." His shout pursued me down the alleyway: "Always sticking your nose in where it's not wanted. I'd like to tear your bloody arms off!"

I followed Michael to the galley. I was shaking.

"Oh, Ben!" He put a hand on my arm. "You will be careful. He wasn't as bad as this even on the *Star of Bengal*. And with this weather... I couldn't bear it if anything happened. I just couldn't bear it."

The Third Man

Despite Michael's reassurance, I returned to the pilot's cabin alone. Smoky and Samuel had promised to follow me up, but when Philip arrived with the mate's summons they had not yet arrived. Carrying Ka'tang's knife, I followed him along the alleyway.

The mate's door, which previously had been wide open, was now on the hook, a few centimetres ajar. My head had started throbbing again. I knocked.

"Come in."

I lifted the little brass hook and pushed through the curtain. No sooner was I inside than the door slammed shut and the bosun seized me by the shirt-front.

"What's all these lies you've been tellin' the mate about me? Little rat! I've a good mind to knock your block off."

I stumbled back. My bandaged toe struck his shin. It was agony. I flung a hand out in self-defence and accidentally stuck a finger in his eye. He gave a bellow of pain and fury.

The mate pulled us apart. "Stop this! Stop it! How dare you, in my cabin. Let go of him, John – I mean Ryland. Let go! His union'll have half the ship out."

The bosun released me. Tears ran from his twisted eye.

My toe was on fire.

"That's enough, the pair of you." While I was below, the mate had changed into his full white uniform, brushed his hair, become a stern figure of authority.

"He's the one started it. Look, he's torn my shirt."

"Be quiet, Bennett. As I recall, it was you who started it, telling lies about Mr Ryland here. Slanderous falsehoods that could land you in a lot of trouble. Accusing him of consorting with criminals."

"Murderers," the bosun said. "My best mate killed by that loony messman, yeah? Now he says I'm knockin' around with pirates, sending 'em signals. I'm tellin' you, Chief, you search my cabin, go on, see if you can find a transmitter." He wiped his eye. "An' how am I supposed to have got down the engine room, fixed them bearings to run red-hot? Anyone see me down there? You want to watch who you're accusing, Mr bloody deck boy Bennett."

I was silent, wondering if Smoky and Samuel had turned up yet.

"Well," the mate said. "What have you got to say for yourself? You weren't so quiet half an hour ago."

"Sorry, sir, I haven't got all the answers. But what I told you, everything, was absolutely true." I drew a deep breath. "The bosun's lying."

"Lying! You little bastard!"

My stomach quaked. Those hairy hands could have squeezed the life out of me.

"I can't say any more, Bennett." The mate was white with anger. "You've heard Mr Ryland's denial. If you choose to trumpet these wild accusations in a statement to the captain or the police in Singapore there's nothing I can do about it. But this I will tell you, and it's an order. You are not to speak about it below decks. I'm not having a dishonest and bloody-minded deck boy undermine the morale and discipline of this ship. If I hear so much as a whisper that you've disobeyed me, you'll be on a charge, do you understand? A charge so damning it'll put an end to your days at sea, I can promise you that."

His dark eyes burned into me. I struggled not to be browbeaten.

"Is that the knife?"

I held it by my stomach. "Sir."

"Let me see."

Reluctantly I passed it across. The mate examined it, turning it this way and that in his long hands: the handle, the sheath, the cord that had gone round Ka'tang's neck. I saw he wore a signet ring on his little finger but Michael was right, if he had worn a wedding ring it was now gone. He drew out the curved blade, tested it with the ball of his thumb, dabbed a finger against the point.

"Deadly weapon in the wrong hands." He passed it to the bosun. "What do you think?"

"Yeah." Ryland grasped it in a fist familiar with knives.

Alarm bells jangled in my head. I stepped back. At the same moment the ship rolled heavily, punched by some gigantic wave. I staggered across the rug.

The mate resumed his seat and lit a fresh cigarette. I watched, unaware how important this small act was to be. He sat directly in front of me. The bosun was behind. I moved so I could see both.

"Goldie come up with you?" A cloud of smoke enveloped the mate's head.

"I'm not sure, sir. You told him to get on with his work."

"Up here by yoursel' then." The bosun's eye was red and watery. The hand holding the knife hung at his side.

"No, Smoky and Samuel came with me. They're waiting outside." I prayed it was true.

"Why?" the mate said.

Ryland swished the curtain aside and half opened the door. "What are you lot doing up here?" He spoke harshly. "Get down below."

"We're waiting for the lad." It was Samuel's voice.

"Well you can wait down in the messroom."

"We'll wait up here if you don't mind, Bosun."

"You'll do as you're damned well told. This is officers' quarters. You've got no business up here."

"Ben is our business." This was Smoky. "Too many funny things been happening to him lately."

"He's our mate." Aaron had joined them. "We're not going down 'less he comes with us."

Ryland hesitated then turned back into the cabin. The door slammed shut.

"You OK, Ben?" I heard Aaron's shout.

"I hope so." My heart was thudding.

"Failure to obey orders." The bosun was furious. "That's mutiny."

"Almost." The mate remained in his seat. "These friends of yours, Bennett. Am I to take it they already know about this incident in Wellington – I should say this alleged incident?"

"What I saw in the hotel?" I wasn't sure who knew by this time. "Probably, sir."

"So despite what I said, your unproven accusations are all over the ship."

"I don't know, sir. I just told Charlie and one or two others."

He reached for his glass of whisky. "Oh, I think we can say all over. If you *just* told one or two people, everyone will know by this time. You're in deeper trouble than I realised, Bennett."

Holding his cigarette between first and second fingers, he raised the glass to his lips. He drank almost daintily, little finger protruding. The cabin lights, switched on for the storm, winked on the bright disc of his signet ring. I stared. Where had I seen that gesture before: the long hand, the cigarette, the golden glass of whisky, the flash of a ring? It was important. A half memory of spaciousness, ferns, a sunbeam, a disembodied hand ... The mate set down his glass and flicked the ash from his cigarette with a thumbnail.

In that instant I remembered:

The Ascot Hotel – the third man!

I raised my eyes to his face. He saw my horrified expression; looked down where I'd been staring; was puzzled.

My eyes flew to the bosun. Down to the knife. Back to the mate.

"What's the matter, Bennett?"

I panicked. "Nothing, sir. I've got to go. Excuse me."

Not even feeling my red-raw toe, I backed to the door, keeping both in full sight.

"Bennett!" The mate's voice cracked like a whip.

"Where you think you're going, you little shite? Come back 'ere." The bosun lunged to grab me.

He was too late. I shoved him aside with all my strength and next moment was out in the alleyway.

"You all right, mate?" It was Aaron.

Before I could answer the mate appeared in the entrance. "Bennett, back in here!"

"No, sir."

"How dare you!" He stood aside to admit me. "In here, this instant."

"No, sir." I backed behind my friends.

He strode between them and grasped my elbow. "Into my cabin. Right now."

"Get off! Let go!" I struggled back. My fists struck him on the neck and chest.

"Hey! Come on, Ben." Aaron was shocked.

"Leave go of him, Mr Mate," Smoky said.

The mate was livid. "You've done it now, Bennett." His eyes blazed. "Striking an officer."

Samuel intervened. "No, sir, you had no right to lay a hand on him. He's a sick boy, you can see that. Very upset about something. You come wading in and start hauling him about. He had every right to defend himself. And there's three of us here as witnesses."

The mate was silent.

"I'll go back if you all come as well," I said. "Or if the old man comes down. But I'm not going in there with him and the bosun."

"Don't blame you," Smoky said. "Not get me in there neither."

"What is it, boy?" Samuel laid a big hand on my shoulder. "What you scared of?"

"The two of them." I hung back. "Mate and the bosun, both of them. I saw them in Wellington with that pirate leader – Ka'tang. And all the chocolates. In a big hotel. They're all working together. They're the ones behind the attack on the ship."

"You know what you sayin', Ben?"

"They want to shut me up. Bosun's in there right now with that knife in his hand."

"He's imagining it all," the mate said.

"Telling Michael to get below. Asking if I was alone up here. Trying to stop me talking."

"It's the knock on his head."

"Ask Michael, I told him. And Charlie. Not about the mate 'cause I've just found out. He's got that ring an' everything." I pointed. "And he's got rid of all his wife's photos and stuff. And he calls the bosun John, like he's a pal. How come just after I saw them in Wellington I got shut in that freezer locker? Why'd he try and put me in a hot bath that could have killed me? Who was in the pool when it collapsed? Why'd the bosun try to send you all down and leave me alone up here?"

"If Tanner had let me give him that injection," the mate said, "we wouldn't be having to listen to all this nonsense."

"You're right, I'd be dead."

"For God's sake, am I giving lethal injections now? It was a mild sedative to keep you quiet when you came round. Once and for all, there's no plot, Bennett. You're over-excited. You're sick, like Jones says."

"All right, but maybe the waiters back in Wellington will remember. The police can send pictures. I'll tell them where you sat. One will remember me definitely 'cause that pirate guy, Ka'tang, he cut my arm and I was bleeding through paper towels. She offered to fetch me a plaster." I showed them the scar. "I nearly left without paying."

"I can't go on listening to all this." The mate called through to his cabin. "Bosun."

Ryland appeared. The knife had gone. "Yes, Chief?"

"Take Bennett below. See he stays in his cabin. Lock him in if necessary."

"I'm not going anywhere with him," I said. "I'll go with Smoky and these. Lampie, if you like, or the second mate. Not with him though, there'd be an accident. I'd fall over the side. He's a murderer, he killed a friend of Michael's back on the *Star of Bengal*."

"Still banging on about that is he?" Ryland snarled. "It was an accident; the police said."

"Oh, for God's sake!" the mate exploded. "I don't care who he goes with, just get the bloody boy out of my sight. When I want to see him again I'll send for him." He turned back into his cabin. "Get below, the lot of you."

My head was thudding so painfully I needed to sit down. Smoky took my arm and slowly, clinging to rails as *Pacific Trader* pitched and rolled in the storm, we made our way below decks to the messroom.

Wet as a Water Rat

EVERYONE WANTED to know what had happened that afternoon in Wellington. So I told the story again and bared my forearm, but I didn't feel too terrific and after a bite of lunch I returned to the cabin I shared with Aaron to lie down for half an hour. He kept me company, repairing some jeans with a broken zip, but I fell asleep and half an hour stretched right through into the evening. When I woke up, Michael had taken his place. Unlike the practical Michael of the morning, he wore eye shadow, a low-neck T-shirt and baggy Thai silk trousers. As I blinked across the cabin he was concentrating on his lipstick.

"What's the time?"

He consulted his watch. "Coming up half past eight."

I couldn't believe it. "Not seen the trousers before. Going to be a party?"

"Who knows what might happen?" He pressed his lips on a tissue. "Can't let a puff of wind and a few spots of rain get you down." He fastened a necklace, slipped on some bracelets and examined himself in a hand mirror. "There! What do you think?"

"Gorgeous!"

"Oh, you sailors say that to all us girls."

"No, really, you look great." It was true.

He was pleased and returned his make-up to a tattered sponge bag.

I was hungry and we made our way to the messroom. The alleyway was wet under my bare foot. Right hand and left, we lurched from bulkhead to bulkhead as the ship rolled heavily. Dinner was long past and everyone had returned to their cabins, all but the eight-to-twelve watch – Smoky, Brian and an AB called Scudder whom I scarcely knew – who sat drinking coffee. All three wore rubber boots and leggings. Oilskins and sou'westers were thrown over chairs and dripped on the deck.

The storm had reached its ferocious climax. It was, we heard later, officially recorded as typhoon Caroline. *Pacific Trader* pitched and rolled so wildly it was a wonder the plates could take the strain. Chains secured the messroom chairs to the deck. Edges had been erected round the tables and wet tea-towels spread on top to stop things sliding around. Big hands were wrapped round the coffee mugs. Thuds and crashes came from near and far where objects that had not been lashed securely fell to the deck. Darkness had arrived early. Beyond the streaming portholes the wind shrieked in wires and railings. Black waves, higher than the bridge, bore down upon us and filled the air with spray.

"Hello there, Ben boy." Brian greeted me. "How you feeling now?"

"Lot better, thanks." I took the chair he spun round.

Michael said, "OK if I leave you now? You'll be safe with this lot. I told Barbara I'd look in, she's shaving her legs again. Don't know why she bothers, hairiest queen on the high seas. Have you seen her chest? I told her, you want to call yourself Queen Kong and go on the halls." He shrieked with laughter. "It's not a friend she needs anyway, it's a surgeon, the place will be awash with blood. It's always the same, fishnets and sticking plaster. Lisa Minnelli hasn't got a look in."

With a swirl of *L'air du Temps* he was gone, leaving me with the three tough seamen in their work clothes who waited to be summoned back into the storm.

"What you were saying before," Smoky said moodily. "'Bout the mate's wife. That right he's got shot of all her gear?"

"Looks like it. Photos, even his wedding ring."

"Lucky beggar. Anyone got them pirates' address? Get 'em to come to Westport, take my old woman anytime." He drew on his skinny fag. "Mind you, they wouldn't stand a chance. Fists like Joe Louis."

Attila wandered in and mewed for attention. Smoky picked him up.

"Strewth, what a weight.!" He settled the marmalade cat on his knees. "Attila the Hun – that's what my old woman's like. You've seen her, Ben. Pirates come round our place, she'd knock 'em dead in the front garden. Give the SAS a bell, come and get rid of the bodies."

Attila stretched his claws and yawned contentedly.

"Cor, your breath! What you been eating, rats?"

I took a handful of biscuits. "What are you doing down here anyway, all three of you? That's the whole watch. Who's up on the bridge?"

"Mate give us an extra smoko," Scudder said. "Wanted a word in private with the bosun."

I sat up.

"Good on him, I say. Got to have a man on the wheel storm like this. Bosun's steering, mate's keeping lookout, we get a break."

"Ring down when he wants us back."

"Midnight'll do me."

"Any idea what it's about?" I said.

"Likely to tell us?"

"What about the old man?" I packed my mouth with biscuit. "I thought he was living on the bridge this weather."

"Mate give him a break, get his head down for a couple of hours."

Smoky said, "Get you a coffee?"

"No thanks, just a bit peckish. I missed dinner. Maybe Kevin'll make me a sandwich."

The rolling ship trapped me in my seat. I waited for it to roll back and came away. After the events of that morning, whatever was being discussed up there in the wheelhouse, it concerned me. My life could depend on it. And if Ryland and the mate were up there, there was nothing to be scared of down here in the crew quarters.

I spotted Aaron heading into the washroom. "Hey." I followed him. "Mate and bosun are up on the bridge having some big confab. Sent the watch down. Will you come up with me, see if we can hear what they're talking about?"

"After what's just happened? In this storm? Are you off your head?"

"But if there's two of us."

"Away into the bar." He vanished into a cubicle. "I'll be along in a couple of minutes."

The bar and the sick bay were only a few doors apart. I'd visited Steve earlier and looked in again now.

Several people had told me how unforgettably brave he had been to tackle the drug-crazed man with the machete. In saving my life, which he had certainly done, he had been seriously hurt. The murderous weapon, which could have hacked off my head with a single blow, had been deflected by the metal steps. Other pirates had dragged the madman back and Ka'tang had shot him, but not before he had inflicted terrible wounds. Long scars, black with scab and bristling with stitches, decorated Steve's chest and back and the side of his face. Heidi and Captain Bell had done a brilliant job but Aaron was right, Steve Petersen's days as Mr Westport were over. Although he must have been devastated, he tried to be upbeat and hadn't blamed me at all.

It wasn't the first time I'd had reason to be grateful to Steve: he had rescued me in the thermal pool. And it was Steve, I was sure, who had saved me when I was being hunted by Ryland and the rest when they were robbing the cargo. It had to be Steve, there was no one else.

As I entered the sick bay, the cabin in which poor Ossie had been imprisoned, he was asleep, possibly sedated to give him respite from the storm. A plastic medicine glass rolled about the deck. I set it where it wouldn't rattle and stood by the bunk. Steve's powerful legs were covered by a sheet and he wore boxer shorts patterned with girls in bikinis. Above the waist he was bare, his golden muscles like a photo from a body-building magazine, but now criss-crossed by those disfiguring wounds. He lay peacefully, unshaven since the attack, his blond hair straggling across the pillow. Aaron looked in and went away again. I stayed a few minutes longer, wretched with guilt, and came away quietly.

Music and raised voices issued from the bar. Aaron had joined a crowd. Someone produced a felt tip and Michael found a corner of Aaron's plaster to add a new message. There were shouts of laughter.

I continued along the alleyway. An open door led down into the engine room with its roar and smell of hot diesel. Directly opposite, a flight of stairs led up to the engineers' quarters. I climbed them and headed for a door that gave access to the boat deck. As I opened it, the gale wrenched it from my hand and smashed it back against the bulkhead. In an instant I was transported from shelter into a maelstrom of wind and rain and towering waves. I stepped out on deck and struggled to shut the door behind me. In seconds my T-shirt was sodden, my old cotton football shorts clung to my legs. Both were black, appropriate for my role as an eavesdropper. I bowed my head against the storm, clung to the handrail on the bulkhead and worked my way for'ard. The noise was terrific: the thump of waves, rattle of spray, snap of the lifeboat covers overhead, shriek and roar of the wind. I stared around in the darkness. Brackish water salted my lips and blurred my vision. The bulkhead came to an end. Before me lay number three hatch so recently raided by the pirates. There was no sign of their presence: the wool had been re-stowed, the boards replaced, the canvases secured. No safety line had been rigged, perhaps because it was possible to get from place to place below decks. I waited, and in a momentary lull dashed the length of the hatch. The ship rolled suddenly. I lost my footing and was flung towards the side rail. The ship rolled back. I staggered the other way, crashed into the hatch coaming, and managed to reach the bridge steps. Gratefully I grasped the handrail, waiting for the raw pain in my toe to ease.

According to what Scudder had said, the mate and bosun were in the wheelhouse. Cautiously I mounted the steps. The wing of the bridge was deserted. The wheelhouse door, a wide sliding door, was shut tight. I peered through a corner of the big windows. All was dark, as it needed to be for night vision. Instruments glowed with subdued light: the engine-room repeaters, gyro repeater, ship's head indicator, angle of rudder. A man stood at the wheel, the binnacle directly in front of him. The dimly-lit compass card illuminated his chest and face. I squeezed the water from my eyes. Though the windows ran with rain and spray, I could see it was the bosun. The angle of light cast deep shadows and gave him the appearance of a demon. A spark of red, small as a firefly, brightened by the for'ard window. The mate was smoking.

It was impossible to eavesdrop from that stormy location. Also, I guessed, from the opposite wing of the bridge. There was, however, an internal route to the wheelhouse, the route I had taken to speak to the captain, the route I had taken when I fled from the pirates. I descended to the boat deck. The ship shuddered under the impact of a gigantic wave and solid spray landed *whop* on my shoulders. It made little difference, I could be no wetter.

I wrung out my shorts and T-shirt in the crew showers and hurried back for'ard. The stairs by the officers' dining room led directly to their quarters. I mounted cautiously and flitted across the alleyway. The much narrower stairs that led up to the chartroom and wheelhouse were wet from the boots and oilskins of the watch-keepers. I clutched the handrail to keep my balance. The chartroom door opened off a little landing. All was silent. A switch extinguished the staircase light. Infinitely slowly I eased the door open. The chartroom was dark and unoccupied. A voice reached me from the wheelhouse. I slipped through and closed the door behind me.

The chartroom was the same width as the wheelhouse and separated from it by the long chart table, above which were big windows, curtained at night to preserve the night vision of the watch-keepers. At each end of the chart table, port and starboard, a door led from one navigating room to the other. These stood permanently open.

What I was doing was foolhardy in the extreme, I realised that, but I was certain that if I were spotted I would be able to beat a retreat before the mate or the bosun could grab me. Safety lay just a short staircase away. All the same, I was very frightened and took time to get my bearings: there lay the current chart, the course recorder, echo sounder, barometer and empty sextant shelves. The port connecting door was nearer. Wet as a water rat, I crept to the threshold – and listened.

Get Rid of that Bloody Deck Boy

I CLUNG to the door post and strained my ears to hear above the noise of the storm:

"... have taken more bloody care. Kept your eyes open." The mate stood by the spray-beaten window, high above the foredeck. "I mean, Jesus, what were you doing, sending up flares? He must have spotted you and followed you. But did you see him? Don't make me laugh. He's no fool, that boy. He might be the biggest bloody pain in the arse since deck boys began, but he's got his head screwed on the right way."

I couldn't make out the bosun's reply, something about *like to unscrew it*. His back was towards me, silhouetted against the dim light of the instruments. He spun the wheel as the ship sheered to starboard.

"He saw everything," the mate went on. "You, Jawa Ka'tang, the chocolates, the transmitter ... sure you didn't send him a list?"

"... saw you as well. You didn't spot him."

"Matter of fact I don't think he did see me, he deduced it somehow, right there in my cabin ... recognised my watch or something. But he was right, wasn't he? And he knows it. Says he's going to tell the old man, and when we get to Singapore he'll tell the police."

"When's that then?"

"What?"

The storm reached a crescendo, shrieking in the rigging, roaring round the wheelhouse. Already they had to speak loudly; the bosun raised his voice further. "I said, when we due to reach Singapore?"

"Singapore? Not make tomorrow night now. Maybe next day, depends on the weather."

"So what are you proposing?"

"What am I proposing? About that bloody Bennett? What the hell do you think I'm proposing? He's got to go. Get rid of him. Over the side. Shouldn't be too difficult this weather. An accident – preferably one that *works* this time."

I knew already, but to hear it said out loud like that chilled me to the bone. All this while – the mate! I glanced behind me to make sure my escape route was clear.

"Not as easy as you think," Ryland was saying. "He's sticking with his pals now. I reckon there's someone even goes to the bog with him."

"We agreed at the start, any rough stuff's your business. My end went like clockwork, you're the one cocked it up. Up to you to put it right again."

"Well, I can't exactly – "

"Wasn't for that new messman – what's he call himself?"

"Barbara."

"That's it, Barbara! Wasn't for him I'd have settled Bennett myself. Hot bath. Morphine overdose. Cocky little runt used to be a medical orderly; hardly turn round but he's in my face. It's up to you now."

A shriek of wind and whack of spray against the wheelhouse windows drowned out their words.

"… work something out."

"I would if I were you. You're the one he saw; you're the one he's got evidence against; you're the one going to end up in jail, accessory to murder. Not to mention if they reopen the case about that steward on the *Star of Bengal*. Me, it's just circumstantial. No jury could convict me on what he's got."

The bosun said, "What about the waiters in that hotel, the Ascot, like he says? If the cops send photos an' they recognise the three of us?"

"If you'd done your job like you were supposed to it wouldn't be an issue. Anyway, I've been thinking about that. If the worst comes to – "

The ship crested a massive swell and rolled far over to port. Parallel rulers skidded across the chart table and landed crash on the deck. I fled to the door that led down to the officers' quarters and grasped the handle, but the two in the wheelhouse had more important matters on their minds. After a minute I returned to my listening post.

"... not all that difficult to disappear," the mate was saying, "start a new life somewhere else. I've always fancied living in Australia anyway: sun, beaches. Still, we'll cross that bridge when we come to it."

After a silence Ryland said, "What you mean, *if I was you ... you're the one he's got evidence against*? You trying to dump me?" His voice was harsh. "We're in this together, Duncan Rose, an' you'd better remember that."

"I suppose so. That's how we started out anyway." A lighter flared. The mate continued, "I've done deals with a few people over the years but never anyone like you. You're just so bloody stupid. I've *never* been in this kind of a mess."

"How d'you mean, stupid? You'd better watch what you're saying."

"You want to know? Well I'll tell you. Picking on Bennett from day one, for a start. Getting in tow with that bloody fool of a cadet. Couldn't keep your dabs off the cargo. Running a personal vendetta against those stewards and their pals. Allowing yourself to be followed. So-called 'accidents' that never worked. How's that for starters? Couldn't keep your head down, oh no, not you." He glanced at the gyro. "For God's sake, you're thirty degrees off course!"

Sullenly, thick hands on the spokes of the wheel, the bosun brought the ship back.

"One bit of luck, that psycho messman, whatever his name was, he got rid of Lenny Rathbone for us. I know you palled up with him but he was a liability. And I managed to persuade Jawa to take your other pal, Fanshott-Williams, off our hands. Not be hearing from him for a while. So that's two problems out the way."

"What about your wife?"

"My wife? You're not serious. You don't think I'd marry someone like Trish Grahame. Couple of cheap wedding rings, who's to tell? No, she was just along for – well, a bit of fun. Silly cow. Swanning round in her bikini. Deserved all she got."

The bosun thought a bit. "So now it's just the two of us."

"That's right, just the two of us."

"And are you planning to get rid of me as well?"

"Pull yourself together, what do you think I am?"

"You asking? Well, I'll tell you; ruthless, that's what you are. An' slippery. An' greedy."

"You reckon?" The mate gave a wry laugh. "Pots and kettles, eh?"

"You've got too high an opinion of yourself."

"If you say so."

"But I'll tell you what. You'd better not try an' double-cross me, 'cause I'll take you with me."

The bows plunged deep into a wave and came up shuddering. A wall of water crashed the length of the foredeck. For a minute the bosun concentrated on his steering.

"Where's the money, anyroad?"

"Somewhere safe. Sort it out when we reach Singapore. Don't worry, you'll get your twenty-five percent."

"Fifty."

"I beg your pardon?"

"I said fifty percent. Straight down the middle."

"We have an agreement, John, right back at the start when I got you this bosun's job. Crooks' contract. Whatever we get, your share's a quarter."

"Well, now I want half. Hundred thou – that about right? Set me up very nicely."

"Don't push it, John, for your own good. I'm telling you."

"Is that a threat?"

"No, a bit of advice. A warning if you like."

"*You're* warning *me*? Don't make me laugh."

"Suit yourself, but remember this, I'm not the one into double-crossing. And I'm not the one with that deck boy's evidence stacked up against me either."

"You think he's the only one got evidence?"

"Who else then?"

The bosun didn't reply.

"Who else?" The mate's eye caught the light from the binnacle.

"Codswallop! There's nobody. I'm clean anyway." He glanced for'ard, keeping cursory lookout.

"What about me?"

"You?" The mate was dismissive. "Would you really give up – what, fifty grand? I don't think so, John. When are you going to see that sort of money again? Anyway, what have you got on me, nothing. Just your word, the word of an ex-con against his chief officer. They'd laugh you out of court."

"You think you're so clever."

"Compared to some people."

"That's all you know." The bosun tapped his left shoulder.

"What does that mean?"

There was no reply.

"What's all this?" The mate mimicked his action.

The bosun wore a loose cotton jacket. He opened one side.

"What have you got there? I can't see. A gun?"

Ryland laughed. "You been watching too many films. No, not a gun. A tape recorder."

"Tape recorder?"

"Player, really. Little job, belongs to Lampie. But it records too."

The mate drew on his cigarette. Briefly the glow illuminated his features.

"Hung it on a bit of cord, see," the bosun said. "Way things were panning out, I reckoned I might need a bit of security."

"All the time we've … ?"

"Everything you just said, all in here." He gave the instrument a little pat.

"I don't believe you. Won't have picked it up."

"Did down below." Ryland set the wheel amidships and held it with his leg. He turned to catch the binnacle light and fiddled with the controls beneath his arm. There was a pause while he ran the tape back then the recorder crackled into life. I strained to catch the distorted voices:

" *… end went like clockwork, you're the one cocked it up … sorted Bennett myself. Hot bath. Morphine overdose. Cocky little runt … could convict me on what he's got …*" Crackling interference. He fast-forwarded. " *… take your other pal, Fanshott-Williams, off our hands …*

think I'd marry someone like Trish Grahame ... when we reach Singapore ... your share's a quarter ..."

The bosun switched off. "Believe me now?" He re-set the controls and let his jacket fall. "Not all that clear but the police will be able to sort it out. So if you've got any more ideas about ripping me off – big shot!"

The ship had wandered far off course. A huge wave, coming on top of the swell, caught us smack on the starboard bow. Water exploded mast-high. *Pacific Trader* slid into the following trough and rolled far over. Distant crashes reached my ears. Ryland was a good helmsman. Expertly he spun the spokes of the wheel; the gyro ticked round; reluctantly the bows swung back to meet the sea head-on.

"Looks like you've got me beat, John."

"You reckon?" Ryland was pleased with himself. "Fifty-fifty?"

"I guess so. Doesn't seem like I've got much choice." The mate crushed out his cigarette. "Never thought you'd pull a stunt like that on me."

"Got to look after number one, Chief."

"Dog eat dog, eh? I suppose you're right." The mate pushed himself from the window. As he moved into the dim light of the binnacle I saw he wore a cardigan and light canvas trousers. "There is one other possibility though."

"What's that then?"

"I keep it all myself."

"Come again?"

"You heard, I said I keep it all myself, every brass penny."

"You reckon? An' what about me? I just stand there and let you, I s'pose."

"No, I dump you over the side."

I don't know where the mate had the knife hidden, but as he passed Ryland I saw the dull glint of steel.

"What?" Ryland half turned. "You take me on, I'd break every bone in – "

The mate was behind him. He drew back his arm and with a savage, calculated thrust, plunged the blade handle-deep into the middle of the bosun's powerful back.

I'm not sure Ryland realised he had been stabbed. At least, not at once. I've heard it said that a stab feels like a punch. All the same, he was shocked. The spokes of the wheel spun from his grasp and he whirled to face his attacker. "What are you – "

The knife was stuck and the mate had to dodge round to pull it free. Twice, so hard that I heard the thud, he drove it into the bosun's broad chest.

And Ryland saw him. His twisted eye squirmed. He tried to speak but no words would come, just a terrible sound in his throat and blood running from his lips. He took a threatening half step – then his legs gave way and he fell to the deck. For a time he thrashed, those brutal hands fluttered like butterflies. Then he lay still.

The Stormy Foredeck

I FLED to the door that led down to the accommodation. The mate, I was sure, must come into the chartroom but he did not. Terrified, I returned to my spot by the wheelhouse.

The knife – Ka'tang's knife, my knife – still protruded from the bosun's chest.

The mate grasped the handle but it was stuck. He put his foot on the body and gave a little tug then wiped the blade on the dead man's jersey. The tape recorder lay beneath his outflung arm. One swift slice severed the cord and the mate pulled it aside.

A pool of what must have been blood was spreading beneath the bosun's head. From where I stood it looked black, glinting in the light from the instruments. The mate looked down, then went to the flag locker at the side of the wheelhouse and pulled out a rolled-up flag – I couldn't see which. He shook it free, two metres long, and swaddled it round the bosun's head. Taking two corners, he tied them in a rough knot to hold it in place.

It was his intention, he had said, to throw the body over the side and then, I suppose, sluice away the blood. He crossed to the wheelhouse door, the port door that led out on deck. Had he looked into the chartroom he might well have seen me. I retreated into the deeper darkness. The storm roared about the bridge. As he slid the door open, it burst in upon us. The spokes of the big ship's wheel, untended, turned this way and that. The gyro tick - tick - ticked round as the ship's head swung off the wind, exposing her flank to the fury of the sea. The mate brought her back on course.

Then he stooped and gripped Ryland by the jacket. The body was heavy. Laboriously he backed towards the open door, dragging the bosun behind him. Ryland's muffled head lolled from side to side. His work boots trailed on the deck. As they emerged onto the wing of the bridge, the wind and whirling spray tore at the mate's cardigan, blew the hair over his eyes, unpicked the flag from the bosun's head.

They passed from my field of vision. I stepped into the wheelhouse and looked after them. The straining figure backed towards the ship's rail. Just three metres away from me, the tape recorder lay on the wheelhouse deck. If I could gain possession of that ...

Pacific Trader buried her head and rolled far over. The recorder slid towards me: two metres. I gathered myself like a cat, and in a momentary lull I crept across the deck. And all would have been well had not the ship, balancing on a wave crest, dropped like a stone into the trough beyond. Something in the chartroom fell with a crash. The recorder slid away. I made a grab, lost my balance, set my hand in the pool of blood and slithered full length.

The mate looked up and saw me in the shadows. Instantly he let go of the bosun and sprang back towards the wheelhouse. I regained my feet and snatched up the tape recorder. It was too late. The mate was upon me. In desperation I flung the recorder full in his face and dashed back into the chartroom. In three or four steps I was at the door by which I had entered, the door which led down to the officers' quarters. It was set in a corner. Whatever had fallen, some boxed instrument, it felt like, had burst from a cupboard and prevented the door from opening more than a few centimetres. Two, three times I smashed it towards me, yelling aloud, and raked at the obstruction with my foot. There was no time. The mate appeared, clutching his eye. I fled the length of the chart table and out through the door to the wheelhouse at the far end. He followed, one arm raised to strike at me. Did I imagine it or did I see the knife in his hand? I swung round the door post and doubled back through the abandoned wheelhouse, past the swinging wheel and slippery pool of blood on the deck.

The mate shouted but what he said I have no idea. Next moment I was out in the storm, running across the port wing of the bridge. Ryland's body sprawled in my path. I leaped over it.

The steps were beside me. I grabbed the hand rails and slid down to the boat deck. The wind battered about me, tearing at my clothes. The bandage on my toe was unravelling. As I reached the bottom it snagged on a corner and tore away the dressing. I was too terrified to feel pain, but the rolling of the ship threw me off balance. The side rail was only a stride away. I hit it with my chest and grabbed hold with both hands. As we heeled far over, the leaping black water was right beneath me. I pushed myself back just as the mate, looking like a wild man with his hair and cardigan flying, came leaping down the steps towards me.

It was a split-second choice. To run aft, where friends offered safety, meant dodging past the mate who, as I saw in the gleam from a porthole, definitely was carrying Ka'tang's murderous knife. I fled down a second flight of steps to the crew deck. The pitching of the ship threw me from rail to bulkhead and by the time I recovered, the mate was slithering down the steps at my back. On the narrow strip of deck there was no way past. I ran for'ard.

Below me lay the foredeck, remnants of the last wave swashing in a corner, streaming out through the rails in a windblown cataract. I hesitated and looked back. The mate came running towards me. I had no choice. The steps were before me. Seizing the rails with both hands, I slid down to the foredeck.

As the ship rolled to thirty degrees, waves slopped through rails normally high above sea level and swilled across the metal deck, splashing round my ankles. Safety lines had been rigged the length of the foredeck, one each side of the hatches. The port line was beside me. I grasped it and started for'ard. The ship dipped her bows. Tremendous spray hit me in the face and chest. She slid sideways into a trough. Black waves, glinting in what little light came from the sky, reared mast-high above me. I struggled on, there was nothing else to do.

Inexorably, ten metres behind, the mate followed.

With a blow that jarred the whole ship, a wave struck the bow. Solid water cascaded over the fo'csle head, burying the capstan, foaming above the rails. I cried aloud and locked my hands on the safety line as it crashed down on number one hatch and surged the length of the foredeck. I had never felt such force of water. I was submerged, buffeted, but somehow maintained my grip. At that moment I think it would have taken a crowbar to loosen my fingers on the rope. The wave subsided.

Coughing salt water, I looked round for the mate. The line was empty. He was nowhere to be seen. Had he gone over the side? My hopes surged. Then I saw him, sprawled against the superstructure at the after end of the foredeck. Whether he was hurt or still had the knife I couldn't tell, but at once it became clear that he did not intend to let me escape. His eyes found me in the darkness. Rising with difficulty, he grasped the safety line. Hand over hand, determination in every step, he worked his way for'ard.

I reached the fo'csle where the safety line ended. Where could I go now? To go up on the fo'csle head would be suicide. The ship buried her bows again. I pressed against the bulkhead where there was a small overhang. The torrent poured past my head, leaving me in a watery cave like the space behind a waterfall. As it ended, boiling on over the hatches and down the foredeck, I fled to the safety line on the starboard side.

Something had changed. In the aftermath of the wave the ship was wallowing, her rolling had become more sluggish and extreme. With no one at the wheel she was swinging broadside-on to the storm. The next wave hit her exposed flank with a crack like an explosion. A tremendous fan of water leaped high as the crosstrees. Further and further she rolled to starboard. A derrick at number two hatch broke from its lashings, smashed to the deck and skittered to the rail. Paint tins crashed about in Lampie's locker. Somewhere beneath me the anchor cable shifted. What may have been happening elsewhere in the ship I had no idea for my ears were filled with the roaring of the wind and sea. Luckily I had tight hold of the safety line for I lost my footing on the streaming deck. My legs trailed. The starboard scupper was under water. The Java Sea slopped towards me.

The ship rolled back. I regained my feet and stared all round. Again the mate was nowhere to be seen. What should I do? I hesitated, then hand over hand I began to work my way back down the foredeck.

The starboard rails had been smashed by the wave: ten metres were buckled, another ten metres were broken off. Hanging from a couple of stanchions, they straggled across the deck. I reached the foremast.

The mate was waiting for me, clinging to a ladder behind the mast house. Like a nightmare, he sprang out and caught me by the T-shirt. I yelled with fright and pulled back but he was too strong. Gripping the safety line with one hand, I beat at him with the other. My fist struck his head, shoulder, chest. It made no difference. The knife was gone. His hands were on my throat. His thumbs dug in, painful, unbearable. In seconds my head began to reel. I let go of the rope and clawed at his face, tore at his hair, scratched, punched, gouged, anything to make those hands release my throat.

They didn't. Then dimly I realised that we had been joined by a third person. Someone else was tugging at the mate, beating him about the head, screaming, "Let go! Let go!"

It was Michael, who had been talking to Aaron in the bar. I was nowhere to be found. In a panic he had followed me to the bridge and found it deserted, stumbled over the dead bosun and spotted the two figures far beneath him.

The ship listed heavily to port. We fell to the deck, tangled as cats, and fetched up against the hatch coaming. Water washed over us. One of the mate's hands was dragged away. I pulled at the other. His nails tore my skin, cut like blades. *Pacific Trader* rolled back to starboard. The deck tilted – thirty, forty degrees.

Abruptly the floodlights came on. The mate's face was right before me. His eyes were murderous, his teeth bared. Michael's fingers dug into his cheeks, his eyes, his nose. With a final heave my throat was clear. Blood was restored to my brain. Sweet air rushed into my lungs.

The dazzling lights revealed the wildness of the scene. Someone gave a yell. Through clearing eyes I saw a black wave poised high above us. In the split second before it struck I flung up an arm, struck the safety line and gripped it fast. The next moment we were engulfed in an overwhelming tumult of water. This way and that I was beaten and flung about. Yet luck stayed with me for the mast house offered a degree of protection and somehow, as the wave subsided and left me stranded, I was still there

But where were Michael and the mate? I looked on every side. The leaping ocean reflected the floodlights and bore down upon us at the speed of a train. The remnants of the last wave boiled along the foot of the superstructure. High above me, little faces peered down from the bridge.

Then I saw Michael. Right arm hanging, he rose from behind a winch. His low-neck T-shirt had been ripped to the chest, his ballooning silk trousers clung to his legs like a second skin. Clearly he was in pain. I worked my way down the safety line to give him a hand.

"Help!" A faint cry rose above the storm.

I looked all round.

"Over here!"

But where? Where had the shout come from?

Michael heard it too. Gripping the rope with his left hand, he limped towards me. I stared. Something terrible had happened to his eyes. The sockets were black. Hideous fluids ran down both cheeks. He came closer. With relief I realised it was his mascara.

"There," he yelled above the gale. "By the rail."

I looked where he nodded and saw nothing but the trailing derrick and broken tangle of rails. I took a couple of steps and looked again. The mate had been washed through the rails left standing and clung to the bottom bar for his life. Only his arms and head were visible, the rest hung down the ship's plates. He swung up a leg and scrabbled for a foothold.

Someone had taken the wheel. Slowly the bows swung back to face the storm. The pounding waves were not so damaging. Even so, if I let go of the safety line to offer the mate a hand, I might be swept overboard myself. He might pull me over the rail. I looked at the sea and hesitated.

Michael, with a broken arm, had no such reservations. Already he was picking his way across the tangled deck. He shamed me. Feeling that I was committing suicide, I crossed to help him.

The mate watched with desperate eyes as we came close. "Hurry! Hurry!" The hands that two minutes earlier had been choking out my life were clamped on the rail. I reached through and gripped his elbow Michael, with his good hand, caught him by a wrist. We heaved. The mate's grip shifted to the second rail. A giant wave came roaring to meet us. I let go and clung to the rails for dear life.

I was submerged and carried away, flung against the broken

rails, the derrick, the hatch coaming, the winch. Frantically I cast about for something to hold on to. There was nothing. Head over heels I tumbled along, smashed into the towering superstructure and was tossed sideways.

The wave spent its force, poured out through the rails and freeing ports, was caught by the wind and whirled mast-high. I came to rest. For half a minute I could not move. Then I tested an arm, a leg, my back. They hurt. I hurt all over, but nothing, it seemed, was broken. Watery blood ran into my eyes, blurring my vision.

I crawled to my knees. Where was Michael? I didn't see him. He couldn't have gone – not Michael!

There were voices above me. I looked. Smoky, Barbara, Samuel and a couple of others came tumbling down the steps to the foredeck. I made an effort and stumbled towards them.

A movement caught my eye. I blinked the blood away. It was Michael. The wave had carried him back behind the winch. He leaned on it to recover. His broken arm was giving him pain. Samuel crossed to support him, strong arm around his back.

"Hello, big boy." Michael managed a smile. "I didn't think you cared."

Barbara joined us.

I said, "The mate's gone."

"No." Smoky nodded up the foredeck. "He's right there."

The mate lay on the deck, close to the coaming of number two hatch. The storm-driven wave that carried Michael and me away had flung him back inboard. He had always been immaculate. Now he lay awkwardly, his cardigan gone, shirt torn open. Unblinking eyes gazed up at the floodlights. Brian and Scudder worked their way towards him. But even from where I was standing it was obvious, by his unnatural stillness and the angle of his neck, the mate was dead.

Sunset and Sunrise

AND THAT was it really. The four who had spread their poison throughout the ship – Jumbo Ryland, Lenny Rathbone, Tony Fanshott-Williams and Duncan Rose – were gone. Captain Bell was back on the bridge. The watch was summoned to take the helm and keep lookout. Tim Nettles went through the ship with working parties to see what could be done to limit the damage. Those of us who had been hurt were attended to.

By four in the morning the wind was easing as Typhoon Caroline turned north-east, lashing the coast of Borneo and moving on towards the Philippines and western Pacific. Forty-eight hours later our battered ship sailed into Keppel Harbour in Singapore.

Dad was standing on the quay when we docked.

He was very nice about everything. In fact, everyone was very nice about it, I mean me being Ben Thomson, a fifteen-year-old runaway, and not Joey Bennett as it said on my papers. By everyone I mean my friends on board, the Singapore police, and Captain Bell who said, "Good God! Fifteen years old! Bloody hell! Come on, sit down here and tell us about it. Heidi, any chance of a cup of tea?"

So I told him everything, just as I had told dad: the weekend away from *Frankie's*, meeting Charlie, the disco, Joey's papers – but leaving Smoky out of it – meeting Ryland at the Eight Bells, how he had killed Curly aboard the *Star of Bengal*, Tony stealing from the cargo, poor Ossie, the hot springs, the Ascot Hotel, the freezer locker, the collapsing pool, Ryland on the radio, the pirates, Ka'tang's knife, the hypodermic, the mate's cabin, what I had witnessed on the bridge and my pursuit around the stormy foredeck. "Good God!" he said again when I had finished. "Bloody hell!"

When dad told him that if it were possible I'd very much like to complete the trip as deck boy, he said it was highly irregular but he'd had good reports of me, which pleased my dad no end, and in the circumstances he'd pull a few strings – no promises, mind – to see if something might be arranged.

Two days later I was summoned to his cabin and told, to my delight, that I was still a member of the crew. "Which means, Bennett, Thomson, whatever your bloody name is," he concluded gruffly, "you've got a job to do. So what are you standing there for, grinning like a bloody schoolgirl just got her first kiss? Get on with it."

We were in dock for ten days, longer than anticipated. The Singapore cargo was discharged and, in that equatorial heat, the frozen bodies of the mate, the bosun and Lenny Rathbone were taken ashore. The storm damage, which was extensive, was repaired and a replacement lifeboat was hoisted into the davits.

Police investigations continued the whole time we were in port. Among other things, they wanted to know who had been responsible for sabotaging the engines. Some of us guessed it was Luigi, who had had plenty of opportunity and been so angry when we asked him about it. We were wrong, it was a friend of his down the engine room, another Italian, an older man whose wife was sick and needed an expensive operation. I barely knew him, although of course I had seen him about the ship, a gentle man named Stefano with a shock of white hair. Ryland had bribed him. The chance to earn some extra money simply by turning off a couple of oil valves had been too tempting. The poor man had no idea what the outcome was likely to be – and now the ship was looted and a young engineer lay dead. Beside himself with distress, he had confessed to Luigi and in Singapore he confessed to the police.

When we sailed, Stefano did not come with us, and some months later I heard he had been given a three-year jail sentence. But there was a happier outcome: when the story of his part in the raid reached the Italian media, an appeal was launched by *Corriere della Sera*, the national newspaper, to enable his wife to have the life-saving operation she needed. Many times the needed sum was raised and the operation was a success. Afterwards she made several visits to Westport to visit her loving husband in prison.

Captain Bell suggested dad might like to take over as mate but I didn't want him to and anyway, his contract in the UK made it impossible. So a new mate and three deck crew were flown out to join us, and with Samuel upgraded to bosun, the atmosphere on the ship was transformed.

For the days he was in Singapore, dad slept in the pilot's cabin. He met my friends. We went out for meals, explored the city and talked a long time. Despite the fact that I had driven him mad with worry, he said he was proud of me. Charlie's mum, true to her word, had written to him. Dad had visited them and was very happy, if that's what I wanted, for me to stay with the Sunderlands and complete my education at Westport High School. I went to the airport to see him off.

Some of the crew needed medical attention. A small cut above my eye, which had been stitched in the storm, was reopened and stitched again. Michael's arm was re-set in plaster. Aaron's arm was x-rayed and pronounced to be healing nicely. A few others, who had been injured by the pirates, were examined by doctors. Steve Petersen, who had saved my life, was admitted to *Singapore General Hospital* which had a specialist unit dealing with injuries such as his and when we sailed he did not come with us. Charlie, to my disappointment, was not yet strong enough to rejoin us in Singapore but he did so in Colombo with a sharp new haircut, lots of stories and a pretty Indian girl clinging to his arm. At once we moved back into the old cabin.

The days passed quickly and all too soon, for me at least, we were sailing up the cold grey Mersey to Liverpool. Sadly, as we signed off and collected our wages, I said goodbye to my many friends – Aaron, Smoky, Michael, Barbara, Luigi, Samuel, Kevin, Philip, Tim Nettles and Attila. But that's the way of the Merchant Navy: once the voyage is over, friends who have been inseparable for six months or a year shake hands, embrace, step into a taxi and disappear from each other's lives. Unless, of course, they've arranged to sail together the next trip.

But for me there would be no next trip. It had been arranged, and I had agreed, that at the start of the summer term I would return to school to complete my education.

Mrs Sunderland, Auntie Meg, as I came to call her, was the best mum a boy ever had – after my gran, of course, who had been a mum to me. Uncle Joe, her little husband, was kindness itself. And Charlie, my best friend in the world, became the brother I had never had. Every evening I took Doctor Death, the big soft Rottweiler, his lolloping run through the parks and along the overgrown lanes on the outskirts of Westport.

It was strange being a schoolboy again, wearing Charlie's old green blazer with a badge on the pocket, after the events aboard *Pacific Trader*.

I had changed over the past five months. Was this Ben Thomson, burned brown by the tropical sun, his hands callused by hard work, the same boy who had paid prefects to forge a letter for him, been hypnotised by Betty's stupendous breasts, and fled through a guesthouse window to avoid the shrieks of Mrs Stringbaum?

For a while I wrote to some of the people I had sailed with, and Michael, the only one to maintain a correspondence, kept me up to date with news of others:

Steve, after a long period of skin grafts and convalescence, left the sea. Always supremely fit, he went to college to train as a PE teacher.

Luigi returned to Naples and got his teeth fixed. Soon, despite being as gay as a maypole, he was being photographed with some of Italy's most glamorous women and became a popular TV star.

Joey and Fizz, who remained my lifelong friends, were the happiest couple in English football. Fizz had two, three and finally four children. Joey, at the age of twenty-three, became striker for Newcastle and was a regular member of the England squad.

Samuel, the finest man on board, continued a few more trips as bosun then took a job as school janitor to be with his growing family and work for the church.

Michael, a big hit with Auntie Meg, was left a substantial sum of money by his grandmother. He and Barbara moved to York and opened a bijou restaurant called Pink Champagne, which became very successful.

Smoky and Dolores resumed their violent marriage. Before we left the ship he had presented me with a beautiful painting of our day at the lake in Fiji – with the other Dolores, the praying mantis, hiding in a corner. Word of his work was spreading and an exhibition was organised at a gallery in London. By the time it opened, however, Smoky was drinking his lager and rolling his fags aboard a tramp steamer, five hundred miles up the Amazon.

Ossie, of course, was no longer with us, drifting in the depths of the beautiful Java Sea. Michael and Barbara arranged a requiem mass at St Mary's in Westport with lots of candles and a good-looking altar boy swinging clouds of incense. Charlie and I went with Auntie Meg. To my surprise it was well attended and I spotted several faces I recognised. Captain Bell read one of the lessons and Michael the other, demure in a soft grey suit, a white buttonhole for Ossie and the merest trace of eye-shadow. A memorial stone was erected close to the plot of his appalling mother:

> Oswald Bagot,
> *faithful son and much-loved shipmate.*
> *Safe in the arms of Jesus.*

And what became of Tony Fanshott-Williams and Trish the Dish, who were carried off by Ka'tang? There was no news of the horrible Tony and I couldn't care less. But by chance, two or three years later, Charlie came across an article in an old magazine which spoke of rumours, passed on by seamen, of a beautiful white woman who was said to be running with a gang of buccaneers in the South China Sea. Can such stories be believed? I hope so, and if it *is* Trish, I wish her well.

As for me? Nothing so exotic. I stayed on at school to take my 'A' levels and mostly enjoyed it – friends, rugby, teenage parties – but the trips I had made with dad and the months I spent aboard *Pacific Trader* had got into my blood and I wanted to go back to sea.

I imagined this would be in the Merchant Navy, it was all I knew, but my plans changed when an officer from the Royal Navy came to talk to the sixth form and show us a short film. I liked what he had to say enough to go for an interview. And later a medical.

Auntie Meg drove us to York for the opening of Pink Champagne. "Ooh, lucky for some," Michael said when I told him my plans. "All those bell-bottoms! A lot of *very* lively people in the Navy, dear – and the straights are even worse! Isn't that right, Barbara? *Pacific Trader* hasn't got a look-in."

Dad put it differently. Now a deep-sea captain on the China run, he flew home to see me. "Just the job for a grand lad like you, Ben," he said as we sat in the lounge bar of the Eight Bells. "A real career. Plenty of action, foreign travel, good pay, good prospects of promotion. I couldn't be more pleased."

So that was it. And on a beautiful October morning, two months before my eighteenth birthday, I kissed Auntie Meg and my girlfriend goodbye at the station, shook Uncle Joe's hand, and set off with a high sense of adventure to start my training at the Royal Naval College in Dartmouth.

Glossary of Nautical Terms

AB : able seaman
alleyway : corridor
azimuth : check accuracy of a compass against the true bearing of the sun or stars
bight : a wide bay; a bend or loop in a rope
binnacle : housing for magnetic compass
bitts : pair of strong posts on deck to which mooring or tow ropes are attached.
booby hatch : small rectangular hatch with raised trunking that gives access to the hold
bosun : petty officer in charge of the crew
bridge : navigating deck (wheelhouse, chartroom, binnacle, etc.)
bulkhead : wall
chippy : ship (or shore) carpenter
coaming : raised metal edge around a hatch for keeping out water
crosstree : horizontal beam high up the mast
deckhead : ceiling
decks : lowest decks : foredeck (hatch1, foremast, hatch 2)
        afterdeck (hatch 5, mainmast, hatch 6, poop)
  crew deck : one above foredeck and afterdeck (crew accommodation, hatch 4)
  boat deck : above crew deck (deck officers, hatch 3, engineer officers)
  top decks : bridge : above deck officers (navigation, captain's accom.)
      funnel deck : above engineers (funnel, lifeboats, ventilators)
derrick : long tubular beam used for loading and discharging cargo
D.F. : radio / telecom. direction finding
donkeyman : responsible for the auxiliary / donkey engine and generators in port

flying wing : projecting wing of the bridge
fo'csle : enclosed section of foredeck at the bow
fo'csle head : raised deck above fo'csle
freeing port : opening in a solid rail to allow water to escape
gyro : gyroscopic compass showing true (as opposed to magnetic) north
halyard : rope for hoisting flag, sail, etc
heaving line : a light rope for throwing
hold : cargo space : lower hold
                                  lower 'tween deck (some with lockers)
                                  upper 'tween deck (some with lockers)
                                  shelter deck (holds 3 and 4)
holystone : block of sandstone (with handle) for scouring a wooden deck
J.O.S. : Junior Ordinary Seaman
lamptrimmer : lampie; petty officer, junior to bosun, in charge of deck stores
marlinspike : metal spike used for splicing etc.
mast house : locker at the foot of the mast
monkey island : small deck above the bridge where a magnetic compass is situated
Pool : the Shipping Federation office, where seamen learn what work is available
poop : raised platform / deck at the stern
quarter : starboard or port side of ship towards the stern
safety line : rigged rope, waist high and taut, to grip in stormy weather
samson post : thick post to support and suspend derricks
scupper : drainage channel and outflow at the side of the deck
shackle : U-shaped metal fastener with screw locking pin to secure wires or ropes
shroud : another name for mast stay
single-up : reduce mooring lines to one
slops : ship's store providing basic clothing, bedding, etc.
smoko : morning or afternoon break
splice : join two ropes by weaving the strands together (end to end / end to middle)

stage : long board / seat with a cross-piece at each end, suspended on ropes
stay : wire guy-rope supporting the mast
steaming light : navigation light when vessel is under way
stem post : flag pole at the bow
suji-muji : suji – a lime and soda mixture used for washing paint
tabnabs : biscuits, small cakes, buns, eaten at break times
thimble : a tear-shaped metal eye around which a rope or wire is spliced
winch : electric motor with revolving drums for hauling ropes and wires
windlass : powerful winch / motor on fo'csle head for raising anchor

In place of the correct nautical term 'companionway', for which dictionaries offer various definitions, I have referred to stairs (below decks), steps (above decks) and ladders, which seem to me more precise and less cumbersome.